The Knight

AND THE

Coveted

BOOK 2
HEALING FATE SERIES

ASHA NYR

ISBN: 979-8-89079-016-3 (ebook)
ISBN: 979-8-9885350-1-0 (paperback)
ISBN: 979-8-9885350-2-7 (hardback)

Copyediting by Misha Carlstedt, Verity Ink Editorial

This novel is dedicated to Rinji Boo Pantsu no Jutsu—a friend with a million bizarre nicknames. During the darkest chapter of this year, one of the darkest ones of my life, they found a roof and put it over my head.

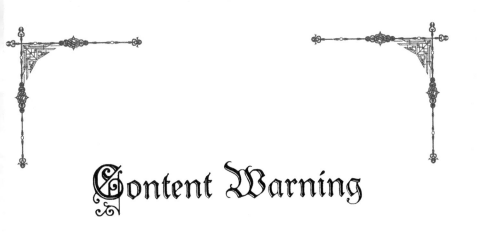

Content Warning

Dear new readers, this novel contains adult content with scenes describing explicit language, explicit sex, human trafficking, and references to both sexual exploitation and suicide. Reader discretion is strongly advised.

The Dragon Knight and the Coveted was originally exposure therapy for the sexual assault I survived. Due to popular demand, I've decided to publish it. More information is provided in the Author's Notes about why this was written. Please note that includes spoilers.

More information can also be found in the Author's Notes of *The Mistake and the Lycan King,* the first book of Healing Fate. Though this is the second book, it can be read as a standalone.

Acknowledgments

Some gratitude runs too deep to put into words. What can one say to those who keep giving them oxygen? I can at least put them here on a pedestal wrought of ink. I only wish I could do more. Renee Sanguinetti continues to teach me, guide me towards a life worth living.

Author Logan Black always makes time to answer my questions—and refuses to leave my shoulder like a fine, grammatical parrot.

Author Hunter Ambrose is a dedicated source of positivity and finds me when I feel forgotten. He is a spark of light in the darkness.

My shifter pack, my beloved reader family… there are far too many of you to name. Never had I imagined creating such a supportive, loving community. To see it grow beyond me to where you are now supporting each other has been a joy to watch. My heart warms just thinking about it. I want to give special acknowledgment to Beta Julie, Callie H., Nurse Moon, and Manon Leah van der Veen, who have all become a part of the heart that unites us.

You will never know how much you all mean to me, but may this give you some idea of that. Thank you. Sunlight preserve you all.

Love,
Author, artist, musician, and unyielding survivor,
Asha Nyr

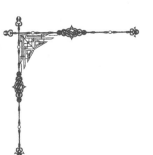

Chapter 1

Sir Keyon

Despite the disappointed cries from the female onlookers, I pulled my clothes on and strode toward the covered cage we'd used to move the liberated slaves. My team had taken turns shifting into our dragons and hauling the cage across the territory. I'd taken the burden on the last leg of the journey as my soldiers were looking a little bedraggled. Yes, I was the knight general, but if I deemed myself above any exertion, I wasn't fit to be a leader. How else would a leader know what was possible for their troops if they didn't lend a hand on occasion?

This particular trip made me realize that it was far more exhausting to move something as fragile as living bodies than anything else. You had to exercise more control over your movements, which put your body in a state of near constant tension. You also needed to stay more alert and aware of your surroundings. I made a mental note to bring more squires on our next den raid; the problem was that we never knew how many slaves we'd find. One of these days, we'd be severely underprepared, and that was a discussion I intended to have today.

Keys jingled and jangled in my hands as I searched for the iron mate to the cage's lock. The weary individuals inside the container were quiet, just staring at my busy hands. I was grateful they weren't clawing at the door. I wasn't feeling up to a good trample today.

Make the women go last so we can stand clear of them, Toast said.

I ignored my dragon and unlocked the door. I waited a moment before opening it to give my traditional short speech to the rescued humans and shifters. "Welcome, Reborn! It may be a citizen's duty to serve the crown, but today, let the crown serve you! We will provide you with temporary housing, food, medical care, and work until you can support yourselves. Orphans will be placed in foster homes until they can be adopted. If they are not adopted by the time they are of age, we will provide them with employment. School is mandatory.

"Females, women, hatchlings, pups, cubs, children—all are to leave first. Form a line and do not go faster than a walk, please! Any strong individuals are welcome to assist in moving out the injured or elderly; otherwise, we'll retrieve them last. You will be met with servants on the left side who will give everyone water and food! There is plenty, so do not rush. After, please stand in the designated area until you're called." I opened the cage door and let the poor liberated souls begin their second chance at life.

The dry grass crunched under my boots, and I frowned at the thought of the shoeless young walking across it. I summoned a servant to my side and said, "Please roll a large tarp out in the waiting area so they're not standing in this sharp, dead grass. Please and thank you." The servant scurried off to perform his task, and I sighed, watching the unloading with satisfaction.

Of everything I'd done in the name of our king, I had to say that this was the project that pleased me the most. Going to war with another country was a bitter experience because you knew you were fighting people who simply wanted to live their lives on their farms or just watch their children grow. Raiding a den full of slave traffickers, however, was a delicious experience. I got to slaughter those who truly deserved to bleed. I'd seen disturbing things in battle... but some of the things I'd witnessed in these slave dens had nearly made me lose all faith in our future as dragon-shifters. Every time I thought I'd seen the worst we were capable of as a species, I was proven wrong in the next raid. I shook myself out of old memories and brought my mind back to the present. Seeing as how everything was going smoothly, I left the rest of the work for the rehabilitation team. I raised a hand, signaled for my soldiers to retire, and strode across the field to make my report.

I groaned quietly to myself at the crowd that blocked my exit from the field. Throngs of women and female dragon-shifters were huddled by the fences, right where I needed to pass. I grumbled under my breath and pulled my gloves from my pockets. Terror radiated from my dragon, and I fought his urge to take control of my movements.

They're waiting for us, Toast warned nervously. *They always know when we're coming. How do they always know? Who tells them?*

They won't hurt us, I said for the millionth time. I wanted to look at the maidens, but it would only agitate Toast. Well, maybe I didn't want to look at them. It was just a tease of what I couldn't have, what I hadn't been able to have since I'd turned eighteen so many, many years ago.

Don't go that way. Go to the other fence. They will swarm and attack!

Not going to happen, Toast.

You wouldn't know until it's too late!

Toast, when was the last time a woman attacked us? I asked, and he went silent, but I could still feel his fear. It grated on me. As much as I felt for him, his gynophobia was a cage, and I was trapped miserably in it with him.

I tried leaving by one gate, but it was immediately swarmed by maidens looking to get my attention. It would have been extremely flattering if I was able to do anything about it, but alas, my dragon had been cock-blocking me for twelve years. To say I was sexually frustrated was the understatement of the millennium. I gave the maidens a curt smile and bowed slightly. "Ladies," I acknowledged and moved to squeeze past them. They sighed and moaned dramatically at my inattention.

I strode down the covered walkway to the palace, wondering if I'd hit a new record for needing to masturbate since returning home. How many minutes had it been?

"If it isn't the world's most eligible bachelor!" a mocking voice called out from an intercepting pathway. I sent a very tolerant half-smile to my friend, Leofwine, before aggressively smacking the shit out of the back of his head.

"You're lucky you're so good-looking that I can't bring myself to break your face, Leof," I grumbled. "One of us has to get laid, and you're our biggest hope."

He grinned and rubbed the back of his head like I'd severely hurt him. His white teeth and long fangs flashed brilliantly against his obsidian skin. The bastard was pretty, and he was well aware. He'd probably gotten laid last night. Bastard.

"How'd the raid go?" Leofwine asked as he escorted me to our meeting.

"Rather well, but some of the big players had left before we'd gotten there. It ended up being a den full of grunts and slaves, so it crumbled like burnt paper. We got everyone out alive, thank the Sun God," I replied and kicked the dirt off my boots before stepping into the castle.

"Feels good to see us freeing those people, but it's disturbing that these rings continue to pop up," he murmured thoughtfully. "We're going to have to expand our team of spies if th—"

"Oh, my darling, Keyon!" a woman's voice called from the upper flight of stairs, and I groaned internally. Leofwine didn't bother hiding his dislike for the woman and glowered at the approaching figure. The twenty-five-year-old dragon-shifter flew down the steps and raced to hug me.

Toast yanked me behind Leofwine like a puppet so Princess Gisila couldn't murder us. At least that was what Toast was certain she'd do. Personally, I didn't mind Toast's actions this time. The king's daughters were all rotten, and I wanted nothing to do with them. Why Gisila thought she'd get a hug this time was beyond me.

Leofwine held his hands up to prevent her from getting past him, and she pouted like a child; she even stomped her feet. What a sexy look.

"Can I help you, Princess?" I asked, slowly coming out from behind my friend. I pretended I'd found a spider on my friend's back to not only cover for Toast's yank but also to keep the princess at bay. "You really must stop going into the cellars, Leof, if you're going to be bringing back all these cellar spiders," I said to my friend, grimacing as I dusted off his shoulders.

"S-spiders?" the princess shrieked, backing up a dozen steps while picking up her skirts and frantically searching her black curls.

My friend shrugged his massive shoulders. "I guess I'll send the servants next time," he replied, not skipping a beat. "They don't usually go for me. They prefer little things like children and young ladies." Leofwine never missed an opportunity to create a lie sandwich, and I nodded along in agreement.

"Princess?" I asked again, raising a brow. "Did you need something?" She was pale, and her face was so pinched it looked like she'd been nibbling on limes all day. She shook her head but held her hand out for me to kiss. Oh gods, I hated this song and dance.

Even if I wanted to kiss her hand, Toast wouldn't allow it. My dragon and I had worked out an agreement where I could place a gloved hand under a female's without contact and bow over it.

I sensed that she was about to jerk her hand up to my lips, but I pulled away just in time to give her a nod and walked off with my comrade. Toast was shuddering inside me, as if he'd dodged an arrow that had been aimed at his heart.

Leofwine and I entered the king's study to make our report and verify our next course of action. Osgar, the king's personal guard, was standing at his side, and he nodded slightly to me in deference. I nodded back, making Leofwine scoff in irritation. He was always complaining that Osgar never acknowledged him. Aiken, resource management, was sitting on the leather couch on the right, covered in what was probably the entire contents of his desk just minutes ago.

"Welcome back!" King Uhtric exclaimed, smiling happily at me. "From the commotion outside, I take it we were successful with our last raid?"

"Yes, Your Majesty," I replied, smiling back at the old, shaking dragon. "We've returned with two hundred and fifty-seven Reborn. They're being processed and cared for right now. It seemed that the slavers knew we were coming because we only found grunts there."

"And since this isn't the first time Keyon's reported it, I'm concerned we may have a security breach," Leofwine added, his playful demeanor disappearing under the call of duty. The king nodded at him with a frown.

"See to that, Leof," he said gruffly. "We can't let them get away. They'll grow like a cancer somewhere else."

"Also, Aiken, would it be possible to get more squires for our next raid? My team was spread too thin upon our return. I'd rather have too many than not enough, especially if the slavers decide to ambush us on the road."

The dragon nodded and wrote furiously into his notebook. He wasn't a male of many words, but he got things done. Our king had a gift for assigning the right people to the right duty. I'd always admired that about him.

"We got a visitor from a neighboring kingdom with a special request," King Uhtric said, handing me a piece of paper. "They're looking for a slave that may be in our region. She was taken as a little girl, and they're hoping that our efforts to clear up these trafficking rings will expose her location. They said she'd be… rather hard to miss."

I looked down at the piece of paper with a description. She'd be twenty-five by now... I had no idea how much she would have changed. Some dragons didn't even end up with the same hair color they had as hatchlings. I sighed at the task set before me. This would be difficult.

"Is she a shifter? A human?" I asked, and the king's face hardened.

"I tried asking that, but they wouldn't tell me. I suspect she's a shifter, but... there's no way to know until you see her what species she is. Just do your best, Sir Keyon. You'll find her."

I groaned inwardly. Would I?

Elpis

"Shh, shh, it's ok, hatchling," I crooned into the dirty heather curls of a thirteen-year-old dragon-shifter as I rocked her in my arms. She was new to the mansion and would be groomed soon for slavery. "I snuck you a treat! Would you like a piece of taffy?" I asked, tilting my head down to look at her inconsolable, snotty face. She nodded and took the piece of candy from my palm. It was warm from being in my hand for an hour, but it should still be good. "That's a good little hatchling," I said and continued to rock her.

"Wh-when did you get h-here?" she asked in between hiccups.

"I don't know. I've been here as long as I can remember," I confessed and realized it was the wrong answer. The little dragon's face scrunched up into utter emotional agony, and she burst into tears.

"Oh nay! Sweet one! Nay, nay, don't cry! Shh!" I soothed a little frantically. If the slaves were too loud for too long, a guard would come in and take them away to be punished. It didn't matter how old they were. "Nay, see, I'm sure we'll get rescued real soon! I know the signs! I've been around a long time, and I heard the signs of rescue!" My flimsy dress had no proper pockets, so I pulled the lie out of the only place I could hide things: my bottom.

I breathed a stilted sigh of relief when she stopped crying. The door to the room swung open, and a guard looked in to see who'd been causing the commotion. I froze with my arms wrapped around the hatchling and felt a shudder trickle down my spine. A bead of sweat soon followed the shudder, made much colder by the chill of our stone room. When I heard the guard approach us from behind, I regretted sitting with my back against the front of the cage, so I stayed still, not wanting to draw attention. I kept the hatchling in my lap and prayed that she'd stay quiet so that he'd leave us alone. They weren't allowed in any cage I was in if I wasn't wearing my chastity belt, but I didn't need them using a slave's disobedience to get access to me.

I heard the guard stop, and I pulled the child against my chest, hoping it would deter him from reaching in and groping me. A gloved hand trapped a length of my hair, and I knew it was time to let the hatchling go. I gave her a smile and pointed for her to go to the other female who was caged with us. Zosime was a good dragon-shifter; she'd comfort the hatchling. She already had the little underfed thing in her lap and was covering her eyes.

I tugged my head to get away from the guard, but he fisted and yanked it, smacking my skull back against the cage. I hissed in pain and watched his other hand lower through the bars to flick one strap of my dress off my shoulder. I gritted my teeth and looked at the far wall. I would complain about this new guard the next time I was brought aboveground. He'd regret this. They knew better than to touch me. Everyone caged in this room was a Slave of the First Water. A guard using one of us to get off was a colossal no-no.

The male's heavy breathing puffed against the side of my face, and I nearly gagged. He groaned when he moved to uncover the rest of my breast but was interrupted by a pair of footsteps who happened to be passing by the door.

"He's sampling the prime merch!" I yelled, and the guard immediately let go of me. He rushed out, and I heard yelling outside, even after they'd closed the door. I smiled sadly, readjusted my dress, and hugged my knees. Zosime looked over at me again but didn't say anything. There wasn't anything to say. I decided to engage with the hatchling again.

"What's your name, sweet one?" I asked and went to sit next to them. The little dragon sniffed, and I reached up with the skirt of my dress to wipe away her tears and snot. She leaned away with wide eyes.

"No, that's a pretty dress..." she protested. I laughed and held her still to clean her face.

"And you're a pretty little dragon," I said, making sure to get rid of all the grime. "Nay, dresses are as common as can be, but you're precious! One of a kind. Isn't that right, Zosime?"

The dragon chuckled tiredly. "One of a kind, indeed. So, you must have a one-of-a-kind name."

"Dagmaer," she whispered, pouting at my soiled skirt.

"My, what a strong name! When they rescue us, you're bound to become one of the king's knights! I just know it!" I grinned and looked playfully around her skinny arms for a muscle to pinch. The little dragon giggled and leaned against Zosime to get away from my tickling fingers.

"Oof!" Zosime got an elbow to her belly, and Dagmaer fell apart apologizing to her. I laughed quietly, and Zosime stuck her lean dragon tongue out at me. I whispered an apology and waved my hands in an attempt to placate her.

Dagmaer settled and looked up at me from where her head rested on Zosime's bosom. "So what are the signs?" she asked, picking nervously at her fingers.

"Hmm? The signs? Oh! The signs of rescue. Right..." I thought quickly. "Well, the very first sign of rescue is the news! If we hear of others being freed, we know that our rescuers are on their way!" I smiled, confident in my choice.

"You know, the slaves at the two southern dens have been liberated," a woman named Dagrun whispered from the corner of the room. She was caged with an older teenager that she'd been mentoring. They were both pleasure slaves, like me.

"What?" I asked in an excited hiss. "Franco's dens? Did they catch him?"

"I hadn't heard anything about that. Just that the slaves were taken, and all his men were killed."

"Oh, how I wish I had sparkling wine, Zosime," I said, turning to her with a wicked grin. "This would be a good one to celebrate."

"So, what's the second sign?" little Dagmaer asked, and I turned away, tapping the ground in agitation. I wanted to keep her spirits up and her hope alive for as long as possible.

"Ah… the second sign is snooping strangers," I said with a nod. "They will send a spy in!"

"A spy!" Her eyes lit up in excitement. She was eating up my lies as if they were more pieces of taffy. If I could give her one more night of optimism, I would. I already felt like my life was over; I was old for a pleasure slave, and who knew how long they'd keep me around before selling my virginity. I'd be useless after that. Males and men were monsters. You couldn't pay me to think otherwise.

The door opened, and I was surprised to see my handler enter the room. Her eyes landed on me, and she gestured for me to come as she unlocked the cage.

"We have a guest tonight, Elpis. You will be expected to serve them," Tofa said while attaching the lead to my collar. I never understood why she had to attach the damn thing; I never tried to run from her.

"Yes, T— Ow! Yes, Tofa!" I said while she yanked on my collar. I frowned, wishing I could growl or hiss, but neither of those came naturally to me. I just had an urge to kick her in the bottom, but that was about it. What a wretched female. Perhaps her own pleasure slave wasn't able to keep up with her.

Tofa dragged me to the prep room where a half dozen maids scrambled to prepare me. I was shoved into a bath and scoured until

I was certain all my skin was gone. They shaved every inch of me, except for my head, of course. I hated when they shaved my privates; the smoothness made me feel like a child. Something about that just felt extra nauseating when I was forced to please someone. It wasn't like the client could see anything under the chastity belt anyway. There could be a topiary under there, and they'd never know!

I was dried, styled, and made-up until you couldn't recognize me anymore. They squeezed me into our two-piece dancer's dress and marched me out to meet the mansion's mysterious guest. *Perhaps it'll be a spy,* I mused to myself.

Surprisingly, I was brought to the kitchen where I was handed a carafe of wine. I knitted my brows when they showed me how to properly pour into a glass without spilling. I wasn't above this type of serving. I was just very confused as to why I was being asked to do it. I'd never done this before and found myself terrified that I'd spill the contents onto someone's lap.

I was shoved toward the dining room, and someone tried to urge me off with an overeager slap to my bottom. Unfortunately, their hand met with the hard gold edge of my chastity belt, and I smirked, walking away from a hissing, cursing male who was likely nursing his stinging palm.

I entered the dining hall and scanned for new faces as subtly as I could. We weren't really allowed to look at people, but I got away with more than most slaves. I began to fill the guests' glasses as instructed, making my way slowly around the large table.

"Ah, there is our lovely Elpis. Our most beautiful dancer, yes?" the lord said, looking down to his lady wife for affirmation. I snorted in my head. Dancer? We just learned to do what the males enjoyed watching. Zosime and I could grind against each other, and they'd still call it dancing. Filthy males.

"We're thinking of sending her to the academy. Would you like to witness a performance?" the lady of the mansion said with a bit of a tease in her voice.

"That's not necessary, Your Ladyship. I'm sure she's a fine dancer," a voice said; it was so beautiful that I nearly dropped the carafe when his notes reached my unworthy ears. It pealed like a warm, low bell. It was a strong and confident voice. It was commanding and drew my attention. Could I risk a peek at the owner of such an alluring voice?

I knit my brows at my own foolishness. Who cared if they had a lovely voice? No, if they were friends with the lord, they were not good people.

Don't be fooled, Elpis! I scolded myself.

I filled the lady's chalice and moved around the table. "Be a good girl, Elpis, and show our guest some of your dancing," the lady said with a grin, gesturing to where the male sat.

I gulped and moved to where I was directed. In a smooth sweep, I straddled the large male without touching him, which wasn't hard to do because he clamped his legs together and leaned away from me. I couldn't bring myself to look at his face as I swayed over him, caressing the air above his lap with my hips. His thighs looked rock hard and so did something else. I was used to that kind of reaction, but I had to congratulate him on being the biggest I'd ever seen. I was sure his women and females were happy.

I almost faltered in my movements when I noticed his delicious smell, and I desperately wanted to take a closer sniff. I couldn't place his scent, and I wondered what kind of cologne it was. I wanted to take one of my old dresses and rub that smell all over it so I could lie on it at nighttime.

What a strange new fascination I have, I thought. *But he just smells so good.*

The rest of the room seemed to fade away as I focused on dancing for the male before me. I wanted to look at him, but there were too many eyes on me.

I noticed his breathing become slightly ragged, and his body tensed. His large, calloused hands gripped the armrests until his knuckles blanched. I wasn't sure what to make of that, so I decided to wrap up my performance and twirled off him.

I barely grazed his hand with mine when he bolted out of his seat, sending the chair rolling away from us. I froze and waited for my next order because I had no idea what was going on, and I was a bit frightened.

"That's enough," the male ground out through his teeth.

"Thank you, Your Lordship."

Chapter 2

Sir Kenon

Something weird was definitely going on here. When Leofwine said he'd gathered enough evidence to sanction a raid of Lord Adelmar's property, I'd immediately put a team of knights, squires, and medics together. Even Prince Cyneric gave me a handful of his men, saying he wanted to see Adelmar in custody as soon as possible so he could pay for his crimes.

The unsettling thing that led to this dinner was the invitation I'd received from Lord Adelmar to visit. He mentioned wanting to discuss some kind of business venture, but I couldn't imagine why a lord wanted to team up with the knight general. We did not perch in the same aeries, so to speak. Since Leofwine and I had a pretty good idea of what was happening behind closed doors at Adelmar's mansion, and it wasn't a secret that I was in charge of tearing down trafficking rings, this invitation was either a trap or a desperate bid to buy my silence.

As I was not a fan of traps, I decided to combine the raid and the dinner. This gave me a couple days to get a sense of the area, the security, and possibly the location of the slaves. That would minimize the risk to my team, which I always kept at the front of my mind. I'd left them approximately six miles away from Lord Adelmar's land with strict instructions to raid only when my signal was given. The lord and his lady wife had—of course—welcomed me with gracious, open arms. They'd shown me around their property and mansion, trying to impress me with all the gold and jewels they had in their collection. I wasn't going to lie; as a dragon, my fingers twitched at the sight of a particularly pretty set of star sapphires, but I knew better than to let them distract me. I had my own hoard I'd collected over the years at home. Also, I had a feeling that a lot of their collection was acquired through bloodshed. No, I had no interest in their tainted treasures.

Dinner was even more awkward. I'd been asked to keep an open mind over the next couple of days while they made their business proposal, and they began putting pressure on my not-so-open mind as soon as we got to the table.

"So, Sir Keyon. Are you mated yet? You have been of age for quite a while," Lady Adelmar inquired, sipping at her iced sangria.

And we never will be! Toast added vehemently.

That was it. I was officially in a black mood. I forced a smile on my face and took a sip of my own wine. It was quite good. Toast was immune to pretty much every poison, so I wasn't concerned about them trying to kill me this way.

Let them try, Toast snarled.

"I am waiting for my fated mate," I said simply. It was the best excuse I could give for why I was never seen touching a female or woman. Even though I doubted I'd ever come across her, I had a small hope that if there was anyone Toast could work to accept, it'd be our fated mate.

"And thank the Sun God that whole fiasco is over! All our unmated went forever without their proper bonds," she replied with a dramatic wave of her glass. "Really terrible that our own princess got pulled into that mess."

I shrugged, not feeling very sympathetic. I wasn't sorry to hear about how her tale ended. The female had been a pest. Well, all the king's daughters were pests, but she'd been the worst. I couldn't count the number of times I'd caught her waiting nude in my chamber. Toast and I had pushed our luck on several occasions trying to remove her without touching her. I smiled at a particular memory where we'd grabbed a straw broom and whacked her out with it.

"Well, I'm still holding out for my mate. I'll put my trust in the sacred bond," I continued.

"Indeed," Lord Adelmar said in a bored voice, clearly not paying attention to what I was saying. He crooked a finger to call a servant over and whispered something in his ear. Not sure why he bothered whispering when I had phenomenal hearing. He was asking to have his favorite readied, and I hid a frown in my glass. Was he about to show his hand now? Seemed early.

"Mates are fine and all, but does anyone truly need a mate?" Lord Adelmar asked smoothly, and his wife pressed her lips together in irritation. "Present company excluded of course, my beloved," he said, tapping his wife under the chin. She relaxed a little but still seemed annoyed. I'd be more than annoyed if I were her; one didn't talk to mates like that. I'd have helped her flip the table.

"What makes you say that?" I inquired, nodding to a servant who placed a large bloody roast before me. I took a bite, and it was fucking phenomenal. So far, this meal was the only good thing about this mission.

"I'm just saying that a male doesn't always have time for a mate. Let's say you mated. Wouldn't your lady wife be unhappy with how long you'd be away on missions?"

I kept my temper in check, but this lord was really tempting my wrath. I wondered if he'd forgotten he was addressing the king's knight general, but I doubted it. He was testing me.

"So, what is your solution for my hypothetical, failing love life?" I asked wryly, swirling the contents of my glass.

"I'm just thinking it'd be nice to have someone at home instead of trying your luck at a brothel," Lord Adelmar said with a shrug.

One of the other nobles at the table spoke up for the first time, breaking the din of clinking utensils and mastication. "Which we know the king is working to dismantle that market as well," he complained with a sneer. He wiped sauce off his double chin, which wobbled when he shook his head disapprovingly.

"And you are?" I asked, taking a casual bite of my meal.

A pig dragon, Toast interrupted.

What have pigs ever done to you, Toast? I replied, suppressing a smile.

"Duke Gero," he said shortly and refused to engage further. I made a mental note to give that name to Leofwine. Everyone here was potentially involved in the slave market.

"So, what do you mean by having someone at home? A girlfriend?" I inquired innocently to the lord. He snorted and shook his head, looking away as though imagining a grand scene.

"Nothing as demanding as that. Just someone who's always available to entertain."

"So, if not a mate, a girlfriend, or a whore, are we talking about a sex slave?" I just went for it, tired of the bullshit.

"Oh, I wouldn't put a name on it right away. You'd be doing them a favor if anything, but let's leave that business for tomorrow. Come now, enjoy your meal!" the lord said and offered a bite of his roast to his lady wife. Her nostrils flared for a second, and the smallest trail of smoke curled out, but she accepted his food and nodded in approval.

A delicious scent meandered into the room, and it made all the hairs on my body stand on end. It was like sweet spring grass after a rain with a touch of agave. Sweet and earthy. My mouth salivated, and I wondered if this was dessert—if it was something new and foreign to me.

Dessert has never smelled so good, Toast admitted. *Smells like they used agave syrup. I rather prefer that nectar to sugar.*

So do I, I said eagerly, hardly able to focus on my dinner now. Why was I feeling so giddy over a dessert course? It was like I was a six-year-old again.

The scent became stronger when a woman walked into the dining hall with a jug of wine. My heart nearly stopped beating, and my lungs almost caved in because she was the most beautiful creature to have ever lived. I was frozen, terrified because of the predator in me. If I moved, I worried that she might run like a swift doe, never to be seen again.

Her unusual, fog-grey hair ran straight over her shoulders and down to her hips, like a cloudy waterfall. Fortunately, her hair was pinned back with gold barrettes at her temples so I could see her face.

It dawned on me that even though she looked divine, she also looked to be in bad shape. She was heavily made-up, but underneath it all, I could see that she was extremely pale; I couldn't tell if that was from illness or genetics, though.

Her large eyes were as dark and sweet as brown sugar, framed in thick charcoal lashes. They were beautiful, but I could see her fear and confusion in them, especially when her charcoal brows were drawn in anxiousness. Behind it all, she looked dead inside, like her hopes and dreams had long since departed.

Her nose was beautiful and sloped up ever so slightly, as though she had the grace of royalty but not the snobbishness. Her pale lips… I could best describe them as gentle. Not too wide and not too narrow, they were full and kind, as though only loving words were allowed past them.

At this point, I was painfully erect, and it felt like all my nerve endings were firing.

Your dick is a traitor, Toast accused.

I think you'll find that you're the traitor to my dick, I snapped back. *You're the one preventing me from living my life the way everyone else gets to.*

I'm doing it to protect us!

Shut the fuck up.

After that exchange, I was surprised that Toast didn't protest my gazing at her body, which looked like it was made for sex. That thought made me uncomfortable—almost sick—and I adjusted myself in my seat, frowning into another sip of sangria. I had no doubt I was looking at a pleasure slave, and I was sure they'd nurtured her body to look the best it could. I tried not to stare at her charitable breasts when she leaned to pour wine into the other guests' glasses. Similar to what fell across her thighs, her breasts were wrapped in a tight, gauzy fabric. Her waist flared into wide, enticing hips, and her legs went on for days.

"Ah, there is our lovely Elpis. Our most beautiful dancer, yes?" the lord said, and I tried to snap out of my haze to pay attention to him. He looked down to his lady wife who nodded an agreement, but I stared skeptically at the slave. She was no dancer. She was weak; she didn't have the musculature a dancer would have, especially at her age. Come to think of it, this slave was rather old to be in this role.

Is that scent coming from her or the drink she's carrying? I asked Toast in confusion.

No woman smells that good. It is from the drink, Toast said flatly, but I sensed his unease. No... that was sangria in her hands.

"We're thinking of sending her to the academy. Would you like to witness a performance, Sir Keyon?" the lady wife asked with a sly edge to her voice. What a joke, sending a slave to an academy. How stupid did they think I was?

"That's not necessary, Your Ladyship. I'm sure she's a fine dancer," I replied, and the slave, Elpis, fumbled with the wine container. I released a breath when she didn't drop it. I wasn't sure what these people did to slaves who made mistakes, but I didn't want to witness it firsthand.

The woman frowned, then filled the lady wife's glass. Lady Adelmar chuckled and eyed my utensil, which I had accidentally folded in half. I fixed it haphazardly, and she said, "Be a good girl, Elpis, and show our guest some of your dancing."

My heart rate sped up as she approached me. What kind of dancing was this? She could dance anywhere. Why was she—

No. Nope. Fuck to the no. Nuh-uh, Toast protested when the slave straddled my legs without touching me. I leaned back immediately to avoid contact.

Do NOT make a scene, Toast. We can't afford to screw around here.

It's the screwing I'm worried about! he argued. What?

You need to pull it together. Do it for the slaves, Toast. This will be over in a minute. I promise I won't let her hurt us, I said, trying to keep my dragon from taking over and destroying the dining hall. One wrong move, and this whole place could go up in flames. Toast was the very last dragon you wanted to trigger.

My body was brutally on edge while the slave swayed over my lap and legs. Her arms, thighs, and torso fluttered like a flag in the breeze and ran like a ripple over water. Even though her dance wasn't fed with strength, she was beautiful and graceful. When she leaned back and gestured to the sky like she was pleading to the gods, my eyes caught on the gold of a chastity belt. That was odd. How could a pleasure slave this old still be a virgin? I was starting to have so many questions, and I needed time to think, but this woman was incredibly distracting. Her scent was also driving me mad.

That smell is definitely hers, I said to Toast. *Is this female our mate? Don't mates have strong, desirable scents?* That was what all my mated friends have said.

We don't have a mate, Toast said stubbornly.

Toast, you have to verify this for me! That's your fucking job, I argued.

Our job is to rescue these slaves! Toast snapped back in a decent argument. Damn him for appealing to my sense of justice. I gritted my teeth and stared at the woman performing over me. I eyed the grooves of her hips that looked like they'd be perfect handholds. Gods, I wanted nothing more than to rip that chastity belt away and impale her virgin flesh with my cock. Fuck! Fuck, shit, fuck! I needed to calm the shit down. It wouldn't be good if Lord Adelmar noticed how much she was affecting me.

See? She's already causing trouble, Toast said, reading my thoughts.

Fuck off, Toast. Be useful or shut your trap.

Fine, I'll be useful. She matches the description the king gave us. She's probably the one we need to escort back, he said sullenly. My eyes jerked back up to her face. I almost wondered how I didn't see it. I wouldn't call her hair silver, but the cool grey was unusual and—in my opinion—close enough. Brown eyes was a yes. Pearly white skin? Well, she was very pale. She also looked like she'd never seen a drop of sunshine in her life. I couldn't imagine that helped with a slave's complexion... or mood. The Sun God gave so we could take; His gift was energy, light, and joy. I wished I could take her outside right now, but our god was already retiring to make way for the Sky Gods' starlight.

The more she danced over us, the more anxious Toast got. The more anxious Toast got, the more anxious I got. I gripped the armchair, trying to restrain myself from doing... something. Shoving her away with a plate? Bending her over the table and fucking her like a rabid beast in front of everyone? My thoughts were as knotted as my stomach.

Her movements slowed, and she spun off of me as though I'd scared her. When her hand brushed against mine, a spark of pleasure raced up my arm, and Toast—thoroughly startled—shot me out of the chair, which went rolling away on the ground. I was shocked because I was expecting a much more dramatic reaction from him. Skin contact would normally trigger him into running away completely, but he stood still and gave control back to me, seeming confused. Fuck, I was confused as well. What the shit?

M-mate. Mate ricks. May tricks... She may... make tricks on... Toast fumbled for words in a panic, sounding like his brain had completely broken. *Mine. Mind... fuck... Women are a... mindfuck...*

The fuck is wrong with you? I asked my dragon, genuinely concerned and a little freaked out over his behavior. Could an inner beast have a stroke?

I was still aware of our audience, and I gathered myself as if I'd just been startled by one of Leofwine's infamous cellar spiders. "That's enough," I gritted through my teeth. "Thank you, Your Lordship." My eyes fell onto the slave, and she was frozen, hands shaking slightly in fear.

My heart sank into my stomach, knowing that I'd caused that. I hoped she wouldn't get in trouble because of my outburst. I'd better try to clean up this incident. I dragged my chair back to the table.

"Sorry about that," I said, clearing my throat. "Your dancer was doing too good of a job. My wings almost popped right out!" The table erupted into approving laughter, and the lord chuckled, nodding to a servant to remove his dish.

"Ever the young, hot-blooded dragon," Lord Adelmar noted with a sickly sweet smile. "Our Sir Keyon knows well the value of a beautiful female."

"Indeed, I do," I replied with a smirk but felt revolted with myself.

Elpis seemed to snap out of her trance and continued refilling the glasses at the table. I noticed a younger noble slide his hand up her thigh to rub what he could touch of her bottom, but the lord snapped his fingers at him in a signal, and the noble stopped, looking surprised. Was this common behavior when the knight general wasn't visiting? Maybe I shouldn't wait another day to scout the area if I could prevent further abuse to this slave. I was one second away from ripping off that man's hand.

Don't risk the mission over her, Toast whined. *She's probably full of diseases.*

What the fuck? She's a slave. She doesn't have autonomy over her body. Whatever state she may be in is not her fault, I raged back at my dragon. *You know what? I don't want to hear from you for the rest of the night. Get lost.*

She's driving a wedge between us already!

No, you are!

I tried like hell to hide my fury at the table. All I wanted to do now was retire to my room. I couldn't stand anyone within twenty feet of me right now. The only one who wasn't pissing me off was the poor slave, who was standing at the corner of the room, waiting for the wineglasses to get low.

"Ah, you must be quite tired, Sir Keyon. It's been a long day of flying for you, no?" Lord Adelmar asked, tilting his head and stifling a yawn of his own.

"It has, Your Lordship," I said honestly. "I am quite ready to hit the nest."

The lord nodded to Elpis and said, "Lead him to his guest room. Take care of him if he is not tired enough." I stood from my chair but was barely able to contain the look of horror that wanted to crawl onto my face. Did he really just command her to please me if I asked for it—in front of all these people? Oh, that was a bold fucking move on his part. He seemed pretty confident on what he was going to try to sell me on tomorrow. He was practically showing his slave off to me.

Elpis's face gave nothing away when she bowed and led me from the dining hall. I strode after her, wondering if I'd be able to keep myself from killing Lord Adelmar when my knights arrived. He was asking for it. He was practically begging for it with how he paraded his 'dancer' around me. How was he so confident? I didn't understand why he thought he had me in the bag. I needed to be extra careful.

Elpis led me to a guest room, and a dragon-shifter was waiting patiently by the door. She was dressed smartly in slacks and a button-up; perhaps she was an administrator. She simply nodded at me and opened the door. Elpis led me in, and the female closed it, leaving me alone with the slave. I noticed that my small, innocent bag of luggage was in here. I wasn't worried that anyone had gone through it. Unless you could perform espionage with socks, there was nothing in there to find.

I opened my bag to pull out some pajama bottoms, hoping Elpis would leave on her own, but I only heard her sit down on the floor. I sighed and turned around, looking down at the beautiful female who was staring expectantly at my shoulder.

"You're free to go, Elpis," I whispered as quietly as I could and made a shooing motion with my hands. She looked confused, glanced down at my stubborn erection, and frowned up at me. She reached to unbutton my pants, but I backed up before she could touch me. I tripped and fell back on the bed, hissing at her to stop.

Her mouth was practically gaping at my refusal to let her 'tire me.' She looked fearfully toward the door again and tried to climb up after me on the bed.

Don't let her touch us! Toast yelped.

I'm trying! She's a female possessed!

I backed away when her hand shot out to hook onto my belt. She clutched at it in victory, but I loosened it, and the belt slid off into her hands. She frowned and threw away the belt. I scrambled for my bag and held it between us as a shield.

"Elpis!" I hissed. "Stop! You don't have to do this! I won't tell them!"

She snorted in frustration and tried to shove away the bag. I didn't want to hurt her, so I let go of the bag but slipped again and fell against the wall. My head smacked against the stone, and I collapsed into a heap.

Did they just fuckin' wax these floors? I grumbled to myself.

Elpis jumped over, and tears started streaming down her face. She turned to look at me from different angles, panicking and trying to see if I was injured. I reached back and felt only a small bump. That would heal in a couple minutes.

See? Women are dangerous!

Toast… do you understand that we got hurt because we were trying to avoid her? Worst thing that would have happened if she'd gotten a hold of us would be getting the best handjob in the kingdom.

He didn't have a comeback for that one this time.

"It's ok, Elpis," I whispered and sat up with a groan. "I'm fine. I won't tell them." She continued to stare back at the door, and I could practically smell the terror emanating from her. "Will you get punished if you don't do anything?" I asked tiredly and scooted up against the wall. She nodded as she stared down at the floor. I rubbed my hands over my face and sighed. Oh gods, this was about to get stupid.

"Alright, Elpis. I'm going to help you, but you have to promise to not make me laugh," I said, raising a warning finger, and she nodded vigorously. Her wide, brown-sugar eyes looked curiously up at my shoulder, and I cleared my throat.

"Ahhh! Oh yeah." I grunted, acting like Elpis's lips were wrapped around my cock. She placed her hands over her mouth and turned away, holding back giggles. The corner of my lips curled up in a smirk, and I kept going. "Mmm, you like that, huh? Like my big cock sliding down your throat?" Elpis was keeling over in a ball, shaking with suppressed laughter. "Ah, yeah. That's how your dragon likes it. Mmm. Mmm. Oh yeah!"

Elpis put a couple fingers in her mouth and moaned to join my fake fellatio performance. "Elpis!" I hissed, nearly laughing. "Don't make me laugh!" She grimaced and covered her face with her hands, but I could tell she was having the time of her life.

"Ahh, yeah, that's it. Don't stop, beautiful. Don't stop; you got it. You got me. You want to swallow? You want a taste of the knight general?" I groaned out and almost faltered when I scented Elpis's arousal. She had scooted against the wall and was pressing her thighs together. Her face was no longer pale. She was no longer laughing.

Flamin' shit! Stop turning her on! Toast cried.

I'm almost done... I said distractedly, incredulous that my vocal acting had affected her so strongly.

"Ahhh, yeah, that's it. Drink your dragon empty. That's a good girl," I said finally and rested my hands behind my head. I stared at Elpis, who was shifting uncomfortably, and felt kind of bad. Well, at least that lady outside would be satisfied. Hopefully she wouldn't be punished for anything that'd happened this evening.

I watched Elpis leave and changed into my sleepwear. Several minutes later, there was a knock on the door, and I opened it to find that the dragon-shifter had returned.

"I'm sorry that our Elpis was not satisfactory," she said, bowing in an apology. "She'll be punished."

"No," I denied, completely thrown. "What are you talking about? She did great."

She narrowed her eyes. "We always check their mouths."

And there it was. There was the next horror. When I thought I'd seen it all... It was like clockwork. I glared coldly at her and ground out, "I gave her water. I'm not a barbarian. Do not punish her. She pleased me."

The woman shrugged. "It's too late," she said and departed. I slammed the door closed and roared into my pillow. Pacing angrily, I tried to contain my rage but simply ended up scorching a wooden table until it disintegrated into a fine black powder.

That female was dead too.

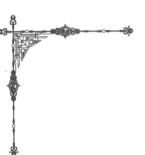

Chapter 3

Elpis

When I left the knight's chamber, Tofa gripped my arm and yanked me back down to the underground floors. When we got back to the room my cage was in, Tofa fisted my hair and pulled my head back to look into my mouth. I held back a whimper and allowed her to check, knowing what she was about to say. She sniffed slightly and growled, then pushed me hard, making me trip over a small cage and fall to the ground. I cried out in pain, grabbed my leg, and saw that it was skinned and bleeding.

"Oh, shut up, shiftless," the woman spat. She walked toward the small cage, opened the top, and gave me a hard stare. My eyes widened, and I shook my head, backing away from her.

"Nay, please! Please! I did what he asked! You heard! You heard us!" I cried. "Please don't punish me! I did what he asked, I swear!"

Tofa looked down at me and shrugged. "Then I guess I'll go back and get the right story. Get in the cage." She glowered at me.

"He'll say I did it!" I appealed, but I was only met with cold, unmoving eyes. I stared at her, breathing hard for several minutes, hoping she'd give in... but she didn't. Tears beaded in my eyes, and I knew I'd lost. I broke out into a cold sweat, and my feet trudged forward slowly and unwillingly. I wrung my hands and pleaded with every muscle in my face. "Please let me out when he says I did it..." I begged, and she nodded, then shrugged. I had no idea what that combination of gestures meant, but I had a feeling that all hope was lost.

It was a bitter misery struggling to do something that was only going to bring you more pain. Getting into the cage was hard, almost as hard as getting out of it. I squatted, curled up into a ball, and tilted until I was on my side. It was the only way to fit in it. My entire being screamed when Tofa closed the top of the cage and locked it. The cold bars pressed in from all angles, and my claustrophobia hit me in full force.

My wild eyes landed on Zosime and Dagmaer.

I'm sorry, little hatchling. I can't be strong for you now.

After Tofa left, Zosime wiped a tear from her cheek, took a long breath, and began singing in a whisper. Everyone in the room joined Zosime's efforts. Tired voices united in pain and sorrow to distract my mind.

We heard that you are out there
In your light we will trust
Your children are in nightmares
Do you remember us?

Please find us under stone
Beneath the rock and rust
Your children are alone
Do you remember us?

Free us from the depraved
By brute force if you must
Your children are enslaved
Do you remember us?

There was a steadying breath in the chilly, dripping room before the last verse, the water condensation a drum to their lament.

If you have but a moment
A last request we plea
Help lost Pelagia ascend
Do you remember she?

The final verse was something we'd added years ago, and we took a moment to grieve before the Slaves of the First Water moved on to the next song. They quietly repeated every song we knew until I grew drowsy. It was a tradition that went back as long as I could remember.

Whenever someone was put in the punishment cage, no one could sleep until the tortured slave did. I didn't know how it came to be, but it had kept me from losing my sanity on more than one occasion. With my claustrophobia, I did worse in the cage than anyone else. I owed these people my life; I was certain of that.

***

When I woke, I realized there was no one to distract me. I tried to think of something pleasant, and my mind went back to the warrior I had been supposed to please last night. Just thinking about him relaxed me, and as soon as I realized that, I clung onto it like a lifeline.

I had never been asked to please an unwilling male before in my life. Actually, I didn't think I'd ever seen an unwilling male until last night. I couldn't figure out why he didn't let me relieve him. He was obviously aroused; there was no hiding that monster from my sights. I smiled slightly into my hand and chuckled. It was really too bad. I think I would have actually enjoyed touching him, which would have been a first.

Great goddess, he was a stunning male. His very presence was overwhelming, like you were expected to either fall into line or get out of his way. He towered over everyone at the mansion with his broad but agile frame, and I swore his biceps were as large as the lord's head. I nearly giggled again, picturing the lord's head next to the knight's bicep so I could see which was larger. I bet that bicep could crack the lord's head like a walnut! How I'd love to see that!

Oh, and how I wished I could dig my fingers into his tousled locks. The deep, rich brown reminded me of roasted chestnuts I'd seen once at the lord's table. The boyishness of his messy hair almost softened his barbaric silhouette. Then there were his bronze eyes. The way his metallic eyes looked at me last night turned all the butterflies in my belly into little dragons. They flew around and breathed fire, stoking and stirring my insides into a rapturous warmth. I smiled and squirmed happily at the feelings he'd aroused in me. If I had to be anyone's personal slave, I'd rather be his. At least I had a feeling he'd never force me.

I loved his scent, I loved his sun-kissed skin, and I was dying to know what his expressive, cocky lips would feel like on mine. I probably shouldn't encourage these feelings, but it was all that was keeping me sane right now. If he was a bad male, I'd deal with that later. Right now, he was my knight in shining scales, my savior, and I hung on to every memory I had of him.

He'd even made me laugh, offering to do something so stupid as pretend I was pleasing him. I hadn't laughed that hard in a long time. I sighed longingly. Of all the males that wouldn't let me touch them, it had to be him.

A thought occurred to me in that moment that sent nausea curling in my belly. Although I'd never seen a male deny a female, I wondered if what I had attempted would have been considered rape. He wasn't willing and did everything he could to stop me without hurting me.

Would he have been traumatized if I'd touched him? Did that happen to men too? If so, why didn't we hear about it? I frowned and tried to scratch an itch on my nose, making my elbow dig painfully into the wires of the cage.

I was now beginning to feel ashamed of how I'd pursued him. Yes, I'd been ordered to... but that didn't make me feel any better. I knew I had been risking punishment, but perhaps one night of torture was worth it to avoid traumatizing someone for life. I never wanted anyone to feel as dirty as I did. Even when I washed, I could still feel other hands on me. Groping hands and demanding cocks followed me like ghosts, reminding me that I was nothing but an instrument for release—used and stained.

I'd learned to drift away and leave my body when I needed to, but... I'd never want to be the cause of someone else having to do that. No... I wouldn't try to force myself on anyone again. I barely had anything to live for now, and I wouldn't add that shame to the anchor that dragged my soul through the dirt. Dagmaer was my latest reason to live, but she was a thin one. She'd have others to protect her if I was gone—if I was lost enough to follow in Pelagia's bitter, tear-stained footsteps.

Sir Kenon

"So, how did you sleep last night?" Lady Adelmar crooned the question over her glass of sparkling wine. I settled down at the dinner table, though it was a bit early to be supping. I was even crankier today than I was yesterday, and my answer was a complete lie.

"Oh, I slept very well, indeed. The guest quarters are most comfortable." I was writhing all night from one thing or another. First of all, my brain was furious over how the slave had still been punished despite my attempt to intervene. Why the fuck did it matter what happened behind closed doors as long as I was "happy with her services?" Was she expected to hold a dragon knight down until I caved under her magnetic charms? She had no chance. Either way, she was going to lose. It was ridiculous.

Secondly, I'd been suffering all night with the sense that something was wrong. It was a mixture of dread and panic; a dull burn and sharp scalding of the mind. Even the room had felt too small—to the point where I almost couldn't breathe. Part of me equated it with being forced to interact with slavers, but another part of me thought it was something else. Something deep and primal.

"Did our lovely Elpis leave you well?" Lord Adelmar asked, raising a brow over an amused smirk.

And the sales pitch continues, I thought with a sigh.

"Oh, she is quite the eager thing," I said, taking a sip of my wine, but when the table murmured an agreement, I nearly choked in rage. It was the same crowd as last night; had everyone here touched her? I fisted my left hand at my side, allowing my claws to pierce my palm and draw blood. I focused on the pain, tried to slow my breathing, and took another sip, buying a moment to collect myself. Toast felt rage on my behalf too, and it didn't take much for him to lash out in my defense.

"Yes, I was most pleased. Utterly exhausted by the time I hit the nest," I finished, hoping that would be enough information for him. I studied the lord over the rim of my glass. Did he think he had me in his pocket now? Did he think that all it took was a night with his best slave to turn me into a sympathizer? What a lark if that was the case. No, there must be more.

"Ah yes, I had no doubt. Oh, here is our little sunrise. Come fill our cups," the lord said, and I scented her before I saw her. Sweet grass and agave nectar coiled about me like a drug; it was much more potent than the wine in my hands. Every flavor was bland in comparison to her aroma.

The slave walked in slowly, gracefully, but I detected a slight limp. The instability wasn't just in one leg, but both. She seemed weaker, shakier. One shin was wrapped in a beautiful blue cloth with bells hanging from it, but I saw the impression of bandages underneath. I could smell her blood. I didn't know how it was possible, but she seemed even paler than yesterday. What did they do to her? What had her punishment been?

The lord held his cup out, and she rushed to fill it, trying not to limp. "We've trained her since she was a small thing, so she really doesn't know how to do anything else. Including stretching before dancing, isn't that right, my silly little Elpis? Did you strain a muscle again?"

She nodded and continued around the table to check for low glasses. So even though they weren't even trying to hide what she was, they were still hiding the punishments and abuse.

"So that comes to expanding upon what I've been showing you today. Since slavery is illegal, there will be so many individuals at a loss with their newfound freedom. They won't know how to survive. If Elpis was cast out, she'd surely die of starvation or at the hands of an abusive male."

Is he looking to off-load his inventory before he gets busted? Toast asked.

Good question.

"Now, if someone offered to take her for a fee, they'd be responsible for housing her or preparing her to live on her own. Whatever they need from her, really. But at least she'd have a home."

"Why would someone give you money to 'adopt a slave?'" I asked, briefly looking down at the grilled trout set before me. I nodded my thanks to the servant... or maybe it was a slave dressed as one.

"Well, the money is for a good cause! It goes toward taking care of the poor creatures that still need a home. If we so happen upon more slaves... we can care for them until lovely do-gooders such as yourself come along," Lord Adelmar said, pasting a poor excuse for genuine concern on his rotten face.

So, Adelmar gets to collect slaves, claim that he is rescuing them, and is accepting 'adoption fees' for concerned parties to take responsibility for the slave's future welfare, Toast summarized with venom dripping from each word.

Yep, I agreed. *He's rebranding, but he's still in the market. He'll generate income by abducting people and selling them.*

Same old story, different skin. The hatchling was just as ugly inside the shell.

"So why not allow these slaves to go through the king's rehabilitation process?" I asked, knowing this would be his biggest hurdle. The lord's eyes narrowed for just a moment.

He was hoping we weren't going to ask that one! Toast snarled with delight. I could almost hear him sharpening his teeth to cut through the lord's spine in one bite.

"Consider this a private service, Sir Keyon. The castle has limited resources and attention must be spread out among many. We simply offer a more intimate, nurturing process for the lost and lonely," he said with a practiced shrug. He then tilted his head and twirled a finger through his trimmed, greying beard.

"We really do have the slave's best interests in mind," Lady Adelmar said with faux compassion, fiddling with her necklace.

They both seem nervous now, I said to Toast. *Look how they fidget.*

Best accept any deals right now, then we could probably send the signal tonight.

"And how do you guarantee that these… ex-slaves are adopted by good people?" I asked, too curious to stop at this point.

"Oh, we'll have a strict referral system in place…" the lord said, looking progressively more uncomfortable with my follow-up questions. The table became quieter, and other guests shifted in their seats.

"Sounds intriguing, I admit," I finally announced, taking a bite of my fish. "Would certainly save me some trouble if you gathered the slaves for me."

The tension around the table released, and it seemed like Adelmar's guests found it possible to breathe again. Some laughed, and discourse around the table went back to a steady chatter.

We need to know if anyone else is involved, I noted in frustration. *This could start an entire new ring of slave abduction and trading. We're witnessing its birth right now!*

I suppose I could try to not kill Adelmar, and we could take him back for questioning. Leofwine's good at getting them to squawk.

True, I mused.

"So, if you're... amenable to this noble venture of ours, I'd be more than happy to make a gesture of goodwill," the lord said, but his eyes were following Elpis as she worked to refill Duke Gero's glass. He was on his fifth, but with how he stared at the slave's breasts, he didn't seem to be draining his cup for the alcohol.

I had to dig my nails into my palm again to keep my rage—and subsequently Toast's rage—in check. I forced my eyes back to the lord's and raised a brow. "What gesture did you have in mind?"

The lord held up a small gold ring with a key attached. I didn't make the connection until I heard a tiny gasp come from the slave at the foot of the table. I glanced over to see shock on Elpis's face. Seemingly without thought, her hands drifted down to her hips. What...?

OH!

"Absolutely not!" Duke Gero protested, sending spittle flying across the table. "My Lord, you said th—"

Lord Adelmar chuckled and swung the key to Elpis's chastity belt around his finger. "I've made no promises, my dear duke. Don't you want our generous venture to succeed? Don't you think our benefactors deserve the very best?" Duke Gero was practically purple and possibly at risk of a heart attack.

Good. Toast scoffed. *I decided I didn't want to sink my fangs into that rotten shit anyway.*

"So, Sir Keyon," the lord said, "would you be our first good soul to adopt a poor slave? Elpis has been here almost her entire life. She needs a kind soul to look after her... free of charge, of course. Who knows what could happen to her if she was released into this dangerous world all alone..."

I was frozen. I admit I had not seen this coming. It shouldn't matter, though... I'd call my troops tonight anyway. This place would be empty by dawn.

"That is a very generous offer... but I'm afraid I must decline. I can't have this coming back to me, you see," I said in a bored tone.

The lord sighed and turned to the duke. "Well, I suppose our original deal stands then," the lord said, adjusting his grip on the keys. There was a moan of dismay from Elpis, who was shaking like a baby deer at the turn of events.

"Then I look forward to breaking her in after dinner!" The duke grinned excitedly, almost bouncing in his chair, and gestured for Elpis to come sit on his lap.

No. No. No. No. No!

"I've changed my mind," I announced firmly in my most authoritative, dominant voice. "I accept your offer." I didn't need to give a reason. Fuck these people. If I was playing a part, I'd play the part as someone who took what he wanted.

The lord grinned, and the duke screamed in outrage, but I was too busy talking to my dragon to care about anyone.

I know you don't like females, but we can also agree we don't like the pig dragon. Let's not give the pig dragon what he wants. The female won't touch us. We'll hand her over to our soldiers when they arrive. She'll go through the intake process like every-one else. Please don't put her rape on my shoulders, Toast.

Toast was silent for several minutes, and I busied myself eating the remainder of my meal. Lord Adelmar tossed Elpis's key to me, and I snatched it out of the air. Elpis slowly made her way to my side and stood there quietly. Her legs were beginning to shake, and I looked up at her. "Sit, Elpis," I ordered, and she collapsed to the floor, exhaling in relief.

See? She'll do what we ask. Just trust me to handle her until our troops come. Please!

Fine, Toast said, caving but sounding frightened. *If she stabs us in the back, it's your fault.*

Totally fair, I agreed, looking down at the golden key in my palm.

I'm going to have nightmares.

I got you, big guy.

Chapter 4

Elpis

I sat next to my new owner in complete shock. Was I leaving this place now? What about the other slaves? What about Zosime and Dagmaer? I couldn't abandon them! Dagmaer's life had just begun! Who knew when she'd see the Sun God again? I listened to the conversations around me, trying to find out when we'd be leaving, but I got no such clue. I guessed that we'd leave tomorrow because it sounded like everything they needed to talk about was resolved.

My worst fears had been confirmed about the knight; he wasn't a good guy. He was content to just let slaves continue to be sold under the Sun God's very nose. Did that mean Dagmaer would be sold? She was a pretty young girl, and I was terrified that the duke would get his grubby hands on her.

Oh gods, I could barely think straight! I was drawn to her hope. I couldn't let Dagmaer get taken! Was there a way I could sneak down and free her tonight? I tried to will the tears away, but I was starting to panic. This was too much! Everything was happening too fast!

A glass of water came into my peripheral vision, and I started, flinching because I thought someone was going to pour it on me.

"Drink some water, Elpis," the knight said in a firm voice. I didn't look at his face, but I accepted the water and drank heavily, draining the cup in one go. I caught my breath and sighed in relief. My parched throat was no longer as raw, and I handed the cup back gratefully. Both times he'd been careful not to graze my fingers. He still wasn't touching me, and I wouldn't complain.

I couldn't believe I was almost Duke Gero's slave. A shudder wracked my body from head to toe. I hadn't even known he'd put a bid on me, but then again, I hadn't known that our lord was thinking about clearing us out either. At least on the floor I didn't have to suffer the duke's disgusting looks. I would have needed five baths tonight to get the stench of his gaze off me.

A giant coat draped over my shoulders, and I was no longer thinking about stenches. I was encapsulated by the knight's scent and nearly melted in bliss. I looked up at his shoulders in question because we weren't supposed to look our owners in the eyes. Why'd he give me this?

"You were shivering," the knight explained with a shrug and turned to talk to another slave.

Oh, that shudder was emotional, but at least I got something pleasant out of it. I tucked my nose to the side and took a deep whiff of the coat. I sighed, and my belly squirmed in delight. It smelled like… something I still couldn't place. I scented male sweat, but I couldn't detect the other elements. I wrapped the coat around my knees and snuggled into it. Mmm, total bliss. All I needed now was some food, and I was set.

A slave handed me a bowl of fish, rice, and vegetables, and I stared at it in awe. Could my new owner read my mind? I peeked up at my owner, whose eyes flickered from me back to the lord. Fiddlesticks! Caught looking. I blushed and dug into my bowl of food, grateful to ease my aching, empty belly. Water, food, sitting, and warmth. I was already getting a good deal. Maybe if

I could put on some weight, I wouldn't be so cold all the time. Oh! Maybe I'd get real clothes!

I was drowsy by the time everyone got up from the dining table. I stood to follow the knight but was pulled aggressively into the hall by a violent hand. A sweaty palm cupped my mouth to muffle my cries, and Duke Gero whispered, "You will take the dagger I put in your pocket, and you will kill your owner in his sleep. If you don't, I will bid on that pretty little girl and see how well she handles serving me in the privacy of my bedchamber!"

He immediately shoved me away from him, and I stumbled, falling to the floor with a thud. I winced, knowing that my tail-bone was going to be very sore tomorrow. My owner rounded the corner in a fury but calmed when he saw me. He looked very confused to see me on the floor, so I jumped up, held back a cry of pain, and shuffled to follow him again.

He glared darkly into the hall, and his nostrils flared. When he snorted, a puff of smoke curled from his nostrils in anger. He must have known that the duke had harassed me. My new owner might not be a good person, but he wasn't stupid. He hadn't even wanted me until he knew the duke did. Was he protecting me?

The knight brought me back upstairs to his guest chamber and closed the door behind me. I stood at the door while he went to open his bag. I wanted to say something, but we weren't to speak until addressed. I squirmed uncomfortably and fisted my hands at my sides until he froze and turned his head to look at me.

"Are you ok?" he asked. I shook my head 'no' and waited for him to give me leave to talk. I curled my toes and shifted my weight from foot to foot. He still didn't say anything, so I sighed and just showed him. I held my hand out so he wouldn't consider me a threat and reached into his coat pocket. I pulled the dagger out, made sure he saw it clearly, and then I threw it at the wall to break it. It did not break. In fact, it just bounced off the wall and headed back toward my toes. I shrieked and jumped away, narrowly evading the rabid length of steel.

I was on my back by my master's feet, panting and looking down to make sure I had all my toes. I collapsed in relief and placed my hands over my face, groaning at my stupidity. I just wanted to show him my loyalty! Besides, I had no plans on letting the duke get his hands on Dagmaer. That piss-poor excuse for a dragon no longer held power over me!

When my attention returned to my surroundings, I realized that the knight was laughing uncontrollably. He was sitting down and clutching at his scrunched red face, occasionally wiping a tear away with a knuckle. I looked up at him from my floor vantage, and a small, amazed giggle escaped my lips. His laugh was extremely contagious, and I got swept into it. I chuckled quietly, but eventually, every boom from his chest trickled down my abdomen to settle between my thighs.

Oh gods, what?

I felt a rush of heat and dampness from my core, so I stood and walked to sit on the other side of the room to hide my embarrassment. How was it that even his laugh aroused me? I tried to focus on something else. I eyed a pile of black ashes in confusion but ended up poking it to draw little shapes on the floor.

Didn't there use to be a table here?

"Yeah, I cremated that table when they told me you were punished," he said when his laughter abated. He sobered and cleared his throat. "I tried, Elpis. I really did. She wouldn't listen. I'm sorry." He looked apologetic, and I lowered my gaze. Owners didn't apologize. This was weird.

"I hope it wasn't... too bad," he added, pulling out several items from his bag. I didn't reply. I didn't regret not forcing myself on him—not that I could have. I couldn't force soup on a dying man; this body was so weak.

I noticed the dagger was still on this side of the room, so I grabbed it by the blade and handed it to him. He took the handle and carefully removed it from my grip. "So, is this a show of your loyalty as a slave or your decency as a human being?" he asked curiously and raised a brow at me. I supposed it was

both, but I didn't know how to answer. He was making communication difficult, not using yes-or-no questions. He didn't
talk like an owner. It was almost as if he knew nothing about
owning slaves, which was impossible because he was friends
with the lord.

Was this a test? No. No, it couldn't be. He'd been nice to
me the other night. Maybe he was just a nice owner? Maybe if I
spoke freely, I wouldn't be punished. He didn't seem to like the
fact I was punished. He even tried to help me break the rules.
Ah... my mind was tired. Too much. This was all too much.

"Okaaay," the knight said with a deep intake of breath. "Let's
try this one. Did Duke Gero give you this weapon?" he asked,
crossing his arms and shifting his weight. He wiggled the blade
from one of his tucked hands.

I breathed a sigh of relief and nodded a 'yes.' Finally!

"Elpis, I need you to speak freely with me. I don't understand
these conversation games. I'll be straight with you, but I need
you to do the same in return, especially if I'm to protect you,"
he asserted sternly.

Ok, good. He made the rules clear. "Yes, mast—" I started
saying, but he interrupted as fast as lightning.

"If you call me anything but Sir Keyon, I'm going to be very
cross with you. Or Keyon. Whatever. I don't care. Just do not call
me your master!" he snapped. He tossed a set of pajamas onto my
lap and turned around to face the wall. "Get changed. Those will
be big, but they'll be much more comfortable than that costume
they put you in. You'll get better clothes later."

I marveled at the soft cotton under my fingers and couldn't
hold back a squeal of delight. I jumped up, took the costume off,
and put on the fine clothing. I had to tie the strings on the bottoms
extra tight, but I got them to stay. I giggled as I walked in a circle
with an extra foot of pajama trailing behind me.

"Don't trip now," the knight, Sir Keyon, said with an amused
chuckle. I grinned back up at him, but then averted my eyes out
of habit. Gods! What was the rule for that now?

I looked around for a spot to settle and curled up at the foot of the bed. I nuzzled into my warm, pajama-clad arms and scented his delicious smell all over them. I smiled and curled tighter. I felt so spoiled.

"Elpis, get on the bed," Sir Keyon ordered. My eyes shot open, and I glanced warily up at him. He wasn't going to use my belt key to get to me, was he? He saw the look on my face and snorted. "I'm not going to touch you. I'm just letting you have the bed. I'll take the floor. That's an order. Go on, get on up there, moonflower."

I balked at the strange endearment, but I scrambled onto the mattress and groaned into the pillow. This was a complete turnaround from last night's sleeping arrangement. Everything about this was amazing! I snuggled under the covers, kicked my feet, and squealed again. I could hear him laughing, but I didn't care if I looked stupid. This was the best moment of my entire life!

"I need to head out for a little bit, Elpis. Stay here. Do not go anywhere, and don't let anyone else in. Make sure you lock the door. I'll be back soon," Sir Keyon's voice said, and I popped my head out of the blankets to see him swing the door shut.

I waited until I couldn't hear his footsteps any longer before crawling out of bed. Now was the perfect time to try to free Dagmaer!

Sir Keyon

I left my guest chamber without a solid plan in place, but I knew I had to find a way to get to the roof or a higher balcony to send the signal. I'd heard enough, and I'd honestly seen more than I wanted to see. I couldn't get the sight of how Duke Gero looked at Elpis out of my thoughts. It was embedded in my memory, and I wanted nothing more than to wipe it from my mind. I didn't care if I had to smuggle her out in a blanket. He'd never put his filthy eyes on her again. If he so much as reached for her, he'd be removed from his hands.

I spied Lord Adelmar strolling down the hall and walked to catch up to him. He heard my footsteps and turned with a wry smile. "That was fast," he teased, and I snorted.

"No offense," I said, falling into stride with him, "but I'd rather taste a fine wine out of crystal than a cup. I'll deflower her when we get home."

"That's fair." The lord nodded with a chuckle. "I almost wish you'd write after. I admit I've always been curious about how she'd taste."

Gross. Toast shuddered.

"It's remarkable you've been able to keep your hands off her for so long," I replied dryly. It was getting far too easy to speak like a slave owner, and I felt like I needed to wash my mouth out with soap. "That aside, any diseases I need to worry about?"

"They lose their value when they're broken in, and she would have been worth a fortune. And as for your question, no. She clears them from her system fairly quickly. Surprisingly fast for a shiftless," the lord answered. "It's one of the reasons why she's our most popular. The guests covet her."

"Shiftless?" I asked, genuinely curious now. "She's not a human?" I really had not been certain.

A short, sharp laugh burst from him. "Does she look human?" He shrugged. "It's unclear what she is. She came to us as a child but never showed signs of a first shift. Her faster healing also makes it clear she's probably not human. As long as she did what we asked and did it well, it didn't matter what she was."

These creatures are disgusting, Toast growled.

I hope you and I can agree that it's appropriate to feel bad for the female, whether or not she frightens you. Yes? I pressed. Maybe I was pushing Toast too much concerning Elpis, but if she happened to be my—our—fated mate, he needed to understand my need to protect her.

Either way, Toast did not answer me. I sighed.

"Well, if I discover what she is, I'll be sure to let you know," I said in a bored tone.

"I doubt the duke would have been so curious."

"Now where did you dredge that muck from anyway?" I asked, perhaps a bit too rudely. I couldn't keep my hatred for the dragon beneath my scales.

"He's not useful on his own... he just has good connections. Believe me, I'd like to be rid of him as well. The dragon is a stain at my table. Alas, he has too many friends in unsavory places. I wouldn't dare." The lord scowled, scuffing his boot particularly hard on his next step as though he was scraping Duke Gero off it. "No doubt there will be repercussions for giving you Elpis, but he would have ruined her in days. Body and soul."

I've seen her eyes, my dear lord. You've already killed her soul.

"Don't tell me you gave her to me to save her." I scoffed in disbelief. The lord's eyes flickered in the dark hallway, and he scowled.

"Yes, I took her, I enslaved her, I raised her, and I used her, but there is only so much monster in me, Sir Keyon," he said in a hard voice.

Whatever helps him sleep at night, Toast muttered.

Even demons crave comfort.

"Enough of this for now, then. Elpis will be cared for," I dismissed. "Now the evening is still early, and I'm looking for a spot to stretch my wings and loosen these thoughts from my mind. You've stretched my comfort zone today, Lord Adelmar. Any suggestions?" I asked, adding a dose of reality to make him nervous and therefore more pliant. He knew I was still much more powerful than him, in title and body. I could snap him like a twig.

"No doubt you could. You've been most generous in coming to hear me out. You'll have to send my regards to the prince for organizing this. I wasn't supposed to mention him, but since it went so well, I can't really see what the issue is..."

What? Toast interjected. *No, that's impossible.*

We've been set up, Toast. This was a trap.

I had to verify. "I'll give your best wishes to the crown prince, then."

The lord stopped and gave me a sharp look. "I think you mean our good Prince Cyneric..."

We stood and stared at the other, two enemies simultaneously exposed. We almost didn't react to the large explosion that came from downstairs. Lord Adelmar laughed darkly and shook his head, looking out the nearest hall balcony like an emperor watching his domain fall to ruin.

"Seems like you and I have a common foe, Sir Keyon, and he's the third most powerful male in the kingdom." He backed toward the open doors, stripping himself of his clothes. He stood on the edge and said, "Do be a male of your word and care for Elpis, hmm?" With those last words ringing in the air, the lord jumped and shifted into a mottled pewter dragon. I stared at his escape, barely able to process what was happening.

One word stabbed through my fog. *Elpis!*

I had to get to Elpis!

I raced back down the hall toward my guest chamber and flung open the door. She wasn't there! I breathed the air in, but her scent was old. She'd disappeared shortly after I'd left. Was she taken? Was it the duke?

"Fuck!" I swore and flew down the stairs in a fury, looking for the source of the explosion. I jumped down several flights to take a shortcut to the ground level and tuned my ears. The commotion was coming from the main hall. Smoke crawled through the rooms while servants, slaves, and guests were screaming, scattering like bugs from a disturbed garden rock.

We hadn't given the signal yet! Toast roared in rage. *Why are they burning the place down? They can't have found the slaves already. There's still people in here!*

I allowed Toast to spread his wings and felt them rip through my shirt. If I didn't allow him to vent, we'd go into a full shift, and there was no room to navigate in here with Toast. He was a biggun.

I forced my way past screaming people, trying not to touch any women. Toast didn't need any more aggravation. I spied some of the soldiers that Prince Cyneric had loaned me, but I couldn't see any of mine. My knights, my Inferno, were they ok?

I grabbed one of Cyneric's men and jerked him to a stop. "Why did you not wait for my signal?" I hissed. "Where are the others? Answer me!"

"Where are the slaves?" the soldier asked, blatantly ignoring my interrogation.

"Why. Did. You. Not. Wait. For. My. Signal?" I repeated through gritted teeth, grabbing handfuls of his coat and lifting him off his feet to face me.

"We were exposed, and your men were attacked. We're here to get the slaves and go!" the soldier growled through his discomfort. I noticed the changes in his breathing, muscles, and heart rate the second he lied. I'd get nothing from him. I threw him off me and strode toward where I suspected the slaves were being held.

I grabbed the handle to the closet, and Elpis's scent was much stronger here! I yanked the door off its hinges and threw it away, hoping darkly that it'd hit one of Cyneric's men. I folded my wings, tore another door down, and jogged down the stone stairs that went underground. Puffs of smoke were curling from my nose in agitation. Her scent was getting closer.

The stairway opened to a room that split into two paths. Two guards immediately stood up to engage me, but I broke their necks. I didn't waste time with slaver guards. They never knew enough to be useful, and I'd long since stopped bringing them back alive.

I looked down one flight of stairs that led to a packed cell, and I sent Cyneric's men that way to work on liberating that crowd. Elpis's scent was in the other direction. I opened a cell door to find a quiet room with smaller cages. Each one held one to three slaves that were in slightly better condition than the ones that were downstairs. These were probably the 'upstairs' slaves—servants and pleasure slaves that needed to look presentable. These were given more care. It didn't seem like much more, though.

My head snapped to the right when I heard sobbing, and a small voice called my name. Stuffed into the tiniest cage was Elpis. Even curled up in a ball, she barely fit in it.

"I don't know who you are, but please let her out! She's not violent! She's being punished for coming back down here after being sold. She tried to lift the keys off a guard, but a pickpocket she is not," a female's voice begged quietly from the cage closest to Elpis's torture cage. "What's going on out there? We've been hearing screams."

"You're all being freed," I said and backtracked to try to find keys on one of the dead guards. I could melt all the locks, but that would take longer, and I was shaking with outrage at seeing Elpis being tortured. I had tunnel vision for freeing her, and my hands trembled violently as I searched the guard's pockets for keys. Aha! I snatched the iron liberators and ran back to unlock Elpis's cage. She was starting to panic, kicking her legs and hyperventilating.

"Shh, Elpis, I'm here. I'm freeing you. I've got you," I said, making an effort to soothe her, and carefully swung open the top. Ah shit, her joints were probably all locked up; how was she going to get out of there?

"What are you waiting for? Pull her out!" the female snapped, and a little hatchling's voice piped in angrily. I could feel Toast's anxiety spike at the thought of touching a female.

I can't! Fuck!

I gripped the corner of the cage and tilted it up, hoping she could maybe roll herself out of it. She whimpered and eventually fell out, hitting the ground with a pained cry. It broke my fucking heart that I couldn't lift her out myself. I clenched my teeth and gripped my chest. Fuck, it actually hurt!

I squatted by Elpis and murmured, "I'm going to get you out of here, but let me just free your friends first, ok?" She didn't say anything, just whimpered as she tried to uncurl her trembling arms and legs. I rushed from cage to cage, unlocking doors as fast as possible. I had no idea how much was on fire upstairs, and the sooner we were out of here, the better.

Once everyone in the room was freed and fleeing, I turned to see the female and hatchling crouching over Elpis's tortured form. They were massaging her arms and legs, trying to get her muscles moving and her blood flowing again.

"They did this to her the other night too. It's too much on her body, not to mention she's claustrophobic," the female snarled angrily, sensing I was behind them. So this was her punishment for doing nothing?

What do they do to these people when they actually do something wrong? Toast asked scathingly.

I didn't have a chance to say anything before Cyneric's men rushed in to forcefully drag away the female and hatchling. "Hey!" I snapped. "Careful with them!" When one of them moved to pick up Elpis, I blew out a thin jet of fire to stop him.

"The king sent me to escort this one," I asserted, taking a step toward the soldier, daring him to challenge my authority. These soldiers were pushing their luck with me. They were getting away with far too much. My knights would never act so disrespectfully.

The soldier stopped in his tracks, but he didn't retreat. He looked calculatingly at me, and I did not like it. Another soldier came in to assess the situation.

It's happening, Toast warned.

I do think you're right. It's too tight in here for a full shift, so I need you to keep it together, Toast. We got this, big guy. Just keep lending me your fire.

You got it.

Chapter 5

Sir Keyon

"We'll take over the escort from here, Keyon," one of Cyneric's men stated. The disrespect of dropping my title was an indicator that I was no longer the one in charge here. Perhaps that was so in the chain of command; not so much in regards to the food chain.

I let Toast's blue flames trickle from my mouth as I spoke. "I think not. I think you better rethink your loyalties here, slaver sympathizers," I said in a low voice, taking a step forward. "Cyneric is showing an interesting side here, isn't he?"

"We're warning you, Keyon. Give us the slave, and perhaps we'll only cut your tongue out," the male replied. "You're outnumbered."

I laughed and took another step forward, getting between Elpis and the soldiers. "When has that ever fucking mattered?" I asked and whistled out a thin thread of blue fire that incinerated a tiny section of the nearest dragon's chest, killing him instantly. It was hard to kill a dragon with fire, but with Toast's potency and my aiming, we utterly destroyed the mold. Several more soldiers filled up the doorway, alerted to the commotion. The soldier who'd been threatening me blanched but set his teeth.

"Is this slave worth dying for?" I asked, cracking my knuckles and elongating my claws and fangs. "Because you will die. I guarantee that will be the outcome for each and every one of you."

The soldiers rushed me, and I blew them back with a wall of blue fire. They couldn't push past that. I stopped and heard Elpis coughing from behind me. The air was getting thin down here from all the fire.

"We can keep this song and dance going, but the longer you push me, the thinner the air will get down here, and we'll all die from asphyxiation. The slave you want so badly is already struggling to breathe." I jerked a thumb over my shoulder. "And I won't let you kill her."

I didn't give them a minute to think about what I'd said. I grabbed the nearest soldier and ripped my claws through a carotid artery, tossing him into the next soldier to block any charge. The rest of the soldiers spooked and ran like rabbits, leaving the scent of piss in their wake. I killed the last lingering traitor and dropped his body to the ground.

Shuffling behind me told me that Elpis was struggling to get to her feet. I rushed to help her without thinking, but Toast scrambled to rear me back at the very last minute.

Sorry, Toast. I was just worried.

He didn't reply, so I turned my attention back to the coughing female. "We need to get you out of here. Follow me," I said and gestured for her to stay close. I led her up the stairs and noticed there was a collapse in the wooden frame. The fire had spread to the closet. Shit.

I motioned for her to stand back as I cleared the flaming debris away, trying to make a path her fragile body could navigate. I lured her out and showed her where she could step until we reached the main hall. It had been slow going and everyone had long since disappeared. Gods, I wish I could have just picked her up and carried her. Fuck! I hoped my Inferno was ok. They couldn't have been overwhelmed by Cyneric's men!

I escorted Elpis out the main entrance and saw evidence that the transport cage had been here. Cyneric's men had just burst in, grabbed the slaves, and left. I had no idea if anyone had even been arrested, but I seriously doubted it. They'd only seemed to care about killing me.

I swore and threw a fallen support beam up in the air to incinerate it with a blaze of fire. I grabbed my hair and screamed. "Fuck!" I shouted and paced. I had no idea what the fuck to do.

I'm guessing you won't carry Elpis for us so we can catch up to either Cyneric's men or to see what happened to our Inferno? I asked Toast, already knowing the answer.

Sorry...

"Fuck! Shit! Fuck!" I cried out again and sat down for a moment.

Well, we're not leaving her behind, I told him. If he was putting his foot down, I was putting mine down too. Leaving our potential mate to fend for herself wasn't a fucking option. With a scowl, I watched Elpis lie down on the dirt several feet away. I didn't want her lying on the filthy road. I wanted her curled in my fucking arms!

Is she our fated mate or not, Toast? I asked again. *I won't stop bothering you until you tell me.*

I was met with more silence, and I fumed. I put my hands in my face, completely at a loss for the first time in my life. I felt like my hands were tied. I stretched my wings and arched my back, trying to get the tension out, but it was buried deeper than flesh this time. I relaxed to find Elpis watching me, but she averted her gaze again and closed her eyes.

"If I go salvage some things, will you be ok out here, Elpis?" I asked. I hoped that I hadn't terrified her with all my screaming and murdering over the last... half hour? Hour? I'd lost track of time. I looked up at the stars and the Moon Goddess. She looked prettier these days.

I realized that Elpis hadn't replied, and I looked at her. "Um, yes," she mumbled. She'd probably nodded, and I just wasn't looking—I should've been, though. Elpis was much prettier than the moon. Pretty wasn't a good enough word. Elpis was beautiful, striking… exquisite.

I sighed and trudged back into the burning mansion to gather my belongings with a raging erection. I grabbed my bag from upstairs and swung by the kitchen to take whatever food I could fit in the rest of my pack. We'd have to clear the area tonight. This place would be crawling with looters soon.

Before I left, I hesitated and went to find the lord and lady's room. Elpis would need clothes. Perhaps the lady had something that would fit better than my pajamas. It had been extremely cute to watch Elpis parade around in them, but they would not do for traveling.

I found the lady's wardrobe and parsed through the dresses. I didn't want to spend too much time looking, so I grabbed three that looked the most suitable for walking and opened the window. I stepped off the ledge and fell to the ground, flapping a couple times to slow my descent.

Elpis screamed, and I shot toward her. "What happened?" I asked, extending my claws and looking around, not scenting any dangers.

Her eyes were huge and framed by a blushing face. "Mmm, sorry! Thought… you… get hurt. Forgot."

Oh. She thought I was just going to hit the ground and break a leg. Cute.

I burst into laughter. "No. Sorry I scared you, moonflower. You've probably never seen anyone use their wings before, huh?" She shook her head and looked away in embarrassment. I looked over my shoulder and flapped them a couple times to tickle her playfully with a breeze. "Here," I said and handed her the three dresses. "Hopefully one of these will fit. Walking will be hard for you in those pajamas."

Her eyes grew as round and bright as the moon when she held up the gowns. Her lips moved ever so slightly, as though she were talking to herself. The corners of her sweet lips pulled back into an excited smile, and she pulled my pajama top right off, exposing her bare flesh to me. My jaw hung loose, and I froze in spot, forgetting all manners of gentlemanly decorum. Just as my gaze was about to rake down to the swell of her starlit breasts, Toast yanked my head around to spare himself the terror of gazing upon a topless female.

Oh, you are simply the worst, Toast. You couldn't have given me one more second? I can't remember the last time I laid eyes on a pair of tits. Those promised to be phenomenal!

You should listen to yourself, Toast snorted. *She's turning you into a barbarian.*

I'm a male with wants, Toast! This is what happens when you deny me for over a decade. You won't even tell me if she's our mate!

Once again, he went silent. He couldn't seem to function whenever we broached that topic. I scratched the back of my neck and turned to face Elpis again. She had her back to me and was fumbling to tie the back. I wished I could help her. It was such a little domestic problem, but I wanted to do it. I sighed longingly and did everything to not choke on my own damn spit when she turned around to face me.

"Mmm, ready," she mumbled, looking away.

Yeah, she was close to bursting out of that gown, but there wasn't anything I could do about it. Elpis was taller and curvier than Adelmar's wife. She didn't seem uncomfortable with it, though. It still covered more of her than anything else I'd seen her wear. She shivered, and goose bumps erupted across her arms and cleavage. I swallowed hard at the sight of her chilled nipples pressing against the fabric.

"Keep the pajamas too, Elpis," I said and handed her my coat again so she could stay warm. She took it gratefully and shrugged it on while hanging onto the spare clothes I'd found. "I know you're tired, but we've got to get a little farther from the mansion tonight before you can sleep. It's not safe here. Can you do that, moonflower?"

She nodded, suppressed a yawn, and began to follow me at a sluggish pace. I took us into the tree line so we could have immediate cover. It'd probably take another hour or two for the unsavory to come sniffing about the deserted, smoking mansion. I'd lead us for that amount of time and then settle so she could sleep.

What a damn fucking shame my dragon wasn't able to carry her back with us. That was going to cost us, and what terrified me the most was not knowing how much. It felt like a race back to the castle for a 'he said, she said' war, and I had a feeling we were going to lose both the race and the war. What was Cyneric doing? What was his plan?

I had to get a message to Leofwine. He was the only one I could trust. I trusted the king, but if he had to choose between my word and his son's...

I shook away that thought. I was tired, angry, depressed, and horny. I needed to find us a decent place to camp. My ears caught the sound of a stream, and I turned slightly left to head toward the water source. We finally found ourselves a decent place to camp, and I set my bag down against a log.

Elpis was about to sit, but I sent out a tiny, weak breath of fire to stop her and said, "Wait, Elpis. I don't want you on the dirt. Hang on." She squeaked and stood still, wringing her hands anxiously. I pulled out a blanket that I'd grabbed from the guest room and spread it out for her. She lay down when prompted, and I pulled the rest of the blanket over her to keep her warm before digging a firepit.

I felt her eyes on me the entire time I was building the fire, but every time I looked up, she averted her gaze. Finally, when I lay down to go to sleep, I wrapped a wing casually over my side. I wasn't cold, though; it took a lot to weaken the kiln that burned hot in Toast and me.

As I rested, I inhaled Elpis's scent, letting her aroma calm me. It settled deep into my mind and massaged away some of

my fears. As if she knew I thought of her, I felt her eyes on me
again as I drifted off to sleep.

⚜

I woke to a small voice calling my name. My eyes snapped
open, and I saw Elpis's form squirming through the tendrils of
a dead campfire. My fingers shifted in the cold dirt as I sat up,
blinked rapidly, and folded my wing.

"Elpis?" I asked in a groggy voice. "Is everything ok?" I
saw that she'd replaced her dress with my pajama top and wasn't
wearing any bottoms except for her chastity belt. I tried to keep
my gaze from roving hungrily down her soft thighs as she rubbed
them together. When she shook her head, it slowly dawned on
me what was happening.

"Oh, shit! I'm sorry! Let's get that cursed thing off. You
probably need to relieve yourself. Fuck, you should have said
something last night. I completely forgot!" I grabbed my bag and
checked the contents, but I couldn't find the key. I hadn't noticed
it earlier with the smoke, Elpis's strong scent, and the commotion,
but I detected the vaguest smell of Duke Gero's grubby hands.
Had he taken it when my chamber was unattended?

"Fuck! It's gone," I swore angrily and snorted out a plume
of black smoke. A small sob came from Elpis's direction, but I
held up a hand. "No, no. I won't let you down. I'll get it off you.
I can easily melt gold, moonflower."

Alright, Toast. What do we do here? I asked. *I can't burn it
off from a distance.* I needed my dragon to come to the conclusion first. I was tired of forcing discomfort on him. He was me,
and I was him. I had to work around his trauma the best I could.

I... I don't know.

We can't allow her to be stuck in that forever.

No... that would be a terrible fate.

So, what do we do?

Toast was silent for a while. I tried to be patient, but Elpis looked absolutely miserable, and it was twisting my heart to bits. I growled impatiently and held a finger up to Elpis to tell her to wait just a bit longer. My claws extended, and I tapped them on the old log. I was about to lose my cool, so to speak.

Do what you must. I'm retreating to the back of our mind and hibernating for twenty minutes or so. Please don't touch more than you have to, Keyon. Please... I'm begging you. I still have access to your memories.

I promise I'll exercise as much restraint as possible, Toast. Thank you. You're doing something very brave, and I won't betray your trust, big guy.

I sighed in relief and walked over to Elpis. "I need you to lie down, Elpis. I need to get close to work on the lock. Are you ok with that?" I asked, and she nodded fervently.

"Mmm, yes. Please hurry." She whimpered and reclined on the blanket, pulling her top up to her belly. I tilted my head and nearly groaned at the sight of her. If her squirming was from another urgent matter, I'd be in a lot of trouble. Fuck.

I knelt and bent over to grab the lock. I put my hands between the lock and her skin to protect it from the intense heat I was about to generate. Gold melted at just under two thousand degrees. I was capable of going up at least another thousand. This would be easy. The hard part was not hurting her.

"You need to speak up if you think you're getting burned," I warned. "No more head shaking or nodding. I want to hear talking, ok?"

"O-ok," she acknowledged with a stammer, and I grunted in approval. I tried not to think of her beautiful, soft skin inches from my face or the fact I could smell the heady aroma of her sex. Gods, I'd give anything to bury my face in between her thighs. Just... obviously not right now.

I clicked my teeth and furrowed my brows in concentration, placing my lips an inch away from the lock. I blew out a small white flame and went to work on the thinnest part of the lock. I increased the heat slowly and kept the flame as short as possible. It was surgical work and not many would be able to do something so delicate. The shackle weakened, became gummy with heat, and fell off her belt, removing the lock with it.

"Careful, don't touch the metal," I said, intercepting her hand with mine, and felt a shock of pleasure run up my arm again. I clenched my teeth and groaned at the sensation but pulled my hand away and ripped the chastity belt off of her. She cried out in joy and jumped up to run off into the woods. I was frozen in place, barely able to process everything that had just occurred.

I collapsed and rolled onto my back, breathing heavily with the sight of her pert, bouncing bottom fresh in my mind. I'd caught only the briefest glimpse of her sex before she'd stood, and I moaned at the memory, grabbing my swelling cock through my pants in overwhelming arousal. I was almost afraid that if I moved, any amount of friction would fill my pants with cum. I stumbled to my feet and wandered behind a tree to find a moment to myself. Hopefully I had time before she returned because I didn't feel like I had much of a choice. Her touch had done something to me.

I loosened my pants, and my heavy erection sprang out into the cold morning air. It was nearly steaming from its radiating heat and covered in pulsing veins. Oh fuck, I'd never been so hard in my life. I spat in my hand and gasped when I fisted it, running my fingers up my length to the shiny head that dripped with pre-cum. It tingled under my grip, but it had fuckin' nothing on whatever sensation I'd gotten from touching Elpis's hand. What the hell had that been?

I closed my eyes and pictured her writhing as she'd been before, on her back and pulling up her shirt. This time, her squirming would be from needing a male's touch—my touch. This time, she'd drag the cloth higher, past her soft belly, to catch the underside of her inviting breasts.

I braced myself against a tree with my palm and leaned into it for support while I pumped at my extremely eager member. I never had enough mental material to work with since Toast tried so hard to keep our eyes away from females, but in the last ten minutes, I felt like I had enough inspiration to last me a lifetime.

Gods, I wondered what the rest of her breasts looked like. Now they were just a tantalizing mystery. What color were her nipples? What would her slopes feel like against my palms? She was blessed with such generous curves; I couldn't imagine they'd be anything but soft and heavy. Fuck, what would those globes feel like against my cock?

I squeezed my length a little harder and imagined dripping and spreading my pre-cum between her breasts to lubricate them. I'd palm their sides to mold them around my dick so I could slide back and forth between them, like I would the warm, wet channel of her sex. I groaned at the mental picture, thrusting my fist up and down my shaft. Would she moan or give out tiny little mewls as I fucked her cleavage? Would she offer her sweet mouth to catch me?

My grip hammered feverishly as the pressure in my cock increased, fed by my feral imagination. Would she arch into my thrusts? Would she call my name and beg for her turn? My sack drew in tight and heavy as my dick hardened further. When I pictured my cock exploding its load across her chest, neck, and lower lip, I came with profound ferocity. Hissing nonsense through my lips, I dug my claws into the tree, ripping out curls of bark. My glutes tightened, and my abdomen lurched each time I spent my seed on the roots. I grunted with each spurt, groaning in ecstasy from the best orgasm I'd ever had in my life.

I barely noticed Elpis's scent through the euphoria of my ejaculations. Between hissing grunts, I glanced back to see her step out from behind a tree, looking for me. Her eyes widened when she saw me and stood stock still, gaze locked intensely on my spurting member. Her jaw dropped.

I snapped my wings out to block her stare, cursing as I contin-ued to release ropes of steaming cum onto the ground. I growled in irritation when my spasms ended and leaned my forehead against the tree. Gasping for air and squeezing my eyes shut to avoid a trickle of sweat dripping from my knotted brow, I blew out a puff of smoke and tried to relax. My muscles were shaking from the intensity of my masturbation.

Flamin' shit. First of all, that was fucking terrible timing; she'd gotten quite the show. Second, there was no way a normal female could have this effect on me. I needed to drag more information out of Toast or I was going to lose my damn mind.

Speaking of minds... mine was a disgusting, filthy bastard. I barked an incredulous laugh at the state of myself. Good gods, if Elpis could read thoughts, she'd be running for the hills, and I wouldn't blame her. I'd even send her off with supplies. Gruff laughter raked the insides of my ribs, and I shook my head. I supposed my punishment was her running across me doing this. Go figure. I chuckled and tucked my calmer cock back into my pants, then went to rinse my hands in the stream before returning to camp.

I admit, I was expecting it to be worse than it was, Toast murmured, returning from hibernation.

We really need to have a talk, big guy, I said *seriously. I only touched her on accident to keep her from burning herself, and I felt that same sensation. Check that memory out, Toast. That can't be normal. She's not normal... at least not for us.*

I need out... Toast sighed uncomfortably.

If that's what you need. Let me warn Elpis first. Hang tight, I said.

I spied Elpis sitting on the blanket with an expression I couldn't quite place. Sadness? Confusion? Something along those lines. "Everything ok, Elpis?" I asked. "Feeling better?"

"Mmm. Y-yes, thanks," came her small response. I wasn't sold, but I'd let her have her privacy. I snorted to myself. Privacy in the woods... ah, no such thing. I wasn't going to bring up the masturbation incident if she wasn't. I felt no shame over the act as I'd desperately needed it, but... I'd much rather forget about it.

I cleared my throat and kicked off my boots. "I need to let my dragon out, so we'll be away from the camp for a little bit.

We won't be far." I pointed in the direction where we'd be. "If anything happens, call and we'll be here in seconds. Are you ok with that, moonflower?"

Elpis nodded, then opened her mouth to use her words. "Mmm... yes. That's fine." She wrapped her arms around her knees, making it clear she'd stay right there.

I undressed and tossed my clothes onto my bag, comfortable in my own nudity as a dragon-shifter. I walked away and began shifting, feeling Toast burst forth in all his grandeur. I watched my perspective shift from the roots to just under the swaying eucalyptus treetops as we reached our full height.

Toast stretched his larger wings in stuttering jerks, enjoying his time out in the daylight. He looked down to make sure his tail hadn't knocked anything from our camp. When his eyes fell upon harmless little Elpis, he released a growling yelp and scrambled away from her.

I thought you'd take us farther away! he accused.

He tripped over his own tail somehow, let out the weirdest choked roar I've ever heard, and rushed off through the creaking woods. The small scales around his neck and spine flared up and clacked with his nervousness.

In the distance, I heard the stunned, disbelieving laugh of a very confused female.

$\mathfrak{C}$hapter 6

$\mathfrak{S}$ir $\mathfrak{K}$eyon

Sorry about that, Toast, I said. *Thought we were far enough.*
Toast didn't reply, but he eventually slowed his escape so
we wouldn't be too far from Elpis. He started pacing, breathing
rapidly, and making soft chuff-like noises through his mouth.
Come on now, big guy. No, no. Don't cry, I implored. *You're
gonna make me cry too.* Watching him suffer was torturous
because I never knew what to do. There was no magic concoction
for what we were barely enduring.

Toast was working through a panic attack, and all I could do
was to try to coach him through it.

*It's ok, Toast. Breathe. Just breathe. Let's count together, ok?
In for one, two, three, four, five, six, seven, eight. Hold for one,
two, three, four, five, six, seven, eight, and then out as slooooow
as you can, buddy. That's it. You're doing great. Let those muscles
feel nice and heavy when you breathe out. Yup, just like that.*

Toast's panic eventually calmed, but he still cried in the way
that dragons cry. *You think I like living like this?* he bawled. *I
don't like living like this, Keyon. I don't like making you suffer*

because females terrify me. I don't like keeping you from having a mate because females terrify me. I don't want us to end up alone because females terrify me!

But why, though? I asked. *I still don't understand what happened and why you won't talk to me about it. You were like this from the day you woke within me.*

I'm just not ready to talk about it...

When then? How can we get better if you refuse to talk about it? We're in a very delicate situation right now. We need to be as strong as possible, big guy.

Soon, I promise... this time, I promise, he sobbed. *I don't want to be like this anymore! It hurts, Keyon. It hurts more than ever! I feel like I can't breathe. It's a cage.*

I sighed, wishing I had a solution.

Maybe I just need to face it, Toast sighed as though he were defeated.

How, Toast?

Remember when Grandpa told us about his neighbor's hatchling who wouldn't go near dogs?

Yeah, what about it?

The neighbor just kept bringing their hatchling around to meet dogs little by little until they weren't afraid anymore.

Oh yeah. I do remember that, but we can't go around asking to pet the head of a restrained woman and walk away, I said, trying to make a point. Toast burst into laughter, which sounded similar to his crying. It was nervous laughter, but I could tell it was releasing a lot of built-up tension. It made me chuckle a little too. Toast just sat in that little part of the woods, snorting and huffing with laughter like a crazed drunkard. Little white flames licked out of his mouth in his mirth.

When Toast calmed down, he said quietly, *She's our fated mate, Keyon.*

Great fucking gods. I had a feeling... I replied. *Proud of you for telling me that, buddy.*

I... don't want to cost us our fated mate. I don't know what scares me more.

Does she really terrify you as much as other females, Toast? How do you feel about her specifically?

It's not as bad... but she still makes me nervous. The bond must be helping.

You didn't run away at the dinner when she touched me. That was impressive.

Well, that's obviously because I was stunned...

OH. Is that why it sounded like your brain had broken? I laughed, and that caused Toast to start laughing again too.

Unfortunately... yes. That's when I verified what she was to us...

She's proven several times that she doesn't want to hurt us, Toast.

He growled a little at that, and his tail thrashed. *That's not how it works, Keyon! My brain can tell me all the facts it wants, but I still FEEL the fear! I feel the nausea and the adrenaline. I feel my heart pound simply from the fact that I have no control over it. I'm constantly at war with my own mind and emotions. It's a lot more complicated than you think! Don't make me feel like shit for being terrified of something as big as my foot. 'Course it's not completely logical...*

Sorry, sorry! I apologized hastily, trying to placate him before he started to get another panic attack. *I obviously don't experience every little thing you do. Sometimes I wish I could, just so I could help better...*

Aaargh! Toast huffed in frustration. *Not to mention this is so fucking embarrassing, having to hide this condition. Worse, as we're in a high position under the king.*

Don't be embarrassed, Toast. Let's just focus on what works and what doesn't. I feel you're about to spiral, so let's pull back, ok? We'll keep it simple.

Right. He snorted out a tiny puff of smoke. *Keep it simple. I can do that.*

One step at a time, I added. *Little tiny hatchling steps.*

Tiny steps, possibly with a limp, he added reluctantly, but we just ended up laughing again.

Ok, so let's get on the same page with a plan now. We need to find a town to send a message to Leofwine. We'll then leave to meet him, but what do we do with Elpis now?

Doesn't seem like it's safe to bring her back to the castle, Toast surmised.

At least until we know more about what's going on with Prince Cyneric. I also... should we check where we left our Inferno? I'm worried about my knights... and the others.

If they left dead bodies, they're charred beyond recognition, Keyon...

My heart sank at that dark thought. Could they have really attacked our own? My Inferno, medics, and squires? I was snapped from my thoughts when we heard my name being screamed in the distance.

"Sir Keyon!" a female's voice screeched in terror. "Help me! Sir Keyon!"

Elpis! Toast and I said simultaneously.

Toast snarled and bolted. He ran back to the camp as fast as he could, arriving in seconds to see three males chasing her in the other direction. When Toast's eyes narrowed on her torn dress, he flew into a rage, immediately stepping on and crushing the closest male to her. His shriek was cut off the moment his life was replaced with death.

The two remaining attackers balked and tried to shift, but Toast wasn't going to risk Elpis's safety for the fun of a longer skirmish. He snapped his teeth down around one male's midsection to paralyze him and tossed him through the canopy to die on impact somewhere else. The third male? Well, Toast just bit his head off first and ate the rest, trying to shield his gruesome activity from Elpis with his wings.

Unfortunately, the meal did not agree with him. He heaved and looked around for a place away from Elpis to puke. *Nope... shouldn't have eaten that. That one was a cat. I'm gonna barf.*

Well, don't barf here! And remove that flattened body. Oh, great Sun God, she's going to be traumatized, I groaned in dismay.

Where is she any— Ahhh! Toast exclaimed, seeing that Elpis had crept closer to him in wide-eyed curiosity. Toast backed up, grabbed the body he'd made a doormat from, and ran off to regurgitate the cat-shifter.

I shifted back when he was done purging the foul thing from his system and nearly ran into Elpis on my way back to where I'd left her. She was gasping for air but seemed relieved. She also seemed like she was having a hard time not looking at my naked body, but I was too worried about her to be pleased about it. A sheen of sweat lathered her forehead and upper chest as she pulled up a torn sleeve. I frowned at it, but at least that was the only part they'd been able to touch. We shouldn't have left her side. That had been risky.

"I'm so sorry, Elpis. We shouldn't have left you alone!" I apologized, wishing I could grab her arms while I said that to show her my earnest. She shook her head and looked at my shoulder.

"Mmm, nay. Not your fault. Thanks for coming..." she said with a tiny smile. The sweetness of her face made my brain stop working, and I couldn't recall the way back to our things. I got turned around for a moment, trying to remember where we'd camped, but finally caught the scent of our old firepit.

This was my fault. Toast sighed when we returned, still not agreeing with Elpis's assessment.

Nope. Let's all drop the guilt here, I replied firmly. *You didn't call those looters to assault our mate. She's safe. That's what matters.*

Yes... Toast agreed, almost shyly.

"Did they hurt you?" I asked Elpis and pointed to her torn sleeve.

She shook her head and answered, "Nay, I'm unharmed."

I breathed out a sigh of relief, and she nodded at my shoulder.

"Why do you keep looking at my shoulder, Elpis? Do I have a spider there?" I asked while pulling on a pair of pants.

"Mmm. Slaves don't look at faces," she said quietly, and I froze once I stood up, only moving to tighten the buckle on my pants. Had it not been clear? Had I not clarified after the chaos? Now I didn't even remember.

"Elpis," I said cautiously. "You do realize you're not a slave anymore, right?" I studied her face as her expression went through a myriad of emotions. It happened so fast I couldn't even keep track of the order. She just ended up looking stunned. Like someone had slapped her, and she didn't know what to do about it. Her hand went to the collar at her neck.

"Yeah, we're going to remove that one too, but it'll be trickier," I admitted, tossing a shirt on and closing my bag. "Iron has a much higher melting point than gold. We should remove that one in the water."

She didn't really react, just held her collar and stared. "Elpis?" I asked. "Can you hear me? None of the lord's slaves are slaves anymore. You're not a slave. You're a free female now. You're free like your friends. No one will ever own you again."

"Mmm. Were you the ones who freed the slaves at the other dens?" she asked. It was the most she'd said at once to me. She also sounded a little sharper now, coming across as more alert and intelligent. Had she been intentionally making herself seem dull-witted? I wanted to learn a lot more about her.

"My knights and I have been performing the raids, yes. We've freed many, but there's a lot more left. Hard to say how many, but I'm worried it's more than I thought," I answered. "Adelmar's plan was deeply concerning to me."

"So, you were a spy," she mumbled thoughtfully but seemed happy about it. I saw a barely concealed smile curl up a lip. I chuckled at her deep contemplation. I supposed I had played a part to get more information.

She placed her hands on her face and choked on a relieved sob. Her brown-sugar eyes finally flickered up to mine. They sparkled with tears and something I hadn't seen on her face thus far—hope.

"The other slaves are ok? Dagmaer… the little hatchling is safe now?"

"They should be," I answered, pushing confidence into my response. I wasn't one hundred percent positive, but I would have hazarded a guess that they'd be brought safely back to the castle to avoid more suspicion around what happened at Adelmar's mansion.

"Mmm, how... Teach me to survive?" she asked breathlessly, and I nodded, feeling warmth in my chest from her request.

"I'll help you get strong, Elpis. Teach you self-defense too," I promised. "We'll sort out a safe place for you to rehabilitate. We just have to deal with some... complications first."

I'd help her. I'd put her first when I could, but... I didn't really want her rehabilitating anywhere other than at my side—preferably in my arms. Could she even feel the bond? I sighed and rubbed my temples. I sensed that this was going to be a rough road.

This is all far too much, I thought to myself while we gathered our things. My heart pounded as I rolled up the blanket, tucking in my new clothes to keep everything together. I barely noticed Sir Keyon gesture for us to be on our way, and I had a hard time staying present while we moved toward his next destination.

Slaves of the First Water had to master hiding their pain, and I tried to mask how shaken I was, but everything that had occurred over the last couple of days was starting to become a lot more than I could handle. I felt like someone was stacking weights on me and that before I was able to get used to the previous weight, another would be added.

Burdened by mental and physical exhaustion, I hoped we didn't have far to walk. I was still sore from being tortured multiple times, and once was usually enough to break me for at least a week. Thoughts of Sir Keyon were what kept me from being utterly destroyed after the first night. Then he saved me from the cage the next...

So much had happened after that... Why had the soldiers attacked Sir Keyon? Through the pain, smoke, and thin air, I barely recalled him mentioning the king and calling those soldiers slaver sympathizers. They'd also set the mansion on fire, apparently. Were my friends truly safe with them?

I'd had it all backwards, and that had given me a spark of hope. Sir Keyon had been the good guy. He had been the spy, but I didn't really know who he was. I was all alone with this stranger. That by itself should scare me, but it didn't. What was I feeling?

I was attracted to him more than ever, but now I felt safe... nearly doted on by the male. I had no idea what it was like to be a free female, but being fed, watered, clothed in pretty dresses and not allowed to lie on dirt certainly felt like doting. He'd come when I called and killed those wretched attackers. I shuddered at how close they'd come to grabbing me, snagging just my sleeve when I jumped to my feet. They'd been so quiet. I should have been more alert, but Sir Keyon hadn't let me down. He'd kept me safe.

What else... Confusion. That was another one. He confused me. Sometimes his actions wouldn't just confuse me; they also made me feel pangs of disappointment. The two times he'd touched me had been by accident, and he'd always recoiled as if I was some slimy creature. Was he disgusted by me? Being too old to be a pleasure slave meant you were no longer pleasurable... and I was at the retirement age. Maybe it was the same in the real world? Maybe females of my age out here were considered undesirable too? Had I lost my chance to find a mate?

I snorted quietly in bitterness. I knew he liked females because he obviously had a response to me. He'd just much rather touch himself than let me do it. When I'd returned from relieving myself, I looked for Sir Keyon. I'd heard him hiss out my name, so I followed the sound and found him doing my job for me. I didn't know what it was like for free females, but I was disgraced. He could've just asked and closed his eyes so he wouldn't have to look at my old, cellulite-covered body. I was still good at it! *Nay! What are these thoughts running through my mind?* I asked myself, slapping my cheeks. Those were slave thoughts, not free female thoughts! I shouldn't want to please a male ever again with the life I've had... right? What happened to me thinking all males were monsters? So why did I so desperately want to please him? Was I broken? Was there truly no coming back from being a slave? How was I supposed to learn how to be a free female?

I began to lose myself in confusing thoughts and rubbed a watery eye. Staring at the knight's back as we walked, I just couldn't figure out what he wanted from me. Why was I even here with him if I wasn't a slave? I was free, right? I should be able to just walk in a different direction from him... right?

I rubbed both my eyes this time and tripped on what felt like a jutting stone. I hit the ground and yelped, immediately grabbing the elbow I'd smacked against a rock.

"Shit! Are you ok?" Sir Keyon asked, turning to see what had happened.

"Mmm, I'm fine," I mumbled and sat there for a moment, trying to look at my elbow. It wasn't bleeding, but it would definitely bruise. I looked to see the knight frowning in concern but sighed when he didn't move to help me stand. I didn't need his help, but the lack of the gesture made my heart sink even lower. I was definitely not even worth touching as a free female. Used. Ugly. Old.

I stood up and motioned for us to continue. The spark of hope I'd felt earlier was now ebbing down a drain. Since my mind was a mess, I decided to leave it for a while. Emptiness was familiar; it was safe.

We walked for several hours before we hit a dirt road. I hadn't been paying attention to where we were going, so I just stared blankly at the scene while he wandered around it. It looked like someone had thrown a bunch of junk off to the side of the road.

I crouched to pick up a helmet that had been sitting upright and traced its swirling designs with a finger. Underneath the helmet was a dark spot that caught my attention, so I put the helmet down and took a closer look.

"Sir Keyon?" I called. I didn't know why, but something in my gut said that this was important. I heard him approach from behind me, and I pointed at the symbol. Someone had burned an image into the back of a piece of bark.

The knight's face darkened, and I moved to get out of his way when he crouched. He picked up the bark and put it in his pocket, then stood up and began searching under other objects. Were there others? I meandered around until I found another symbol on the back of a tree. I called him over and pointed at that one, which he worked to dig out with his claws.

I searched around while he pried the image out of the tree, but I spotted no more of them. Placing the bundle I was carrying on the ground, I sat on it while I waited for the knight to do what he needed to do here. Eventually he sighed and came over to sit by me with a grim look on his face.

"The good news is that I'm not seeing enough blood to suggest that anyone died. There's also no sign of incinerated bodies," he said while massaging the spot between his drawn brows.

"Mmm, these were your soldiers?" I asked quietly, and he nodded.

"My group of knights, my Inferno. I also had squires and medics here. I just don't know where they went. They were supposed to show up at the raid… and that's where the bad news comes in to play." He reached into his pocket and brought out the first symbol I'd found. "Each of my knights has unique metal stencils they use to leave messages. This one belongs to Sir Stroud. You know what this symbol means? It's his symbol for 'traitor.'" Sir Keyon stared at it with a scowl. "So now I know that something happened here, and Sir Stroud found a moment to place this metal piece on wood and use his dragon's breath to brand a message. This says that someone had turned on my knights."

Sir Keyon put the bark back in his pocket and pulled out the small chunk he'd carved from the tree. "This one," he said with a more worried expression, "is Sir Gerfrid's symbol for poison."

I swallowed heavily, and my hands suddenly felt clammy. I wiped my palms down my thighs and felt dread in my belly. "Mmm, poison is a bad man's sword," I murmured. Sir Keyon's bronze eyes flashed with anger, and he nodded in agreement. He put the chunk of wood away and rubbed his face with both his hands.

"But seeing that symbol now... it doesn't matter if there's no blood around. They could all be dead from whatever poisoned them. All their attackers had to do was remove their bodies," he said into his palms, his shoulders quivering. "They could all be dead," he repeated with a waver in his voice.

When I heard a wet sniffle escape him, I reached over to pat him on the shoulder. That was a mistake, and I really should have thought twice about it. He jerked away from me and backed off like I'd bitten him. I lowered my eyes, held up my palms, and rushed out an apology. "Mmm, I'm sorry! I won't touch you ever again! I promise! Never, ever, ever! I'm sorry! I'm sorry!"

He backed up a couple more steps, but I dared not look at his face. *Stupid, stupid! Oh goddess, I really messed up this time!* I opened my mouth to apologize again, but Sir Keyon burst through his clothes, and his dragon took to the sky. Wind pelted me from his departure, and I scrambled backwards toward the tree line, covering my head to keep the wind-strewn debris from flying in my face.

I gasped and grabbed at my stinging chest. Tears brimmed in my eyes at what felt like the ultimate rejection. Stumbling like a drunkard, I turned and ran. I raced through the underbrush, crying without a clue as to what I was doing or where I was going.

Was this the world that was waiting for me outside slavery? I didn't know what I was doing. How was I supposed to navigate this? I began to hyperventilate when my panic escalated. Where would I go? How would I feed myself? How would I protect myself? Had I screwed up leaving where he'd left me? Would he be glad to see me gone? So many questions. I'd had nothing but questions since I'd been freed, and I'd been too overwhelmed to ask any of them.

My feet slapped on the forest floor, kicking up cold dirt and detritus. Sometimes I'd step on something sharp, but I just kept running through the woods. I was fueled poorly by pure adrenaline and despair, and I knew my body would regret this later. My soul was just too battered to fight any longer. My heart writhed in pain. I didn't know why it jabbed me so, but it was agonizing.

Hopes and losses, hopes and losses.

I wished I could just sink into the shadows and never be seen again. No one would miss me, and maybe I'd get to see Pelagia once more. I cried openly, almost as if asking nearby predators to just have at me. Cut me to ribbons.

Just make the pain go away. I beg of you.

Chapter 7

Elpis

I eventually collapsed by a large tree that had grown out from around jutting boulders. My fingers clutched at a tree root like it was a pillow, and I hid my face, pressing it painfully into the rough surface. It received my gasping until I ran out of sobs to cry.

"Why?" I wailed to absolutely no one. "Why does it hurt so bad?" I clutched at my chest and squeezed my eyes, draining it of the last few drops it had to give. What was this yearning pain in my body? My head and neck throbbed, and I raked my fingers over my collar.

"Get off! Get off me!" I shrieked, scratching at the iron that offended me so. I knew it was useless, but I pulled at it. I even tried prying the lock off with a branch, but it slipped and cut a long bloody line down my cheek. Hissing in pain, I crawled around the area, looking for anything I could use to get it off of me. I gave up trying to bash the lock's shackle with a rock and collapsed, defeated.

Defeated and thirsty. I licked my lips, and the reality of what I'd done came to me like a slap. I'd gone absolutely mad and ran from the person who was going to teach me how to survive. I sat up and looked around, suddenly quite afraid. Even though I'd made enough noise to let every single meat eater know where I was, I stood still as if I had a chance of escaping their notice. I needed to keep moving. I needed water too.

I walked as fast as I could without making extra noise, certain that I was being followed by beasts that hid their footsteps in the roars of my terrified heartbeat. I paused at one point to crouch by a berry bush, hungry. Perhaps these could provide a little water. I plucked the red berries and popped them in my mouth while I kept paranoid eyes on the woods. After I ate my fill, I stored a handful for later.

As I did not feel like I was made for tree climbing, I decided to head toward higher ground to see if I could spy a water source from a distance. During the hike, I starting giggling, feeling pretty good for the first time. I huffed and puffed up the hill and fell into laughter when I got to the top. A glorious sunset took my breath away, and I plopped onto the grass to watch the novel scene.

"Hey, Sun God!" I yelled at the top of my lungs, giggling. "It's been a while! Haven't you wondered where I was all this time?" I pointed an accusing finger at the shimmering ball in the sky. "You forgot about us! Do you know how many times we sang to you? Do you know how many times the"—I cackled hysterically—"other slaves had to listen to my out-of-tune singing? That's the true crime here!"

I narrowed my eyes as the sun split into two wobbly suns. "Hey, where'd your friend come from?" I asked, annoyed at His rudeness. "This was a private party! Is that there a lady god with you? You better treat Her right!" I shook a finger at the sun. "You males know nothing about females! Show Her you care! Don't just say it! Words are words are words!" I thought for a second and asked, "Do suns have cocks?"

I fell back to study the darker sky. "Same goes for you…" I said drowsily, not sure who I was talking to this time. "Words are words!" I announced to the birds that chirped past me. I giggled and began mumbling the last verse of the lament. "If you have a moment, a last request we plea... Help lost Pelagia ascend..." I looked up at a cloud that was getting closer and closer and asked, "Do you remember she?"

I pointed a finger up at it. It was quite large and quite brown for a cloud. "Filthy cloud, get away from my hill! You're killing the view!" I shouted. The ground vibrated when the cloud landed, and I huffed, closing my eyes. "You could stand to lose some weight, cloud. Go pee somewhere. Don't pee on my hill, though. I just got here. I need a pee-free hill!" I succumbed to cackles and spread my arms.

"What the fuck?" the cloud said to me.

"You wash yer tone!" I slurred. "Filfy mowf forra cloud. Fershame!"

"Uh... are you ok, Elpis?"

"How'd you know ma name? You a spy!" I laughed and snorted, which made me laugh even harder. "Like Sir Keeeyon!"

"I am Keyon..."

"Liar!" I accused and yawned, rolling onto my side. I felt the berries I'd stashed in my cleavage fall out and roll onto the grass. "Nooo..." I complained but couldn't bring myself to go after them. I was so sleepy. If the sun was going to bed, I probably should too.

"Elpis? Elpis, did you eat these?" the cloud said closer to my face. I tried to swat the cloud away and rolled onto my other side. "Fuck! Elpis, you need to throw up right now!"

"Yooou throw up," I bit back and giggled. *That'll show 'im!*

"Shit, shit, shit, shit," the cloud continued to hiss.

"Iz fine..." I grumbled and fell asleep.

<hr />

All I felt when I woke was dampness. Then came the coldness. I was cold and wet—sticky too. I moaned and rubbed my eyes, trying to figure out how one opened their eyes after they'd been glued shut. Oh, there was a new sensation... a throbbing headache.

"Elpis?" Sir Keyon's voice broke through my foggy head. I slowly sat up and licked my chapped lips. Oh, I desperately wished I had some water right now. When I managed to pry one eye open, I spied a stricken Sir Keyon staring at me by a campfire. Squinting, I fought to remember what happened earlier.

"Elpis?" he repeated as he stood and came over, looking ashen-faced. "How are you feeling?"

I groaned and held my throbbing head. "Like I insulted the Sun God," I answered, cringing. The large male offered a canteen of water, and I snatched it, trying to drain it in one go.

"Elpis, slow down! Don't choke—" he started saying, but water sloshed over my face from my zeal, and I sputtered. As I coughed and choked, I accepted that I was not looking particularly put-together. I felt like death itself. No, I felt like what death would feel like if death died.

Once my attempt to breathe water was complete, I handed the canteen back to him and plucked at my sweaty dress. "Ugh... what happened?" I asked.

"How many of these berries did you eat, Elpis?" he asked severely, holding up some berries that looked rather familiar.

"Oh... I had some of those. I don't know... maybe thirty?" I speculated, and his lips parted.

"Just seven of these," he said scathingly while holding up a singular berry, "can kill a hatchling! I honestly don't know how the fuck you survived. Never, ever eat these again!"

Oh, he looked furious. He even had bits of smoke curling from a corner of his mouth. I gulped and eyed the innocent-looking berry. "I almost died?" I asked hesitantly, not really wanting to know.

"No," he said and ran his fingers through his tousled chestnut hair. "No, I watched over you. You didn't even come close to dying. You should have, though. These are highly toxic, Elpis!"

I frowned. "They just made me feel... really good," I admitted. "Then I just got sleepy." Sir Keyon threw his hands up in the air and then covered his face, shaking his head.

"Gods, I almost lost you because of a stupid…" he mumbled into his hands, and I couldn't make out the rest of it. What was he saying? I didn't understand this.

"Why'd you come look for me anyway?" I asked. "I thought it was pretty clear I should go."

The knight's posture slumped, and he dropped his hands from his face, just staring at me by the fire. I couldn't tell if he looked sad or worried, but it was one of the two. I could almost see his mind working for something to say as his metallic gaze flickered between his hands and the campfire.

"It's my job to keep you safe, Elpis," he asserted in a low voice, staring up at me through his dark eyelashes and messy locks. The firelight flickered over the beautiful, unique curves of his nose and lips.

"But why? If I'm free, I should just… go be free, right?" I asked, confused. "I don't understand any of this."

"And that's entirely my fault," he said with a sigh and brushed back his hair. "Yes, you're free, but… society works differently. You should have never been a slave to begin with, and since society let you down, we have programs that help Reborn get back on their feet—to help them become independent and able to control their own lives."

"Reborn?" I asked. "What's that?"

"You, your friends, every slave who's been freed," he answered, picking up a twig and anxiously snapping off tiny pieces. "The truth is, Elpis, someone is looking for you, and I was supposed to escort you back to the king. I don't know who it is, but it could be your family."

"My family?" I hadn't thought about them in ages. They were just… blurry feelings.

"Do you know your last name?" he asked me, and I shook my head.

"Nay… I don't really remember anything from before…" I picked up my own twig to mirror his nervous habit.

"So Eudokia doesn't ring any bells?" he inquired, tilting his head and staring at me curiously. His lips were left parted, and I couldn't stop staring at them.

"Nay, it does not. I am Elpis Eudokia?" That was odd. Having a surname made me feel... less slave-like. "It makes me sound like... a person."

Sir Keyon burst into laughter and nodded at my silly little observation. I stared at where his winsome lips curled into his smiling cheeks. What a perfect little spot to kiss that would be. He stared back at me when his chuckles subsided, but his smile didn't disappear; it just softened into a smaller, gentler one. It was a smile that made my chest hurt, and I almost reached up to massage the ache.

I watched the ball in his throat bob when he swallowed. "So... as I was saying. I was supposed to escort you back, but I think it might be too dangerous to go straight there right now."

"Because of those other soldiers?" I asked, and he nodded.

"I'm concerned that Prince Cyneric is becoming a slaver sympathizer, and... I really need to get more information before we go back. I'm not willing to put you in danger. You're my... charge," he said with an uncomfortable clearing of his throat. He looked down at the twig as though it was the source of his irritation and tossed it into the dark of the night.

"I'm sorry I touched you. I'm sorry that I make you uncomfortable. I'm sure you're not happy to have a charge like me," I apologized, unable to look at his face any longer. I was starting to recall that feeling of rejection, and it poked at my heart, reminding me how much it could hurt me.

Sir Keyon heaved a colossal sigh. "No, Elpis. None of that is you. My dragon and I, we are in a... unique situation right now. Please don't take my sudden movements personally. Actually— Elpis, look at me—I'm begging you to not take it personally."

I looked up at him as he'd ordered, and his face was showing genuine grief. It was stricken, fighting to keep my eyes locked on his magnetic ones.

"Please, Elpis, little moonflower, do not take it personally. Just... be patient with me. Can you do that?"

I didn't know what I was being patient for, but he seemed desperate to hear a 'yes,' so that's what I gave him. "Yes, Sir Keyon. I can do that."

"Just Keyon, moonflower."

"Yes, Keyon. I can do that."

Keyon's posture relaxed after I agreed to be patient with him, and he looked as if a burden had just fallen from his shoulders. He then leaned to pass me a small plate that contained cooked meat and some kind of bar with nuts and dried fruit. He must have eaten his meal a while ago because he mostly just stared at the fire while I shoveled food into a tender stomach.

How dumb of me to eat poisonous berries. I counted myself lucky that he had found me before something else had. When I finished eating the real food, I shifted uncomfortably in my clammy dress. Then I spied my spare clothes at my feet, which drew my attention to the blanket beneath me. Had he moved me? I reached behind to loosen the dress's laces and glanced over to see if Keyon was watching. He was staring at my chest but then glanced up at my face and turned to give me privacy. I could still see his profile as he looked into the fire. A bitter expression was written across it. I didn't know what to make of it, but I remembered his request and tried to not let it jab my heart too deeply.

I grabbed the pajama top from the pile of clothes and pulled the dress over my head. I slipped the long top on and left my legs bare, already too warm from eating those berries and from my proximity to the fire. I did cover myself back up with the blanket, though, since Keyon looked so uncomfortable.

Why, though? Certainly, it couldn't be a propriety thing. Shifters didn't worry too much over nudity in general; at least that's what I thought I knew. I sighed and closed my eyes. Being a slave had been simple. You were simply asked to do something, and you did it. You either hated it or you didn't. Lord Adelmar's guests made it clear that they either liked you or they didn't. I frowned and buried my face in the blanket. I desperately didn't want to think about any of those males right now. I shuddered, remembering how they'd touched me.

"Elpis?" Keyon's low voice broke the silence of the night, soft and uncertain. It yanked me from my discomfort, and I felt like I could breathe better.

"Hmm?" I hummed into the blanket and turned my head in his direction, but I kept my eyes closed.

"Can I… try something?" he inquired hesitantly, and I opened my eyes to look for his face. He had nested himself a little closer to me than the previous night, and if I reached out, I could probably poke his nose. That would—of course—likely result in something particularly disastrous.

"What are you wanting?" I murmured, staring back at him. Despite all the bunching, rippling muscles and the intimidating, leathery wing that he'd rested over himself, he looked so vulnerable in that moment—vulnerable and fearful. The puffs of his apprehensive breaths vibrated the grass by his chin.

He swallowed before finally asking, "May I hold your hand?" His lips pressed flat, and his brows drew up into a hopeful but nervous expression. His warm bronze gaze flickered between my eyes as though he was searching for my thoughts or wishing he could read my mind. It was the smallest little request, but he made it sound like the largest demand you could ask of someone.

Little did he know, I'd have a hard time denying him anything. I'd never felt that before, but I liked it. I liked being able to offer something instead of it being taken from me by force. I supposed that was my first real epiphany since being freed; having options was empowering. It was also easier to give in because I found myself admiring him. Even when he pushed me away, I kept getting drawn back, like a moth to a campfire.

I met his eyes, slowly reached out to fulfill his request, and placed my hand on the ground between us, palm up and patient. He released a breath and gazed at my palm for a moment. His eyes then focused so intensely that it was almost like my hand was the doe, and he was the hunter. I heard him take a ragged breath, and his large hand lifted, slowly moving to hover over mine.

When a little moth landed on my thumb, he stopped moving, and we both burst into laughter. I think we both realized we'd been holding our breaths. The moth flitted away, startled by our vibrations, and Keyon chuckled from deep in his belly. "I think we offended his delicate sensibilities."

There was less tension in the air after that. The laugh had slightly relaxed him, and he began to lower his hand again. First, I felt the tips of his curved fingers brush against my palm to spread and flatten. Then I felt the warm pressure of his rough, heavy palm on mine. I smiled softly at him as his eyes closed tight and his breath caught. He was so affected by my touch. Why was that, and what could make him and his dragon struggle over such a simple thing? This was by far the easiest thing I've ever been asked to do, and I'd gladly do it again—only for him, though.

Under the heat of his touch, I felt the pulse of a heartbeat, but I honestly couldn't tell if it was his or mine. It was running a little fast and could be from either his anxiety or my excitement. I was loving this, but all it did was make me want more. It made the valley between my legs ache as much as my chest. My neck throbbed too, but I think my collar was pressing in too much.

I felt a deep urge to rub my thumb delicately along the side of his hand but resisted, not wanting to startle him. This was such a fragile moment; I felt like anything could ruin it. A falling leaf or another wayward moth could end it all, and the last thing I wanted was for him to fly away from me again. His gentle gaze was fixated on where we touched, and I held onto a hope that he was trying to anchor himself to me as much as possible. I could dream until I was proven wrong, I supposed.

After a little while, his arm began to shake, and he slowly withdrew his touch from mine. It was a reluctant move but decisive. I sighed in disappointment as my hand became cool again. I was going to miss his touch now that I knew what he felt like. The ache in my chest grew twofold at the void he'd left in his wake.

Keyon tucked his hand by his chin and stared over at me again. I couldn't tell what he was thinking or feeling as he simply said, "Thank you, moonflower."

I gazed back and hummed in response. I sighed once more, closed my eyes, and said, "You can have my touch whenever you wish, as often as you wish, however you wish, Keyon. Sleep well." It was an open and honest invitation. It left me vulnerable, but I'd rather offer for the future and never hear back than to offer in the moment and be rejected. Perhaps it would give me a little buffer against feeling too old, too used, and too undesirable. It could just sit there as an unanswered question I could maybe forget about over time.

"Good n-night," he replied, a touch flustered, and I curled into my blanket. I then rested my hand by my nose so I could fall asleep to the scent of his hand on mine.

Sir Keyon

I felt an intense need to be close to Elpis after I had been convinced that she was going to die from eating those poisonous berries. I couldn't believe that she'd survived eating as many as she had, and I'd sent at least a dozen prayers to the Sun God to thank Him for keeping her alive. If our fated mate had died because we couldn't handle a pat on the back... we'd never recover. This had been a severe wake-up call for Toast, and he said he was ready to start trying right then and there.

Once Elpis had fallen asleep, he'd allowed me to roll her onto the blanket to drag her to a safer campsite. I'd kept a paranoid ear on her breathing and heartbeat, terrified that any second one of those would stop. What Toast wouldn't let me do was put my finger down her throat to make her puke—which I'd done for soldiers in the past who'd been poisoned—so all I could do was wait to see if she'd survive. We had no idea how many she'd eaten. Perhaps it had only been a couple since she'd stored some in the... top of her dress. Perhaps she was a squirrel-shifter...

After hours of nervously watching her sweat while she digested the toxins, we were beyond relieved to see her awaken. We'd only left once, and that was to kill some dinner as fast as possible so there'd be something for her to eat if... when she recovered.

Toast had already been near inconsolable when we'd found her and was downright miserable when she'd asked why we even came looking for her. He'd begged me to not share his problem yet, so I kept it vague but made sure to be clear that our reaction wasn't her fault. As much as she triggered his phobia, he was equally fearful of her rejection.

That was when we talked about our first hatchling step. Toast and I agreed that a touch was too small, and a hug was too big, so we settled on holding her hand if she'd allow it. I wasn't sure how she'd interpret the request as it would probably sound childish out of context, but there was no way to find out other than to try. If Toast was willing to go that far, I'd be willing to ask on our behalf. I was already dying to put my hands on her skin and was excited to finally have Toast's permission to do so.

He'd been so anxious when I reached for her that he tried to hold my breath without knowing it. The moth incident had relaxed him as much as it had me. Something about seeing the tiny insect finding safety on her skin gave him the small degree of comfort he needed to see his hatchling step through to the very end.

I was more prepared for the tingles of her soft touch this time and eased both Toast and myself into it. Pressing our skin together had been nearly euphoric. Her cool palm radiated a soothing sensation that almost lulled Toast into a sense of security. I felt our hearts beating together and pleasure flowed through my veins. Staring at where we touched, I could only marvel at how such sensations could span across a simple interaction.

I couldn't allow myself to be too disappointed when Toast needed to stop. I was surprised at how long he'd managed to control his anxiety and made sure he knew how proud I was of him.

First hatchling step done, Toast said in relief. He was a little shaken but sounded... slightly different. Curious perhaps? It was hard to tell when he was experiencing a myriad of emotions.

Turning my appreciative attention back to Elpis, I said, "Thank you, moonflower." She simply hummed but eventually replied, saying something that threw me completely off guard.

"You can have my touch whenever you wish, as often as you wish, however you wish, Keyon. Sleep well." I glanced up at her with wide eyes, but she was already curling up to sleep.

What... did she mean by 'however' you wish, K-Keyon? Toast stammered.

I... don't... I didn't really know what to say. *I don't know if that came from a place of want or if it's the slave in...* I couldn't finish my thought. It felt offensive to her, but I was just so fucking uncertain about what she actually wanted for herself.

I stuttered out my own stupid-sounding good night and tried my best to fall asleep, but I was kept up for hours thinking about all the ways I could have her touch. That vague offer was going to drive me mad.

Chapter 8

Sir Keyon

"I'd like to make it to the river today," I said, half to myself, as I mused over my sketch in the dirt. "From what I remember, there's a small town on the other side." I prodded the little house drawing with a stick, as though I were commanding tiny, invisible forces. "We just have to follow it north a little bit... cross the bridge." My voice dropped to a mumble as Elpis leaned across from me to look down at my sketches. My eyes became glued to the round swells that created her tight cleavage, and I forgot what I was saying. It suddenly occurred to me that as much as I enjoyed staring at them, I didn't want any other males leering at her overflowing assets. She was my fated mate, even if she didn't seem to realize that.

"Gotta get you some proper-fitting clothes," I mumbled without thinking, watching her breathing strain the fabric. She looked up at me, and my eyes flickered to hers.

"I don't have any coin..." she said quietly, fidgeting with her fingers.

I smirked at her and pulled my bag over to rummage through it. "Oh, you have pleeenty of money now, Elpis. You'll be starting your new life with a nice bit of savings." I removed the solid gold chastity belt from it and walked a safe distance away to dig a hole in the dirt. I placed the metal garment over the hole and withdrew a step. I drew in a breath and unleashed blue fire upon it, forcing the metal to soften and fold under the thrall of my heat. Pacing around it, I nudged all the gold into the hole so it'd melt into one solid piece. Once I was satisfied with its compact form, I snorted out a victorious plume of smoke and picked up the large nugget.

"There. Much less offensive now," I announced proudly. "And much more sellable."

"Wow…" I almost couldn't hear Elpis's murmur of amazement, and I puffed out my chest, pleased at the compliment.

I tossed the scalding gold lump in the air and caught it in a hand, smiling over at her. "A tiny fraction of this will buy you proper clothing and necessities after we sell it to a blacksmith or merchant. Much easier to sell a nugget than an illegal chastity belt." I gestured to her neck and added, "We'll do the same thing with your collar later when we reach the river. Plenty of good iron there. I'm sure you'd also like to have that cursed thing off as soon as possible."

She sat up straighter, and her sweet eyes sparkled with delight. Elpis grabbed her slave collar and said, "Yes! Yes! I want this awful thing off! I'm so excited!" She bounced slightly in her elation, and I had to avert my gaze this time. Otherwise, I'd definitely have to sneak off for a second critical round of masturbation.

I'm ready, Toast reminded me, and I smiled at his determination. After grabbing my bag, I held out a hand for Elpis. She looked up at me with surprise in her eyes and slowly put her hand in mine. Her soft skin and the pleasant tingles excited me a bit too much, and I jerked her up from the ground faster than intended. She stumbled forward from the force of my pull and had to brace herself against my chest.

I sucked in a sharp, excited breath when her soft breasts pressed against me, but Toast got spooked. *Be careful! Back up, back up, back up!*

Her eyes widened, and her soft, pale lips parted. I quickly let her go before Toast could take control and push her. A nervous laugh escaped my mouth, and I said, "Sorry about that, moonflower. You're just such a light little petal."

She blushed a faint peach and took a step back herself with a small smile. Then she turned to pick up her bundle of clothes and blanket and awaited my lead. I made a mental note to buy her a proper bag to carry her things in as well. Once I verified the right direction to go in by checking the position of the sun and where the moss grew on the trees, we began walking.

I glanced down at her and mentioned something I'd noticed. "You don't hum before you talk anymore, Elpis."

She raised her brows, and it seemed like she'd just realized it herself. "The other slaves and I only talked freely to each other. We weren't supposed to talk to non-slaves. If you recall... I struggled when you didn't ask yes-or-nay questions. I found that if I started with a small noise, I could work my way up to a word, but it was very difficult."

I fought an urge to give her a playful nudge and said, "I think those berries knocked that habit out of you. You were yelling at me, calling me a fat cloud and shaming me for cursing. You said a lot of things actually. Had quite the bold mouth on you!"

Her eyes widened in horror, and she shifted her grip on the bundle. "Nay, I did not!" she protested, obviously in denial.

"Oh, you most certainly did," I teased. "I would have found it extremely entertaining if I wasn't worried about you dying." I then proceeded to tell her in great detail everything that she'd said and enjoyed mortifying her until she finally broke into laughter with me.

It was early evening when we reached the river and found a decent place to settle. I started a larger campfire for Elpis since we'd both need to wade a bit into the water to remove her iron collar. She had a one-track mind when she dropped her bundle, bouncing anxiously on her toes while looking out at the water.

"Have you even seen a river before, Elpis?" I asked, fairly certain she hadn't.

She shook her head, eyes locked on the current. "Not that I can recall. I was usually either in the mansion guest rooms or the underground cell."

Scorching, violent fury swelled in my chest at the thought of her under another male's control, and I was surprised to hear Toast growl as well. I fisted my hands and spat a blue flame at a tall weed to vent some heat, incinerating it instantly.

I angrily shucked my shirt off and removed my pants, leaving only my undergarment on so I wouldn't have sopping clothes to dry. I looked over at Elpis and caught her staring at me. She averted her gaze and started untying the back of her dress, the sight forcing an odd sound out of my throat that carried notes of hesitation and alarm.

"Euhhh… Elpis, why don't you keep your dress on for this... You have some dry clothes you can wear after we get that collar off," I suggested and shifted my weight uncomfortably.

The light in her eyes faded, and she looked like I'd just publicly shamed her. She opened her mouth to say something but shut it just as fast. Wilting, she turned to walk to the river, but she couldn't quite hide the subtle tremble of her lips and the moisture in her eyes.

What did I do wrong? I asked Toast, not sure why I even thought he'd have the answer.

I don't know... Thought she'd take it as preserving her dignity. Also, one more barrier between us. He shuddered slightly at the thought of her body touching mine. I groaned and rubbed both hands down my face.

Well, hopefully she'll cheer up with the removal of the collar, I said with a modicum of hope and followed her to the river's edge. *How do you want to do this, Toast? You going to hibernate again?*

I'll... stay for a bit and leave if it becomes too much, he decided.

Hatchling steps, big guy.

I waded in and sat so I was chest-deep in the water, then gestured for Elpis to come over while I took a deep breath. "I'm going to need you to sit on my lap here, Elpis. I need to get close to that collar and sweep cold water on your neck while I work. This is going to get pretty hot." I winced internally at that last sentence, wishing I had worded it differently.

She waded over to me, and I parted my legs slightly, preparing to cradle her sideways. I gritted my teeth until I was certain they'd crack and settled her on my lap, hoping she wouldn't feel my erection through her dress skirt. I leaned her back until her collar was just above the water. When I cupped my hand under the lock, I realized that I needed my other hand to do this, so I released my dragon wings to support her back and angled them carefully to prevent them from billowing in the currents.

I cupped the lock on her collar with my left hand to protect her skin as much as possible then began to blow a white flame. I increased the heat to just under three thousand degrees, then used my right hand to keep her hair back and slosh water onto her neck and chin. The tingles from touching her were calming, and I hoped it would help Toast tolerate her proximity.

Hot steam rose from my efforts, and I tilted her head away, worried she'd burn from that as well. "Are you doing ok, Elpis? Any burning?" I asked, focusing intently on one spot so the metal would weaken as fast as possible.

"I'm fine," she responded, staying as still as stone.

I grunted in approval and continued working, heating the metal while making sure she stayed cool. The iron began to get gummy and bend, so I started pulling on it a little, urging the metal to stretch and weaken further. I twisted and pulled it under my blue flame until the iron melted enough for me to rip it. I grinned and displayed the melted lock for her to see, and her hands flew to her neck. Knowing what a meaningful moment this was, I allowed her to free herself, and she began to cry, rubbing her naked neck in disbelief.

"It's gone!" she exclaimed, alternating between sobbing and laughing. "My neck feels so light. So naked," she murmured, tracing her throat in awe. My eyes followed her drifting fingers, and I eased her off of me so she could go back to get dry. Once she waded out, she asked, "Are you coming?"

I nodded and waved her off with a hand. "I'll be there. I need a minute."

Can one die from blue balls? Toast asked.

If it's never happened, I'll be the first, I thought darkly. *How'd you handle that experience, Toast?*

I took a ten-minute break, but I stayed for most of it, he reported.

I'm... really surprised. You're feeling ok?

I'm a bit nauseous and anxious, but I think I'll be ok after a sleep, he admitted. *I probably couldn't have done it without that tingling mate touch.*

Good job, buddy. You're making progress.

Good luck with that erection.

Euhhh... thanks.

Once my body had calmed itself, I turned toward the riverbank and climbed out of the water. Elpis noticed my approach and sat up from her curled position on the blanket, then she went back to staring at the inside of the collar with a melancholic look on her face. She was getting easier to read by the day, which surprised me, but I was grateful for it. It helped me connect with her.

Before getting any closer, I blew some cooler yellow fire over my arms and legs to evaporate the water droplets that were streaming down my body. Elpis glanced at my activity before returning her gaze to the iron pieces in her hands. I wanted to playfully flick some water onto her, but she didn't seem very receptive at the moment.

"Lost in thought?" I asked and settled across the campfire from her. I couldn't see her face very well with how her head was hung. Her long, damp hair left the shoulders and chest of her pajama top soaking wet, and I wished I could dry her hair for her, but she wasn't a dragon-shifter. She was not very fire-resistant.

I watched the top of her head bob as she nodded. "I have a question that is hard to ask, but it is torturing me," she said weakly. Well, that made me nervous.

"You can ask me anything, moonflower," I said steadily and pulled on my pants while I waited for her to summon the courage to say what she needed to say.

"I don't know what's different about being a free female. As a slave—"

"A Reborn," I corrected, interrupting her. She was no longer a slave.

She swallowed hard and continued, "As a... well... nay. What I'm trying to say is that I'm considered old. You saw that I was about to have my virginity sold, and then my value would have dropped. Undesirable. Old, undesirable, and used."

"That's a myth," I snapped unintentionally and lit a little branch on fire with an angry spit. I picked it up and tossed it into the campfire. "They would have you think that because they impose those restrictions on themselves. If they can't enjoy a female after her first time, then I feel sad for them. I'm not an expert, but a female doesn't change; the entrance just stretches a little, then it heals. She's not dirty. The female body is meant to wash out what is put inside. No, the female organ is a work of art and brilliant design. And you mention old?" I barked a disgusted laugh. "Old is subjective. You'd be considered a child to a hundred-year-old male."

She stared at me with stunned eyes, unable to comment or move. I fed the campfire a twig and said, "I'm truly afraid of what some of your facts are based on, Elpis. I will try to clear up what I can, but you're anything but old and undesirable. Once you've lain with a male, you're not used. You're not any less pure. All it means is that you had sex."

"Oh…" she said simply but sullenly. She tossed her own stick into the campfire. "So, it is not too late for me to find a male? A mate? I haven't lost my chance?"

A heavy dose of jealousy pooled into my abdomen, and I bit back a growl. My fangs tried to lengthen, itching to mark my mate, but I restrained the urge. I wanted to run into the woods, shift, and pull up trees by the roots, but I just sat there and answered her question instead.

"No, Elpis," I said through my teeth and eventually loosened my jaw so I didn't sound like I was mad at her. "You have all the time in the world. You'll be desirable until the day you pass on to the Sun God." I didn't meet her eyes when I said that; maybe it was too exposing. Either way, she needed to know there wasn't some kind of dreadful countdown.

I rubbed my eyes, feeling a little bit of panic coming my way this time. Why didn't she react to the bond? Couldn't she feel it? Even humans could feel it, though it wasn't as strong before mating and marking. I didn't want her looking around at other males, trying to figure out which one she wanted. I wanted her to only look at me, for fuck's sake!

Before I realized it, I was standing up and walking over to her. *Toast? You doing this?* I asked, taken by surprise.

I'm practicing, he grumped as he had me crouch before Elpis. *Hold her hands. She's upset. I'll… tolerate it.* When he removed his control, I wobbled a little bit and fell on my ass. I'd have been embarrassed if I wasn't so stunned by Toast's initiative.

"Whoops," I mumbled and scooted to sit closer to Elpis. She eyed me warily through tendrils of her long, damp hair, and I put both my hands out, palms up in invitation. She tilted her head slightly and frowned but slid her slender hands into mine. I took a deep breath and closed my eyes in pleasure. The tingles settled deep into my skin, and I found gratitude in how it calmed my anxious and jealous mind.

"You don't feel that, do you, Elpis?" I murmured quietly and gently squeezed her hands. "The tingling?"

"Nay... I feel nothing but your grip," she said with a small amount of concern. "Did you injure your hands?"

I chuckled and opened my eyes to gaze down at her. *If by injury you mean smote by the mate bond,* I thought with a smile. "Something like that," I replied evasively and looked down at her hands. Her slender fingers looked like they've never worked a day in their life... it was so deceptive. Her work had included some of the most difficult labor a female could ever be forced to endure.

"We have a scholar at the castle who works with our doctors," I said softly, turning her hands until her palms faced skyward. "I'd see her come with the doctor on occasion when someone from my Inferno would get injured. I learned a lot just from listening to her talk about her research. Did you know that our skin replaces itself once a month?" I stroked my thumbs over her palms as I stared at all the tiny wrinkles there, so different from my own.

"N-nay, how's that possible? It always looks the same."

"The skin sheds so finely we don't even notice it, but it's always renewing itself. You know what this means?" I asked and looked up to smile encouragingly at her face.

"Wh-what?" she breathed. I had her complete attention.

"It means that in a month or two, all your skin will have never known an unwanted touch. The skin that remembered the mansion will be completely gone," I answered, hoping it would help remind her that she'd always be her own person. Unowned. "These hands will only have touched what you chose to touch."

"Wow," she gasped and stared down at her arms, amazed. "That's incredible!"

"May I feel your arms, Elpis?" I murmured my question, wanting to move past hands now.

"You kn-know the answer to that," she said, biting her lip.

"Right… whenever, as often, and however… whatever that last one means." I mumbled that last part out loud without thinking and cleared my throat nervously. I could feel my face heating up, which was unusual. I normally had much more control over that.

Resting her left hand on my knee, I took her right arm in both hands. I traced my fingers around her bony knuckles and wrists, then dragged a forefinger up the inside of her cushiony arm to its crook, pushing the fabric of her sleeve along as I did so. I watched as all the tiny, pale hairs on her skin stood on end. Toast wasn't telling me to stop, so I kept going, wishing I could just get lost in her body. I was in a place of paradise, finally able to explore a female.

I slid my finger up her bicep and stopped when the sleeve bunched too much to proceed. Her breath caught when I completely wrapped my hand around her arm and slid it down until I reached her wrist. I palmed her hand and held it again. "You're so soft. Are all females like this? I can't even remember anymore," I murmured to myself. When I scented her arousal, I fought to keep my composure. She shifted delicately and avoided my gaze.

The turn of her head swung a damp lock over her eye, and before she could get to it, I brushed it away from her face. I gathered all the hair that was slung over her right shoulder and placed it behind her, wanting to see the curve of her neck now that the collar was gone.

"How does your neck feel afte—" I began but noticed something quite unexpected when I leaned forward to get a closer look. "Elpis," I asked with apprehension, "did you always have symbols on your neck?"

"I do? I don't know… I don't recall ever seeing my neck before it was collared. Do they look like these?" she asked and pointed to the inside of the iron collar. I grabbed it from her and held it up to her neck to compare. The symbols were mirrored but identical. It was like the collar had stamped them on over years of pressure.

"They do, Elpis. They're the same..." I said, uneasy. I traced one with my thumb, and Elpis jerked a little bit. "Shit, did that hurt?" I asked, and she shook her head.

"Nay, you just surprised me."

"Sorry..." I said quietly and moved to squat behind her. I lifted her hair there and spied the line of symbols continuing. "They go all the way around, but I don't know what they mean. Looks like witchwork. Did Adelmar ever have witches come by the mansion?"

"I-I don't know. I don't remember any," she replied nervously. She shuddered as I ran my thumb over the symbols, and despite the topic, I suspected she was getting as aroused as I was. I sighed, realizing I should stop touching her now. Toast did marvelously and deserved a break.

Well done, Toast. You helped me discover those markings. We need to learn more about them.

Then let's not melt the collar for money. We'll provide for her anyway. We don't need the coin.

Can't believe how well you're adapting.

What does not adapt ends up dying. He sighed. *I don't like the sound of her asking about looking for other males. It is putting a lot of pressure on me to work harder, and I am very stressed.*

I'll do what I can. It'd help if she recognized us. I don't know why she can't.

Let me get us dinner, Toast said, changing the subject. *I want to provide.*

Alright, one minute.

I got up and walked away from Elpis. "Toast wants to find you dinner."

Play it cool, idiot! Find us dinner. Find US dinner! Don't make me sound like some lovesi—

"Toast?" she asked. "Who's that?"

"That's my dragon's name," I said with a devilish grin, stepping out of my pants again. "Terribly ferocious name, isn't it?"

Keeeyon! Stop!

"It's a fine name!" Elpis said with a tilt of her chin. "Without it, bread would always be cold, and who likes cold bread?"

You know, I'm not certain if that's a compliment or not, Toast said thoughtfully. *It sounds like a compliment, but like… a compliment for a baker.*

"You flatter him," I chuckled, slipped out of my undergarment, and walked off to shift. Toast quickly returned to Elpis with a mouthful of fish, which he proceeded to drop about ten feet away from her. He got a little spooked when she waved at him, and I shifted back to prevent him from having another panic attack.

Under the fear, I could tell he was still pleased as shit to provide. Toast was also quite upset when we had to toss most of the fish back in the water because we couldn't eat twelve salmon between us. At least they were still alive, which was a relief to Elpis.

After dinner, Elpis curled up in her blanket, and I nested near her again with a wing slung over me. She extended a hand out between us, yawned, and said, "Sleep well, Keyon. Thanks for taking the collar off. It feels amazing—like I'm a brand-new person." I watched her eyes close, but she didn't withdraw her hand.

I hesitated, then placed my hand over hers and left it there. The corners of her lips curled up into a tiny smile, and I grinned into my other hand. Closing my eyes to rest, I simply said, "Good night, moonflower." Neither of us moved our hands.

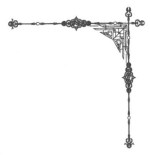

Chapter 9

Elpis

I woke to find our hands still entangled. Keyon's fingers had slid between mine and dug into my palm like it was the last handhold on a cliff. It didn't hurt. If anything, it was comforting and made my belly flutter with tiny dragons again. My eyes slid up the steep slopes of his arms that looked as hard as my old iron collar and stared at the defined, corded muscles of his broad shoulders. I couldn't see much else because of the wing he'd rested over himself. He couldn't have been cold if he'd slept shirtless. A mischievous part of me was tempted to crawl under that wing and share my body heat regardless.

Sexy little tent. The words came to my mind out of nowhere, and I nearly snorted out a laugh. I tried to angle to see his face, but it was mostly tucked away under his other hand and his messy chestnut hair. It was even more of a mess than usual from drying overnight. I sighed and squeezed my legs together. I needed to relieve my bladder, but I held it, wanting the moment to last just a little longer. I wasn't ready to let go of his hand.

I liked touching him, but I was starting to prefer him touching me, like he'd done last night. I'd especially liked it after he'd fought off my fears of being old and undesirable. I knew he was just escorting me, but I was starting to wonder if there was more. Something was changing, but it was happening very slowly. I wondered if he'd ever explain the reason for me needing to be patient. I think the patience was paying off, though. He seemed more attentive and engaging by the day, even if his actions were still a mystery to me.

I slowly tried to pull my hand away, but his grip tightened, and he mumbled into his other hand. "Zno trainin' today."

I sandwiched my lips between my teeth, my belly convulsing with suppressed laughter as I struggled to escape his grasp. I twisted and writhed, but it was like being shackled.

"Keyon," I said in a low voice, tugging again. "Wake up!"

He responded by mumbling and pulling on me this time. His yank forced me to scramble toward him, narrowly avoiding stepping on one of his wings.

"Keyon!" I said a little louder with a laugh. "I need to pee! Let go!"

His eyes snapped open to find me awkwardly balancing over him. He released me immediately, and I sighed in relief, shaking my freed hand. Both his palms raised a little, as if I were holding him at sword's point, and he stared intently at my face, his jaw rigid.

"I-I'm sorry," he said brusquely. "Did I trap your hand?"

"Which was fine, but I really, really need to pee!" I said in a rush and ran off into the woods to relieve myself.

When I returned, we ate a quick breakfast and began following the river. After about three hours, we reached a wide stone bridge that led to a town. It was the first town I'd ever remembered seeing, and I froze halfway across the bridge, unable to tell if I was excited or frightened. I tried to swallow, but my mouth ran dry. On a wide cobbled street, sandwiched between shops, were dozens of tents and hundreds of people.

Assaulted with unfamiliar noises, sights, and smells, I took an uncertain step backwards. My skin crawled unexpectedly, and I wrapped my arms around myself. The last time I'd been around a crowd was at the mansion. Adelmar would host large parties that the pleasure and sex slaves had to work. Those were long, excruciating evenings where the guests pawed and groped until they dragged you to a dark corner or hallway to service them. Bowls were placed in discreet locations where we could throw up our stomach contents in case the constant swallowing became too much to handle.

Servicing one guest a night was something I could endure and detach myself from, but servicing multiple was pure misery, and I always had a line. Being Adelmar's favorite, he'd send me back down earlier than the others and reminded me that it was a compliment to be so coveted. He wanted me to be proud of myself, like he was of me.

Dagrun and I would talk quietly the rest of the night across our cages. We'd talk about anything to distract ourselves, even make up little stories about bugs that happened to skitter across the cold floor. If we slept, we'd have nightmares. If we stayed awake and stewed in our thoughts, we'd cry all night. Sometimes Zosime would hold me if I crumbled, and I did the same for her.

When Keyon realized I wasn't following, he halted and turned with a concerned look on his face. The male backtracked and hesitantly placed a hand on my arm. "Are you ok, Elpis?"

I couldn't reply for a moment; my mouth was so dry, and my chest had turned into stone. I slid a hand up to a belly that was aching with anxiety. I didn't know why, but the stress was making me feel like I was aging faster.

"That's a lot of people, Keyon," I whispered hoarsely. My face iced over, and I struggled to keep my breathing slow.

He looked back over his shoulder, licked his lips, and said, "Yeah, it's a farmer's market. Businesses set up tents to sell directly to the townsfolk. There's also entertainment, but that's mostly for the hatchlings."

"Keyon? Do... free males touch females?" I asked, bringing my fingers to my mouth. "They're not supposed to, right?"

He scowled, looked back again, and a small growl rumbled from his chest. "Without her permission? It happens more than it should, but it's illegal. No one will drag you away from me, Elpis. If anyone tries to touch you, I'll rip their hand off."

My eyes widened. "Is it legal to rip hands off?" I gasped.

He flattened his lips and growled again. "Not really..."

I would have laughed if I didn't feel so sick to my stomach. My forehead broke into a sweat, an uncomfortably cold one, and I swept the moisture away with my fingers. Keyon slid his hand down my arm to grab mine. "I won't let anything happen to you, moonflower. Stay close, but know most of these people wouldn't wish you harm. They're just families living their lives."

I nodded, swallowed heavily, and followed him the rest of the way across the bridge. I grimaced as we entered the marketplace and could almost feel hands on my arms, thighs, and waist. Keyon guided me through the thinnest sections and directly into a shop. There weren't as many people in here, and they were all women. Keyon's own hand became sweaty, which made me look up at him. He didn't look so good himself.

We approached a pretty young lady behind a counter, and Keyon said, "This lady"—he squeezed my hand—"requires several complete sets of clothing and a heavy cloak. Can you help her with that?"

The young lady eyed him up and down and grinned playfully. "I can help with anything."

"Excellent," he replied graciously, then turned to me and said, "I'll be just outside. I need some... air." He nearly jogged out of the shop, and I let out a small, helpless whimper.

I turned back to the shopkeeper, who smiled and said, "Let's find you some clothes, then, shall we?" Suddenly, I didn't want her helping me, but I followed her to a changing room where she took my measurements.

"That male doesn't happen to have a mate, does he?" she asked when she peeked at my neck. She curiously regarded the symbols on my neck, then continued writing on her notepad. I shook my head despite desperately wanting to lie and say he was mine. She grinned and continued working, looking pleased with herself. Jealousy hung hot and heavy in my belly, and I fought off a deep frown. She was being nice to me and didn't deserve my ire.

"Yes, these clothes you have on do not do you justice," she said with a laugh. "Let's get you looking gorgeous. What's your favorite color?"

My favorite color? I had never thought about that before in my life. I twisted my lips in thought, but the first thing that came to mind was Keyon's copper eyes. That was something I liked looking at. Maybe that was my favorite color? "Copper?" I said shyly.

She nodded and looked me up and down, though not quite like how she'd done with Keyon. "I can see you in our rose gold. That's close. I think we'll do lavender and raspberry too."

She bustled off and returned with a basket of items. Three dresses, several cloaks, bras, panties, nightgowns, something she called stockings, and socks. The dresses felt significantly more comfortable, and she cooed over the fit. When I looked in the mirror, I was absolutely stunned to see myself in something so pleasant and normal. One of the dresses would be nice and warm for cold weather, while the other two were a bit more on the flirtatious side. I felt a little bit more like a free female wearing something feminine instead of obscene.

"I've never worn anything that fit before," I murmured, tearing up at how unreal it seemed.

The lady looked down at my dirty, bare feet and asked, "Reborn?" I nodded, flushing slightly. She frowned, shook a finger, and said, "You have nothing to be ashamed of. You are bloody gorgeous and an inspiration to women everywhere. Now you're going to wear our dresses and hold your head up nice and proud!"

I laughed through a sob and nodded again, feeling too choked up to say anything. The shopkeeper led me back to the counter, and I caught Keyon's eye, letting him know we were done. He stepped warily into the shop, and the young lady told us the amount. He dug some coins out of a purse without batting an eye and gave them to me.

"Is that a lot?" I asked Keyon, concerned. "I'll pay you back." He shook his head, then gestured to the shopkeeper. I handed the coins over, and she passed some smaller coins back in exchange. While she wrapped my items, Keyon explained what had just happened and how much each coin was worth. I furrowed my brows, focusing intently on what he was saying so I wouldn't forget.

He handed me a pretty little embroidered purse and said, "That's to keep your coins in. Go ahead and put what you just received in there."

"But these are yours," I protested, confused, with the small coins still piled on my palm.

"Use them to buy your shoes. Let's test what you just learned," he said with a smile. I dropped the coins in the pouch, deeply touched by his generosity and willingness to teach. I hoped I didn't seem too stupid.

The shopkeeper said, "Here you go!" and handed me a bundle tied with twine. I gave her a thankful, genuine smile, even if she did plan to steal my... court Keyon. I suppressed another surge of ugly jealousy and turned to leave. However, before I stepped outside, she grabbed my arm, surprising me. The female cupped my ear and whispered, "I snuck some extra things in there, free of charge. Go get him!" She giggled and pushed me back toward the exit. My mouth hung open, and I stumbled but finally caught up to Keyon. What was that? Had I read everything completely wrong? I was so confused.

When Keyon held out his hand, I took it, following along in a daze. He continued to walk me through the market, placing himself between me and everyone else as much as possible. It wasn't that hard because his unyielding warrior's body parted the crowd like a king. Looking about, I noticed a lot of women staring at him and grew increasingly more agitated over it. Most might have been innocent gawkers, but one female tried to catch his eye while licking her lips suggestively. When he didn't acknowledge her, she turned and sneered at me. The female mouthed something, but I couldn't read her lips. The hostile interaction had my arms shaking, and an intense urge to headbutt her stupid face or kick her in the shins possessed me.

Keyon must have noticed my distress because he pulled me against his side and wrapped his arm around my shoulder. My behavior was embarrassing, and I didn't know why I was feeling so aggressively territorial. We weren't a couple. I didn't even know if he had someone at home.

We entered another shop that had a mix of male and female customers in it. Leather products filled shelves from top to bottom. Bags, belts, and shoes of many styles and colors lined the room and hung from hooks. Once again, Keyon took me to the counter where an older male was cutting leather.

"Good afternoon. We're looking for a pair of boots and slippers for this lady," Keyon said as he glanced around the shop. "We don't know her size, though. Is that something you could help us with?"

The male grunted and jumped off his stool. "Come, come," he beckoned and waddled over to a stool. His gruff demeanor softened when he saw my dirty, scratched feet. "Let's take care of you, sweet one," he grunted with a wet sniffle and pulled out some string to take measurements like the other lady had done. Once he finished, he gestured to follow him to the back porch, which made Keyon stick to my side like a guard dog.

"Wash yer feet here, then come back inside," he grumbled, placing a bucket and some soap by me. I sat down and scrubbed at my feet the best I could, grimacing at the little cuts I exposed once the caked dirt had been rinsed off properly.

Keyon frowned at the scrapes, grabbed the bundle from the clothing store, and said, "Let's get some socks on to protect your feet." He shuffled through the items delicately until he saw something that turned his face red.

"What's wrong?" I asked curiously. Did he not like the dresses?

"Nothing," he stated rather quickly and continued rifling through items until he pulled out a pair of soft cotton socks. He handed them to me and rewrapped the bundle. I shoved the socks on and moaned in pleasure. I've never felt such softness under my feet! Keyon chuckled, then held out a hand to help me stand. I tiptoed in long strides back into the shop, trying to keep the socks as clean as possible.

The older man held out a pair of soft boots and flat embroidered slippers. "Try the deerskin boots. They're the softest I have and good for walking distances," he said while coughing. "Excuse me."

I pulled on the boots and suppressed a pleased groan. Oh my goddess! I couldn't stop touching them. "They're amazing!" I breathed and jumped up to walk around when he prompted. "They're exquisite," I gushed and turned to the man. "You're incredible!"

"I think that means we'll take them," Keyon said with a grin. His eyes glimmered with amusement when I tested a hop, but I stopped jumping when I noticed several people staring, and I rushed to sit back down on the bench. I had the same reaction with the slippers. They were so light but so protective. It was almost like being barefoot!

The shopkeeper let me keep the slippers on while I bought them so I didn't have to go barefoot again. When I tried to pay for the shoes, I accidentally gave him enough to buy twenty pairs instead of two. "Try again," Keyon said, nudging me with an elbow. I frowned and moved the coins around, trying to remember what he'd taught me. I handed the shopkeeper my second attempt, and he let out a wheezy guffaw.

"Perfect," he said, trying to keep a straight face, and handed me a bundle. I grinned haughtily at Keyon over my success while he purchased a rucksack. The older man offered me a hug, wished me luck, then returned to cutting leather. I was stunned by the gruff sweetness and the lack of sexual intent in the embrace. I didn't recall the last time I'd gotten a genuine hug where the giver expected nothing in return. It was like getting a hug from a female, and I wondered if that was what being hugged by a grandfather would feel like. It was nice... I liked it!

"He gave you those slippers for free," Keyon said when we were clear of the shop.

I gasped in dismay. "Nay! I didn't give him enough? Why didn't you tell me?"

"Did you see the look on his face? You made the old male's day! He wanted to help you out, plus business is booming because of the market. He's not hurting for money," Keyon said with another joyful grin.

"Ahh," I uttered with a shake of my head. "Such a sweet person. I feel bad, but I'll accept it! Wish I could give him something in return."

"Like I said, Elpis," he reminded me, gesturing to the crowd, "most of these people are just kind souls living their lives. Many find their own joy in giving to others. It's just a small piece of society." I nodded but still feared straying from his side. I felt a lot more vulnerable here in the open market than I did in the shops.

We stopped next at what looked like a blacksmith's shop. I grimaced when I saw a large, sweaty male working on a sword that was so hot it was glowing. That looked dangerous! A younger, brawny male who looked like he may have been the other male's son walked out to greet us, wiping his hands with a stained rag. He smiled at Keyon but grinned when he spotted me. I slunk closer to Keyon, not liking that I couldn't read this other male's enthusiasm. Was it sexual? I was starting to doubt my observational skills since the dress shop.

"Hello! Welcome, welcome. Lovely day for a market, wouldn't you say? What can we help you with?" he said to us both.

Keyon fished the gold nugget from his bag and handed it over to the male. "We're looking to sell this gold nugget. Get some things at the market and start a savings for this lady. Is this smithy in need of any gold?"

"Oh yes, we could always use gold. Jewelry does very well at the farmer's markets," the smith said and gave me an odd, appraising look before he fetched a scale. He placed the gold nugget on the pan and wrote something down in a fat ledger. He hesitated, looked up at Keyon, and then walked over to interrupt the older smith in the back, who'd just placed the red-hot sword in water. Hissing steam drowned out their conversation, and I inched even closer to Keyon, pressing against his side.

He looked down with a concerned frown and asked, "Are you ok, Elpis?"

I shook my head and whispered, "Was he eyeing me? I can't tell anymore."

Keyon glanced at where the smiths were talking and murmured, "Didn't seem like it to me. Keep an open mind and keep observing, but always listen to your gut. I'm here, though. You're safe." He wrapped an arm around me and squeezed my shoulder. I relaxed a little bit but couldn't keep the worry off my face.

Both smiths came back this time, and the older male pulled out a safe. He counted out a number of coins that were the highest value Keyon had shown me and passed them to me. I fumbled for the lovely purse Keyon had bought and stored the coins.

"You've got the coin for the weight, plus a donation for the Reborn," the older smith said as he locked the safe and stored it. "Always glad to see the knight general's hard work paying off for them poor souls." He held out a hand for Keyon to shake that was so thickly calloused it looked like he was wearing leather gloves.

Keyon seemed pleasantly surprised and accepted the male's hand. "Surprised you recognized me, sir…?"

"Sigeberht," he answered, then stroked his short, neatly trimmed blond beard. "I visit my twin at the castle. He works at the smithy there."

"Sigivald?" Keyon exclaimed, then started laughing. "I should have known. You're not identical, but you're very similar. He does exceptional work."

"I help out too when I'm there." He grinned slyly, and his pewter eyes gleamed. "We do love to gossip over the forge. Glad to see you're actually spending time with a lady."

Keyon snorted. "I'm just escorting her. Don't read too much into it, Sigeberht."

My heart sank into my stomach at those words. An urge to leave and find a place to be alone hit me fiercely, but I couldn't do that. On top of it all, I was embarrassed by the dismissal, and my face ignited.

Stop it, cheeks! I moaned miserably in my head.

"Well then, maybe Sigeweard here could take her to dinner tonight?" Sigeberht suggested with a grin.

Sigeweard raised both his palms and turned to dramatically depart. "Leave me out of your games, Father. I'm out!"

I didn't know what upset me more, them talking about me like I wasn't there or the two rejections I'd just experienced. My cheeks blazed now, and I pressed my lips together while scrunching my nose in an attempt to restrain tears. When had I become so bad at hiding my feelings? I'd never struggled this much before my rescue. Had I worn my slave status as a mask? Maybe once that was pulled away, I was more raw and naked than I realized.

Thankfully, no one seemed to notice the change in my demeanor. Keyon lowered his voice and shifted the subject. "Since Sigivald is a very vocal supporter of the king... you may want to tell him to be... careful about what he says and does."

Sigeberht's face fell and grew serious. "Is he in danger?"

Keyon inhaled deeply, glanced around, and said under his breath, "I don't know what's going on, but you see Elpis right here? She's the only one I was able to free from the last raid because someone from the castle interfered and tried to have me killed. I don't even know if my Inferno's still alive. I'm not going to give you any details to protect you and your brother, but... if you see him face-to-face again, just... tell him to watch what he says. I have a feeling that loyalties will be tested very soon, and I'm scared for my people."

The older smith scratched his right arm and nodded with a set jaw. "I'll be sure to visit him soon, Sir Keyon. Check on my nieces too." He held his hand out again to Keyon and said in a gruff voice, "You have a friend and ally at this smithy. Sunlight preserve you."

"Sunlight preserve you," Keyon returned, shook his hand, and guided me away from the smithy.

Chapter 10

Elpis

Keyon must have noticed my listless behavior because he said, "You must be exhausted. We'll make one more stop, book a room at the inn, and get some food. Does that sound ok?"

"Mm-hmm," I hummed, not feeling like talking. Keyon reached for my hand, but I avoided it and pretended that I needed to adjust my skirts. I didn't look at his face and fidgeted with my fingers instead.

"Oh, right. I forgot." Keyon paused in his steps for a moment before moving to a quiet spot away from the colorful, noisy booths. He grabbed the rucksack he'd bought and reached for the bundle and boots I'd stuffed under my arm. The male placed them neatly in the bag, which he passed to me with a small smile.

"Here, this is yours too. We just need to get you some essentials, then we can rest. Just a bit longer, Elpis."

"Thanks…" I said and slung the bag over my shoulders. Ah, this was much more convenient. It was nice to have free hands at the moment. I felt like I could defend myself a little better if someone tried to grab me. "I like this bag…"

Keyon guided me into a larger store that seemed to offer a variety of household items. A portly gentleman greeted us and asked if we needed any help.

"Yes. Can someone help her pick out an assortment of general feminine necessities? I'm not... versed on the subject, and she doesn't have any yet," Keyon explained.

The male glanced at me before yelling, "Adelais! A customer!"

A beautiful young female rushed in, holding her skirts away from her heels. Her long blackberry curls bounced with every step. "Yes?" she asked, out of breath.

"Before you leave with that shipment, can you help this lady pick out essentials? She doesn't have anything at the moment, so you may have to explain some things."

"Oh! Yes, happy to do so!" she said and waved for me to follow her. She picked up a wicker basket and pointed to little bottles and bars of soap, explaining their use. I was able to pick this up a little faster, having watched the servants bathe me time and time again. I eyed the straight razor with a little trepidation, and she laughed when she saw the expression on my face.

Adelais snuck me back to a private space with a bucket of water and soap, then explained how to use the razor without bleeding to death. I nicked myself once but slowly got the hang of it, so we added the blade to the basket. By the end of her tour, I had a decent amount of items, and she escorted me to the front to complete the purchase.

"Found everything?" Keyon asked, and I raised my hands a little.

"I think so?" I said and opened my purse nervously. I wanted to get it right this time.

Adelais told me the amount, and I picked through the coins, but my brain stopped working. Maybe I was just tired or still stressed from the smithy encounter, but I panicked, my brow growing dewy once more. When Keyon's hand landed on my shoulder, I nearly jumped out of my slippers.

"Hey, just breathe. It's ok. Want me to go over the amounts with you again?"

I nodded, both embarrassed and relieved, and he dug out a variety to explain again. Finally, I handed the correct amount over to the female and muttered, "Sorry about that..."

She gave me the sympathetic look I was starting to see a lot of around here and said, "Good luck out there. The world's a big place, but you'll do just fine, sweet one."

I looked up at Keyon and asked, "How does everyone know?"

He twisted his lips in a sad smile. "Some people are just very observant, but they mean you well."

I nodded and placed my nearly full rucksack on the counter to store the items. The lady dropped something else into my bag, but she did it so fast I couldn't tell what it was. Another gift? I guess I'd find it later.

I swung my bag on and shyly said, "Thank you for your help..." The female waved it off and wished me luck again.

We stepped out, and I released a massive, weary exhale. I was exhausted already, physically and emotionally. My stamina here was lacking. Keyon squeezed my shoulder and said, "Let's get a room at the inn so you can rest a bit. Then we'll eat." Though he didn't try to hold my hand again, I stayed close, nearly bumping into him a couple times.

We entered a long, three-story building and were greeted by a very distracted worker. The poor thing was balancing a tray, dragging a chair, and had a notepad in her mouth.

"Nooking foa roo?" she asked breathlessly through the pad, and Keyon nodded. How he knew what she said was beyond me! She put down the tray, removed the notepad from her mouth, and ran to grab a ledger. "We're pretty booked up from the market, but we have a suite available. It's a little more expensive than the normal room, but the cheaper ones are all taken..." she said, looking certain that we'd turn and leave.

"That's fine," Keyon said and handed her some coins after they went over the prices and services. I eyed his purse. He wasn't even putting a dent in it! I tugged on his sleeve.

"Can I pay for my half?" I asked, but he looked offended.

"I'd rather you didn't. Technically, this is still an escort, so you shouldn't be paying for anything," he answered, sounding slightly grouchy. Turning back to the servant, he asked if they could have some food sent to the suite. She nodded, gave him the room number, and rushed off to the kitchen to place the order.

Keyon led me up the stairs and unlocked the door to our room. "Wowow!" I yapped and ran into the suite. I abandoned my bag on a canvas chair and dashed into another room to investigate. A huge bed! I dove onto it and bounced once before settling. I rolled off and ran into another room. A tiny kitchen! Wow! I barely heard Keyon's laughter from the entryway as I explored the suite.

"It's like a small mansion," I whispered before rushing to find the bathroom. Ah, there was a porcelain tub! I needed a bath so bad. "Keyon?" I called out from the bedroom. "Can I take a bath?"

"Don't ask permission. Just go take one!" he yelled from the other room. "Free women control their own bathing destinies."

"Thank you!" I shouted unnecessarily, grabbed my bag, and scrambled excitedly to use the new items from the store. It was good she'd told me what each one was because I couldn't read, and I was able to identify the shampoo, conditioner, and body wash. There was a bottle in there I didn't recognize and realized that must have been what she'd snuck in earlier.

"Keyon?" I asked and walked out to the room where he was seated, drinking water. "What's this? She put it in there but never told me what it was, and I can't read." I handed him the bottle, and once his gaze landed on it, he choked and sprayed water everywhere.

"Oh my goddess!" I panicked. "Should I pat your back?" He shook his head and held up a finger, telling me to wait. I fidgeted worriedly while he struggled to clear his throat and breathe. After a couple minutes, he coughed out the last of it and leaned back with a groan, closing his eyes.

"Are you ok?" I squeaked, wishing I hadn't shown him the bottle now. Was it bad?

"Yup." He cleared his throat one last time. "I'm all right, Elpis."

I stood there for another long moment, waiting. "So... what is it?"

He scrubbed a hand over his face and rested it over his eyes. "She gave you lube, Elpis. I'm guessing she wanted to empower your... other destinies." Whatever I could see of his face was bright red, and he muttered, "The women in this town, I swear to the Sun God Himself..." He returned the bottle to me and said in a gruff voice, "Anyway, it says it's warming and tingling... so... yeah... enjoy it... or... not... whatever... I guess..." I backed up quietly while he continued to mutter and escaped to my bath.

I tossed the bottle into the bag, frowning. I'd never touched myself in the way the sex slaves described. I couldn't really imagine getting in the mood when I was sitting in a cage with another female in a cold room full of depressed slaves. Not only did I not know enough about it, but I also didn't really feel like trying because my instincts were screaming for something else. I didn't think I'd ever get the sight of Keyon's erect cock out of my mind, and I blushed madly at the memory of catching him in the midst of his finishing.

What a gorgeous beast! my mind howled. I had to agree with it. I grabbed my heated cheeks and shivered.

The food arrived as soon as I jumped out of my accident-free bath. All products had been used correctly, and no bleeding occurred under the wrath of the straight razor! My muscles were sighing in relief, and I felt like I'd finally washed away the last of the mansion. Wrapping a towel around myself first, I burst out of the bathroom to get to my brand-new clothes, squealing like an excited hatchling. Keyon watched me pass with a bewildered expression.

"Food... is... here..." he announced falteringly.

"Coming!" I squawked from the bedroom. I yanked open my rucksack and spilled the entire contents of the dress shop onto the bed. Oh gods, what should I choose? I put on the underwear and melted when I snapped on the bra. What a difference support made, oh my goddess. My bosom had never known such happiness.

I wriggled into the rose-gold dress and ran my hair through a comb. Then I shoved my feet back into the slippers and opened the bedroom door a crack to see where Keyon was. He sat with his back to me, eating slices of meat and cheese from a tray. I cleared my throat to get his attention.

When Keyon turned, he raised his brows. I jumped into the room with my hands on my hips, proclaiming, "I am a brand-new free person, and my name is Elpis... Eukadoka?" I had started quite confidently but ended on a very uncertain note. Shit! I forgot my own last name!

Keyon laughed, a deep rumbling sound that made my toes curl in my slippers. He stood and walked over to where I was. "Eudokia," he said with a chuckle. "You were very close, though."

"Eudokia, Eudokia, Eudokia!" I chanted, furrowing my brows. I couldn't forget my own name! Keyon was watching me with a slight smile, and his gaze ran over my outfit.

"You look nice, Elpis," he said with an expression I couldn't decipher. "I'm glad you got what you needed here. You deserve more, much more, but that'll happen when we find you a place to... settle," he said, hesitating at the end. He then perked up and gestured to the table laden with fruit, cheese, meat, and bread. "Come eat! The food's quite good."

I hurried to sit and shoveled food into my mouth, despite Keyon telling me not to eat so fast. How could I resist such delicacies, though? We saw many of these foods at the parties but were never even allowed a taste. When I popped a piece of cheese into my mouth, I groaned, palming my cheeks in delight.

"You have no idea, Keyon. You have no idea what it's like to go from what I was... to this. I feel like I've been put into a different person's life!" I shared after swallowing. I picked out a different cheese and wrapped it in a thin slice of meat.

He studied me with understanding eyes and a sad smile. "No, I definitely don't know, moonflower, but based on the faces you're making, I can definitely imagine." He moved his stare to the food on the table and fidgeted with a grape. "Nothing makes me happier knowing I was the person who could show it all to you."

𝔖ir 𝔎eɲon

Elpis was always beautiful, but right now, she was glowing. Her sudden happiness made her bloom brighter than any moonflower under the glowing night sky. I tried not to stare at her while she ate, but it was too hard to avoid. Everything was so precious to her. I'd never seen anyone appreciate plain bread the way she did.

I got a fun idea and grabbed a slice of bread. Holding it out with a thumb and forefinger, I blew a gentle fire over it until it was a nice golden brown.

"Toast!" Elpis cried out, laughing.

What? Toast asked groggily. *Someone say my name?*

Go back to sleep, Toast. Just feeding Elpis.

Nah, I'm awake now…

I held up a finger to Elpis and placed some meat and tomatoes down on the toast. I sprinkled the top with pieces of cheese and hit it with another breath of fire to melt it. Elpis was watching what I was doing with rapt attention, her nostrils flaring. I handed the melt over to her and leaned back with a smirk.

"Careful," I warned, smug as fuck. "It's hot."

Elpis blew on it and took a conservative bite. Her eyes widened, and she didn't bother to finish chewing to speak. "Mohm my moddesh, mishish amazing!" She kicked her feet excitedly and ate it as fast as she could without burning her tongue. I made her another one, immensely pleased by her enthusiastic response.

I think it is becoming enjoyable to feed her, Toast said cautiously. *Providing feels good.*

Oh, I'm loving it. Look at her face! I replied happily. *You're doing well today, Toast. You keep surprising me.*

I kind of have to, he said darkly. *You saw all those males watching her! I'd rather endure her closeness than let one of those beasts get any ideas.*

I think you're enduring better than you're letting on.

It… It's not an easy thing to admit, Keyon. I don't want you thinking I'm having an easy time of it just because it's getting easier to bear.

You know I wouldn't, I answered. *I just want to make sure we're both being honest with ourselves. That's all.*

Right… just… you keep those males away, and I'll keep… adapting the best I can…

You know I will, I growled possessively. I must have growled out loud because Elpis gave me a startled look. "Sorry," I said to her, popping one last grape in my mouth. "Was just thinking about something."

"About what?" she asked curiously, nibbling on an apple. Her soft, pale lips were pressed tight around its skin. Oh, how I fucking wished my cock was that apple… minus the chewing part.

I shook my head and cleared my addled brain. What was I saying? "Oh, uh." I thought quickly and did find a somewhat truthful reply. "I just realized I forgot to post a letter. We're going to have to step out one more time before we can fully retire. We can eat dinner downstairs later so we won't have to leave once we get back."

"Ah…" she said simply and placed the apple back down, perhaps to finish later. "I'm ready." She tossed her damp hair over her shoulders, and once again, I wished she was a dragon like me so I could dry it for her.

We stepped back out onto the street, and it looked like they were setting up for the night market. It'd be fun to show Elpis around after dark, but I was afraid it'd be too stressful for her. Toast was also becoming incredibly fired up and territorial. This was the first time he'd ever had to be wary of males as well as females, so going into a crowd now was absolutely pushing his limits. I had to make this errand fast.

I hunted down the post office and grabbed some flowery stationery to write my message:

Dearest Leofwine,

My lover, my life, my sunset sky! I simply can wait no longer to see thee! I've been burning for your touch for two... no... has it been three weeks? I can't be sure as time slows between our dalliances! I wish I could fly to thee, but alas, my sad human feet know naught but dirt. Please, oh please, come see me!

Your Amorous Lover, Berhta

I hesitated, then turned to Elpis with a grin. "If I gave you a piece of paper, do you think you could copy these symbols? I'll teach you reading and writing later, but this could actually be helpful for me," I asked.

Elpis appraised the page with a raised eyebrow and said, "I could try... looks fun." I grinned excitedly and handed her a fresh sheet of the flowery stationery and a pen. I showed her how to hold the pen, then unleashed her. Oh, this was fantastic. Not only would the wrong hands be unable to recognize my handwriting, but it'd also confuse the shit out of Leofwine—which was always a bonus.

I watched as Elpis finished copying the letter. It was a beautiful disaster, but you could definitely tell what it said. "It's perfect!" I praised her. "I wish I could just keep it and frame it for myself."

She blushed and pivoted bashfully. I paid to have it posted and expedited, then left the office with a bounce in my step.

"What was the letter for?" she asked.

I pulled the original out of my pocket and read it in a very feminine voice, which had Elpis staring at me like I was a madman before she broke into laughter.

"What in the goddess? Berhta?" she gasped between giggles.

"One night," I shared, leaning down a little to speak under my breath while grabbing her hand, "my friend, Leof, and I got outrageously drunk. And I mean, we were flat-out hammered. He'd just told me this funny story about how one of his spies used the wrong code word in a message so when his supply drop came, he received a box of wigs instead of scent removers. Funniest shit Leof's ever seen happen, and apparently now when they complete a successful mission, they take the wigs out to the taverns.

"Anyway, I digress." I waved my other hand to move on to my point. "That night, Leof and I came up with our own code in the form of love letters. I was laughing so hard, I nearly pissed my pants at one point."

Elpis was snorting with laughter now and pointed to my letter. "So I'm guessing that letter does not mean what it says it does."

I shook my head with a grin. "Nope. Not at all." I let us into the suite when we returned and said, "It basically says that he needs to meet me at the mountain cabin in two to three days. I wasn't sure about how long it'd take since we'd be on foot. It'll be easy for him to fly and check."

"Wow, you'd never know," she said thoughtfully. "You sound quite practiced writing love letters."

Is she digging for information? Toast inquired. *Signs of jealousy are good, right?*

Not good for her, I replied.

"Writing that kind of stuff is easy," I replied dismissively to Elpis.

She didn't seem satisfied with that response and pressed, "Is it? You don't have someone you... write to?"

Yes, definitely digging. Maybe she'll be less distracted by males now. Encourage her! Toast implored.

"No, Elpis, I don't have any females at home waiting for me if that's what you're asking," I answered a little dryly. "Or males," I added as an afterthought, in case she thought I had another preference.

Her lips parted like she was about to say something, then she shut them. She stood, fidgeted, and said, "I'm going to take a little nap... I'm a little worn out..."

I heaved a sigh and leaned back in the chair to close my eyes a bit too. I was looking forward to leaving town. The crowds were putting an odd pressure on both her and Toast. In turn, that was stressing me out as well.

Maybe it's time you try to say hello to her again when we leave town? I asked Toast.

I'm not sure I'm there yet...

Alright. Hatchling steps, big guy.

Hatchling steps.

I woke Elpis after it was dark so we could eat dinner. Keeping her hand securely in mine, I led her downstairs, deeply enjoying the leeway Toast was able to give me. The restaurant downstairs was more of a tavern than anything, and it was packed. I managed to find a table in a relatively quiet corner, and a waitress arrived to take our orders. When I opened my mouth to ask Elpis what she chose, I realized she couldn't read the menu.

Not wanting to embarrass her, I asked, "Would you like anything to drink, Elpis? Water? Wine? I'm guessing not sangria." I raised an eyebrow and chuckled.

"Definitely not sangria," she agreed with a laugh. "Never, ever again."

Chapter 11

Sir Kenon

While Elpis was thinking about her options, I turned to the waitress, who was regarding me salaciously, and ordered. "Let's have your house ale, mead, cider, and two glasses of water. We need a bit more time to peruse the menu."

"You seem to be… thirsty tonight," the waitress commented in a sultry voice and turned to leave, swaying her hips. Elpis jerked in her seat as though she were about to tackle the female. Fury hardened her expression, and if she were a shifter, I was certain she'd be sporting claws and fangs right about now. Hoping it would mollify her, I ignored the waitress and started explaining items on the menu for Elpis.

"What are these symbols here?" she asked, pointing to the side.

"That's the price. I'll teach you numbers too. They're super easy," I said.

When I translated some of the prices, she gasped. "Some of these cost more than my boots!"

"They make fancier meals during the market so they can inflate prices. It's expected, though not ideal for folk with less to spare."

"Ahh..." she said simply but turned her nose up in disapproval. I chuckled, loving her show of morality.

The problematic waitress returned, carrying a tray with our drinks. "So," she said in a provocative voice, leaning over to set the drinks on the table. "Do you see anything you'd like to... try?" She angled herself in a way that gave me a view down her shirt, and Toast began making gagging noises. I could feel his anxiety spiking. We'd just gotten here, and he was already alarmed.

I kept my eyes firmly on Elpis after that and gestured to her. "Ladies first. Have you decided, moonflower?" Hopefully my term of endearment for my fated mate would give the waitress a hint to back the fuck off of me.

Elpis glared at the menu and said, "I'll have the roasted chicken." She set the menu down and moved her glare to a knot in the grain of the table. If she stared hard enough, I was afraid the table would catch on fire.

The waitress nodded and regarded me. "And what will you have, handsome? The veal or the prime rib?" It was a veiled insult at Elpis, and I was starting to get extremely pissed at her for disrespecting my female.

Fucking whore, Toast snarled. *Doesn't hold a fucking candle to our fucking mate. Elpis is a hundred times prettier than this fucking idiot.* I hid a smile at his impassioned rant. This was a new side of him, and I was glad to see it, but it was a dire threat to my composure.

Choosing not to play the waitress's game, I kept my eyes on the menu and said, "I'll have the roasted chicken too. My moonflower has good taste."

The waitress wrote it down and sauntered off again. I lined up the beverages in front of Elpis and said, "Now we are definitely not going to drink all of this, but I got these for you to try. See if you like any. They are alcoholic, so don't drink too much, ok? You probably have no tolerance."

She studied them curiously and tried the ale first. "It tastes like grass," she announced after a sip, not showing like or dislike.

"I've never tasted grass, but I imagine this is what grass would taste like." I snorted and pointed to the next one.

"This is mead. It's basically wine made from honey. Very sweet."

"Honey? I've never had that!" she said excitedly and tried a sip. "Mmm! Interesting. Now I just need to know what honey tastes like." I chuckled at her clever little remarks and pushed the last one forward.

"This is cider. It's like apple juice, but they add alcohol to it, so technically it's called hard cider," I explained. She grabbed it and guzzled with gusto.

"Woah, woah, Elpis!" I said, laughing as I tried to take it from her. "Slow down!" She avoided my grasping hand, took another swallow, and set the stein down with a thunk.

She leaned forward while gripping the beverage and whispered, "This is the one. Who knew apples could be so sinful?"

"You mean this is the half of one," I corrected while reaching once more to confiscate it. "You are going to get a hangover if you finish this." She heaved a disheartened sigh and slumped, letting me take the beverage away from her.

Give it back, Toast whined. *She's so sad.*

She's going to get drunk.

So? You get drunk all the time.

I have a tolerance. You want to see her throwing up in the morning?

No...

"I'll tell you what, Elpis. If you're feeling clearheaded after dinner, you can have some more of this, ok?" Great gods, it was hard to resist her gloomy face. I needed to build up a pout tolerance.

"I suppose that's fair," she said, cheering up a little.

"Just be prepared. This is going to hit you in a little bit," I warned with a grin. "Your inhibitions will go down the drain, and I don't want to see you dancing naked on any tables, alright?"

She looked horrified and crossed her arms over her chest to cover her breasts. "Understood," she squeaked.

Not that you wouldn't like to see that, Toast teased.

Was that permission, Toast? I asked, half joking.

No comment, he said a little too hesitantly.

Interesting, I thought privately, mildly surprised.

The waitress returned with our food, and I noticed that a note was placed under my fork. The waitress leaned over to say, "Enjoy," and moved to pat me on the arm. Toast reacted faster than me and jerked my arm away from her. I frowned at the female and opened the note right in front of her. The female raised her chin but seemed shaken by my rejection.

"A room number and a time," I muttered. I met her eyes and blasted the note with a small flame, disintegrating it. "Apologize to the lady here. You've disrespected her."

Her lips were parted in an aghast expression, but she turned to Elpis and mumbled an apology. The waitress left as quickly as possible, ditching the saunter for speed. I glanced at Elpis to find her baring her teeth, and she promptly stomped a foot as though to keep herself from tackling the other female. This was new. I furrowed my brows as I watched her response. She then fisted her hands and lowered her head, closing her eyes.

"Are you ok, Elpis?" I asked in concern. "I wanted to do that earlier, but I wasn't sure if she'd spit in our food. Maybe we should have just left."

She sandwiched her lips between her teeth and forced a deep breath. "I'm fine." She snorted in irritation. "Just didn't… like her."

"It's ok to not like someone," I said, trying to validate her feelings. "She wasn't behaving appropriately."

Elpis nodded, sighed, and dug into her food. It wasn't long before she'd forgotten the incident because she was moaning over the roasted chicken like it was sex. I adjusted my pants in my seat, clearing my throat while running a hand through my hair.

When we finished eating, I went to the counter to pay, but Elpis wandered off to another table where a human father and his daughter were seated. They were sharing a loaf of bread with some cheese and looked a little on the thin side. I stared as Elpis dug out the most valuable coin from her purse and handed it to the father, who immediately broke down into tears. She handed one to the daughter too, not knowing that children that young didn't normally carry their own purses.

I was rendered speechless by her gesture, and I'd never been more grateful and proud that she was my fated mate than in that very moment. It made me want to throw her over my shoulder and pleasure her all night. I groaned and pinched my nose, then turned to hand some coins to the bartender. When I left the counter, I was approached by another female trying to garner my attention. Toast moaned miserably in my head, just wanting to go back to the suite. I tried to move around her, but the slinking dragon-shifter blocked my path.

"Where you going, big guy?" she purred, alcohol riding her breath, and tried to place a hand on my chest.

I stepped back and pressed my lips together in irritation. Elpis walked over, staring daggers at the female stalking me.

"Fancy a stroll with a real female?" the dragon-shifter asked.

"I've already got a real one, thanks," I returned gruffly. Toast was starting to panic, and I stepped around the female to escort Elpis back to our room. If I didn't get away from this shameless, intoxicated dragon, he was going to make a scene.

"You? Ha!" she said to Elpis. "I don't smell anything. You're not even human. You're just a shabby shiftless. You couldn't handle this dragon if you wore fireproof lingerie. Stick to your breed, sweet one," she sneered, leaning into my fated mate's face. Elpis was breathing hard again, shaking and fisting her hands until her knuckles blanched. When she bared her teeth, I knew that she was at a breaking point. My hand shot out to grab hers, but I didn't get there in time.

Elpis yanked on the dragon's hair, headbutted her, and then kicked her in the shin—hard. The female cried out and fell into a waiter, who proceeded to spill drinks all over a table full of gamblers. The gamblers proceeded to round on the waiter, but a handful of other males intercepted the assaulters. It wasn't long before the entire tavern became a madhouse, so I picked Elpis up, slung her over my shoulder, and fled to our room.

I deposited her onto the bed and paced, not sure whether to laugh or yell. I could not believe what had just happened. Elpis sat up and crossed her legs under her dress, fidgeting with her fingers.

"I'm sorry..." she whispered. "I don't know what got into me. I just... felt... I don't know." She looked so ashamed, and I didn't want to come down too hard on her. I knew that it was the fated mate pull making her territorial. Why didn't she recognize who I was to her, damn it? I didn't want to tell her. What if she didn't believe me? What if... Augh! Too many what ifs!

"Part of me thought that if you were threatening to rip hands off, I could maybe kick someone..." she mumbled defensively. That got me. I broke out into laughter, my nerves totally shot, and grabbed my knees.

"Ahhh... Elpis, I don't know what to say to that. We can't go around assaulting folk, but... I can't hold you to a double standard. I'd probably punch someone who'd grab you." I laughed and sat on the bed with my face in my hands. "Oh gods, what a mess."

She was silent for a while as I chuckled the nervousness out of my system. I felt two small hands grab my shoulders to rub them, but Toast jerked me off the bed, startled within an inch of his life. I whirled to stare at Elpis, breathing hard. She was curled up with her hands on her face.

"I'm sorry, I'm sorry!" she whimpered. "I won't do it again! Please don't leave!"

I could only stare at her state, feeling hopeless and heartbroken. We couldn't keep doing this.

"I j-just thought since you h-held my hand and carried m-me...
I c-could give you a b-back rub. I th-thought... Y-you s-s-seemed
tense. I just... I'm sorry, I'm sorry, I'm sorry!"

"Elpis..." I began, not knowing what to say. Toast's trauma
was not mine to share. I walked out of the room, spitting weak
flames in my distress.

What the fuck do I do? I thought to myself as soon as I heard
her start crying.

Keyon... Toast said miserably. *Just... just tell her. I just hope
she doesn't judge me or... Keyon, she's going to think I'm weak!
Pathetic!*

I doubt that, Toast, I replied, falling into a chair to gather
my wits. *She's kind. Kind people don't see anyone as pathetic.*

I'm scared. We're going to lose her.

No, we won't.

We will! he insisted, panicking again. *All my hard work will
have been for nothing!*

Do you trust me, Toast? I asked. He was silent for a long while.

I guess... he eventually said, albeit dubiously.

Do you trust me? I pressed. His answer wasn't good enough.

Yes...

Then hibernate until tomorrow, and I'll deal with this, I
directed. He didn't reply, but I felt him sink into the recesses of
my mind to hide. It was time to tell her.

I strode back into the bedroom and sat on the bed next to her
crying form. Taking a deep breath, I stroked her arm to get her
attention. "Hey," I said gently. "I need to share something with
you, Elpis, but it's going to be very difficult for me."

Her sobs subsided, and she froze for a moment before looking up at me.

"What's that?" she asked quietly as she wiped tears from her
face. Damnation, her eyes were already red and swollen.

"First of all... I'm sorry for all the times my behavior upset
you. None of this, Elpis, is personal. I don't know if you noticed,
but I didn't let any females touch me tonight. Did you notice that?"

She thought for a moment, nodded, then sat upright. Moving her gaze to her slippered feet, she kicked them off, sending them flying across the room. They smacked into the wall, and she winced. I folded my hands and took the dive. "When I turned eighteen and my dragon arrived... Toast, he... arrived with some trauma. I don't know where it came from, and he still hasn't told me. He's promised to tell me soon due to... certain changes, but that conversation has yet to occur," I explained, more nervous by the word. It had seemed so much easier picturing this conversation in my head. Now I felt like my heart was going to drop into my stomach. I was even becoming a touch ill, and I went to fetch my canteen, taking little sips of cool water to combat the nausea.

"It doesn't matter if they're young or old, mated or unmated. Toast is... afraid of females." I winced and took another sip, wishing it was ale this time. Maybe I should have had more to drink before sharing this. Elpis's brows drew in, and she looked confused.

"But you're not?" she asked. "Why can't you touch females? Toast is not in his body right now."

Right... she's never shifted. She doesn't know what it's like to have a beast within her. I had a dirty thought for a moment and shook my head. *Stop it, brain!*

"When a shifter comes of age, their beast awakens inside of them. It's a... shared experience. He can access my memories and experience things as I do. So if I even get close to another female, he can get pulled into a panic attack." I paused for another sip and steadied myself. "Some shifters with... more powerful beasts can have a bit of a power struggle if their beast disagrees with their actions. Toast is probably the toughest dragon you'll meet, and he basically yanks me away from females and women who get too close, especially if he's startled." I gave her a meaningful look when I said that last word.

Elpis raised a hand to her lips, and sorrow flooded her eyes. I didn't know what I was expecting, but I wasn't expecting that. Extremely nervous now, I wiped my sweaty palms on my pants.

"Oh nay... can you apologize to him for me? I'm so sorry. I wish I had known sooner!" she said, tearing up again.

"Oh gods, Elpis, please don't cry. Don't cry. It's not your fault. It's extremely personal, and he never tells anyone. Literally only two other people know about it. That's it," I implored, grabbing her shoulders to try to catch her gaze. "He wanted me to tell you now because you were so upset."

Elpis began wailing, and I sighed, groaning. "That poor hatchling!" she cried, blotchy-faced and miserable. "I wish I could hug him to bits, but I can't! I caaan't!"

I chuckled at the sad irony and shook my head. "Minus the hatchling part, I think he'll appreciate the sentiment, Elpis. He thinks you'll judge him and find him pathetic."

Her sobbing only intensified after that, and I handed her the canteen. She was a sensitive soul; I'd give her that. Toast was probably going to feel bad for making her cry. Mediating this was tedious, and I wished they could just talk directly. That would involve either mating and marking her or adding her to my Inferno. Unfortunately, neither of those would happen any time soon.

Elpis calmed and sniffed. "I would never. I think we're kindred spirits. I have my own fears. I was terrified all day long. Fears aren't funny."

I settled my hand on hers and smiled. "You did very well today, Elpis. I think you handled everything much better than expected. Toast did well too."

"Really? I felt so stupid today," she muttered, staring at her feet again.

"Tell me why you felt stupid, and then tell me why you don't need to judge yourself so harshly over it," I said and waited for her answer.

She pursed her lips in thought. "I felt stupid for forgetting the coin values. I guess it's expected, though. I just learned about it."

I smiled triumphantly and patted her hand. "Exactly. Mistakes are almost required when you're learning," I said with a chuckle.

Then I sobered and slid my hand off hers. "So..." I swallowed hard, hating to admit this last thing. "Do you remember when I asked to hold your hand and touch your arm?"

She nodded and gazed expectantly at me.

"Well..." I sighed and looked down at my hands. "That was me trying to slowly get Toast used to you so he'd panic less around you."

Her mouth dropped open, and she said, "Ooh..."

I shifted uncomfortably, feeling like I was about to vomit from a swell of stress. "Do you know what a fated mate is, Elpis?" I asked casually, picking at some invisible blemish on the canteen.

She shook her head. "Nay... never heard of it. Adelmar has a mate, his lady wife. That's all I know."

All my courage plummeted down the drain. She didn't know. *Nope! No way! Definitely not saying anything more on that topic. Backing the fuck out.*

"Ah, anyway... I hope this clears up my behavior. I hope you understand that it's truly not personal. Toast just... struggles. He's working really hard to get better."

"It actually does make me feel better, even though now all I want to do is hug Toast." She frowned sadly. "Maybe someday. If I'm not around for it, bring him by." She fidgeted and curled her toes, still staring at them.

"I will..." I sighed heavily, willing myself to believe that she'd eventually want to stay by me even without proof of the bond. How could I prove it to her?

"So, what do you need to work on next?" she asked, her tone shifting from sadness to curiosity.

"Hmm?" I asked, a bit sullenly. I was exhausted.

"Where do you want to touch me next? We could do legs," she said and wiggled her feet, "back, face, or torso." She pointed to her breasts and tilted her head. I was now wide awake.

"Uhh... Elpis, you don't need to feel obligated... you're not a pleasure sl—" I objected, certain my face was on fire. Smoke had to be billowing from my ears.

"I know I'm not!" she snapped and shook a finger at me. "Don't say that again. I'm a free female, and I'm offering! I'm free to offer, right?"

"Y-yes?"

"Is that a question?"

"Yes! I mean no!"

"Then where do we start?" she asked, raising her chin. Oh gods, now I was feeling as terrified as Toast. When I fumbled for an answer, she lost patience, stood on the bed, and tugged the dress over her head.

"Elpis!"

"Better decide fast. Otherwise it's all coming off!" she threatened, staring me down with her hands on her bra straps. "Toast isn't gonna like that!"

"Legs! Legs!" I cried out, unable to process her boldness. Oh my gods, I felt like a shy sixteen-year-old again. Why was I panicking so much? My heart was trying to burst out of my ribcage with every thump. I palmed my face and drew a stuttering breath. Even my arms were shaking. This had been so much easier to do when she didn't know why I needed to do it.

"Hey… it's ok, Keyon. Look, it's just skin," she comforted, and I peeked over at her hand, one that was currently poking at her knee. "Just skin and muscle. Well, not a whole lot of muscle." She laughed and smacked her thigh, making it ripple a little.

Oh gods, please don't tempt me further, Elpis.

She offered a hand, and I hesitantly accepted it. Delicate fingers led my hand to her shin and left it there, then the female reclined to watch me.

I took another deep breath, exhaled as slowly as possible, and ran my palm down her shin, reveling in its smoothness. Her skin was actually starting to look a little healthier. Maybe a couple days outside had been good for her. It wasn't darker, but the paleness had more depth to its color.

I ran a thumb over her bony ankle and across all the tiny little veins of her foot. I curled a forefinger under the arch, and she jerked her foot away, laughing. "Don't you dare!" she squealed, shooting me a playful glare that promised a slow and painful death. I chuckled and wrapped my entire hand around her ankle, sliding it up to her knee again.

"You have beautiful skin, Elpis," I murmured and palmed a circle around her kneecap. She didn't say anything in return, but I heard her heart quicken. I cupped the back of her knee, lightly massaging the muscles and ligaments there.

I hesitated before sliding my hand up her thigh to her hip, just tracing the edge of her silken undergarment. I could tell she was aroused and wet for me. It was a damn shame I couldn't do anything about it. I was already struggling to control myself.

I lay down next to her and just stroked her upper thigh, staring at its softness. I gripped and squeezed it gently, watching in fascination as the fair flesh bulged between my splayed fingers. She was so different. So sweet, so soft... like a plush, downy blanket.

"I'm not as firm as I used to be..." she whispered with a frown. "Sorry..."

I snorted. "Elpis, someday you'll see the beauty I see." I ran a thumb over the smallest bit of cellulite and stretch marks. "You're an adult female. This is normal. What matters is being strong and healthy."

She didn't respond but just looked thoughtfully at me while I caressed her leg. She raised it to put her knee on my hip, and I narrowed my eyes. "Elpis, be careful," I warned.

"What? Just giving you better access," she said innocently. I studied her for a moment, but she seemed genuine.

You're going to be the death of me. Death by blue balls.

I cupped the inside of her thigh and curled my fingers, brushing them down to her knee and back up again. I slid them higher to where her inner thigh met her undergarment, and her breath caught. My knuckle slid too close and collected some of her wetness. When I looked up at her, she was staring back at me with a flushed face. Her heart raced, and her lungs heaved just shy of panting. Elpis's brown-sugar eyes were deeply dilated, and from her shaking, I could tell she was trying not to squirm. I had half a mind to check in with Toast and ask him if I could pleasure her, but I knew what he'd say. We just weren't ready yet.

I sighed and removed my hand, choosing to rest it on her hip. She was so ready for me, and it was so fucking hard to pull away. When her eyes trailed down, they landed on the bulge in my pants. There was no hiding it, and it was unavoidable. I wasn't ashamed, but I couldn't do anything about it. I guess I could go masturbate in the bathroom. Her hand moved toward my swelling cock. It wanted to be freed so desperately, but I shook my head at her.

"I'm really good," she whispered. "I could get you there in the blink of an eye..."

I sighed and closed my eyes. *I'm pretty sure you just touching it would make me explode everywhere.*

"If it was just me, I'd say yes in a heartbeat, but we're not ready, Elpis. Toast isn't ready," I replied softly.

"I understand," she said. "I'll be here when you are."

"That's a very big, personal promise to make someone, Elpis," I said with a low growl. "You're not a thing to be used."

"Nay," she said with a yawn. "I'm not."

Chapter 12

Sir Keyon

I patted her arm, rolled off the bed, and said, "Get some rest. We'll leave town tomorrow." I trudged out of the bedroom, adjusting my tortured cock in my pants with a frustrated grunt.

"Someday, big guy," I muttered, not sure if I was referring to my dragon or my cock—perhaps both. One did kind of control the other.

I stripped and threw on some pajama bottoms, then released my wings, stretching them wide like I was trying to push my anxiety out with them. Elpis's feet slapped purposefully through the suite, and I watched her collect every single pillow and blanket she could find. When she disappeared back into the bedroom, I crouched to settle by the chair for the night, but her footsteps came right back and made a beeline for me.

I gave her a questioning look when she held out a hand for me to take but got distracted by her nightgown. It was an opaque satin and went down to her ankles, but it left little to the imagination where the shape of her breasts was concerned. They swayed and jiggled freely with every movement, and her nipples pressed excitedly against the fabric. Those little vixens.

Oh, come on, Elpis. I was just starting to calm down!

"Just take my hand," Elpis urged gently, and I frowned at her fingers. Was this a trap? An Elpis-sized trap? I grabbed her hand, stood, and let her drag me to the bedroom. My brows shot up when I saw a massive wall of pillows and blankets running down the middle of the bed.

"Look!" she said excitedly, crawling under the covers on one side and flailing with her arms and legs. "I can't attack you! You can safely sleep in the bed! I don't want you on the floor again. It's really comfy."

I gawked at her dramatic rendition of a female unable to assault an unsuspecting male and thought it was the cutest fucking thing I've ever witnessed in my life. As silly as it seemed, Toast would probably really appreciate this gesture. She was earning his trust directly now by her actions.

I swallowed heavily at her adamant optimism. She deserved so much better than what we could give her. She truly was the best. "You're a remarkable female, Elpis Eudokia," I said softly, struggling to not choke on my words. I retracted my wings and slid under the sheets on my side of the bed. She was right. It was blissfully comfortable, so fucking nice to get a break from the forest floor.

I blew out the lamp and stared into the darkness. "Good night," Elpis said, yawning.

"Sleep well, moonflower," I replied wearily, wishing I could give her so much more than words.

Predawn filtered through the curtains, filling the bedroom with a dim blue glow. I lay on my back and stared drowsily at the ceiling. The night had been rough. I'd kept waking, finding out that I had knocked over a bunch of pillows and blankets to sleep closer to Elpis. My body was adamantly drawn to her, and I wondered if I should have just stayed on the floor.

Good morning, Toast said cautiously.

Hey Toast, I said tiredly. *How was your sleep?*

Not as interrupted as yours. We're going to be tired today...

Yeah, I know.

Last night went... better than I thought, he admitted. *I was so certain she'd be disgusted.*

No, Toast. All she wanted to do was hug you and apologize. She's very fond of you, I said, and Toast grew quiet for a while. I gave him time to think and rubbed a crusty, bleary eye. I really needed to take a bath before we left. Great gods, I must smell dreadful.

There was a lot of tension last night... Toast noted.

Yes, Toast, we got a little wound up, but I didn't do anything. I stopped before the temptation became too much. I wouldn't violate your trust like that.

I appreciate that... he murmured, seeming lost in thought. *She is good to us, Keyon. M-maybe we should think about rewarding her.*

What does that mean? I asked, intrigued by this line of thought.

I... I agree with your thoughts on how... she deserves better. I don't... Toast struggled to find the words, and I let him work through his feelings. *I feel good that she's relieved, knowing my... phobia. I want her to keep feeling good. I w-want her to be happy.* He began to get anxious, but he wasn't having a panic attack, not yet.

Hatchling steps, big guy. What do you want me to do? I asked plainly. *No one here is rushing you into anything. You're already pushing yourself pretty hard.*

He was quiet for a while, then seemed to come to a firm decision. *Keep her happy, Keyon. Just... don't mate her. Don't join with her... I'm not ready. If our mate wants to let off some steam... just... keep her happy. I don't want us to lose her.*

For the love of the Sun God, Toast, she's not that kind of female. She's not going to hate us for not touching her, I said as calmly as I could. I wanted to admonish him for misjudging our mate, but he was too delicate for that right now.

I said what I said, Keyon. Just... warn me before you do anything, he replied nervously. *Oh, and if you get a finger stuck in her, I will never sleep again for the rest of my life, and I'll hate you for an eternity.*

I couldn't help it. I burst into quiet but appalled laughter. *Toast! Where the fuck did you hear that garbage? That's not possible. Your imagination is a complete asshole, big guy.*

And if you could check for teeth first, that would real—

Oh my fucking gods, Toast! Not. Possible.

Then why are their nether parts called lips? Where there are lips, there are tee—

We're done talking about this, I snapped decisively. *I've heard your request, I'll follow it, and I don't want to hear any more talk about teeth, so help me. You do know I had sex before I turned eighteen.*

Don't remind me... he replied, making a gagging noise.

Ok, well, since you've given me permission, I'm going to cuddle our mate now because I think she'd like that. Too late for take-backsies, I asserted and swept all the pillows and blankets off the bed. A complicated swirl of approval and discomfort came from my dragon as he tucked himself away.

I scooted up to Elpis and gently laid an arm over her waist. With her silky hair in front of me, the temptation to nuzzle into it was too great, and I savored her sweet and earthy scent. The mate bond swept over me, and I closed my eyes, basking in her presence. I was almost too excited to go back to sleep. I couldn't wait to tell her how well Toast did. She was going to be so happy about that.

Elpis stirred under me and mumbled, "You laughed earlier. Everything ok?"

I nodded into her hair and whispered, "Yes, now go back to sleep. It's still early."

"I worked so hard to build that wall, and now you're the one attacking me," she grumbled.

My face heated up in embarrassment. "Sorry, Toast gave me permission, and I got a little zealous," I said, realizing too late what I'd done. I rolled away from her, but she grabbed on and came with me, hugging me from behind like a squirrel.

"Iz too late," she said drowsily into my back. "Yer warm and you can't escape now," she finished with a yawn. I smiled into the pillow, grateful that she hadn't considered my approach unwanted. That had been a little risky on my part.

She murmured, "The slave cages were always so cold... Zosime and I would cuddle like this all the time, but it was never enough..." She didn't sound sad recounting the memory, but I felt a pang in my heart. "I think if we'd been human, those conditions would have killed us."

"Fuck..." I groaned and turned to face her. Tucking her arms between us, I pulled her close to keep her warm. "It kills me we hadn't gotten there sooner, Elpis."

"It's just a memory now. I have nightmares, but I'm happy as long as I wake from them," she whispered, nuzzling into my chest. "You smell good."

I laughed and shook my head. "Not possible. I'm planning on a bath before leaving." She shrugged and stayed burrowed into my chest. Her fingers slowly traced around my muscles as she rested, and I watched them warily. When she ran a thumb over one of my nipples, I flinched and released a low, warning growl.

"Careful what you're doing with those hands, Elpis," I rumbled into the top of her head.

"Am I allowed to touch your chest now?" she asked, and I sighed, humming a yes. I endured her tingling, delightful touch but was not unaffected. Groaning silently, I accepted that I would have to deal with an erection in the bathtub later. I'd have to take care of this one. I was too fucking pent-up.

Her fingers traced down my abdomen, circling around individual muscles like she was trying to memorize them. On several occasions, she'd touch a sensitive spot, and I'd jerk my hips in surprise, shuddering from head to toe. She palmed my chest and dragged it all the way down until her middle finger hooked into my belly button. She let go to rake her fingers through the coarse hair that led to my very aroused cock. I jerked again at her touching such sensitive skin, and when she reached the waistband, I slid out of bed with a groan.

"It's t-too good, Elpis. I need to go. I'm just going to wash now. Feel free to keep sleeping. I'll wake you up later," I said and rushed out before she could say anything.

I turned on the tap and watched the tub fill with piping hot water. With my own soap in hand, I eased into the bath, sighing in pleasure. One of the best parts about ending a mission was taking a soak at home. It was unfortunate that this wasn't the end of my mission, but I could pretend for a second that it was.

I closed my eyes and grabbed my cock, which had grown to excessive proportions. It throbbed in my hands and yelled at me for neglecting it, so I gripped it hard and began sliding up and down. Between the heat my cock was generating and the hot water, I felt like I was being embraced by fire. I tilted my head back and moaned, breathing out a flame to mentally redirect some heat.

I pictured this suite as the home I shared with Elpis to start our family. Last night had ended differently in my imagination. When she'd lifted her leg to place it on my hip, I'd ripped her undergarment clean off her. I pictured pressing against her sex for the first time, parting her gently to prepare her for our joining. I clenched my jaw, feeling a wave of arousal at the thought of her juices flooding from her core to help ease my iron-hard cock into her channel. I'd push inch by fucking inch to bury myself to the hilt, then watch her face glow with deep satisfaction at how I filled her. Then I'd begin pumping into her tight lit—

There was a knock on the bathroom door, and I withered in misery. I was cursed. My cock and I were cursed.

"What is it?" I asked, trying not to snap. "Only come in if you understand what you're interrupting, female."

The door creaked open, and Elpis's head popped in, eyeing how I languidly pumped at my swollen cock in the bath. I looked right back at her, unashamed, and said dryly, "We really need to stop meeting like this, Elpis."

Elpis stared at my cock. "Am I allowed to touch it now?"

"What?" I asked with an incredulous laugh, continuing to idly pump at my length. I absolutely refused to lose my erection and momentum over this interruption. I stared her down as I rubbed the engorged, nearly purple tip of my shaft.

"If I could touch your chest, does that mean I can touch your cock now?" she asked all too innocently. She was serious.

"Euhh…" I hesitated, thrown for a moment. "Only if that pleases you." Toast wanted me to keep her pleased. Did this count? She walked cautiously in like she was stalking prey, and I growled a warning when she got closer. "Just don't start something you can't finish, female. I. Am. Very. Pent. Up."

"I never do!" she said confidently, and another pang struck my heart. Even though she responded like she didn't care, I wished I hadn't said that. Of course she never did; she'd never had a choice.

I lathered my hair while watching Elpis sit by the tub and reach into the water. The closer her hand got, the tighter my abdomen wound, and suddenly, I was extremely nervous again. Her left hand grabbed the base of my cock while the right went straight for the tip. The tingles from the mate touch nearly made me explode on the spot, and I moaned with pleasure. Her palm rested on the head, and she draped her fingers down along the shaft before dragging her fingers up, pressing inward. I bucked my hips and groaned. What the fuck was that!

"Great fucking shit gods what!" I exclaimed from the odd technique and the pleasure it generated. My claws extended and scrabbled to grip at the porcelain tub, but it was too slippery. I glanced at her, near panting as she repeated the stroke. She was just staring demurely through her eyelashes. No doubt she was putting everything she learned into this.

"Fuuuck!" I leaned my head back and scrubbing my palms over my eyes. I braced myself with my feet against the base of the tub and raised my hips into her hand. When she lured my cock completely out of the water, her hands returned, but they were lubricated this time. Her right fist slid downward, twisting and squeezing along the way, and the left fist started at the top just before the other one reached the bottom so it all felt like a never-ending stroke.

"Great gods, Elpis, what the fuck!" I gritted through my teeth, awash in ecstasy and arousal. I didn't think I was going to last much longer, but I really wanted to keep enjoying this moment—this impossible moment. She slowed, and I opened my eyes, watching feverishly as she lowered her mouth, aiming to take me between her lips. I could hardly believe it.

A rapping at the suite's front door had her lips stopping an inch from my tip. "Ignore it," I begged with a growl. She moved to take me in again, but the knocking turned relentless. I bared my teeth, snarled, and dunked my hair to rinse it out before leaving the bathtub. I very nearly opened the door without a towel to show the asshole exactly what he was interrupting.

I was extremely glad I didn't.

With a towel wrapped around my hips, I opened the door to find a ten-year-old hatchling fidgeting anxiously. He looked over his shoulder before rushing into the suite. I closed the door behind him and tilted my head. "Are you ok, hatchling?" I asked, confused and a bit concerned. He was squirming as if he had to pee and worrying his hands around his little hat.

"Sigeberht sent me, sir. He wanted me to tell you there are soldiers in town asking about you and the lady," the hatchling said, jerking his head at Elpis.

"Soldiers?" I asked, pulling my chin back in surprise. "The king's soldiers?"

"Ah... didn't specify, sir," the hatchling said. "Just told me that you needed to leave town now. There's coins on yer head."

"Oh my goddess," Elpis whispered and ran to the bedroom.

I grabbed several coins from my purse and handed them to the young male. "You were brave coming here, hatchling. Run along but don't draw attention. Give Sigeberht our thanks when it's clear."

I opened the door, and the hatchling darted out as fast as a falcon on the wind. I tossed everything into my bag, threw on my clothes, and checked the suite windows to see which one would be the best for our escape. Leaving through the front would just increase the number of witnesses or the odds of running right into the soldiers. I opened the kitchen window to find it over a short alley. Good enough.

I snatched Elpis's bag from her and tossed both of ours down into the alley. Then I climbed through the window and whispered, "Get on my back, Elpis. Hurry." I spread my wings as she crawled over me and wrapped her legs around my waist. I jumped off the ledge, flapped several times to slow our descent, and let her off me. We grabbed our bags and walked toward the town's east exit to avoid drawing additional attention. I kept my ears open for the soldiers, and we found ourselves leaving town without incident.

"If they came from the castle, they've already traveled through here," I murmured mostly to myself, thinking out loud. "They likely won't sweep through the area, but we should keep to the trees as much as possible until we reach the mountains."

"Why are they after us?" Elpis asked anxiously.

"I'm guessing they still want to kill me and take you. What the fuck is going on?" I brushed my wet hair from my eyes. "I can't tell if they want you specifically or if they just need everyone from Adelmar's mansion. Did they only want to kill me because I was in their way, or did they have orders to kill me? As far as the coins on my head, am I wanted alive or dead? Ahh! I have so many questions! I really hope Leofwine can answer some of this shit. I can't imagine the king ordering something like this. He used to trust me completely. Is he well? Fuck!"

Elpis's hand slipped into mine and squeezed it. I calmed down a little as the bond swelled into me, offering pleasure and comfort. I heaved a sigh and let my shoulders drop.

"We'll figure it out," she said confidently. "I won't let anyone hurt you!"

I looked down at her with a wry expression, and I could see that she was trying not to laugh. "I am so relieved to have your protection, moonflower," I replied dryly.

She waved her hand magnanimously. "Anytime, sunflower!"

I snorted. "Please don't." She cackled and grabbed her stomach. However, her laughter was cut short by a wince, and she clapped a hand to her forehead.

Alarmed, I asked, "What's wrong?"

"Headache," she complained, wincing again. "Just came out of nowhere."

"Do you want to stop? We could find a quiet place to rest," I offered, hating that I couldn't offer her relief through our bond.

"Nay… it's ok, I— Ow!" She added her other hand to her forehead and stumbled. I grabbed her arm to steady her and looked around to make sure we still weren't being followed. We'd put a little distance between us and the town, but I didn't want to stop yet.

Permission to carry her, Toast? Mate's not well, I asked.

Granted… I hope it's not serious.

I could help her if it gets worse. Just giving you a warning.

I see. Thanks for letting me know.

"Elpis, I'm going to carry you a bit so you can close your eyes. I just want to get a little farther from town," I said, stopping and facing her.

She worried at her lower lip. "I know you're built like a muscly god, but I'm a female of average height. Are you su—"

"Great gods, Elpis." I leaned down to pick her up with ease. "You're like lifting a newly hatched. I'd juggle you, but I don't want to make your headache worse."

"Liar." She laughed weakly against my chest. "But I won't turn down this very soft pillow."

"Liar." I snorted back, making her giggle. A hiss of pain fell from her throat, so I decided to stop talking.

I walked with her almost all day, stopping to give her bits of food and water. By the early evening, she started writhing from pain, and that was when I began to get deeply concerned. I set her down on her blanket and built her a nice, big fire. Sensing game nearby, I had Toast bring back a deer, which I proceeded to butcher and cook over the fire.

Elpis was curled up in a ball and crying softly while I tried to feed her. "What pain are you feeling? Is it just your head or...?"

"M-my head hurts. Everything is brighter and louder. I feel like throwing up..." she described with quivering lips.

"Hmm, sounds like a migraine," I murmured and brushed her hair from her face.

"N-never had one be-f-f-fore," she said with a shiver. I frowned and took the leap.

"I can help you with this, Elpis, if you want me to," I said quietly.

"Do it! I can't tolerate it anymore," she sobbed.

"Ok well, first you need to stop crying because the more dehydrated you get, the worse your head's going to get," I warned gently, handing her the canteen. She took several long, greedy gulps and put it down, sighing and nodding.

"Now I'm going to need you to take your underwear off, Elpis," I said with a sigh. I steadied her hips as she stood and reached under her skirts to remove them. I didn't know if I should be grateful that she seemed to trust me enough to do it or worried that she did it without a question.

I fetched her bottle of lubricant from her bag and settled behind her. Positioning Elpis between my legs, I leaned her against my chest while snaking a hand under her skirts. "I'm going to make you orgasm, ok? The brain releases chemicals that will help your headache feel better. You're going to have to do half of the work, though. Do your best not to focus on the pain and think of something or someone you like—anything that arouses you. Just try. Can you do that?"

She nodded and leaned her head back, trying to relax. I could tell she was nervous. That was ok because I was fuckin' nervous too. I hadn't done anything like this in ages.

Alright, Toast, I'm going in, I warned him.

Chapter 13

Elpis

Keyon squeezed a dollop of lubricant on his first two fingers and lowered them to my core. I was in too much pain to flinch, so I just watched what he did with muted fascination. He had large, rough hands, and seeing his calloused fingers landing so delicately on my sensitive skin made my belly flip from arousal. This male could decimate a foe, but he chose to treat me like a glass rose—or a glass moonflower, I supposed, as he would put it. Something about the tenderness in his touch lit a primal instinct in me. Something that wanted to let him mount me in exchange for his sweet dedication and protection.

Instead of pleasure, the migraine forced a wave of nausea through me, but I tried to stay focused on what he was doing. I didn't know how long I could watch because my migraine had spread behind my eyes, but I desperately wanted to. I knew I'd be acutely fired up if I weren't in so much pain.

His attentive fingers circled around my sex, dipping in between the different folds and sliding across the middle. My stomach contracted when he hit several very sensitive spots, and

I reached for something to brace myself. When I found Keyon's legs, I gripped them tight.

A puff of warm air brushed the left side of my face, and Keyon's smooth voice crooned into my ear. "Relax, moonflower," he whispered. "Spread your legs just a little bit more. Yeah, that's better." His voice was so soft and so close that it spurred my arousal, causing lightning to splinter from my ears to my belly and core. I let out a sobbing cry, almost unable to handle the stimulation. His voice... Oh, how I worshipped his confident, masculine voice.

His fingers continued to rub around in circles, and I began to get used to his touch. It was so intimate and exposing that, for a while, all I could think about was if he liked what he saw. For some reason, that was very important to me. My pubic hairs were growing back, but they were still short and prickly. I hoped that wasn't a turnoff. It's not like I had chosen for that to happen. What did other females look like?

I groaned through a wave of pain as my head throbbed, but I kept trying to turn my attention back to what Keyon was doing. It wasn't very hard, but it was almost giving me whiplash. I raised a hand to rub my temple for a minute while he tended to me.

His hand rubbed in circles, spiraling closer to my opening. Finally, he dipped in the tip of his forefinger, and I gasped at the invasion. I tensed and returned my other hand to his leg from the shock of it. Keyon's other hand slid around my waist to gently rub my belly. The action soothed me and sent warmth spiraling into my heart. He was tending to my emotions as much as my body, and that spurred some primal instinct. Perhaps it was better I was ill because otherwise I'd be tempted to turn around and ride his cock, not that I knew how to do that.

His finger slid in slowly until it was fully in, then he curled it and pulled it back out, dragging the tip through my channel on his exit. I bucked my hips at the sensation, uncertain what to make of what I was feeling. Everything was so intense! When he rubbed around my entrance again, I noticed that his fingers were dripping with lubrication, and I realized that the moisture had come from me.

"Look at your pretty nectar, moonflower," he murmured into my ear, making me shiver uncontrollably. "Look at how shiny and wet you are for me. You're practically dripping with need."

This time, I moaned from a wave of arousal instead of pain, my belly clenching and flipping from his provocative words. He slowly plunged his finger back in, and I heard the slick sound of my arousal meeting his knuckle.

"Mmm," he groaned lustfully into my ear. "And would you listen to that sound? Who knew you could hear a female's desire?" He punctuated his point by lightly pumping his finger, making the slick noises fatten into squelching sounds. He groaned again, and I could feel his erection on my back. He was enjoying this too!

"You're doing well taking my large finger, female," he grunted close to my ear. "I wonder what else you might be good at taking someday?" He nuzzled his nose against my ear, and I arched my back with a whimper, beginning to go mad with desire. The pain lost its grip, left behind because all I could think about was him. I was surrounded by his masculinity. His massive, tanned, and carved arms were working in front of me, and his enormous cock was swollen against my back, twitching and throbbing. It was so hot that I could feel it through our layers of clothing.

He added a second finger, and I squirmed beneath his slow invasion, releasing a desperate cry. "Hmm, you like that? Are you enjoying my thick, battle-worn fingers raiding you? Are you enjoying the knight general's attention, female?" he growled and lightly bit my ear. I gasped and arched again, nearly sobbing from bliss. I was overrun with emotion and thrilled with every word that sprang from his sensual lips.

"More!" I whimpered. I wanted more!

"More what, moonflower? Finger fucking or dirty talking? Or both?" he whispered.

He started rubbing outside my channel, starting from the top and running down the sides. His fingers travelled in rotating patterns and seemed completely honed in on my body's reactions. "Let's find out what you like, female. Let's see where you like to be touched. Ravaged." Whenever I leaned into what he was doing, he stayed there for a while. If I relaxed, he'd move on to try something else until I reacted again. For someone who hadn't touched a female in a long time, he was completely in control. It was like he was in my head—like we had a deeper connection.

"Mmm, you are so beautiful. So wet. It's a pity I can't just fuck you right now," he murmured, lapping at my ear. His tongue was warm, soft, and wet. I gasped at his unexpected words and experienced a colossal surge of arousal, which made me feel like something was building within my core. My mouth hung open, and my head leaned back as my mind searched for that feeling, desperate to hang onto it.

"Oh, you like it when I talk about fucking you?" he groaned and pressed into the swollen flesh at the apex of my sex. I gasped and clawed at his legs. "Well, I like to think about fucking you. You have such a fine, tight pussy, but thinking about plunging into it risks me coming all over your beautiful dress." I nearly kicked my legs as I tried to arch into his hands. I was gasping for air, unable to stop panting. He leaned his mouth in closer so his lips brushed my ear upon each syllable. "I'd just paint that entire dress white…"

"Keeeyon!" I whined.

"Mmm, yes? Have we found a winner here?" he whispered and rubbed more into the swollen flesh. I scrabbled at his legs, whispering and chanting his name like a prayer. The sensation growing within me itched and writhed, like it wanted to blossom and be free. I wanted to water it and let it bloom. I needed it to bloom!

"Would my moonflower like to come?" he growled and licked my ear again. "Would she like to spill her beautiful nectar all over her dragon's hand?" He continued to rub at the same pressure and pace, making the itch swell intolerably. I wept and nodded in desperation.

"Keyon! Keeeyon! Please!" I begged. I was so afraid to lose the sensation. I was close to something… I just didn't know what! I just knew that I wanted it with a fierceness I've never experienced.

"Gods, Elpis, you are so fucking enticing. Look at you writhing under my hand. I can barely keep myself from mounting your perfect body," he rumbled, continuing his ministrations. "I want to pound into you and spill my seed. Claim you for myself. No one but me would ever touch you again."

"Ah..." I moaned louder as I got closer to blooming. "Ahh..." I arched more, and my muscles clenched. A short, disbelieving mewl escaped from between my lips as new sensations unfurled.

"That's it. Come for me, Elpis, my moonflower. Come for me. Your knight general commands it," he snarled.

I was slammed by a new experience—ecstasy. Pleasure rolled through me in a hot, engulfing wave as my core blossomed. I threw my head back into a hard chest and yelled. "Ahhh! Ahhhh! Ahhhh!" I cried through each wave of pleasure that assaulted me. A finger rubbed into my flesh, prolonging the pleasure that swirled through me. Each rapturous surge sent me arching and bucking as I tried to savor the experience.

A hand moved to massage a breast over my dress, and I leaned into it, enjoying the combination with the rippling, carnal euphoria. The blossoming slowed, and I faded back into a hard chest, panting and smiling like a fool.

My head fell to the side, heavy, and I savored Keyon's scent. He smelled so good, and it was starting to remind me of something, but I couldn't figure out what it was. My heart pounded like it fought to recover from the experience, and the dragon's hand slid from my breast back to my belly, stroking it gently with his thumb. I listened to his own heart and breathing, lulled into a sense of complete contentment.

"Good work, Elpis," Keyon said softly, his demeanor returning to normal. "How do you feel?"

I'd forgotten I had a migraine. When I checked in with my body, I realized I was completely fine. "I... feel much better!" I said with surprise. "Just sleepy," I added with a yawn. He chuckled, a low rumbling noise that would have melted me had I not been so tired.

"That happens when you orgasm," he replied. "Let's get you to nest now." He adjusted the blanket and covered me up when I lay down to sleep. "Wake me if you need anything. I'll be right here, moonflower."

He placed the canteen of water between us and extended a wing over himself as he settled to sleep. I felt bad he'd never gotten a chance to finish today. He said he'd been really pent up too. I'd have to take care of him soon.

He had the most glorious cock I'd ever seen, and I was quite keen to try it. What would it taste like? Which of my techniques would he like the best? He had been very receptive to them in the bath. I smiled broadly, remembering the shock on his face and the profanities that ran from his mouth. It was so funny that it took all my effort not to laugh.

In the meantime, I needed to rest, and I tried not to think about all the naughty things he'd said to get me to orgasm. I was unique-looking, but did he really think I was beautiful? Did he want to claim me as his own? I wondered how much of it, if any, was true. Would I ever know?

Suddenly, I wasn't so happy about him leaving me somewhere to rehabilitate. I didn't like the thought of being away from him. Maybe it was because he'd saved me? No... I didn't think it was hero worship. It felt deeper than that. Well, I had time. I'd see where these feelings would lead. I just hoped it didn't leave me heartbroken. I was ready for something to turn out right for once.

⚜

I wasn't sure why, but I was incredibly shy when I woke the next morning and remembered what Keyon had done to make me feel better. Maybe it was because it was the first time I'd ever received pleasure instead of giving it. I'd certainly made some odd noises and moved in strange ways. Maybe I was feeling self-conscious about that. As I quietly nibbled on some food, I wondered how similar the female orgasm was to the male one. We certainly didn't seem to emit anything other than our natural lubricant. Maybe I'd ask Keyon someday.

"So where are we going again?" I asked as we walked. "Some kind of cabin?" My strides required more effort when our route turned into an incline, and I hoped I could keep up today. Traveling had been a brutal reminder of how out of shape I was.

"Yeah, that's right. I own a cabin on the mountain, and it's one of the places Leofwine and I agreed would be safe to meet at should anything happen. Since something did happen, that's where we're going," he said with a sigh, pocketing his hands. How they fit in there I'd never know.

"And after the cabin?" I asked curiously, looking up at him.

"I don't know. Outside of what's going on at the castle, I'm anxious about those symbols on your neck. I don't think anything like that should go unchecked," he said with a worried expression and brushed some locks away from his eyes as he looked straight ahead.

I ran my fingers down my neck. I couldn't feel anything. It was just smooth skin.

Soon? my mind thought, and I wondered if it would be. "Who could look at it?" I asked.

"I'm not sure… we might want to go straight to a coven. There's just so much happening right now. At least the king doesn't have jurisdiction on coven grounds, so if we were in trouble, we could be safe there, at the very least." He looked down at the ground for a moment and kicked a rock out of his way. "I wish I could be in multiple places at the same time. I feel like we're in for a long haul, Elpis. I'm really sorry. I really wish I could get you somewhere safe to live peacefully."

I supposed that I was a burden. Without me, he could just fly to any location. The realization stung, and I grabbed my chest. I was slowing him down.

"Maybe I could hide somewhere in the wild while you go fly off to see what's happening?" I offered. He bristled at that and shook his head aggressively.

"No fucking way," he growled. "I'm not leaving you on your own. Forget that completely."

"I could stay at the cabin," I suggested, but he shook his head again.

I sighed and tried to think of another idea, but nothing came to me. "I'm sorry, Keyon. I hate that I'm slowing you down. I can tell how stressed you are," I said morosely.

"I can cope with stress, Elpis," he replied sternly and tensed. "I can't cope with harm coming to you. I'm not going to let you get hurt."

The notion was sweet, and I was reminded that I still wanted to relieve him. That would help with stress. Maybe when we stopped for lunch? I blushed at the plan, not sure why I was so bashful about it now. Great Moon Goddess, I'd pleasured many… this shouldn't stir me so much.

The closer it got to midday, the more nervous I became. It occurred to me that I'd never initiated a session, just ordered to clients who were already erect, and Keyon had already been working away at himself when I volunteered. Would he react well, or would he decline? I guess I'd find out soon.

I wiped my sweaty palms on my dress when we stopped for lunch, fixated on my plan. We ate some of the meat he'd roasted last night, which was still pretty good. I wasn't sure how long meat would last—probably not much longer. I suppose that Toast would hunt for us again.

When Keyon finished his meal, I scooted over to him and placed a hand on his knee. His gaze slid to my hand, then moved to meet my eyes. "Whatcha doing there, Elpis?" he asked casually, but there was a hint of nervousness in his voice.

I let my palm travel up his thigh. "Finishing what I started?" I breathed out, making sure to keep my torso low but tilt my chin up so he could look down my dress. I'd made sure to tie the bust particularly tight before this and lift my breasts enough to maximize my cleavage. I trailed my fingers over the growing bulge in his pants and watched his throat bob as he swallowed.

My palm cupped his covered erection and slid upwards, pressing pleasure into his length. I repeated the act with the other hand, alternating until his head tilted back to the sky. I pulled at the strings of his pants but was interrupted when sobbing cut through the forest. I groaned and went limp, resting my forehead on his thigh. "It's not fair!" I complained. Keyon swore every single profanity I'd ever heard in my life and gently moved me off so he could stand and secure his pants. I followed behind as he irritably hunted for the source of the crying.

Our frustration evaporated when we saw a female dragging a male's body through the woods. She was crying, in a near panic, and a hint of madness was riding the sounds escaping her throat. I recognized her curly blackberry locks at once and raced to her.

"Lady from the store!" I cried, accidentally spooking her. "What happened to you?" The female dropped the male's arms with a shriek, crumpled into a ball, and covered her head. "Nay! I won't hurt you. It's just me. It's the Reborn you helped! Elpis!"

"Reborn?" she asked with a sob and hazarded a peek. She held her arms out like a hatchling, desperate for comfort, and I gave it to her. I dove into her arms and hugged her fiercely, rocking and shushing her while she shed her tears. I held her inconsolable form for about a half an hour while she wailed. I knew what her sounds meant. I knew what her body was saying. All the sex slaves came in like this after their first time. This female had been raped.

She hung onto me as if I was her world and nothing existed past me. She seemed to be blocking out everything else, and how she had managed to drag a male during all of this was beyond me. As I kept her in a tight clutch, I glanced over at Keyon, who was investigating the still male. He looked up and met my eyes with a dark expression.

"He's dead," he mouthed so the female didn't have to hear it out loud. She probably knew that already.

Stricken, I petted her hair and asked, "I can't remember your name. I'm sorry... What was it again?"

She buried her face more into my chest and sobbed. "Adelais…"

"Oh… that's right. I remember. What happened, Adelais? So I can help you."

Her body shivered as she bawled, but after a little while, she calmed enough to share. "B-Bertram and I w-were making a d-delivery to the castle when some s-soldiers came and s-started asking questions," she said, shivering with broken nerves. "They w-wanted to know if I s-saw a R-Reborn traveling with the knight g-general."

I looked worriedly up at Keyon, who flinched at the mention of his title.

"I l-lied b-but th-they could tell I w-was lying and threatened to k-kill Bertram!" She fell apart for another minute, shaking and sobbing in despair. "I tried t-telling the truth and s-said I didn't know where you were, b-but they killed Bertram anyway and…. and…" She hung her head and completely collapsed against me, losing all her strength to stay upright. I kept her propped up and waited until she was ready to continue.

She whispered hoarsely, "Once they believed I knew nothing, they… they…" She gripped my dress like she was hanging from a cliff. "They took turns and left!" she shrieked the last words out and fell apart. With a shocked, broken heart, I held and rocked her, moving my gaze to Keyon again. He was livid—wings out and blue flames licking the corners of his mouth.

"Were they the king's soldiers, Adelais?" he asked as gently as he could through his rage. She nodded, and he swore, walking away so he could vent his fury.

"When was this?" I asked as I stroked her hair.

"Yesterday evening," she said between sniffs. "I dragged Bertram off the road because I didn't want anyone looting his body."

"That must have been so hard, Adelais," I murmured. She nodded, and I could tell she was beginning to fade. Her body was here, but her mind was going somewhere else, somewhere she thought was safer—the numb place. "Should I take a look at you, Adelais? Clean you up a bit?" I offered.

She nodded vacantly, and I laid her down. When I collected the canteen, soap, and a sponge, I returned to Adelais and lifted her skirts just enough to care for her. I sighed sorrowfully when I noticed that her underwear was missing. Pouring some water on the sponge, I lathered it with soap so I could wipe her clean. I removed as much as I could of the blood and emission, wishing I could rinse her out too. Hopefully there was a bath at Keyon's cabin. I certainly wasn't going to leave her here.

The sounds of a large creature digging came from behind, and I turned to see Toast burrowing into the ground forty feet away from us. He delicately pulled Bertram's body into the deep hole and buried him. Toast then launched into the sky and scorched the top of the tree he was buried near, making sure to put out any fires he created. When he landed, he went toward a tree to shift, and Keyon came out from behind it, fully clothed.

"So," Keyon said as he came toward us, "I've created a body tag for Leofwine. I'll tell him about Bertram, Adelais, so he'll come back here to recover the body and return him to his family."

"Thank you," Adelais whispered.

"I'm guessing you're not a dragon-shifter since you're still out here. Cat?" he asked, picking up his bag again. I handed him his canteen, and he stared sadly at the sponge in my hands.

"Yes..." She was barely here.

"Alright, well, you're coming with us to the cabin, then. We should arrive there tomorrow. My colleague is meeting us there; he'll take you home. He's one of the best people I know, Adelais. He won't hurt you, ok?"

"Ok..."

"Alright..." Keyon sighed and retreated to give Adelais space. I knew Toast didn't like eating cat-shifters. Would he be ok traveling with one? I helped Adelais to her feet so we could begin our hike up the mountain. My heart was breaking for her.

Chapter 14

Elpis

I made sure to keep a good distance from Keyon as I helped Adelais up the mountain. She was fine for a while but eventually started limping. When I asked if she wanted to take a break, she just shook her head and kept her stare on the ground. I wondered how fast or slow cat-shifters healed. Was this normal for them? I couldn't be sure… I wasn't an active shifter myself, and I'd swear that Keyon was indestructible. I wondered if injuries of the mind slowed down injuries of the body… If so, Adelais would need twice as much help.

Night fell after a long slog of an afternoon. It was more exhausting than usual due to Adelais's presence and state, but no one could blame her for that. Those soldiers… something needed to be done about them before they hurt anyone else. This couldn't be normal behavior for soldiers since Keyon was beyond furious. He looked ready to raze an entire army.

I held Adelais as Toast hunted. He returned with a goat this time, and I made sure to catch his attention before he could shift back. "Toast, you are the best dragon ever!" I praised. "You are

wonderful, and thank you for feeding us, you handsome thing!"
He stumbled back a bit and then shifted into Keyon, making
Adelais bury her face in my shoulder until he was done dressing.

"You've put Toast into quite the dither, Elpis," Keyon said
with a weak chuckle and dragged the goat over to cook. He
worked differently this time, shredding out thinner pieces of
meat and roasting them quickly with his dragon fire so we could
eat sooner. He stopped cutting pieces when we had a large pile
of roasted, shredded meat but reached into the goat to pull out
what looked like its liver. He cooked it thoroughly, waited for it
to cool, then handed it to me to give to Adelais.

"That will help with any blood loss, Adelais. You should try
to eat it," he said gently. "Liver is good for you." She took it from
me and chewed slowly, staring blankly into the fire.

"Thanks for feeding us, Keyon," I said while rubbing
Adelais's back.

"My pleasure," he replied, glancing at me before moving
the carcass.

When we settled to sleep, I put Adelais between me and the
fire and held her from behind so she'd feel safe. I wrapped the
blanket around us both and stared at Keyon as he settled much
farther away than usual. I felt a pang of longing in my heart,
knowing he had to distance himself because of Toast and poor
Adelais. He wrapped a wing over himself and stared at me for
a little while. It was like we were holding hands with our eyes
because it was all we had. He was too far from the campfire for
it to illuminate his beautiful copper irises, and I found myself
already missing them. There was a tug in my chest that made me
want to go to him, but I just squeezed Adelais tight and made an
effort to fall asleep.

⚜

We made a big push in the morning to get to the cabin and
finally arrived there just past noon. It was a large, two-floor cabin,

and I was surprised to see that it was made from stone. Our feet crunched through a thick layer of pine needles, and I looked skyward to see that much of the blue was blocked by sprawling tree branches. This area was quite private, and I could definitely see how it made a great hideaway.

"Can you even see this place from the air?" I asked Keyon, huffing as I carried some of Adelais's weight.

Keyon glanced up and said, "If you're looking hard for it and know it's here. I've tried to keep this place a secret." He unlocked the door and gave Adelais a wide berth so she could enter. "Take her to one of the guest bedrooms, Elpis. They're upstairs on the right," he directed, and I helped the female cat-shifter up the stairs. "Feel free to run her a bath," he added as an afterthought.

I opened the door to find a quaint little bedroom with a large bed. This whole place was solidly built and felt nicely protected from the chillier mountain air. Not even the mahogany floorboards creaked as we walked her to the en suite. I turned the knob on the bathtub and steaming hot water flowed from the faucet.

"Keyon, you wealthy bastard," I swore, running my hands under the tap and grinning at Adelais. "You're going to love this. I can't wait to take a bath later myself!"

She smiled weakly and ran her fingers through the water. I grabbed my bag and removed the soaps for her, then looked through my spare clothes, humming in deliberation.

"Adelais?" I called. "I'm going to leave two dresses and an undergarment for you, but I don't know if they'll fit. I could try to wash the one you're wearing?"

"No…" came her voice from the en suite. "I'm going to burn that dress."

"I think that's fair," I replied sadly. "Enjoy your bath! I'll be downstairs."

"Elpis?" her voice called, and I paused, humming a question. "Thank you…"

"You're welcome, Adelais. You're safe here," I promised and left her room. I brought my bag back downstairs and found Keyon going through the pantry.

"We have plenty of rations here, but I can always get Toast to hunt for us too," he said, collecting a handful of bars from a cabinet. He handed one to me while unwrapping another for himself.

I gnawed at the bar, grateful for a change in diet. "I put a bath together for her and left a couple of dresses for her to try. Hopefully something will fit," I said with a helpless shrug.

"You're a generous soul, Elpis," Keyon said, staring at me while he ate his bar in the kitchen. One bulging arm was crossed over the other, and both rested on his unyielding, carved abdomen. I licked my lips and looked down to study my own bar. Something was definitely happening to my body. The longer I was around him, the harder it was to keep from throwing myself at him. I think yesterday had broken the dam; now I knew what he was capable of doing to me. Oh, how I sorely wanted to repay the favor.

I went to go eat on a soft couch, eager to get away so he wouldn't scent my arousal. I stared out the window for a while until I noticed some of the trees swaying. Was a dragon approaching?

"Keyon?" I called, and he rushed to my side, looking out the window to see what I was looking at. A smaller black dragon landed about eighty feet from the house.

"There he is. That's our Leofwine!" Keyon said, turning to me. I didn't realize how close his face was, and his eyes flickered down to my mouth before he backed up and left through the front door. I watched as the shiny onyx dragon shifted into a tall, strong male. He was leaner than Keyon, and his build told of different strengths and skill sets. He moved like a creature of the night, graceful and silent. He was quite beautiful, but not as beautiful as Keyon.

I heard footsteps come down the stairs, and I turned to see Adelais wearing my raspberry dress. "That was fast, Adelais. Didn't want to soak longer?" I asked with a smile.

She shook her head and wrapped her arms around her body. I jumped up and grabbed my spare cloak to drape around her shoulders. "I didn't want to be alone," she confessed. I fetched a bar from the kitchen and pulled her to sit on the sofa with me so she could comfortably eat.

"Looks like Leofwine's here," I informed Adelais, pointing at the window. He was dressed now, and they were approaching the cabin porch. When the door opened, Adelais sniffed the air, panicked, and stood to run, but she tripped on a little coffee table. Shaking like a newborn foal, she scrambled to get up and pressed herself against the wall by the stairs, frozen in fear.

Leofwine entered after Keyon and stilled when he saw Adelais.

"Mate…" he whispered, but it wasn't with excitement. It was with heartbreak. Leofwine's breath caught, and he looked grief-stricken at the sight of the female cowering before him. Keyon must have warned him about his guest. "Mine," he said quietly and strode toward her. What was happening? What was Leofwine doing? Why was he saying she was his?

Adelais burst into tears and fell to the floor. "Don't look at me! Don't look at me!" she screamed and covered her head, hyperventilating. Leofwine lifted the cat-shifter and cradled her to his chest. I was totally lost. Why… what?

He glared at Keyon and asked, an edge in his tone, "The king's soldiers? Truly?" Keyon nodded and closed his eyes before tiredly scrubbing his hands over his face. Leofwine, clearly overwhelmed, stared down at Adelais.

"Mate," he repeated, his face and voice softening.

"Adelais," Keyon supplied helpfully.

"Adelais," Leofwine murmured longingly and stroked the back of her head. "I wasn't expecting to find my fated mate here… but now that I've found you, no one will ever lay a hand on you again. I will get justice for you, my mate. I swear on my life. Those soldiers will pay, and I will find out what's going on if it's the last thing I do."

Fated mate? Keyon mentioned that term before, but I still didn't know what it meant. Adelais calmed significantly under Leofwine's comforting. She sniffled and finally lifted her gaze, meeting his eyes for the first time.

"M-mine?" she asked, choking on a sobbing laugh. He nodded and grinned, his pearly white fangs glinting smartly off his skin. When he brushed a tear off her cheek with a thumb, I spied a tiny bit of wetness in his own eyes. I was going to start crying at this rate myself; it was too romantic.

"And I'm sensing I've caught myself not a dragon, but a kitty cat," he said with a hint of mischievousness. Surprisingly, he coaxed another giggle out of her. "I'm hoping for a black panther. Those are the sexiest of the big cats." He raised his brows in anticipation.

"Black jaguar," she corrected with a shy smile.

"Same thing!" he dismissed triumphantly, and she smacked him on the chest. "Ow! Kitty's got punches!" Adelais giggled but began weeping again, rebounding into grief. She had to be so overwhelmed.

He smiled down at her, but there was as much sorrow as love in his eyes. Somehow, he felt her pain—I could tell. He reluctantly dragged his gaze from Adelais to address Keyon.

"Keyon... I have to go. I... I have to get her to a doctor or I'm going to lose my mind. I'll be back though, I promise," he said with desperation in his voice as he carried her to the door. Keyon opened it with a sigh and watched his friend shift into a dragon to fly off with a suffering Adelais.

"Just one more day, Keyon." I comforted him with a pat on the shoulder. "He'll be back. At least we got Adelais help, not that I understood a thing that just happened between them. Ah! Everything is so confusing!"

Keyon shut the door and began pacing in the hall, running his hands through his hair. "I'm happy for them and relieved for her, Elpis. Don't get me wrong. I'm just so fucking anxious about our situation, and I wish I didn't have to wait another day to talk to him."

"I understand," I said sympathetically, watching him traipse about the cabin. He stopped and rubbed his face, groaning in frustration.

Now's the chance for footwork, my brain thought, confusing me. Why would I think about footwork? What was footwork? I shook my head as I attempted to clear my mind. Maybe I was more worn out than I thought.

I grabbed my bag and held it up for him to see. "Where should I put this?"

He paused, frowned, and seemed to get stuck in his head, like he was deliberating. After a moment, he waved for me to follow him. "We have another guest bedroom. If Leof returns and needs to stay over, he can use the one Adelais was in."

"Well, where are you sleeping?" I asked, having a feeling I wouldn't like the answer.

He hesitated and admitted, "The master bedroom."

Disappointment settled its heavy weight on me. I didn't have an excuse this time for sleeping next to him. He was just my guard and escort. We weren't together. However...

"What about your practicing, though? Don't you need to practice being around a female?" I asked hopefully. "Practice sleeping next to one?" It was probably the strangest thing I'd ever suggested, especially out of context.

"I mean yes, but I thought you'd maybe like your own personal space. Just trying to be a gentleman about it." He cleared his throat as we stopped in front of the guest bedroom.

"Oh nay." I rejected the idea with a firm hand. "I'm all about helping." As soon as the words popped out, I winced. They sounded so stupid.

The corner of his mouth twitched, and I had a feeling he saw right through my terrible performance. I was starting to realize that I was a terrible liar around him.

"How... noble of you, Ms. Eudokia," he said in a low, droll voice. Keyon's copper eyes burned into mine, and I fidgeted under his scrutiny. He gestured for me to follow again and opened a door to a larger bedroom. It was lovely. A large mahogany bed with deep-blue sheets was tucked against the wall, and large sliding windows framed with blue curtains led to a cozy balcony. It had everything someone like Keyon would need, even exercise gear and armor.

"Ahhh," I breathed, placing my bag against the wall and running to flop onto the bed. "You're so lucky to have a place like this! I'm so jealous!" I rolled around on the luxurious mattress, squealing more than I should. I turned my gaze to Keyon, who'd fallen quiet. He was just leaning against the doorframe and smiling softly, like he was daydreaming.

"So, what are we working on next?" I inquired. That snapped him out of his thoughts. His focus honed in on me, and he licked his lips.

I continued with a shrug. "We have a day to wait. Might as well work on helping Toast." Counting on my fingers, I said, "We still have back, face, and torso, I think." I looked up at Keyon to see what he thought, and his cheeks ruddied. The male was a mix of nervousness and aggression. I didn't think I could blame him; he was under a lot of stress.

"I don't know if I can handle it, Elpis. I feel like I'm about to explode," he growled, fidgeting with his clawed hands. His shoulders twitched, like his wings were about to burst out at any moment.

"I'll take care of you after, or before if you wish. Or both," I offered simply, tilting my head and waiting for his reply.

He chuckled darkly. "I don't know if I could take another unfinished session," he said, pacing slowly toward the bed and flexing his tanned, strained muscles. I shivered at the predatory look on his warrior's face, wishing he could just mount me and claim me as his own. Who knew when he'd ever be ready for that, though. If he'd even want that.

"So, which is it?" I asked, trying not to be so flustered that I'd lose my ability to talk.

He hesitated and looked away, saying, "Back is fine."

I twisted my lips and narrowed my eyes. "Are you suuure? Are you sure you don't want to work on my chest? You seem to stare at it a lot," I pointed out, teasing him a bit.

"I do no—" he protested, and I shushed him. I loosened the ties on my dress and pulled it over my head. In one swift motion, I unhooked my bra and threw it across the room, letting my breasts spill out for his inspection. They hung eager and heavy, waiting for two hungry dragon hands to get them nice and toasty.

"Fuckin' gods, Elpis," he said with a pained expression and crawled onto the bed to straddle me. I lay down, giving him room to hover over me, and savored every change in his facial muscles. He just stared for a while, like he couldn't believe I'd done something like this. Well, I had been a pleasure slave, so I knew how to please. Keyon was the first I'd ever wanted to please of my own volition, so I'd give him everything I had to give.

Reverently, he palmed my waist and slid his rough hands up my body. His touch was warm, and the contrast chilled the rest of my body. I shivered and goose bumps pebbled all over my flesh. His palms moved up my ribs and slowed before they reached my breasts. He was savoring the moment. Perhaps he was trying to memorize me.

His thumbs pivoted to meet in the middle, then followed the bottom crease of my breasts in a focused motion. When his hands framed my breasts, he slid his palms to finally cup them and lifted their heavy weight.

I let out a soft, relieved sigh, and he responded with a satisfied, guttural groan. Keyon's breathing became heavy, ragged as his large, rough hands squeezed and pushed my breasts together. He swallowed heavily and licked his lips again, trying to be subtle about it.

"So soft, so round, so perfect," he murmured under his breath so quietly I almost missed it. He released my breasts and watched with fascination as they sprang back into place. Keyon placed his thumbs on the flushed skin around my nipples and rubbed in circles. Whether he intended it or not, pleasure shot down to my core, making me jerk under his kneading. The thrilling sensations had me moaning and squirming under him, and I grew wet from his carnal attention. His nostrils flared, and I knew he could smell me. He growled, emitting a low rumble from his chest, and his wings burst from his back. Then he closed his eyes, twisted to crack his neck and spine, and returned to studying me.

Keyon grabbed each nipple with his forefingers and thumbs, slowly pinching and pulling to see how they moved. He never hurt me once. He actually seemed more in tune with my body than I thought possible. The male was making me feel things I'd never felt. Sensations shot repeatedly into my belly and sex, making me writhe unashamedly beneath him. No one had ever treated my breasts so preciously.

Unexpectedly, an ugly memory reared up, one of someone handling me sloppily. I froze as disgust whirled in my chest. The discomfort spread to my belly, and suddenly, I felt uncomfortable in my own skin. It crawled, and my breathing shallowed. My nipples felt dirty.

I hadn't expected this. I thought that if I lay with a male I liked, I wouldn't be invaded by bad memories. This was an unpleasant revelation. Would I not be freed?

Keyon noticed the change right away and turned my face to look at him. "Elpis? What's wrong?" he asked, deeply worried. His copper eyes flickered as they studied mine, trying to find the answer in my gaze.

"Nay, just a bad memory... Keep going, Keyon," I replied, forcing a smile. He shook his head and reached down to pull me into his arms.

"No can do, moonflower," he said softly.

I buried my face in his chest, nuzzled, and took a deep breath. Then I pushed him away from me. He looked confused and hurt until I said, "Then I'm going to do what I'm comfortable with right now," hoping he'd accept my gift if I said I was putting myself first. I grabbed him and pulled him off the bed, forcing him to stand while I unbuckled and lowered his pants to his ankles.

"You don't have t— Ahhh..." he began as I slid his undergarment down and eased my mouth onto his cock. I grabbed his buttocks and held them firmly while I slid my mouth forward to take as much as I could. He was wide, wider than I anticipated, and I wasn't sure if my goal was attainable.

He tasted like earth and fire—like smoke and salt. His cock was also extremely warm, which was something I'd never encountered. I dug my fingertips into his butt, warning him to stay there, and gripped as much as I could of whatever wouldn't fit in my mouth.

After years of doing this, I no longer needed to say 'purple' to get the right shape of my lips. I formed a suction and started pumping my head back and forth along his shaft. Whenever my mouth retreated, I slid saliva down with my hands to lubricate the rest of him. He released a deep, gratified groan and rested his hands on my head, shivering. "Fuck! Elpis, that feels so fucking good! Uhnggg!"

I almost interrupted my technique by smiling but stayed focused to move on to the next. I folded my tongue back so he'd slide onto it and back into a tighter space. He jerked in surprise and moaned, "Oh my fucking gods! Uhng! Hnng! Shit!"

Once again, I had to keep from smiling. His noises were amusing, but they were also flattering. I felt deep satisfaction from pleasing him and was ready to give him more, so much more. I hoped for euphoria. His responsiveness was even arousing me. I felt powerful.

I took a deep breath, moved my hands back to his buttocks, and hoped for the best. As I leaned forward, I straightened my neck to force his cock past my mouth and into my throat. It was an extremely tight fit, and I was dismayed to realize that I wouldn't be able to do this for as long as I desired.

"Shit! What the fuck! Elpis! What!" Keyon cried and fisted my hair. I brought my lips almost all the way to the base of his cock, then withdrew. I took another breath and repeated the process, suppressing my gag reflex to squeeze him into my throat. I was forced to go slow with him, but I think he enjoyed it all the same. I could easily hurt myself with his girth, so I needed to be careful.

I hummed the next time I pulled him in, and his hips quivered. "E-Elpis! If you don't remove your mouth right now, I'm going to come in it!" he warned frantically. "Fuuuck!" I pulled him onto my tongue and shook my head, then tucked him back into my throat, humming again.

His legs shook uncontrollably, and his fingers tangled themselves in my hair. "Hnng! Elpis! Ah! Fuck! Shit!" he cried, and I could tell he wanted to pump his hips. My nails dug in as a warning not to, and I slid him back into my mouth. After that, I stopped pulling him into my throat and returned to pumping with my mouth and hands, swirling my tongue around his tip.

"Ahhhnggg..." His body shook and tensed with anticipation.

He released like an inferno, roaring and jerking his hips forward instinctively. My mouth was flooded with his seed, which was much hotter than expected; I almost choked in surprise. I'd never experienced hot seed! I swallowed what he pumped into me, extremely pleased with myself but was astonished by the intensity of his release. My hands worked to prolong his pleasure, and he responded well.

He kept pumping spurts into my mouth, occasionally moaning my name or swearing a list of profanities. I sucked down everything he gave me; it was hot, salty, and strangely smoky tasting. I relished it.

When his last ejaculation hit my tongue, I swallowed and slid my lips off him, letting go with a wet slurp. He stumbled back and fell onto the bed, gasping for air. His chest rose and fell, fighting to deliver oxygen to his orgasm-addled brain. I smiled and crawled onto the bed next to him, extremely happy with how the session went.

I lay down and stared as he scrubbed his hands over his eyes and blinked feverishly at the ceiling. His cheeks carried a healthy glow that one only got from pleasure, and I felt like I'd stamped my name on him. When his hand went to his chest, he looked over at me in disbelief.

"Fuck!"

Chapter 15

Sir Kenon

I blew a smoke ring out my mouth while I contemplated what had just happened. It was a good thing Toast had been hibernating when Elpis decided to go down on me. I hoped I'd get a chance to talk to him before he watched those memories. He was probably going to have nightmares of Elpis biting off my cock or something crazy like that. I sighed and blew another smoke ring, then puffed a bullseye through it. He did tell me to keep her happy, and she was pretty insistent on taking me in her mouth…

Sun God's fire! That had been pure ecstasy. I rubbed an eye and placed both hands under my head, partially aware of my pants still hanging from my ankles. My cock was completely sated, fainted over a thigh like a sleepy reptile on a sunny rock. Elpis jumped off the bed to retrieve her bra and dress. Her butt and breasts jiggled as she squirmed into her clothes, making my cock twitch at the show. I sent it a death glare.

Don't you fuckin' dare get riled up again. Let me enjoy this moment of peace, I seethed at it.

Elpis returned to the bed and sat next to me. "Why is your cum so hot?" she asked bluntly.

I coughed and said, "Excuse me?"

"Your seed, your ejaculate. I've never experienced anything like that," she replied. "Your cock is also quite warm."

"Euhh. Well, Toast and I run hotter than other dragons. Toast is what you'd call an absolute dominant in dragon hierarchy," I explained and reached down to put my pants back on properly.

"What's an absolute dominant?" she inquired, resting her chin on her fists. Great gods, she looked incredibly cute doing that.

I puffed my cheeks and blew out a rush of air. "Ah, where to even begin?" I mumbled thoughtfully. "Only one absolute dominant is born every couple of generations. Toast and I are the absolute dominant from our batch of generations. We're naturally much stronger than every dragon but the king. If the king dies and has no heirs, we're on a list to be potentially picked as the next king. The sun's godling, Corona, is the one who chooses the next king."

"But you said there was a prince named Cyneric..."

"Right. Our current king has four heirs," I said. "If the king has heirs, they are all called relative dominants. They're no stronger than the average dragon."

"So, what's the difference?" she asked, enthralled by the topic. I was getting distracted by her large, brown-sugar eyes and had to pause for a moment to recall what I was saying.

"Ah. For this next part, keep in mind that every dragon has a dormant gene called the Royal Gene, but only dominants truly have a chance of having it activated," I explained with a sigh and rubbed my temple. The topic was tedious at best. "A king is the only dragon with an active Royal Gene. It makes him the strongest dragon alive so he can protect his people.

"Once the king dies, the Royal Gene is activated in the eldest heir. That means the late king's eldest son or daughter becomes the next king or queen. They become stronger to continue protecting their people. Relative dominants beget relative dominants until their family line ends.

"To put it rather darkly," I continued blandly, "being a relative dominant just means you become king or queen if all your older siblings die before the king passes on."

Elpis made a disgusted face, and I chuckled. "Being royalty isn't so romantic if your siblings are power hungry."

"So... the king is the most powerful, then you?" Elpis asked innocently.

"Me and Toast. There are other absolute dominants out there from older and younger generations," I said, trying not to flash a knowing grin. She was very aroused by that, and I wanted to fuckin' preen, but I just stretched my wings a little and refolded them. "That's why you won't see other dragons blowing blue fire. They can't generate anything that hot."

That's when I thought of something I hadn't thought about in forever, and my heart plummeted. It was never on my mind because just getting close to a female was impossible. I didn't really want to share it, but... I could only keep so many secrets from my fated mate. She had a right to know. It was a pretty devastating topic and one of the reasons why I really needed to know what Elpis was. I needed to know for sure.

"The major drawback is that it's pretty impossible for us absolutes to have hatchlings with non-dragons. Like you noticed, our... seed is pretty hostile for the average egg to handle," I said quietly and casually averted my gaze. I couldn't look at her because I felt that I'd let her down as her mate. I could daydream about her giving me hatchlings, but the reality was likely impossible. How could I have forgotten about that? Fuck!

"Oh," she said just as quietly.

"I can only wonder if that was an intentional decision made by Corona. So that only dragons could initially be heirs to the throne," I pondered while staring at the mahogany ceiling.

"Sounds likely," Elpis's voice said, sounding sadder than ever. "Ex-excuse me." Her voice wavered as she walked out of the room. "Forgot to... do... something," she lied.

I closed my eyes and laid an arm over my face. *Toast, are you there?* I called out to him.

I can be. Is it all over? he asked cautiously.

Yeah, it's safe to come out, I replied with a sigh. *Long story short, she lured me over with her tits, then she froze up from a bad memory. I got worried and told her we'd stop, but she dragged me to the edge of the bed and went down on me. She was pretty adamant. Anyway, spoiler warning, she didn't bite my dick off. Everything is fine except now she knows we probably can't have hatchlings and is pretending it doesn't mean anything to her because she doesn't know we're fated mates.*

That was not a long story short.

I did the best I could, big guy. I'd completely forgotten about the compatibility issue.

We won't be able to give our mate what she wants... will we lose her? Toast asked, sounding extremely tired. He'd been running a marathon at a dash, and I was worried he'd snap.

I don't have an answer, Toast. I'm exhausted too. I just want some fuckin' answers. If I could have an answer to one fuckin' thing, then maybe I'd be ok.

You all think Leof is arriving tomorrow, but he didn't say when, Keyon.

Shit... you're right. I think we just assumed.

What will we do if he doesn't show up? We can't just wait around.

I guess we could leave him a note saying where we went. I hate leaving notes around, though.

It's not secure, Toast agreed. *I want to take our mate to the coven... but so many women. I'm so tired, Keyon. I'm hanging by a thread.*

I believe you, big guy. What do you need right now?

I don't know... An island in the middle of nowhere, he lamented, and I burst into chuckles.

If I could, I'd give that to you. It sounds nice. Would trying to meet Elpis help or hurt you right now?

Ehhh... I think that would be pushing it. Plus, she clearly wants to be alone right now.

You could cheer her up. She likes you.

She does, doesn't she? he preened a little at that. *More than you, I think.*

Probably. I laughed. *You do bring her food, you big provider, you.*

I am a big provider, Toast said proudly. *The biggest!*

I rolled off the bed and searched for Elpis. I heard her sniffling in the guest bedroom, so I called out, "Elpis? Where'd you go? Toast wants to say hi!"

Don't make me sound so eager! Be cool! Toast hissed.

I snickered and pretended to look around the kitchen when I heard Elpis's feet patter down the stairs. She'd wiped the tears from her face and seemed in better spirits. The female must be eager to see Toast again, and that warmed my heart.

I walked outside, stripped, and shifted into my dragon form. Toast landed on the soft earth, sending pine needles flying in every direction. He kept a large distance from Elpis and huffed a little smoke when she got too close.

She took the hint and backed up but continued to smile up at him. "I missed you!" she said and Toast shuddered, partially from nerves and partially from joy. The scales around his neck and spine rattled slightly as he lowered his head. He didn't go closer. He just wanted to see her from a different angle.

Elpis searched the ground for something, then picked up a pinecone. She posed victoriously with it. "I bet you can't hit this with a flame, Toast!" she taunted and lobbed the pinecone in the air. I could feel Toast's version of an eyeroll, and he spat a flame that incinerated the cone in one hit. Elpis gasped and cheered in amazement, jumping up and down like a hatchling at a puppet show. He was a little taken aback because it was such an easy target, but he'd entertained our mate, and that pleased him.

She picked up another cone and threw it higher this time. Toast sniped it out of the air, and she laughed as bits of singed cone rained down around her. I heard Toast's snort of dragon laughter and was amazed by it. I didn't think he realized how much he was enjoying himself. Even though Elpis was far away, and he didn't need to look at her to play, he was still enjoying interacting with her. This was new, and I was beyond fascinated. I could absolutely watch these two play all day like this.

Elpis ran around throwing pinecones for a half an hour before she fell over, completely exhausted. Toast ran off to fetch a goat for Elpis, and I shifted to my human form. She was still laid out on the ground when I grabbed the animal to prep it for dinner. Her eyes were closed, and she had a peaceful smile on her face. That perfect vision took some weight off my heart. I was just so damn glad we were able to distract her from crying.

We ate, and I let Elpis decide where she wanted to sleep. I stripped down to a pair of pajama pants and climbed into bed with a groan. I was so fucking tired from such a chaotic day. I closed my eyes but smiled when I felt the weight on the bed shift. The tingles on my back told me that Elpis had decided to cuddle up against me, and who was I to deny her?

Good job today, Toast, I said. *How'd you feel after some time out?*

Much better. I feel... less stressed, he confessed. *It doesn't make sense, though.*

I wonder if you're getting extra strained from hibernating too much. Maybe you're spending too much time away from our mate?

I... don't know. It's possible?

I mean, I'm getting a lot of time with her for your benefit, but I'm just wondering... There could be two things at play here.

Food for thought, Toast agreed.

Good night, big guy.

Good night. Tell mate good night.

"Toast says good night, Elpis."

"Good night, Toast. Good night, Keyon."

"Sleep well, moonflower."

I found myself waking up with Elpis's grey hair brushing my chin. I breathed in her scent of sweet, dewy grass and agave nectar. As I looked down upon the top of her head, I noticed some of her locks were appearing less dull. Instead of a flat, foggy color, the strands were brightening and becoming more reflective. It was like how a stray dog would grow a shiny, healthy coat after a month of loving care.

I wouldn't describe it as silver. Our mate wouldn't be as cheap as silver, Toast said out of nowhere.

Morning, I greeted, holding back a yawn.

I'd say that was more of a palladium, Toast said proudly. *Sturdy stuff!*

I could never tell the difference, I admitted, *unless I got to test the weight. But no, her hair is less grey now. It's warmer and shinier. I'd say it looks more like white gold.*

Toast hummed. *I suppose you're right. Unplated. Speaking of which, I can't wait to show her our hoard. We'll show her all the different kinds of metals and tell her why she's the most precious.*

When'd you become such a poet? I teased.

Shut up.

How are you handling this cuddling, Toast? You're not hibernating right now, obviously.

I'm... tolerating it as long as she doesn't make any sudden moveme— Ahhh!

I jumped as Elpis reached behind her to stroke my erection, which I hadn't really noticed had brushed against her while I was talking to Toast. "Where'd this come from?" she asked sleepily. "We didn't do anything."

"Shit, Elpis! Give a male a warning! You just scared the fuck out of Toast!" I exclaimed while grabbing my pounding heart, flustered.

"Oh nooo!" she lamented and covered her face. "Tell him I'm sorry. I was still waking up! I forgot!"

"I will when he comes back out of hiding." I sighed and readjusted my pajama bottoms. Her touching my cock had made it worse. The reptile had awoken.

"I suppose you've never slept with a male, but we get erections while we sleep. In the morning too. There're a lot of stupid nicknames for it. I suppose my favorite one is 'morning wood,'" I grumbled.

"And your least favorite?" she asked, shoulder shaking from giggles.

"Slumber lumber," I growled. "Just sounds stupid. Maybe cuz it rhymes."

She curled into a ball and laughed heartily. Maybe I didn't hate it so much if it made Elpis laugh. Her hand reached back again, but I was prepared this time and shifted my hips away from her.

"Where'd you go? Why can't I relieve you?" she asked. Did I detect a pout?

"I am giving Toast a break since you scared the scales off him." I growled, trying not to laugh at her searching fingers. They patted around the mattress like a chicken looking for seeds.

"So, I ruined it for myself," she bemoaned.

"Yourself? You mean me! Do you really enjoy doing that sort of thing?" I asked skeptically.

She shrugged and stopped searching with her hand. "Maybe," she said vaguely. I hummed a disbelieving note and crawled out of bed. I bathed, got dressed, and headed out to see if Leofwine had arrived yet. I didn't scent him in the cabin or outside and sighed anxiously. We'd wait a day, and if he didn't show up, we'd leave. There was too much to do, too much to sort out, and I was especially worried about Elpis's neck markings.

"So, what do we do while we wait?" Elpis asked, staring out the window for any signs of Leofwine.

"I suppose I'll start teaching you, I guess," I said, realizing that I had everything I needed here to do that.

"Oh! Teach me what? Reading?"

I nodded and held up a finger. "But first, we're going to start your physical training. I want to get you stronger, Elpis. I want you to have every chance of surviving if for some reason we're separated." She hummed an agreement and waited patiently for me to direct her.

I moved the table out of the way so I could show her how to do push-ups and sit-ups. She couldn't do a single push-up, so I showed her a modified one, and she was able to do five.

"Not bad for a start!" I praised after she collapsed with shaky arms. "We'll get you doing the normal ones in no time." She merely whimpered in response.

The sit-ups were too difficult, so we went through a series of squats, lunges, and planks. She ultimately ended up prone on the floor with a ruddy face, huffing and puffing. I smiled down at her and chuckled as she gave me a little salute. Beads of moisture dripped from her brow, and I realized her dress had gotten all sweaty. Perhaps I should lend her something of mine next time. I'd hate for the workouts to ruin her clothing.

"Go take a bath, and we'll start teaching you to read," I said, nudging her playfully with a foot. I helped her to her feet, and she wobbled up the stairs to bathe. I stepped out onto the porch and watched the sky.

Where are you, damn it? How's the king? What's the second prince up to? Am I wanted dead or alive? Why the fuck are soldiers raping citizens?

That last one really troubled me. The king's soldiers were always the best of the best. They were strictly trained, and we never kept anyone who showed the slightest signs of being problematic. It was almost like those males were mercenaries in soldiers' clothing, and that thought was deeply disturbing.

Elpis eventually drew me from my dark thoughts, and I led her to my study to begin instruction. I'd never taught anyone how to read and write before, but she seemed to absorb what I was saying. Elpis was a sharp female, and I had no doubt she'd be a fast learner. She had been wasted as a slave all those years; she had a beautiful mind.

The afternoon turned into evening with still no sign of Leofwine. I'd switched over to teaching Elpis numbers by that time and kept looking out the window in agitation.

"I hope he's safe," Elpis said worriedly. I hadn't thought about that, and guilt crept into my chest. What if someone discovered he had left to see me?

"Leof's cunning," I replied, meeting her soft, brown gaze and trying to soothe her concern. "If there's trouble at the castle, I'm sure he's staying clear of it, especially since he has a mate to protect now."

She nodded and pursed her lips while copying the numbers and coin values I'd written on the parchment. I smiled as she focused intently on what she was doing. Her right cheek would occasionally tense as she wrote, and sometimes her lips would move, like she was silently repeating what was on the page. Her penmanship was still delightfully atrocious, but she'd improve. Even so, I wanted to frame everything she'd written.

I prepared more goat for dinner and found some other items in the pantry to feed Elpis. Fortunately, I had seasoning in the cabin, so the meat tasted much better. However, she stopped eating soon after I'd served her and winced noticeably.

"Ah." She grimaced and grabbed her head.

"Another headache?" I asked, surprised. I moved to her side and placed the inside of my wrist against her forehead. I was trash at detecting fevers, but she didn't seem to have one.

"Yesss," she hissed and bared her teeth in pain. "Shhh. Ah, it hurts!"

I frowned and pushed her plate closer. "Eat a little more and drink some water. I'll get you some medicine," I said and rushed upstairs to find the medicine cabinet. I grabbed a bottle of anti-inflammatories and ran back down to coax Elpis into taking two of them. She was bent over the table, sobbing and pawing at her head like her skull was going to burst.

"Shit!" I rushed to prop her upright, holding her while I gave her the pills to swallow. She chased the medicine with water and continued to cry.

"It hurts! It hurts! It hurts!" she wailed, clutching at her forehead.

"Elpis!" I urged gently. "You have to stop crying. That's going to make it worse!"

She didn't respond and just continued to paw at her head. I gathered her into my arms, grabbed a bowl in case she puked, and carried her up to the bed so she could rest. I got her into a pair of pajamas and tucked her under the blankets, making sure she knew where the bowl was.

"Give the medicine some time to work, Elpis," I said worriedly while stroking her hair. "Is this the same thing as last time? Louder sounds? Brighter lights?"

She nodded and bit down on her lip as though it'd help stop her sobs.

What is wrong with our mate? Toast asked.

I don't know.

The coven can also treat the sick, Toast reminded, and I nodded. My heart squeezed painfully as I watched Elpis writhe. She reached out and grabbed my sleeve, but Toast refrained from bolting this time, even though he was startled.

"Do what you did last time, please!"

"Just wait for the medici—" I began, but she interrupted me with a cry.

"Nay! I can't take it anymore!" she shrieked, and I flinched from the volume.

Just do it, Keyon... it's... medical, Toast said in resignation.

I sighed and crawled under the sheets with her. Maybe I was getting too much into my head, but I just didn't want to feel like some ass taking advantage of her in a vulnerable state.

I slid up behind her and pulled her against me so her back was pressed to my chest. "Alright, moonflower." I nuzzled into her ear and whispered, "Are you ready for me to make you feel all better?" She nodded and whimpered. That whimper was likely from pain.

Poor mate, Toast said. It startled me.

I thought you'd be hibernating by now.

I don't know...

What does that mean?

It just means that I don't know if I will or not. I'm... confused right now.

Ok. Well, you can be confused, but I'm going to tend to our sick mate, I said and slid my hand under her clothes and between her legs to fix her headache.

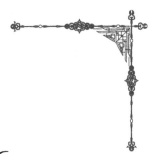

Chapter 16

Sir Keyon

I cupped Elpis's sex at first, just letting her get used to my hand on her intimate mound and absorb its warmth. She squirmed a little bit and brushed her bottom against my cock, which forced me to scoot back a little. I set my jaw, focused, and doubled down on my task.

After a swipe down the middle to collect a little of her slick, I slid my finger straight into her opening, startling her as I'd intended. I wanted all her attention on what I was doing, not on her pain. I pressed deep into her warm channel, not bothering to hide the aroused groan that escaped my lips.

Don't get excited, Keyon. We're doctoring her, Toast warned.

This helps her get there. She responds well to my noises and dirty talking, I argued, trying desperately not to laugh. Toast was totally disrupting my focus, but he'd never stuck around this long. I never would have imagined he'd be awake while I had my finger in a female. I actually never thought I'd get near a female. I was weirdly proud, but… fuck, I didn't know if I could handle this kind of multitasking!

Elpis gave a slight moan, but I couldn't tell if it was from the migraine or my invasion. She was hard to read right now.

"I like your pretty little moans, female," I murmured into her ear. "It's just evidence of how much you appreciate my thick finger in your tight little hole." I pulled my finger almost all the way out, then pushed it back in, squeezing another moan out of her. "Mmm, there it is again. That's two now. Are you saying you want two fingers, little female?"

Ok, but does she really need two? Toast pressed conservatively.

Toast… arousal is important for orgasms. Kinda hard to get there if you're not aroused. The more turned on she gets, the sooner this'll be over.

Toast was silent for a moment, then pondered, *So, have we considered a third finger?*

I ignored his recommendation. Elpis's hips continued to squirm against my hand after my offer of a second finger, and I smiled into her neck. "Is that a yes? I'll take that as a yes," I whispered and plunged a second finger in, curling both of them to stroke against her inner wall. She whined and arched, forcing her butt against my growing erection. How many more times would I have to move away from her lovely bottom. Would she notice?

"Careful there, little female. Your motions are waking the beast in my pants," I growled, and she shuddered. She was definitely very aroused now, perfuming the room with the scent of her natural lubrication. She tried to reach behind to grab me, but I blocked her hand with a thigh.

Don't let her grab us! This is a medical procedure! Toast panicked.

"Ah, ah, ah," I scolded Elpis. "This. Is. Your. Treatment. Moonflower." I pumped my two fingers in with every word to emphasize. "So. Take. Your. Medicine. Like. A. Good. Female!" I growled into her ear.

She wailed in pleasure from my thrusting fingers but continued to reach for my pants.

Can't we tie her down or something? Toast asked frantically. *This is not normal patient behavior!*

Her arousal hung heavy in the air now like a dense fog, but I tried not to give in to her demands. I snarled with lost patience and tossed the sheets off the bed. Ripping off her pants and undergarments, I dragged her hips to the edge of the bed, and pried apart her soft thighs.

Good idea, she can't reach us down here. Wait, what are you doing, Keyon?

Kneeling on the floor between her legs, I reprimanded her. "You are being very difficult tonight, female," I growled, starting to feel a little feral from all the lust she was radiating. The sooner this was over with, the better. "And because you've forced me to come down here, you lose out on all the dirty talk tonight," I informed.

Why won't you be able t— WOAH. I'm out! Please don't get your tongue stuck! Oh my gods, oh my gods, oh my go— Toast yelped and disappeared to hibernate.

Good riddance, I thought vehemently. That had been too distracting.

I held her thighs open and considered my strategy. The trimmed hairs around her sex allowed me to see her better, and she was simply ravishing. Stunning might be a better word for it because I might have been staring at her longer than I realized.

I grazed a thumb down one of her glistening folds, already slick from desire. I'd never tasted a female before, but I'd been craving Elpis for quite a while. I licked her moisture off my thumb and shuddered. I didn't know if the mate bond had anything to do with it, but she was delectable. Aside from a sweet and earthy flavor, she still had that hint of agave, strangely enough.

I leaned in and ran a tongue down the middle, parting my moonflower's little petals. She squealed quietly and started, clearly not expecting my mouth on her. I imagine no one could have done this for her if she'd been wearing her chastity belt all the time. Knowing that I was the first to taste her was arousing, and I growled possessively into her flesh. I buried my face in between her legs and began lapping at her folds, remembering the patterns she seemed to enjoy the most. She didn't fight me or protest; she whimpered and whined with every stroke of my tongue.

Feeling creative, I shifted my tongue a little to make it slightly longer. I turned my head, breathed out a little fire to warm it up, and then dipped it into her channel. My adapted asset drew a surprised gasp out of her, and I glanced up to see her hands sliding all over her body. They went from caressing her throat to under her pajama top to grope her own breasts. She was completely incapable of staying still, and the corner of my lip curled in a smirk.

Who needs warming lube when you're with a dragon? I thought smugly.

She bucked her hips, and I moved my left hand to her pelvis to keep her in place. The right hand went to the swollen flesh at the apex of her sex, where I began rubbing. I knew that once she'd been properly stimulated, that little spot was her undoing.

Between sliding my tongue inside her and rubbing her sensitive clit, it wasn't long before her legs started shaking. I maintained the same patterns and smiled when she fully tensed under my ministrations. The calm before the storm was my favorite part of pleasing her. The anticipation was brutal.

Then Elpis climaxed. Her pale lips released a long, explosive moan, and her body lurched into rhythmic spasms. I removed my tongue and shifted it back to normal but continued to rub at her flesh. I wanted to watch her euphoria. The way she moved was a reminder of when she danced for me at the mansion; her motions were just as smooth and flowing in her pleasure. Her sweeping undulations told of her rapture until they calmed with the volume of her cries.

I took one last moment to stare down at her in her glorious post-orgasm glow. Her long charcoal eyelashes fluttered open as though she was waking from a dream. When our eyes met, I smiled gently and helped her back into her pajama bottoms, then pulled the sheets over her again.

I sat on the bed next to her and asked, "Are you feeling better, Elpis?"

She nodded shyly and looked at her fingernails. "Yes... thank you. I'm sorry I kept reaching for you. I don't know what got into me..."

I shrugged and said, "It's ok. You probably just weren't thinking straight."

"I promised I'd never try to force myself on you again," she replied bitterly. "I'm failing that goal."

"When did you force yourself on me?" I asked, rubbing my eyes tiredly.

"The mansion..." she whispered.

I frowned and scoffed. "That place doesn't count. That place was a fucking nightmare, Elpis." I placed a finger under her chin to force her to look up at me. "Do you know why I call you moonflower?"

She mumbled, "Cuz I'm pale."

I chuckled and crossed my arms. "I mean, I can't argue that observation, but mostly no." I brushed a lock of hair behind her ear so she couldn't hide behind it. "Moonflowers bloom at night when no one is around to see them. Most people don't know how truly beautiful they are because they only see the sleeping flower on their own time during the day.

"The people who had you didn't know what they had. It's like a fisherman tying a diamond onto a fishhook, thinking it should be used instead of bait because it's shiny. They didn't even stop to think about its value—that they could buy new gear, a boat, and open a shop.

"Those slavers put you on the wrong pedestal. They only chose to see what the sun hit: naked skin. But," I continued, poking her gently just under her collarbone, "on the inside where it's dark, that's where you truly bloom. You're clever, brave, joyous, and kind. Now, I didn't know that much about you at the time, but I could tell you were brave and loyal by handing that dagger over. You're smart enough to have a wicked sense of humor, if you recall that terrible voice acting session. And your kindness is exposed by your gratitude." I stroked her cheek with a thumb.

"I call you moonflower because there is more to you than what anyone has ever tried to see. You're not who you think you are, Elpis. You're better."

My words had the opposite effect. Instead of smiling, she started crying. Ahhh... fuck. I was additionally confused when she sat up to hug me. She latched on tight like a squirrel during a storm, and I froze for a moment before choosing to gently stroke her back.

"Th-thank you." She sniffled and burrowed into my chest.

"I... you're welcome, but you have to stop crying, Elpis. You're recovering from a migraine. You know, I actually should get you some wate—" I started saying while trying to stand, but she hung on so tight that she stayed attached and became airborne. She wrapped her legs around my hips, and I couldn't pry her off me.

"Elpis," I chastised, unable to keep from laughing. "Let me get you water." She shook her head, and I threatened to walk away with her, which didn't faze her for a minute. So, I ended up trudging downstairs with Elpis stuck to me, giggling like a hatchling, which ultimately got me laughing. I returned her to bed with a glass of water.

"I certainly hope you are less trouble tomorrow, moonflower," I teased with a smirk. "Get some rest. I'll be in shortly."

"Good night," she said quietly and snuggled into her pillow with a sweet smile on her face.

I walked into my study, pulled out my maps, and sat down to figure out the quickest route to the Solar Coven.

Elpis

I woke up to find that Keyon had already gotten out of bed, so I bathed, dressed, and ran downstairs to find him rearranging items in his bag.

"Are we going today?" I asked hesitantly. "Where are we going?"

He glanced up at me while he stuffed rations into a side pocket. "Solar Coven. If I can't get intel from Leof, we need to do something about those marks around your neck. I'm extremely uncomfortable not knowing what they're for."

I put my hands to my throat again. I kept forgetting they were there. "Think they're causing the migraines?" I asked, feeling around as though I could find them by touch.

"Well," he grunted as he pushed a chunk of clothing into the bag, "you didn't get them before we removed the collar, right?"

"Nay..." I murmured softly. "I've never had a migraine before that."

"If those markings are making you sick, Elpis..." He stopped and sat back, looking at me with a pained expression. "I'm afraid only a witch might be able to help, and I don't want to be days away from a coven if your condition worsens."

I nodded, grabbed some food, and went back upstairs to sort out my own bag. I felt miserable being the cause of such a large trip that had nothing to do with his escort duty. I had to keep reminding myself that he was just my guard. We didn't have a future. Whatever I was, I was the wrong species... and that devastated me.

That's why I was boggled by how I'd acted last night. I needed to do better at keeping my hands to myself when it was unwanted. The spike in my desire reminded me of when I was a bit younger. It was like the day I became a woman; Zosime said that something would change my behavior. What was that word again?

Horn gnomes? my brain supplied. What? I shook my head, hoping I wasn't going mad from the symbols on my neck. This wasn't the first time I'd heard a rogue thought since the collar had been removed. Maybe I should let Keyon know.

I met my escort downstairs, and we left the cabin. "There are two routes to get to the coven," Keyon said as we journeyed farther up the mountain. "The first route goes back down to the main roads and swings up north. Unfortunately, the Solar Coven is way up on the clifftops, so you either fly or you learn how to mountain climb," he said with an irked expression.

"The second route," he continued, scratching at his nose, "takes us farther up this mountain and through a small but wealthy community. We go past that, continue north, and veer west toward the cliffs where the coven is."

"Not an easy place to access..." I muttered.

"Easy for a dragon, but no, not for someone like you," he said with a sigh. I cringed and flushed at those words.

Someone like me.

I fought the urge to apologize because I knew what he'd say, but I was starting to feel like my very existence was an inconvenience. I bit back tears and wondered if the horn gnomes were responsible for making me feel this way—for me thinking it'd be better if I was gone. Had Pelagia thought that way? I felt a pang of regret. I hadn't prayed for Pelagia in a while. I should do that when the sun began its descent.

"I'm tempted to see if there's anything warmer we can buy you in that town, but I'm also concerned we'll be recognized. We'll be safe once we reach the coven, but that doesn't mean we won't be surrounded when we need to leave."

"I can tolerate it," I said listlessly. "I still heal better than a human, and I'm used to cold places."

"Doesn't mean I want you to suffer, Elpis," Keyon replied, regarding me with a stern expression.

"The only thing that can make me suffer is a cage," I returned absently and pulled my cloak around me. It was chilly on the mountain, but if I got sick, I'd get better. I wasn't concerned about it. I just wanted this trip to be over so there'd be one less burden on Keyon's shoulders. If the witches could stop my migraines, that'd be great too. A day would come where Keyon wouldn't be able to help me with them anymore.

Eventually we rounded a huge outcrop and came upon a gated courtyard. Behind it were mansions, fancy restaurants, and upscale shops. There didn't seem to be any roads that led to this place, so it must only be inhabited by dragons.

"This gate didn't use to be here..." Keyon noted with a scowl, kicking the golden bars of the gate that kept me from walking into town. A guard noticed Keyon and marched over to yell at us.

"Save your dragon's breath. We're going." Keyon waved him away and walked aside with me. "This doesn't look good," he said, flipping off his hood and brushing his hands through his chestnut locks. "This has always been a wealthy neighborhood, but there's never been a reason for gatekeeping. There's a low crime rate here, and only dragons have easy access. Why make it harder to enter?"

"To slow you down," I said simply and scratched the back of my leg with a boot. "We saw stuff like this at the mansion. Slavers need time to hide their slaves, and if you wheel a cage up here like you said you did for the mansion, that gate is going to give them enough time to do just that."

"Buying time," he murmured, putting his fingers to his lips in thought. He stared at the town for a moment, then looked down at me. "We'll go around, but I'll need to come back to this when my mission with you is over."

"I could help..." I offered.

Why did I say that? When he was done escorting me, I'd be... well, I didn't know where I'd be.

"Ever the moonflower," he said with a smile but shook his head. "Not putting you in danger. I don't want you getting within a mile of a slaver. In fact, let's go right now. I'm not comfortable hanging around here."

We gave the town a wide berth as we tried to find a route past it. It took a while, and we had to do some difficult climbing through the cliffs and evergreens, but Keyon helped me through it. Watching him jump up to ledges and turning around to pull me up with his monstrously strong arms was thrilling, and I was grateful for the constant breeze that blew away any scent of my arousal. I couldn't help it. He always had such an intense look in his burnished eyes whenever he needed to touch me, whether it was opening his arms to help me down or holding me while descending with his wings. I often felt myself holding back sighs because my brain was getting stuck on sex. I wished the horn gnomes would disappear.

I found myself shivering a little when the sky blushed into oranges and yellows. Keyon grinned and pulled me around a corner to an incredible view. We were right on the edge of the cliff and facing the sunset. My brain didn't know how to process that kind of distance. Just leaving the confines of the mansion had been a challenging adjustment. The world was so big.

"Ah! Oh my Moon Goddess," I gasped while taking a step back, overwhelmed.

"I've got you. You won't fall," Keyon said, grabbing my shoulders. "Look at that view, though."

It was quite the view indeed. Shadowy evergreens, highlighted in gold from the setting sun, spread as far as the eye could see and blanketed the rolling hills. The Sun God hung low in the sky, allowing the ever-busy Sky Gods to prepare the stars. How busy the skies must be at sunset and sunrise. So much to do in so little time.

"My whole life, all this was out here, and I never knew. It was just the mansion and the dark stone of the underground," I said in wonder. The more I looked at the sky, the more I fell under its thrall. Any clouds that dotted the sky were purple on top and red on the bottom. I didn't even have the words to describe the kinds of purples and reds I was seeing. They just... glowed. They burned so bright that I swore I could see them when I closed my eyes. The rest of the sky was a blend of luxurious golds and deep, deep blues. It all fit together like a masterpiece.

Keyon moved behind me and wrapped his arms loosely around my waist. "And now you're here. You'll be able to see sunsets whenever you want now," he replied, sounding deep in thought.

I wondered if Pelagia saw the sunset before she went. Pelagia... I was closer to the Sun God now. Maybe He could hear me better? I closed my eyes and spoke the verse. I was not good enough to sing it and not nearly brave enough to sing in front of Keyon.

"If you have but a moment, a last request we plea. Help lost Pelagia ascend. Do you remember she?" I implored of the Sun God and wiped a tear from my eye. Perhaps she'd already found comfort or a path to reincarnation, but I wasn't taking that chance.

"Who is Pelagia?" Keyon asked hesitantly, flexing his fingers a little.

I whimpered miserably and said, "She was a slave around my age. We were friends and used to cage together. Pelagia... struggled more than anyone with being a slave. Perhaps it was due to the fact she could still remember her old life with her family. She'd been taken at an older age than most.

"When she turned sixteen, they began grooming her to become a sex slave... not a pleasure slave, but a sex slave!" I said vehemently, and tears began flowing freely down my cheeks. "She was so young... so young. She became so distressed that she started pulling out her hair and scratching at her skin until she bled. Tofa eventually put her in shackles when she wasn't being supervised. I'm ashamed to say that part of me was relieved when Pelagia was shackled. I didn't want her to hurt herself." I cried at the shame I felt and rubbed my eyes. Keyon lifted me and sat down, placing me in his lap and wrapping his cloak around both of us. He didn't say anything, just listened.

"Th-the day came that Pelagia was called to a guest's chamber for the first time. They had to pull her k-kicking and screaming from the cage. L-later"—I released a heavy sob—"we found out that Pelagia had escaped the guest's room and flung herself from the mansion's r-r-roof!" I collapsed against Keyon's chest in my grief. "Th-that was when Tofa s-started standing g-guard outside of g-guest rooms. They became more paranoid about slaves taking their own lives after that."

"Fuck..." Keyon murmured and pulled me against him while I cried. I squeezed my eyes shut so hard it hurt, wishing that my memories of Pelagia had been nothing but a bad dream. I clutched at his shirt, trying to anchor myself in the comfort he offered so freely.

"It sounds like every second matters for slaves," Keyon said, as though to remind himself. "I need to get back to my duties as the knight general with these raids... if that's even possible anymore. I promise I'll do my best for you, Elpis. For Pelagia," he vowed and stroked my arm with a thumb.

For me? I didn't understand that, but I was too worn out to press further. It was cathartic to get it all out, though, under the embrace of the wind, the Sun God, and a kind ear. I just sat limply against Keyon, staring at the sunset and mourning the loss of a friend.

Chapter 17

Elpis

I regretted my big talk regarding the cold weather, shivering like a fool while Keyon worked to build me a blazing campfire. I held up my blue-tinted fingers and sighed in relief as the flames worked their magic. The only problem was that this fire kept popping out little excited embers, and I had to kick a couple off my feet. Fortunately, I didn't get burned, but it was close.

Keyon eventually convinced me to sleep next to him since the night had gotten dreadfully frigid on the mountain. I fidgeted nervously as he laid my blanket down and raised a wing so I could join him. He piled several cloaks on top of me, snaked an arm around my waist, and pulled me against his warm chest. He felt warmer than usual, but I couldn't tell if he could control how much he radiated or if he just seemed hotter compared to the night air.

When he cocooned us with his wing, I asked, "Can you tell Toast I'm sorry for getting handsy the other night?" I couldn't recall if I'd apologized directly to him.

"He knows, Elpis. He actually stayed for most of that session. You definitely gave him a challenge," Keyon said with a chuckle. "I'm rather proud of him."

"I think something is wrong with me, but I can't remember the word Zosime used. It's like how I felt when I was younger. My mind seems to think the word is horn gnomes, but that can't be right," I muttered and bit my lip. Keyon buried his face in the back of my neck and burst into laughter. His entire body rocked with his mirth, and I was starting to feel aroused again. Aroused and embarrassed. Red-faced, I protested, "K-Keyon, stop!"

"I-I'm sorry," he said, breaking into another fit. "That's just... the funniest shit I've ever heard in my life!" He turned, coughed, and resumed laughing. "Horny gnomes," he wheezed in a high-pitched voice and removed his hand from me to—I assume—wipe some tears from his face.

His laughter was slowly breaking my frown, but I stood my ground. "S-so what's the right word?"

"Hormones," he gasped out and returned his arm to my waist, pulling me closer, which almost pulled a moan out of me. "They're called hormones."

"Whore moans? I suppose that sounds more familiar. Ugh..." I grimaced. "Must have been named by slavers..."

"What? Wh—OH!" He burst into raucous laughter again, and I withered, wondering what I'd gotten wrong this time. After all this, he could barely breathe and explain himself, so I just flattened my lips and stared into the fire. At least the fire wasn't smart enough to think I was stupid.

After a concerning bout of wheezing, Keyon managed to breathe enough to spell the word out with me. He chuckled one last time, saying, "Remind me to teach you about homophone phrases later. Trust me, it has nothing to do with prostitutes. Gods, you're precious." He nuzzled into the back of my head, and I tensed from the affectionate gesture.

I was so confused. What were we? I closed my eyes and tried to focus on falling asleep. It was simultaneously easy and difficult. In his arms and under his wings was the safest I'd ever felt in my life... but knowing I couldn't be a proper mate hurt, and it made me want to run away from him. My thoughts became a mess, but every pull and nuzzle from Keyon relaxed me. I wasn't sure how much longer I could handle this. My heart was starting to ache as much as my sex. How much of this was hormones, though?

Despite last night's bout of conflicting emotions, I was reluctant to leave Keyon's embrace. We ate, packed up, and kept walking north. At least we were past that town. That town... even thinking about it made me shudder. The town's air almost tasted like poison, and I was certain that there were slaves hidden underground. I wasn't sure exactly how I knew... but I just did, and I was willing to bet my life on it.

"Will you someday tell me how the raid on that town went... if you ever get to it? I don't know where I'll end up living, but I'm curious about the outcome," I asked Keyon as we traversed a narrow path. Several plants tried to hook onto my dress, and I had to pause to rip them out, wincing at the stings my fingers received. I shook my hand, and they healed almost immediately. Huh. That was faster than normal.

"I'll let you know, Elpis," Keyon answered as he led us through a winding pass. "I don't plan on losing touch with you unless you want me to."

What does that mean? I screamed in my head. My brain understood three variations so far: no relationship, intimate only, and relationship. Keyon fit in none of these categories. It just felt like it was cycling through all three at different points in time.

I let out another withering sigh and continued to trudge along behind him. The sooner we got to the coven, the sooner...

"I just had a thought, Keyon," I began rather reluctantly. He looked over his shoulder at me with a raised eyebrow. "You could just leave me at the coven. You said I'd be safe there from the king. Maybe they'll let me rehabilitate with them."

I balked at his scowl. "No, Elpis. I'm not leaving you with witches."

"Why?" I all but shouted. "I won't slow you down anymore! The sooner you sort out what's happening at the castle, the sooner you can go back to freeing slaves! I'm not worth so many lives!"

His muscles tautened as he prowled ahead, and he looked like he wanted to shift. Keyon was silent for a while as we travelled but finally said, "We'll discuss this later at the coven. Let's get all the facts first. We don't even know if they'll want an outsider there."

Someone like me. An outsider.

After a quiet lunch, we picked up the pace, and Keyon led me west for the rest of the day. I wondered if we'd make it to the coven by nightfall; it was getting pretty late in the evening. I was feeling more emotional than usual and craved a reprieve. A good pillow to cry in was very much needed so I could vent some of these feelings. I knew better than to drown in negative thoughts that couldn't be resolved immediately.

Stupid horn gnomes, my brain muttered. I was taken aback by the rogue thought because that was old information.

Hormones! I said loudly, trying to get my brain to remember the new word.

Whoops, my brain replied, and I was so startled I stumbled off the path. Having lost my balance, I fell against a boulder and fought a wave of pain that blossomed in my forehead. I clutched at my chest as my heart raced with adrenaline, then snapped my eyes shut when everything became too bright to look at. What was happening to me?

"Woah! Elpis, what's wrong?" Keyon's voice asked, and I felt his arms stabilize me. I groaned and moved my hands to my head, knowing what was coming.

"Voices, then migraine," I said shortly through a clenched jaw. "I can't see! Too bright!"

"Voices? Is that your beast, Elpis?" Keyon asked worriedly.

"I don't kno— Ahhh!" I cried, and my knees buckled. I pushed Keyon back as I knelt to puke, but nothing left my stomach. The dry heave only made my migraine throb harder, and I sobbed in agony, collapsing to writhe on the dirt. Keyon immediately picked me up and—based on the jostling movements—began running. I was a limp corpse in his arms, unable to mumble a single coherent sentence. I hung on as long as I could until I eventually fell into a black sleep.

⚜

"—but am I doing the right thing, Coven Mother? Are you sure?" Keyon's voice came to me before my vision did.

"If you ask me if I'm sure one more time, I'm going to kick you out!" a woman's voice grumbled. "Questioning a coven mother... disgraceful."

"Oh, calm your bosom, Gunel," another woman said in a sultry voice. "He's just worried about his fated m—"

"She's awake, Tesni. Mind what you say," said another in a sing-song warning.

I moved my right hand to rub my eyes open and stared at the four people hovering over me. A quick glance told me I was in a small guest room. This had to be the coven.

"Are we here?" I croaked to Keyon, nervously eyeing the three strangers. He knelt by the bed with a glass of water, and I took it gratefully after sitting up. So far, my headache seemed gone.

"Yes, we're at the Solar Coven, moonflower. These are the coven mothers; they're basically the leaders here." He smiled gently and patted my knee through the sheets.

"Basically?" an older woman with ashen hair reproached. "We are the leaders!" Keyon heaved an exhausted sigh, as though he'd been dealing with difficult people all day. He pointed to the grumpy, oversensitive one and said, "This is Gunel."

"I can introduce myself!" she snapped, and Keyon backed off, raising both his eyebrows and hands in surrender.

"Aren't you too old to have an attitude?" I reproached. This Gunel's crankiness was contagious. Before words could leave her livid face, I apologized, "Wow, that was rude. I'm sorry. I've been very... hormonal lately. You were setting me off. Don't be mean to Keyon."

Gunel didn't look mollified by my gesture. Oh well, I guess I'd be cursed for life. I sighed and slumped but was intrigued by the other two laughing.

"Yes, I think you did come to us in the nick of time," a tall woman said. She must have been over six feet, and she was absolutely beautiful. She was like a glorious, tanned godling. "I'm Tesni, and this is Arevik, the youngest coven mother ever." She beamed and slapped her hand on the back of a young male with platinum-blonde hair. At least, I thought it was a male—or a man—but I must be wrong. I was confused and was about to ask but held my tongue. The free world had so much to teach me, but navigating it while trying not to insult anyone was terrifying, and I wondered if I'd catch up to everyone else someday. Either way, I was liking Tesni and Arevik much more than Gunel.

"I'm Elpis Eud— Nay... Eukod— Nay, that's not right either. Eudokia!" I blushed furiously in embarrassment, hating that I kept forgetting it.

"You're bound to be a little groggy, sweet one," Arevik said, reaching to retrieve my empty cup. She refilled it with a jug of chilled water and handed it back to me. I sipped at it this time, trying to cool the raw flesh in my throat. I must have screamed more than I recalled.

"Yes, removing symbols can take a toll on the patient," Tesni agreed.

"They're gone!" I gasped, once again feeling for them with a hand like a fool. I withdrew my hand quickly and was relieved to find no judgment in the room.

"Oh, they're gone," Gunel verified, crossing her arms and giving me a pointed look. "And you're going to suffer dearly for what's been done to you."

Keyon sat beside me on the bed and held my hand, but his presence couldn't prevent the ice that melted and trickled down my spine. It settled into my stomach like a cold seed, and out curled a tendril of fear. "What... do you mean?"

Keyon holding my hand wasn't enough. I leaned into him, nudging his arm over my shoulders so I could have something between me and the witches. Keyon's intimidating, muscular limb made me feel a little safer. He ended up outdoing my efforts by dragging me into his lap and wrapping both arms around me. I sighed in deep relief, feeling warmth and protection emanating from him. In that moment, I didn't care what we were. I was just glad he was here.

Arevik sent a scolding look to Gunel, and Tesni pulled up a cedar chair from the small desk that was tucked away in a corner. "That collar did a real number on you, sweet one," Tesni said, crossing her long legs and resting her chin on her palm. "You might have cleared yourself of that doozy-of-a-curse eventually after Keyon removed your collar, but it would have been torture. It was a real nasty one."

"We also found one on your head that was hidden," Arevik said softly.

"You found it, sweet one." Tesni snorted at Arevik. "Don't be so modest."

"What were the curses?" I asked quietly, so quietly that I barely heard myself. I cleared my throat and asked louder. I fisted my hands because they were beginning to shake, and Keyon seemed to respond right away, rubbing my shoulder with a hand to soothe me.

"The first one on your neck was the humdinger," Tesni informed. "We could tell it was placed on you at a very, very young age. It was meant to suppress your beast and kill you if you mated."

I gasped, and my hands flew to my face, hiding my gaping mouth. "Why?" I breathed. "What... Who...?" I couldn't wrap my head around it. Who would do such a thing to a child? Keyon embraced me from behind and rested his chin against the top of my head. It was not a brilliant place for his head to be because I was shaking almost violently at this point.

"Someone needed you to stay a virgin." Gunel scoffed. "That word needs to be wiped from society."

Tesni's lips pressed together, showing a long history of tolerating Gunel's outbursts and interruptions. "Yes, indeed," Tesni said. "Now I forgot what I was going to say…" She placed a hand to her forehead and closed her eyes. It looked like she was the one getting a headache this time.

"The second curse?" Arevik suggested, placing her hands behind her back.

"Right! Yes. Arevik found the second curse, which was an attempt to skirt around the dangers of the first curse. It was meant to keep you from recognizing your fated mate so you'd be less encouraged to mate. Weirdly enough, it was totally pointless. Not having a connection to your beast prevents you from recognizing your fated mate. Sloppy cursing. You were a mess."

I frowned. "I don't understand. What is a fated mate?"

Tesni sighed at Gunel's exasperated groan. Arevik jumped in to explain. "The Moon Goddess pairs the gods' children. They are two souls destined to be together. They are two halves of a whole. When they meet, they complete each other. Best friends and lovers rolled into one. Soul mates. They are simply meant to be—as per Her plan—to keep Her children safe and thriving. It is intended for Her wolves and lycans, mostly shifters, but it benefits us all."

"That sounds nice…" I said numbly, a bit dazed from all this new information. Was I in a dream? "How do you know if you've found your fated mate?"

Keyon tensed behind me, and I had to wonder why. Was he nervous? Was he afraid I'd find someone else? No, couldn't be that. He'd have his own to look forward to someday. That thought really depressed me, though. Maybe it was just the hormones.

"Oh, you'll know," Tesni said with a laugh. "It'll take time for you to recognize them, though. Your beast needs to recover a bit before you'll be able to tell who it is. Just touching them will calm you and light up your skin with tingles. You'll also become extremely amorous." Tesni gave me a very obvious wink.

"I'm already feeling amorous," I grumbled crankily. "How much more amorous can one get?"

"Yes, that brings us back to the suffering you'll endure," Gunel said darkly.

"Don't scare her!" Arevik snapped. Her calm and light-hearted demeanor was getting ruffled.

"It's not that bad," Tesni countered. She turned back to me and said, "When a shifter goes through puberty, their beast is supposed to be there with them. It doesn't matter that they're in their dormant phase before you turn eighteen. You were blocked from yours completely. They're a part of you... They're half of your very being. Your beast never went through that phase, and she's going to want to make up for years of missed cycles."

"I thought I was always a shiftless. Not that I knew what that meant... I just thought I was broken," I murmured, more to myself than anyone in the room. Keyon squeezed his arms for a second, reminding me that he was there.

"No one is broken," Gunel said sharply. "People get injuries, but no one breaks. That's catastrophizing. You'll only feel worse about yourself, so stop exaggerating!"

"Right..." I said blankly, feeling more exhausted by the sentence. "The curse was an injury... and you all healed me... thank you."

"Well, let me just get to the issue at hand," Tesni said, holding up a palm and laughing nervously. "If I could just... stop getting interrupted here." She looked sympathetically at me. "Your body is going to dive right into estrus, sweet one, and it's going to be bad. You're going to go through several waves of... heat. We warned Keyon about it already, and he's aware he's going to have to drive other males away from you."

"Why would males need to be driven away?" I asked, confused. Gunel just burst into dark laughter, which felt very ominous.

"Because you're going to lure them in with your scent. Your body is going to make your fertility known," Gunel said with another strained laugh. What in the name of the Sun God was wrong with this witch?

"They w-wouldn't force me, would they?" I gasped, appalled.

"That's why Keyon's there. But he'll be a problem too," Tesni said. "You two are going to have to have a difficult conversation."

My face erupted into flames, and I covered it with my hands. Oh my goddess, this was so embarrassing. The implication... Though I couldn't imagine anyone else I'd rather spend my estrus with, what about Toast? What about what Keyon wanted? Oh gods, what should I say? He was just my escort! He had things to do!

"Wh-what if I just... was locked up during my cycle?" I asked through my hands. Keyon tensed again, but I had to ask. I had to go through my options. The world did not revolve around me.

"Well, good luck finding a place because you can't stay here. We also don't have a dungeon that could keep out that monster." Gunel pointed behind me at Keyon and snorted. "Also, even though we're a coven, we have males and menfolk here. We'd rather not have that kind of trouble."

Someone like me. An outsider. That kind of trouble.

I withered and did my best to will away the tears. Crying wouldn't help, at least not now. Maybe into my pillow later.

"You must think we're heartless," Arevik said sadly, "but we have to think of our own."

"So, what am I?" I asked miserably. "I don't feel like a wolf or a cat. I certainly don't feel like a dragon. My beast just sounds... slow."

"She's just waking. Give her time," Tesni advised, expertly evading my question.

"But what am I?" I pressed, removing my hands so I could look her in the face.

She shrugged. "Sorry, you have to discover that one yourself," she said. "Keyon came here to get you healed, and that's what we did. We don't share our divining knowledge. To do so might interfere with Fate."

"Unlike that Lunar Coven." Gunel scoffed haughtily.

"Maybe we should have gone there instead, Keyon," I mumbled. He chuckled and hummed in response.

"In the meantime," Arevik said more jovially, "rest a bit before you head out. We'll send some food for you."

"Thank you," I replied, forcing a smile. I was grateful but terribly tired.

The witches nodded and filed out of the room, leaving me alone with Keyon and my fears. Should I leave his lap or was it better to not look at him? I decided to move off and face him... except I couldn't bring myself to look at the dragon-shifter. I couldn't even bring myself to say anything! I just mindlessly traced a finger along the stitching in the blanket.

"Talk to me, moonflower," he urged in his beautiful, clear voice. "What are you thinking?"

"A lot of things," I said, my voice barely above a whisper. "I'm so embarrassed."

"Don't be..." he urged, placing his large, weathered hand on the blanket between us, like he wanted to hold mine. "It's not your fault." He had scars on his hands that I'd never noticed before now. He'd seen so much of the world and I so little. I felt deeply vulnerable, exposed and naked, like everyone knew what to expect but me.

"M-maybe we should go our separate ways, Keyon," I proposed, even though it crushed my heart to suggest it. "I can't force you into such an intimate situation. I can't do that to Toast. You both have more critical things to take care of too."

"Don't... please don't say that," he pleaded, suddenly very emotional. It tugged at my heart, but I didn't know why he was so upset.

"Why? You have your mate out there somewhere, and I have mine," I explained, broaching a topic I hadn't wanted to discuss, not yet. It was incredibly painful. Perhaps I'd gotten too attached to him because I felt more dead inside with every word that came from my mouth. Pushing him away was agonizing.

"Elpis, what do you want? You ask me, but this is about you. Do you want me there?" he pressed anxiously.

"I don't mind you being the one..." I murmured, blushing brighter than Keyon's fire and flustered beyond words. "I just worry... it's not right to ask someone to do this. I should just leave and find a cave somewhere to ride this out... This is also far too trivial for someone as important as you."

Keyon seemed to get increasingly agitated, like he was on the verge of panicking. He reached out and grabbed my hands. "Please let me do this for you! I'll protect you, I swear. I'm sure Toast will manage. You've already helped us so much. Let us return the favor. Please, Elpis. Please!"

I hazarded a glance up at him, and he looked on the verge of tears. I swallowed heavily. "I don't understand this... I don't..."

"And if you're not a dragon, Elpis, and something happens, you won't have to worry about pregnancy with me..." he said with a slightly bitter laugh.

Right, that...

"Am I really going to be that out of control?" I asked worriedly. "This all seems so extreme."

"We'll see... hopefully it won't be as bad as they say." He smiled half-heartedly.

"What if you fly off as Toast when I go through my... heat?"

He scowled and shook his head. "Look, I'll fight it the best I can, but I'm not leaving you unguarded."

Why is it everything he says makes me want to him to ride me? I thought miserably. *Stupid hormones.*

I placed my hands over my face, embarrassed by my thoughts, and groaned. "Where are we going now?" I sorely wished I knew where my life was headed. The future was so hazy.

He puffed out his cheeks and blew out a breath. "I don't know. I guess back to the cabin? Maybe Leof will show up." He shrugged and shook his head. "At least we got some answers here and took care of those curses. That took a huge load off my mind." There was a knock on the door, and a young lady brought in two trays of food. We thanked her, and she bustled out to do her next errand. I picked at the freshly baked bread, cheese, and fruit on my plate. It smelled wonderful... It was too bad I had no appetite.

At least not for food, my beast said unhelpfully.

Chapter 18

Sir Keyon

Elpis and I ate in silence, though she really didn't do much eating. She picked at her food, seeming equally strained. I was becoming an emotional wreck trying to deal with our current situation. I desperately wanted to tell Elpis that she was my fated mate, but the coven mothers warned me against it.

Her connection to her beast had gotten too twisted, frayed, and strangled by the curses. If I tried to convince her that we were destined for each other, and she unintentionally pushed herself too hard to connect with her beast to activate our bond... there was a risk of the connection to her beast snapping outright. The mind was a fragile thing, and the thought of Elpis losing her beast as soon as she'd discovered she had one was simply too devastating to bear. Just accidentally tugging on her beast right now could hurt it. They both had to be ready. Elpis had to ease into her bonds as naturally as possible. They'd never seen anything like this before, and we all agreed that it was best to be patient than risk her health.

Maybe I could convince her to let me guard her until her first shift. That was when she'd know I was hers. She'd already brought up going separate ways, and that scared the fuck out of me. I'd never known terror like that. I'd not known it in battle, and I'd certainly not felt that level of fear from Toast's panic attacks. No, I had to convince her to stay without making her feel rushed. I could tell she was drawn to me, but she was becoming too self-sacrificing, and that wasn't acceptable.

Toast, you've been quiet. I need you to talk to me, big guy, I said, dreading this conversation.

I'm here... I heard it all, he replied. He didn't sound nervous, just depressed.

What do you think of all this? Do you think you can hold me back if she goes into heat? You're quite good at yanking me away from females. It sounded like something I'd say to joke around, but I was serious. Toast was an absolute dominant. If anyone's dragon could hold them back, it'd be mine.

Probably... but do we even want to? He sighed like he was giving up a lifelong dream.

What do you mean? I asked, puzzled. I bit slowly around a piece of cheese, turning it into a circle while I waited for his response.

If we don't mate her, she'll think we're rejecting her. You know that, right? You see that on her face, right?

Since when did you get so good at reading Elpis? I asked, extremely curious about this change. It didn't sound like he was talking out of paranoia like he usually did. He sounded like he was seeing pretty clearly.

I don't know. Just happened slowly. Probably after we played with the pinecones. It was a... connecting experience.

Hmm... I guess I'll try again to make sure she's honest with me about what she wants. She's very difficult when it comes to that.

Keyon... I don't know what to do anymore. We're at a threshold here. We've reached a crossroads. If we mate her and emphasize that we'd like to stick around until her first shift, maybe she'll be more inclined to stay near us. If we don't... we continue with our strange interactions and confuse her even more.

So, you want me to say, 'Hey, can we hang around and see if we're destined because we like you?' I asked, becoming more distressed. W*ouldn't that rush her? Gods, I can't find a safe way to do this! And how long is all this going to take? We have so many things to do. I'm worried about our people, Toast.*

Who's more important right now? Elpis or… well, whatever is happening out there? We don't even know. It could be resolved by now, Toast argued.

Elpis is our life, I reminded myself. *Our present and future. Fuck… I know, I know.*

Let's just see what happens in the next couple of days, Toast said. Somehow, we'd switched roles, and he was comforting me. I had no idea when the fuck that'd happened. *My trauma isn't forever, but Elpis is. We have to be honest with ourselves… remember that was you who said that.*

Right… Ok, Toast… Good talk, big guy, I said, only feeling slightly better.

I looked over to see that Elpis had eaten half her food and was staring listlessly at the rest of it. "We can pack that up if you'd rather finish it later," I suggested, and she nodded.

"Good idea." She crawled off the bed to stash the food in her bag.

"Are you ready to leave, Elpis?" I asked, anxiously watching her stiff movements.

"I am. Let's go," she said and opened the door. Arevik and Tesni were waiting on the other side with patient smiles. They were seated at a small table, drinking tea.

"All ready?" Tesni asked and started guiding us out of the building. The inside was beautiful; it looked like the building was carved right out of the heart of the mountain. I wished we could have stayed a bit longer. I was sure Elpis would have loved to explore the coven.

"When it's all over," Arevik said, as though she'd read my mind, "I'd love for you both to visit again. Don't take this as a sign of disfavor."

"Yes," Tesni piped in, "and I'd love to do a follow-up on Elpis's health too. Make sure y—" Arevik cleared her throat to interrupt, and Tesni subsequently coughed. "Yes, here's the exit. The large torches will take you straight out! Sunlight preserve you both." Tesni's farewell blessing was repeated by Arevik.

"Thank you," Elpis said humbly and gave both the coven mothers a loving but lethargic hug.

"Thank you both. I'm deeply in your debt, Mothers," I said, bowing instead of offering a hand to shake. Toast may be more accepting of Elpis but not so much anyone else. "I see that Gunel's not here to see us off. Tell her it's been... a pleasure." I raised my brows, smiled, and turned to depart the coven grounds. The door closed behind us, and on the other side, the two witches burst into muffled cackles.

"What in the Sun God is wrong with those women..." I muttered and reached down for Elpis's hand. I held my breath, and my stomach cramped with worry. Would she take it?

Please... Please don't pull away from me, Elpis.

She looked at my hand and slowly accepted it. I sighed in relief and strolled to the huge rock archway that marked the threshold of the Solar Coven grounds. I looked back one last time, taking in the stone paths and the succulents that covered the ground. I smiled at the passive-aggressive garden; the witches certainly didn't like people straying off the path. Elpis and I would stick to ours the best we could.

Once we were a mile from the coven, I sensed we were being followed. Before I could confront the stalker, they stepped out from behind a redwood and lowered their cowl.

"Great gods, Gunel. Why the fuck are you following us?" I growled and placed myself in front of Elpis.

"So disrespectful," Gunel said with a scowl. "Your generation... so rude to your elders..."

"What is it, Gunel?" Elpis said, staring past me at the witch while clinging onto my cloak.

Gunel's scowl relaxed, and her expression dropped into one riddled with guilt. "I'm here to give you... information.

Information I'd rather my sisters not know I have," she said in a lower voice, coming closer and looking over her shoulder.

"Which is?" I asked, fairly certain she wasn't lying but unclear about her motives.

Gunel's shoulders drooped, and she gestured tiredly to Elpis. "That second curse on your head. I... that was me. I did that when you were a child."

"What?" I snarled, enraged. I took a protective stance. Was she a threat to Elpis?

"What...?" Elpis gasped. "Why? How? I was at Adelmar's mansion as long as I can recall."

"He summoned me..." Gunel explained, shifting uncomfortably and looking at the ground. "It was not during the proudest chapter of my life. I... owed him a favor. He said he found you at a slave auction and was intrigued by your odd looks but realized you were already sold to a male named Franco."

"Yes... I know that name," Elpis said cautiously, paying close attention to the witch.

Gunel continued, smoothing her skirts nervously. "When he poked around and overheard that you were to be... bled dry once you reached adulthood, he stole you."

Elpis released a whimper and staggered. I steadied her and glared at the witch, seething that someone had planned such an atrocity with my female—if this story was even true. Elpis was my life, my precious gift from the Moon Goddess! I huffed a blue flame, trying to vent my rage through pure heat.

"He said it was the dumbest and most dangerous thing he'd ever done," Gunel recollected, "but he and his mate had just lost a hatchling, and... his common sense went out the window. When he brought you back, he intended to just keep you as a slave and away from Franco. Then... when he decided he wanted to change your collar, he realized that something was off about it.

"That's when he asked for me to visit. I couldn't get a good look inside the collar to understand the full depth of the curse and wanted to consult my sisters, but Adelmar refused. He didn't want anyone else to know about your existence, so I offered to place a second curse down to try and delay the inevitable."

"And that's why I was the only one put in a chastity belt…" Elpis whispered to herself.

"Why didn't you just take the collar off?" I asked. "I melted that fucker off immediately."

Gunel's lips pulled in, and she kicked at a small rock. "Adelmar was afraid! Wanted to let the sleeping curse stay asleep… I wouldn't have been able to undo it myself anyway. I know that now. Many poor decisions were made over your curse. Mine was practically pointless… without your beast, you wouldn't have been able to recognize your mate anyway. I just hadn't had enough information to work with," Gunel rambled, seemingly lost in her memories.

Elpis became extremely agitated as facts sank in and created more questions. "Why did Adelmar just hand my belt keys over to a male? He almost gave me to another slaver! That could have killed me! That would have killed me! Thank the gods that Keyon's not one to force a female!"

"I'm not Adelmar…" Gunel said, accepting Elpis's growing fury with surprising tolerance. "You'd have to ask him."

"So, why are you telling me all this?" Elpis shouted. I angled slightly to pull her against me. "To sleep better at night?"

"I know who placed the first curse. I'm not proud of knowing this person, but if you want to find the ones who are still hunting you and end them before they end you… this is how," Gunel murmured and held out a rolled parchment. Unless she was a master of her body, I detected no lying—about any of this. I scoffed internally, doubting that Gunel had any sort of self-control.

I snatched and unrolled the parchment, noting that it was only directions. I glanced up to see Gunel ambling away from us. She turned one more time and said, "I'm sorry your life began like this, Elpis. I've made… dreadful mistakes." Her eyes flickered to me, and she muttered, "Take good care of her, Sir Keyon." She walked toward the nearest tree and disappeared.

The air had never been more silent. I knew I had to act fast, though. I turned to Elpis and dropped to a knee, grabbing her hands firmly and shaking them so she'd look at me.

"Elpis," I said urgently, staring at her confused face in worry. "Elpis, listen. One thing at a time, ok? I'm here. I'm here for you. We'll sort this out, I swear on my life. Just breathe." I searched her eyes and waited for her to nod and take a deep breath. "Good. Good job, moonflower," I said encouragingly. "Now what we're going to do is set up camp. Then you'll eat a little more, ok? Tomorrow, we'll look at our options, and we'll do what you want to do. I'm with you, one hundred percent. Do you hear me?"

She nodded again and just collapsed to her knees, hugging me as tightly as her weak arms could. I returned her embrace and rubbed her back. "It'll be ok, moonflower. It'll be ok. I've got you."

Elpis

I nibbled on my leftovers while Keyon built another roaring campfire. I watched him split firewood with ease, mesmerized by his prowess. Every movement he made seemed to preserve the trance that'd engulfed me. I didn't want to think about anything else because I knew one more piece of straw might break my back.

Keyon was the safest place for my mind to be. None of his crowded back muscles wept, none of the cords on his neck strained, and none of the might in his arms trembled. I gave myself permission to stare at his butt too. I knew from one of his many shifts that he had nice, tight butt muscles. It had been a brutal day. I was allowed to be a little shameless, I think.

You're not the only horny one, my beast said flatly.

What's your name? I asked, eager to catch my beast in a talkative mood, but she fell silent. *Too horny to talk, I suppose,* I grumped to myself. She'd better not be doing anything unsavory in the back of my mind.

Keyon sent me the smallest smirk when he caught me staring, and I pulled my hood over my head. At least it was cold enough to use the cloak as an excuse to hide my embarrassment. It wasn't like he was naked, and besides, he stared too. It was only fair.

"Warm enough?" Keyon asked, settling next to me and wrapping his arm around my shoulder to share his cloak. It was the little familiar things like this that made me nervous. It was like he knew something that I didn't, and it gave him confidence while I was left in the dark.

"Moonflower?"

I jolted slightly. "O-oh! Um, yes. I'm comfortable."

"Good," he said softly and paused for a moment. "Do you remember the moment Leof saw Adelais?"

I nodded. "Yes, she was terrified. Poor Adelais..."

"But do you remember what he said?"

"He said she was his. He mentioned she was his fated mate... Oh..." I connected it with what Arevik had told me. "I'm seeing their meeting in a new light now. I understand now. That was significant, wasn't it? Their lives changed in that moment, didn't it?" I said in wonder. "They became complete."

"'Mine' and 'mate' are the two most anticipated words in a person's life. If you're lucky enough to run into your fated mate... it's a dream come true. You were there to witness something very rare, very precious, Elpis. I thought you'd appreciate it more now. You remember how they looked at each other? Despite all the sadness, it was still the happiest moment of their lives."

"Must be nice... to belong with someone," I said quietly. I yearned for it. I wanted something like that, desperately.

"You'll find them, Elpis. I have a good feeling. Who knows, maybe it'll be me?" He chuckled and nudged my shoulder playfully.

Oh, how I wish it were true and that I was a dragon.

"That wouldn't be so bad..." I mumbled my confession with a blush, grateful once again for my hood. "I suppose I'll find out whenever the sleeping ninny wakes up," I muttered, trying to keep my longing for him out of my voice.

"No rushing her, Elpis. She's recovering," Keyon ordered firmly. "She's been through a lot too."

"Right..." I replied thoughtfully.

We sat in silence for a while, and I considered removing my cloak. I was getting a little too warm. Keyon took a deep breath before speaking. "So... I spoke to Toast about our... situation."

That immediately put me on edge, and I froze where I sat.

"He thinks he may be able to hold me back, Elpis. He's pretty strong," Keyon said.

"Oh," I replied and winced internally. I'd just sounded as disappointed as I felt. Fiddlesticks! Fiddling fiddlesticks!

"I'm not comfortable with getting your answer when you're in an altered state of mind, so I need to know now. What do you want me to do when you go into heat? What do you want me to do if you end up... urging me? I just want to prepare for the extreme-case scenario. I'm not saving myself for anyone, Elpis. Toast is only comfortable with you right now, and he's... willing." Keyon took a deep breath. "Do you want me to take you?"

That last question felt like a lightning strike. My heart almost forgot how to beat, and my stomach twisted into sizzling knots. My face may have even lit on fire, and I nearly waved a hand to fan myself. "I appreciate you th-thinking it through. I cer-certainly wouldn't have thought that f-far ahead," I stuttered, flustered within an inch of my life.

I worried at my hands in my distress. What did I want? My body was already screaming for him. Should I let it have what it wanted? Maybe I owed myself a little happiness, a little pleasure, as fleeting as it might be. Keyon seemed... keen enough.

"I s-suppose it'd be an opportunity to expose Toast to it... to help him," I said, unable to speak the truth. I wanted to slap myself silly. What a stupid response. Poor Toast was becoming my scapegoat!

"I'm afraid I'll need a yes or no, moonflower," he said gently, rubbing my shoulder with a thumb. I smiled abruptly, thinking back to when he'd freed me, and I hadn't caught on yet. He knew I was more comfortable with yes-or-no questions.

"Y-yes? Yes… if I press the matter… then I give my consent," I said in a tiny voice and pulled my knees up to my chin. I held my breath, and he released his.

"That's all I needed to know. At least we're prepared. It's been an exhausting day, and I'm ready to nest," he said with a yawn, standing to stretch before settling. Like he did every night, he released his wings and raised one for me, offering a spot next to him. I was so pleased that little dragons fluttered in my belly again.

I tried not to seem too eager when I changed into my warmer pajamas and curled up next to Keyon. He lowered his wing to tuck us in and trap his body heat for me. It was bliss. It was like I could be anywhere, and he'd always shelter me, rain or rime. His palm landed hesitantly on my waist, then slid around to pull me against him. He nestled his head into my hair, and I fell asleep, hoping the Sun God would sleep in tomorrow.

⚜

I woke up covered in sweat, panting from an incredibly erotic dream. A dragon had flown down from the sky to cage me, but he turned into a man and… did barbaric things to my body until I crumbled in ecstasy. As the dream dissipated, my mind sharpened. Anxiety struck me hard and fast.

I froze in place, knowing that what I'd been fearing had finally arrived. I gritted my teeth through a wave of arousal and ran my hands over my body. Everything felt swollen and sensitive. My breasts and sex ached, and I nearly let out a whimper when I discovered that my underwear had been soaked through with my desire.

I squirmed out of Keyon's grip and crawled out from under his wing. I knew that I'd consented, and I knew that I wanted him, but this was so much more embarrassing now that it was actually happening. I didn't feel like myself at all; my body was a stranger to me. I was feeling parts of my body that I wasn't used to feeling, like the muscles that were clenching within my core.

I collapsed around the corner, breathing hard, and crouching on all fours. I placed my face on the cold mountain stone to let its chill ease my swelling, then I groaned and arched my back, sticking my rear up for absolutely no reason. There was no one there. I rolled onto my back and grabbed my breasts for no reason as well. None of this made sense, and I was miserable. Hot, aroused, and absolutely miserable.

I whined, almost in tears from discomfort, but I couldn't bring myself to bother Keyon. The thought of waking him up for sex was horrifying to me. So I panted and prostrated under the stars and the eyes of the Moon Goddess, occasionally flipping onto my back and repeating the process all over again.

I grew too heated and ripped my clothes off, simultaneously freezing in the frigid mountain air. The wind on my sensitive skin was brutal, and I worried that Keyon would wake and scent me, so I moved farther away into the trees. In the striped darkness, I started walking, feeling lost, vulnerable, and alone.

I stumbled farther through sparse trees and rocky paths in my growing delirium. I was losing myself to my heat. I wanted hands on me, a male on my back, and fangs in my neck. I whimpered and started running into the night, unsure of many things except for the fact I was going wild.

Race the breeze, my beast urged. *We need a male. Find a male.*

My mind was too far gone to understand her words. All I felt was the wind and the deep ache in my body—the void that needed to be filled. At the same time, I felt fear. I felt like prey, and I knew it was the worry of being followed.

There was a shout in the distance, then a roar and a crashing from where I'd run. Something was chasing me, and I gasped for air, torn between fleeing and giving in to whatever wanted me so badly. I fought for breath and grabbed below my left rib. A stitch had formed in my side, and I squealed from the pain. I was a weak beast, and I had doubts about my survival. I'd been caged and kept from the wind for far too long.

A virile growl from behind spurred me, and my fear turned into excitement. A thread of my arousal dripped down my thigh, and the growl turned into a snarl. A male was chasing me! Perhaps he'd be tough enough to look out for me while I grew stronger. Perhaps he'd provide. Could I risk stopping?

I turned sharply around a corner and jumped down a small outcrop. The footsteps were close now, nearly on my heels, and I was expecting breath on my neck any moment now. I moaned, and my legs finally failed me. They buckled and I crashed down into pine needles and grass, but I couldn't even think about the pain of the impact.

I writhed on my back again, burning out of my skin. No rubbing of my thighs together could free me from the ache and the rebellious muscles of my core. I arched deeply, palming my neck, breasts, and belly in a rapturous tease, wishing my hands were someone else's.

A colossal shadow fell upon me. It blocked the moonlight, and I rolled onto my knees, prostrating at their feet and whimpering. "Female," the masculine voice growled, feral yet clear as a bell. "Didn't anyone tell you not to run? Creatures like us enjoy a good chase." I stared up at the shadow, only seeing blue flames flicker within a fanged grin.

I whined and lowered my head again, arching my back for the male who'd clearly won the chase. The figure prowled to my side, and a rough palm landed on my lower back. Lips brushed against my ear, and a low, inviting voice purred, "Is it time now, moonflower?"

Chapter 19

Elpis

The beast hovered over me while I panted into the soil, lifted my hips, and spread my legs per my instincts' demands. The male caressed my back slowly, almost reverently, before curling his fingers and raking down it. I felt no cutting, only lines drawn by razor-sharp claws. He was so brutally powerful, yet so tactful. I shuddered and a trail of my arousal streamed down a thigh.

The male took a sharp intake of breath, and I heard the rustling of clothing being removed. His warm mouth returned to my ear, sending small puffs of smoke to mingle with my foggy pants. "I'm the one who caught you, female. I'm the one who gets to mount you. I state my right to claim and mate with you. Here. And. Now," he uttered with a husky, guttural growl, dragging a single claw down my spine to graze over the folds of my sex. Gaping at the rush from his declaration, my body responded by igniting my libido. A wave of lust rippled through me, and I shivered violently, already trembling from the cold air.

A strong male wants me! I moaned low in my head, barely able to think more than simple, primal thoughts.

I must have spoken aloud because the male responded in my ear. "One of the strongest. An absolute dominant," he asserted in a rougher, superior tone as he wrapped his arms around my torso and flexed. I sobbed into the dirt and continued presenting, dying to have one of the strongest pick me. For his protection, I'd give him everything.

Pick me! Choose me!

He bit the back of my neck to keep me still and slid his warm hands to anchor on a breast and the curve of a hip. He groped and squeezed my flesh, groaning erotically into my spine. The noise sent a jolt of pleasure down my back to pool into my core, and I cried out in carnal need. I dug my fingers in and tried to encourage him to mount me, shifting my hips over to where he was. He growled at my provocation, released my neck, and yanked me off the ground.

I felt a lurch and squealed to find we'd left the ground. The male landed on a moonlit ledge, and I whimpered in fear at how high we were. I looked around, and there was no path down to the ground. The only escape from this male was to leap to my death. This meant he'd chosen me.

The male placed me down on a pile of his clothes, and I landed on all fours. I scurried away from the edge, but he held me in position so we both faced the expansive view of the starlit mountains. He leaned over me and murmured, "At ease, female. You're under my protection now. My wings are your wings." He licked up my neck, and I whined louder, desperate to be mounted. My body was a swollen, heated mess, and I was painfully in need of relief. "Time to let me in…" he groaned, lapping at my neck and panting in turn.

He widened my already spread thighs and tilted my hips toward his. One fist gripped my hair like a rein, and the other hand slid two clawless fingers down through the folds of my sex. I gasped and tried to back up into him, but he deftly spread me and slid his fingers into my channel. With deeply anchored fingers, he pushed his wet hand forward to keep me in place. I moaned at his invasion and jerked slightly, wiggling my hips to temp more from him than his fingers.

"Ahh." He hissed and pulled his fingers from my heat. "Dripping. Your nectar's everywhere," he rumbled in approval, and I heard a slick rhythmic sound, like he was stroking something with his wet hand. He tightened his grip on my hair, and a broad, unyielding object pressed against my sex. When two fingers parted my folds to allow its entry, I felt a tightness at my sex's opening, and my entire body tensed in nervous anticipation.

"Loosen, female. Let me in," he growled and caressed my bottom suggestively. He massaged my inner thigh, but my sex clenched instead of opening. "I refuse to hurt who I mate."

A palm came down on my bottom, slapping me lightly enough to startle me. I bucked in surprise, but the split second my body relaxed from the scare, the male squeezed past my entrance. Heat rolled through my body, and I twisted my torso in euphoric arousal. I felt my body release more slick so it could further encourage the male's entry. His hands flew to clasp the handles of my hips and wrench me back to meet his next thrust. Assisted by my wetness, he slid in another inch, and I scrabbled at the stones on the cliffside to find an anchor, overwhelmed by his descent.

"Look. At. You. Ta-king. Me. In!" he grunted, slipping deeper with every syllable. Electricity sizzled down my arms and belly at his admiration. My abdomen clenched, and my core tightened around him. He cried out in pleasure and lurched forward to bury himself to the hilt, forcing a guttural noise from my throat. I shuddered and pawed at the ground, whimpering at the fullness of his sex. It was a massive, long rod, fully embedded in my abdomen to establish its territory. Even its broad girth was pushing my limits. I pressed against his hips, his groin, and rubbed encouragingly. My body was on fire, and I needed him to finish the claiming.

"Oh, you need more. I know, I know," he snarled and adjusted his hips. His sack rested heavily between my thighs, and I continued to press and rub against him. "I'm the one to fulfill your heat. Only me. Do you understand?"

I whimpered and ducked my head.

"Only me! Is that clear, female?" he snapped, and I nodded enthusiastically. "Good..." he whispered and rubbed my bottom tenderly in approval. I moaned loudly and sensually at his warm touch, shivering additionally from the cold. He growled and traced his claws down my goose-bumped back. I felt him angle differently as he leaned slightly one side, and the crawling vines nearby were engulfed in flames. It wasn't enough to warm me completely, but it took the edge off the chill. Either way, I was focused on the scorching heat of his hands on my back, his thighs behind mine, and his sex within me.

He adjusted his grip on my hips and slowly began to pull his thick cock from my channel. I lamented at his departure, and as his head slid along my inner flesh, my core clenched to try to keep him inside me. He growled and jerked back, then rocked forward to plunge inside again. I gasped at the pleasant surprise, thrilled to have him returning. He repeated the motion until he was gliding smoothly, and it wasn't long before he was swiftly sliding in and out to the edge. Every pump into me stoked a flame, and I became more and more lost to instinct.

I could have easily been pushed forward by his forceful thrusting, but he kept me safely in place. I didn't know if I was shocked or terrified staring off the cliff's edge because everything but pleasure and lust was drowned beneath my hormones. Every slam of his hips made me lurch forward, seeing more of the ground when all I wanted was to see more of him. So far, I'd been focused completely on touch and sound. When I turned my head to look at the male behind me, I moaned at the sight.

He was glorious and god-like. His short, tousled locks swept forward with each thrust, and his muscles were covered in a sheen of sweat, highlighting every sculpted curve with agonizing sharpness. His neck was corded from his exertion, and his pecs and abdomen constricted just before his hips came crashing into me. The bulk of his biceps and forearms drew taut and worked feverishly to give me what I needed. His body spoke for him and told me it'd provide.

He glanced up when he noticed I was watching and growled softly between grunts and pants. A drop of sweat trickled down his clenched jaw, and his provocative eyes flashed in the dark, catching just a razor's edge of moonlight. He subtly showed off his elongated fangs and huffed out a lick of blue fire. I didn't know how I could tell, but I knew he was trying to show me that he could possess me more than other males. Deeper than other males. More completely than other males. Arousal crashed into my belly, and I cried out to him, still keeping our gazes locked.

I want him, I want him, I want him! my mind screamed in a frenzy.

The male reared his head back and hissed out a burst of blue fire. I watched the swell in his throat bob as he tilted his head down to stare heatedly at where we were joined. He glanced back up at me through dark, furrowed brows and growled more aggressively. His hands dug in, gripped me tighter, and slammed us together.

I had to turn back and maintain my grip on the ledge because his thrusts had become almost violent. The slaps where his hips collided with my bottom grew louder and wetter, and I started wailing from the pleasure of our primal act.

"That's it, that's it, that's it," he snarled as he ravaged my heat and ravished my body, his thundering raising by the word. "Perfect. So perfect. So perfect for me!"

Yours, yours, yours! I chanted in my mind.

He sped up, sliding along my gripping channel until he hit the very end of my depth. I bucked at the sensation and braced myself for the onslaught. A roaring cry exited the male's mouth, and he began to thrust harder and faster than I thought possible, bottoming out with every pump and tensing until his excited quivering rattled into me. He lifted and tilted my hips so that every slap rolled into the apex of my sex, making my eyes snap shut from its intensity. I gaped at the blooming sensation and petals of pleasure slowly unfolded until all were unfurled.

My head tilted upward, toward the silent sky, and I sobbed as an orgasm rolled through my body. The male yanked my torso up so I was arched against him, and with one hand on my hips and the other on a breast, he slammed in several more times before he shouted one last carnal roar. His wings snapped around us in his spilling of seed while our bodies rocked with pleasure. He released a strangled, euphoric cry, and his mouth crashed down onto my neck, sliding to where it met my shoulder. He bit savagely, and through the severe pain of piercing fangs, I gasped as a smaller wave of pleasure rushed through my orgasm.

With a mouth on my neck, he pumped his hips in time with my quaking, delivering his thick promise. His seed was hot! It was so hot! It flooded my channel, and for a moment, I thought I'd been scalded. There was no pain though, only pleasure. I moaned and tossed my head, feeling my muscles milk him until he was spent. He massaged my breast, and his other hand slid up my body to wrap around my waist. In a sensual change, his groans became softer moans, and his hips pressed gently against my butt, as though he was savoring our last moments locked together.

A moment longer, he clung passionately to me and wrapped us a little tighter in his wings. I was surrounded by him; he was everywhere—inside and out. His grip loosened, and he pulled his hips back, allowing his heavy cock to fall out of me. Some of his hot emission trickled down a thigh, joining my desire and sweat, but I didn't think anything of it. We were done...

The male spoke from behind me but not to me. "Fuck... Toast..." He hissed as he traced a finger over my neck.

I was still in a haze but managed to mumble, "What?"

"Later," he said with a sigh and buried his face in my hair while trying to catch his breath. He helped me up slowly and lifted me into his arms as he prepared to get us back to our campsite. I was glad for it—mine didn't feel like they'd work with how much I had braced myself. He looked around, made sure the fires he'd lit had died out, and jumped from the ledge, flapping enough to land gently on the pine needles and grass.

We returned us to our site, and I nearly passed out on his chest, exhausted from what felt like a fever dream. The campfire blazed under his stoking, and I found myself being dressed, though not before my thighs had been wiped down. I was too tired to wonder why he was upset, wincing as he regarded me, and just wanted to go to sleep. He pulled me tight when we lay down to sleep but still seemed hesitant. Everything was fine. We'd mated... Everything had gone according to plan. Right?

Sir Kenon

Elpis was fast asleep against me, and all I could do was repeat the memories of the last... hour? Two hours? I could honestly say I'd lost all sense of time during our reproductive collision. When I'd awoken earlier, I was terrified to find Elpis missing. Even Toast went into a full-blown panic over her disappearance. He'd been doing so much better and now seemed to care about her as much as I did. We were equally beside ourselves.

I scrambled to my feet to find her and had been thunderstruck by her lingering scent. I knew immediately that she'd gone into heat, and she was fucking missing. That scared the shit out of me, and I raced to follow her potent trail, crying out her name.

The stronger the scent of her and her pheromones became, the more I sensed something getting tugged at within me—something ancient and primal that was between Toast and me. It was like a melding of us both, but at the same time, it was something completely new. Perhaps it came straight from where the absolute dominance had been residing within Toast.

I wasn't quite sure, and it almost hurt my brain to try and pick it apart. Perhaps it wasn't meant to be deconstructed. We were still a singular shifter—one individual between the two of us.

It overwhelmed my senses to the point where I hadn't been able to hear Toast, and it roused a roar from my lungs to warn the fleeing female that I set my sights on her. The tugging turned into clawing, and I knew then that its escape was imminent. The emerging instinct gave me a burst of energy, and the essence of my dragon saturated my veins. It provoked my fangs and claws, encouraging me to catch my female and latch on until she let me claim her. If I was forced to wear her down first, then so be it.

I growled in excitement when I finally caught sight of her. Lust flooded my system at the sight of her bare, bouncing flesh. She seemed to be afraid and confused in her race for freedom but also excited. Had she known I was in pursuit? Had she been challenging me to catch her—to mount her? I grinned ferally, knowing in that moment that there was no female who could outrace me. In my overstimulated mind, I saw her as particularly weak but judged that her fertile, luscious body was made to be mounted. When I scented and saw evidence of her readiness drip down a thigh, I snarled at the call of her sweet nectar, and saliva flooded my mouth. My chest, abdomen, and groin clenched in agonizing arousal, and I felt like my entire body ignited.

When she finally gave up and fell, I slid to a stop and decided to enjoy her dance of need in the grass and pine for just a moment. She was tortured by her heat, and I was the one to corner her. My control slipped when she groped her own soft breasts, and my fangs itched viciously to release their venom.

I vaguely remembered stripping and speaking into her ear while she presented herself for mating. I wasn't even certain who came up with the words that left my mouth. Likely me, but the memory was such a haze. I remembered teasing and groping her heated flesh to coax bestial pleads from her soft lips. She wanted a strong male to protect her, to choose her, and that was exactly what she was about to get from me, for I'd pick no other. I latched onto her with my jaw to goad her further. I savored her begging, and her shifting her hips to get me to mount her was so fucking beyond erotic that I completely lost the last ounce of my control. In less than a heartbeat, I snatched her off the ground.

That dragon instinct drove me to pick a perch where she couldn't escape so I could rut her, as my mind had put it. I picked the best view of the landscape to show her my attention to detail, to prove that I would give her the finest nest for our offspring with the finest view.

I nearly chuckled at a particular memory where I'd deeply regretted not having my hoard of treasure to show off. I was so surprised by how ridiculously ancient that instinct was. Either way, in that moment, I was certain that being an absolute dominant was way more than enough.

I glanced over to stroke Elpis's hair in her sleep. She was dead to the world and rightfully so. She deserved to rest for a week.

I'd ridden her like crazy... finally able to have sex again and with my fated mate. That was a fucking dream come true. The pleasure was incomparable, absolutely unimaginable, and I nearly finished multiple times while I was inside her. The poor thing received me at my hardest for her first time, and only Elpis could get me that large—like after I'd removed her chastity belt. I held back another chuckle and played with a strand of her shiny hair. It nearly glowed now in its luster.

Thank the gods I hadn't hurt her. I'd been so worried about my unyielding girth, even in the midst of my lust. I looked for blood after we'd mated but found none. Not every female had a significant hymen, and Elpis must have gotten lucky. She probably would have failed the rot that was the 'virginity test.'

You should try to sleep. We're running off adrenaline at this point. Toast's voice meandered into my head.

Toast... I can't believe you made me mark her. What were you thinking? I asked, too tired to sound accusing.

It's not permanent... It's a partial mark. I didn't inject deep enough. You were too far gone to hear me. I'd just come up with a solution to deter other males a bit... that's all, he defended.

He was unnervingly calm. Had us mating with Elpis settled him somewhat?

So you took control. I cannot believe you had the balls to do that while I was fucking her, I replied, almost shaking my head in amazement. *How the fuck did you pull that shit off? That's miles beyond your comfort zone.*

That... instinct grabbed me as much as it did you. I just had more control because I'm our dragon half... he explained. *Her pheromones completely exposed our primal drive. It was... incredible. And you can call me ballsy, but you're the one who came in her.*

I sighed and grimaced. *I lost... control. To go from a sex drought to a fated mate was... overwhelming. I was surprised she didn't comment on that... She probably expects the incompatibility to spare her. I have to say, I've never been more torn on hoping she's a dragon.*

All I have to say is... why would the Moon Goddess pair an absolute dominant with an incompatible mate? It doesn't make sense. She must be one of us. We really need to keep an eye out for signs of pregnancy, Keyon. Keep her safe.

We'll... We'll find out. I just hope she forgives us for marking her.

Partially. Partially marking her. Just enough to mark our territory. We can always finish it or redo it later.

Gods... so much to explain to her.

I made an effort to sleep then, unable to shake the exquisite images of our pulsing, writhing bodies until I was fast asleep.

∗∗∗

I woke around the same time Elpis did. She rolled toward me and rubbed her eyes while I stretched a stiff wing and took a deep breath, feeling anxious as soon as I recalled last night. I needed to tell her about th—

What. The. Fuck! Toast said, borrowing my profanity for whatever disturbed him.

What's wrong? I asked sleepily, trying to spot what Toast had seen through my gaze. My eyes fell on Elpis's neck.

It's gone... Toast pointed out, aghast. *It's fucking gone. My partial mark is gone! What the fuck? Where'd it go?*

I pushed her hair back to get a better look while she blinked tiredly at me. Nothing. No fang marks. Her skin was pristine. I didn't know why, but I felt deeply... something-ed. Offended? No, that couldn't be it. Emasculated? No, still felt pretty fucking masculine. Robbed? Yes... I was loath to say it, but perhaps I felt a little robbed. I frowned as my fangs itched to lengthen and do it properly this time.

"Are you ok?" Elpis's soft voice asked. I looked down to stare into her shiny, clear eyes. Her hair and skin glowed this morning, and she looked healthier than ever. Her pretty face tugged a smile out of me, and I think for the first time, I had to truly fight a magnetic urge to plant my lips on hers.

"Yeah... Yeah, I'm fine," I said and ran a hand through my messy hair instead of kissing her. I turned and blew out a breath, not sure if I was relieved about her neck's unexpected purging of our mark. It was possible she would have seen my marking as overstepping. Still though—as Toast had put it—what the fuck?

I reluctantly released her from under my wing so she could rise and get ready for the day. I slowly realized that she was still releasing the same pheromone, but it wasn't as strong. Unfortunately, I was not immune to it and had to do some controlled breathing to calm my libido. I scrubbed my face with my palms and growled. This was going to be a challenge. I'd have to make an effort to stay upwind of her.

When Elpis returned, I asked, "How are you feeling? Are you sore?"

Blood rushed to her cheeks, and she shook her head. "N-nay... I'm all better. I've been healing faster as of late."

"Your beast is probably the cause. She must be strong!" I said with a grin, feeling deep pride in my female's inner strength. My enthusiasm made her smile, and she packed her bag, showing she was ready to go. I handed her a ration bar, and she wrinkled her nose.

"Nay, thank you... not very hungry," she said and looked expectantly up at me. "What's our plan?"

"Like I said last night, we're taking care of you," I said, poking her playfully in the shoulder. "Would you like to find this witch and let me beat up your enemies? I'll do it for free."

She laughed and pivoted on the balls of her feet to swing shyly. Her mood became solemn. "Ah... I fear that they'll come for me eventually. If... If I was worth buying only to sacrifice, I can't imagine they've forgotten about me. I still can't process it," she said, her expression growing haunted. "It's possible, but I don't think I'll ever be able to shake that shadow. It looms." She shuddered and looked over her shoulder for just a second. "I've learned so much and have been held back in a cage for so long. I need to catch up to my life. I feel so far behind everyone else. I don't know if that makes sense, but it makes me anxious."

"It makes all the sense in the world," I said, laying a soothing hand on the shoulder that she'd just looked over in fear. I dearly wished she could feel the bond and receive my comfort. In her dark, concerned eyes, I saw her woes and craved easing them all.

She glanced away, flustered. "I'm... driven to learn more, but I can't expect you to come with me. You have s—"

"Elpis, we're past that," I said in earnest, bending down to look her straight in the eyes. She flushed more and leaned back a bit. "We're going to get your answers and crush your foes. I'm following you to the ends of the earth, and from there, we'll fly, alright?"

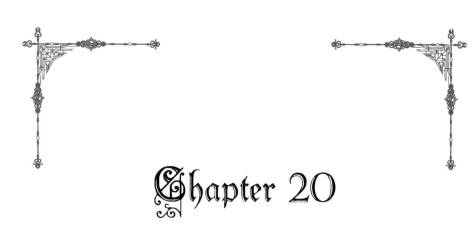

Chapter 20

Elpis

Keyon pulled out the parchment that Gunel had given us, and rubbed his chin, which was getting a little scruffy, while he read the directions. "This is farther up north," he mumbled and rolled up the paper to stash in his bag. "I haven't had much need to go that far north with my Inferno since it's a quiet, rural area. No large reports of thefts, burglaries, or assaults of any kind."

Keyon's expression spaced out, and I assumed he was chatting with Toast. "Oh come on, Toast!" he shouted angrily, spooking me into a backwards shuffle. He never replied out loud. I wondered what was going on in there? Keyon paced, and I retreated to give him more space.

He looked up with a pained expression when he noticed that I'd moved far from him. "One minute, Elpis. I need to let Toast out," he warned and shucked off his clothes in an irritated rush. I grew heated looking at his glorious, naked frame and swallowed heavily. Muscles flexed and stretched, lit by a flattering morning glow.

That rode us last night, my beast saw fit to remind me.

Yes, he did... I replied mindlessly, staring at his tanner, sculpted figure without shame.

Keyon shifted into Toast, and the monstrous dragon shook itself, then stretched like he'd come from a slumber. I always forgot about how much he towered over me, and—once again—I found myself in awe of his presence. His copper and bronze scales gleamed magnificently in the morning glow, individual scales flickering to pure white whenever one caught the sunlight at just the right angle. He folded his massive wings neatly at his sides and turned to face me.

Was Toast testing his tolerance again? Keyon and I got as close as two people could get last night, but what about Toast in his own body? Would he be able to carry me now? I stood still and patiently, giving him an affectionate smile as he neared.

"What a brave dragon you are," I murmured quietly, trying not to startle him. It didn't work. He flinched, but at least he didn't run away from me. I released a breath and chose to keep my mouth shut. Toast stopped about ten feet from me and growled miserably. His hulking, layered muscles were tense and shaking, and it broke my heart. I wiped a tear away as he stared at me. I knew it wasn't personal, but it still hurt. It made me feel like a poison, and it wasn't one I could clear. It was his battle, his challenge to face.

He was so close, though. If he could just move ten more feet. I sat down to appear smaller and stared at the weeds on the ground so he wouldn't feel like prey. I folded my hands and waited patiently, keeping his clawed hands and feet in the corner of my eyes. He slowly lifted his hand and placed it closer. I held my breath as he took another step, but then he backed up harshly and shook his head from side to side. He reared back, and he began making chuff-like sounds. The calls were so heartrending that the only thing they could be were sobs.

I rubbed away the tears that were now falling freely from my eyes. Why was this so sad? Why did his crying tear me apart? I sobbed and placed my palms over my face, unable to resist the pain. I cried for a moment longer before I was startled by large arms wrapping around me. I relaxed when I realized it was Keyon. I hadn't even noticed him shifting back and getting dressed.

"He's ok, Elpis. He thinks he'll be there soon. He just—once again—needs more time." He sighed in frustration, and his head sank onto my shoulder. He was miserable too. I turned and kissed the side of his head, then froze. Oh gods! What had I just done? That urge blindsided me! I turned my head away and grimaced.

"S-sorry." I laughed nervously. "H-hormones," I blamed, sniffled, and cleared my throat, patting his head to warn him I was about to stand. He backed away, but I spied him red-faced and grinning.

Oh, Moon Goddess, please let me keep some dignity through my heat. Grant me some self-control, please!

Dear Moon Goddess, grant her less control around that stud. Please and thank you, my beast prayed in deep betrayal.

What's your name? I asked, trying to get more than one reply from her this time. Nothing. Was she honestly too tired to say more? I wanted to push her but ended up stamping my foot like a child. Augh!

Keyon grabbed his bag, and we started walking north again, where he pointed out an easy-enough pass that would lead us back down from our high altitude. He kept offering me food, but I kept declining until around lunch, where I only nibbled on a little. I was much more thirsty than hungry and ended up needing more breaks to relieve myself.

I thought that walking would be a good distraction, but all it did was heat up my already warm body. The discomfort and ache between my legs were relentless. Thankfully, it wasn't anything as bad as last night, and I was terrified about the next large wave.

I also noticed that Keyon kept more distance between us than normal, and it made me a bit cranky, but at least the breeze kept sending his scent to me. As the hours progressed into the late afternoon, we descended into a pine forest and noticed signs of civilization. Keyon herded me into a clearing to give a lumber mill a wide berth. As he continuously tested the wind, I realized he was trying to keep others from scenting me. My chin trembled, and a tear dripped from my eye in gratitude. I nearly gaped at my over-hormonal reaction. Great gods, I was an emotional mess!

I sped up to thank him but ended up rubbing into his arm with my head and shoulder instead. He started in surprised, and I froze, looking away and unable to meet his gaze. Oh gods, no! I tried to suppress the growing symptoms of my heat, and my mouth opened to apologize, but the only sound I heard was a furious snarl.

Keyon and I whipped around to see a large male approach us. He looked like the kind of male who'd work at a mill. Massive, burly, and raw. He looked... furious?

"C-can we h-help you?" I asked in a stutter, moving behind Keyon, who was calmly undressing. The stranger snorted dismissively at my words, yanked his shirt off, and released his wings. I watched his knuckles crack as his claws lengthened, and my heart rate accelerated at his aggressiveness. Were we in danger?

The shifter's walk turned into a hostile prowl aimed directly at me, like he wanted to abscond with me. Keyon moved to intercept him, and they stood chest to chest. His wings snapped out to block the shifter's view of me, and I listened to their combative exchange.

"She's unmarked and in heat. She's fair game. Back off or challenge me." The aggressor growled. I was horrified by his intention and crouched behind a tree, partially to protect myself but partially to keep my scent from making things worse.

"No. She's under my care. Return to what you were doing, civilian," Keyon stated calmly, his tone laced with dominance and authority, as though Toast had added his voice. That had a rather unfortunate side effect on my heat. My sex grew hot, and arousal soaked my undergarment at the voice of one of the strongest males fending off another dragon. I covered my face in humiliation and peeked through my fingers to notice that both males had snapped their heads around to stare in my direction.

In a dirty move, the aggressor swiped at Keyon's face while it was turned, and I screamed. He jerked his head back, but the other male managed to rake several bloody lines down his temple and cheek. That was when everything fell to chaos.

Both males shifted and exploded into their dragons. Toast hovered imposingly over the smaller, clay-colored one, but what the smaller one lacked in size, it made up for in what looked like yellow venom dripping from its fangs. The winged giants clashed, and even the tree I was leaning against vibrated from their body slams.

Toast growled one last deadly warning, a sound that rattled my bones, but the smaller male refused to leave, so he lunged and ripped the membrane of the dragon's wing to ground him. The smaller one landed a bite on Toast's shoulder but was struck senseless by a kick from Toast's hind leg. Toast spun and hooked the bottom of the aggressor's jaw with his tail. In a bizarrely smooth wrestling move for his size, his tail flipped the dragon up and onto its back. Toast immediately climbed atop and pinned its limbs, then wrapped his maw around its throat.

The fight was over barely after it'd begun, and I was panting… from something. It was either fear or arousal—I couldn't be sure. All I knew was that my heart was slamming against the tree I was clutching like an overzealous lumberjack.

Something unspoken occurred, and both males shifted back to their human forms. Keyon stood and watched the other dragon-shifter run back in the direction of the mill. I was nearly vibrating with a need to run and check on my protector, but I was afraid to move and spread my scent everywhere.

As he approached, I noticed his skin was slightly jaundiced, but he seemed otherwise fine. I couldn't find the bite on his shoulder or the rakes on his cheek. "Were you poisoned?" I asked in a worried hush, looking up at him from my hiding spot. I squeezed my thighs together as my heat peaked.

Keyon stared at me from under his messy chestnut locks, picked me up, and placed me against the tree. He dug his claws into the bark and grinded his hard body against mine, cock clearly engorged and ready to ease my heat. Staring down at me through his caging arms, his lips parted in focus. He rolled his hips into me, like he was a male showing off his massive erection for approval. "Oh gods," I whispered and placed my palms on his chest.

"I'm fine," he ground out in a strained, husky voice. "His dragon had King's Poison venom, which only slightly sickens me, but it'll clear out in a bit."

I leaned into his chest and nuzzled, distressed he'd gotten injured but aroused that he'd protected me. We were a mix of sensations, and he whispered, "I want you, Elpis..." Keyon's hands slowly lifted up my skirts, and I leaned my head back to whimper. Oh gods, yes. Sweet relief under a knight's tending.

He leaned down and groaned into my ear, whispering, "I've got you... It's ok..." He hoisted me up against the tree and wasted no time in getting to me. He tore my undergarment down the middle, grabbed my thighs, and leaned into me, spreading my sex open with the glossy head of his cock. He pushed against my tightness, using his pre-cum and my arousal to assist the stretching of my skin. Keyon pumped slowly and carefully until he squeezed through and filled me. We were trembling with fulfilment at the moment of our joining, and I slid my arms around his wide chest, having a feeling we wouldn't be able to savor this mating as much as we'd like.

Keyon moved quickly this time, and I noticed him sweating more than usual. I worried about the poison draining his energy, so I spurred him on the best I could. The sooner we were done, the sooner I could help him recover.

He panted heavily as he pumped into me, slapping my flesh loudly with his groin and sack. His body worked urgently to finish, and his pelvis rubbed relentlessly into my sex until I was sent over the edge in a gentler bloom. He immediately released a relieved, guttural groan and spilled his seed. His hot release drowned my core, and we pulsed together, my inner muscles rubbing out the last spurt of his burning offering. I moaned from the deep feeling of completion, loving how warm his release stayed after it'd pooled within me.

Brief as it was, every intimate experience with Keyon was still the most satisfying experience of my life. There was nothing more euphoric than our matings.

He gripped me tightly, and we fell back into the grass. His embrace kept me sweetly on top so I wouldn't get scraped or bruised. Still joined, I clung fiercely to him, not wanting to separate. He was breathing hard, but when I looked him over, I noticed that even though he was covered in sweat, his color looked much better.

"You healed me, Elpis…" he panted. "That venom always takes several hours to clear out. You're the only explanation." His hand ran up my neck to slide into my hair and massage my scalp affectionately. He licked his lips and stroked my cheek with his other hand. "Whatever you are," he said between breaths, "you're something special."

The words filled me with warmth, feeding some hidden yearning. I allowed myself another moment to rest on top of Keyon and bask in his admiration. I knew I should remove myself, especially from his cock, but it was incredibly hard.

Very hard, my beast agreed.

I meant difficult! Emotionally! I corrected. *Oh my goddess, you are just...* That was enough incentive to get off the knight general's lap. I stood and took a peek at my undergarment, frowning at the hole Keyon had ripped along the crotch to gain access to me.

"Sorry, I guess I ruined those, didn't I?" he apologized with a grimace, then stood to dress.

I removed the torn undergarment with a sigh. "Maybe I just shouldn't wear any until my heat is over," I grumbled under my breath. "It's not like I can even keep them dry."

Keyon growled over by his bag and muttered, "Fuck."

"Everything ok?" I asked, sliding on another pair and picking up my bag.

"Uh, yeah," he replied hastily in a low voice. He looked up and brushed his hair aside. "Ready?"

I nodded, and we continued our journey. I was a little sore; I probably could have asked to take a longer break, but I knew I'd heal soon enough.

Our feet crunched through the pine and undergrowth for hours, and we did our best to avoid people. Keyon lost his patience when a second dragon came out of the woods to hunt me, and he didn't even give the challenger a moment to speak. He just shucked his shirt off, lunged forward, and spat out an intimidating surge of blue fire.

"Fuck off!" he roared and took a violent step toward the male before releasing his wings and spreading them. I hadn't noticed before, but his wings were larger than other males' as well. It probably had to do with Toast's monstrous size. Perhaps this aggressor wasn't as strong as the previous one because he paled and retreated. I breathed a sigh of relief, glad that Keyon hadn't needed to put himself in danger this time.

As we passed through farmland, we received several more challengers before the evening arrived, but none of them wanted anything to do with Keyon's blue fire. I was sure it didn't help their nerves that we were so close to their crops. Since we'd been interrupted multiple times already, the knight ended up keeping his shirt off and his wings out as he escorted me, which was progressively becoming a problem for my hormones.

I could have been enjoying the landscape a lot more without my estrus. The crowded muscles on Keyon's back made for the only scenery I wanted to study, and my body was terrible at hiding it. He'd glanced several times over his shoulder to give me a heated stare with dilated copper eyes and parted lips, then he'd shudder and turn back to focus on where he was walking.

When we found a private space for a campsite, Keyon became agitated over how to provide food. He really didn't want to leave me to go hunting and agonized over the decision.

"What if I wore your clothes while I stayed hidden?" I suggested, and he froze in his steps. "So I'd smell like you for a little while?"

He perked up, looked at me, and said, "That's a really good idea. Let's do that." He undressed and handed me his clothes to wear while he was gone. I changed into them quickly, noticing they needed to be washed and were a little sweaty but somehow still smelled agonizingly delicious.

I was slowly able to pick out the scents I'd been noticing for a while. I probably would have an easier time identifying the smells if I had more knowledge of things outside of what I'd been exposed to in the mansion. The scent on his clothes was something like... the smoky, spicy wood Adelmar had in his study. I think Adelmar called it... I couldn't recall. I think it started with an 'in.'

Insult? my beast suggested.

No...

Incest?

Oh my goddess, no! I shouted, appalled. *Why would you even th—*

Incense?

Yes! That's it, I exclaimed. *Thank you... I think.* I palmed my face, wondering if my beast's brain had gotten permanently damaged somehow. *I worry about you, nameless thing.*

The other scent I recognized more easily was ginger. Sometimes I'd steal little ginger candies from Adelmar's parties to give to Zosime later. She loved them. Oh, I sorely missed her and hoped the little hatchling was with her. I sighed, feeling melancholic for a moment when my ruminations were interrupted by a thunderous crashing in the woods.

There was a roar that I immediately recognized as Toast's, and I shuffled to hide behind a thick, sturdy tree. A terrifying screech echoed through the area, and a blue-black dragon stormed into our campsite. It went for my bag, shook it, and then threw it away savagely. It sniffed a couple times and spied me but was dragged viciously back by a copper dragon.

My mouth released a combination of a whimper and a squeal, but I was too scared to move. If I ran out and ended up under a rampaging dragon on accident, I'd be flattened. I shrieked at the top of my lungs when claws wrapped around my waist and ripped me away from the tree. There was a colossal lurch as the dragon that carried me took to the sky, and I was almost convinced that the forceful jerk was going to snap my neck. Pressure assaulted my ears as I was lifted higher, making me fear my head would burst.

I shrieked for Toast, not knowing if he could hear me. He was still fighting the blue-black dragon but looked up after I screamed. If he was fighting the dragon, who had snatched me? I twisted a little to find that a different dragon had absconded with me—smaller and glossy. No wonder I hadn't heard it during the din of the dragon fight.

Oh goddess, what do I do? I screamed to my beast, desperate for advice. If I made trouble for this dragon, it could just drop me. Would Toast be able to catch me in time? Had the other dragon been a planned distraction?

My beast remained silent, and I felt deeply betrayed. Not even a word of encouragement or comfort. I screamed and snapped, rising into a raging fit. I yelled every single curse word I'd heard Keyon say and pulled at the tiny scales on the dragon's hand, ripping off one at a time. I was too angry to think. I was furious at my own defenselessness. I was completely useless! Powerless! Fuck this!

The dragon raked at me to make me stop ripping its scales, and I received deep gashes down my arm. I screamed from the deep, hot agony and heard Toast roar just above us, muted slightly by the wind. The dragon carrying me lurched as Toast's jaws crunched down on its wing, and our ascent faltered. The dragon shrieked as it plummeted, letting me go while it scrambled to find any sort of wind resistance with its remaining membranes.

I was buffeted by the gale of my descent and screamed so sharply that I thought my throat would tear. My tears flew up instead of down, and I tried to make peace with my life in case I died. The treetops rose to my feet, and my body prepared for impact. My hair stood, my skin pebbled with terror, and my heart raced to get as many beats out before it stopped forever.

Like a sudden eclipse, I was surrounded by a warm cage before the snapping of branches told me I'd gone through the treetops. My cage thrashed, and I was thrown into it, hearing dirt, rocks, and debris scatter upon the final impact.

I sobbed, traumatized, and felt around the darkness for an exit. As the dust in the air cleared, I smelled the incense and ginger. Realizing I was in Toast's grip, I cried and clawed at his fingers to escape. I needed to see if he was ok! I could hear his breathing and his thundering heart, but what if he'd broken a leg or wing? What if he'd been impaled?

Toast's clawed fingers released me, and I found myself by his grimacing maw. He was on his side and panting. He made a couple muted, chuffing sounds that I barely heard over his strained breathing, and I launched myself at his snout, clutching and sobbing my eyes out, unable to believe we'd survived the fall.

"You saved me!" I wailed like a child and fell to my knees, holding onto Toast like my last breath. He let me stay like that until I stumbled back to get a look at him, rubbing at my swollen, burning eyes to clear them. "Are you h-hurt?" I asked breathlessly, frantically looking him over. There was blood but no injuries. He nodded and then shook it. I didn't understand, but... at least he didn't seem to be dying.

I collapsed by his head, holding myself with my arms and rocking. Toast's hard, scaly face leaned into my body in a nuzzle that I imagined was as delicate as he was capable of giving. He released a heavy exhale before his body finally relaxed. I turned into him and stroked his snout, spacing out and shaking now that the adrenaline was fading.

Toast angled to watch my trembling, and he pulled back to shift into Keyon, who rushed forward to collect me from the ground. I listened to his thrumming chest with a wobbly lip, and he began to jog—I assume—back to camp. How he could navigate was beyond me, and I just stared at the blurry, passing trees until Keyon shifted me to one arm to drag a dead deer with the other. Toast must have caught it before the attackers arrived.

He dropped the carcass by the fire and wrapped my blanket around me. Once I was bundled, he pulled me into his chest and stroked the back of my head. I rested against him, unable to do anything but let my lungs and heart work. It'd been too much. I still couldn't believe we were alive, or that it'd even happened.

"Toast saved me," I croaked out finally. My throat was almost gone from the earlier screaming and crying. "He was able to grab me, Keyon."

"And you healed him," he murmured into my ear and tightened his grip on me. "Healed us. Again."

"What was wrong with him?" I whispered with a cough.

"Lacerations. Fractures in his tail, hind legs, wings, and neck," he said quietly. I whined, sobbed once and tried to keep my lungs from hyperventilating. Poor Toast!

"I'm sorry," I croaked, pulling back to look at him with a devastated frown. "You got hurt because of me. It's too much to ask for someone who's not your mate."

"That you know of," he said kindly. It was kinder than I deserved. "And no female should be taken advantage of in her heat. You know I'd stop it if I saw it."

I nodded slowly at that. It was true. Keyon was a true guardian of the people. He was well suited to his role.

My stomach chose to growl in that moment, and Keyon squeezed me before standing up and grabbing the deer. "You must be starving. You hardly ate today," he said and began to butcher cuts for the fire. I nodded again and clutched the blanket for comfort while he worked naked. Guess he wasn't cold.

He hesitated a moment while he removed a cut from the deer's thigh. "I noticed, Elpis, that both dragons couldn't see very well. Their mobility suggested partial blindness. I guarantee it wasn't because it's night. I'm wondering if your beast had something to do with that," he said and glanced up at me while he cooked.

"I... don't know. She was very quiet. I felt pretty abandoned by her, to tell you the truth," I confessed, meeting his gaze for a moment. He nodded solemnly and looked thoughtful.

"Maybe she was busy helping instead of talking?" Keyon guessed.

"Maybe..." I sighed. "I'll try to ask her... if she ever starts answering my questions."

"She might not know the answers yet," he replied with a shrug. "She'll get there."

"Like Toast..." I said, unable to keep the small smile from spreading my lips. It pulled a big grin out of him, and his handsome face shone with excitement.

"Exactly," he said, handing me my meal and began working on his. I thanked him quietly. After a moment, his eyes unfocused before widening in surprise. He licked his lips and nodded, then met my gaze. Keyon's expression grew wary, uncertain, but the rest of his body relaxed with relief. His face was moving through so many expressions that I could only imagine what he was thinking. He must be talking to Toast.

Keyon's eyes widened a bit, and he took a deep breath. "I think he's ready to talk about it now."

Chapter 21

Sir Keyon

〰〰〰〰〰〰〰〰〰〰〰〰〰〰〰〰〰〰〰〰〰〰〰〰〰〰〰〰〰

"Are you sure, Toast?" I asked my dragon out loud for Elpis's benefit, since he'd be sharing with her as well. Elpis had moved closer to my side, wrapped in the blanket, and listened with rapt attention.

It's time, Keyon. Elpis… finally got through to me. I'll always regret that it took her abduction to do it, but at least it's over. She doesn't scare me anymore, Toast said tiredly. *I could have saved us so much grief had I just been able to trust her from the start. Yet no matter what, she came back to me. Healed me. Cared about me.*

Do you want me to share this with her? I asked him.

You should share all of this. I have nothing to hide, not after tonight. He sighed. I repeated his words to Elpis, and she scooted forward to lay her head on my knee, staring up at me with glittering, emotional eyes. I picked at my cooked meat and cleared my throat, preparing to repeat Toast's words to Elpis.

When I awoke on your eighteenth birthday, I began the process of catching up on your memories, familiarizing myself with you and getting to know the life that was waiting for me. I ... was distracted right away by a memory that had a curse on it, so I ended up watching that one first. Perhaps if I'd watched them in order as instinct told me to, I might not have been so traumatized, but we'll never know. It felt like luring a hatchling over to a stage with candy, only to end up making them witness an execution.

Toast occasionally paused to give me time to relay his story to Elpis, who seemed to absorb every word as though it was the most important tale to ever be told.

When you were a nine-year-old hatchling, Toast revealed, *there were a lot of rumors about you—us—being the next absolute dominant. The adults saw the signs... you were more mature than others, stronger and sharper. You didn't really know what it meant, so you just kept being yourself.*

It drew more attention to you over time. Mentors gave you extra attention, lots of hatchlings wanted to be your friend, and sometimes, the little females would fight over you.

I didn't remember much of my youth, and I certainly didn't recall being that popular, but I supposed I wouldn't if some of it'd been locked like Toast had said.

Toast continued. *Our father often took you with him to the castle when he was summoned by the king. You wanted to be the knight general too when you grew up, so he thought it'd be good to expose you to castle life once in a while. When he had to attend private meetings, he'd drop you off to play with the young princes and princesses. You liked it at first but grew to hate it after a couple weeks when the king's hatchlings found out that you might be the next absolute dominant.*

The princes Odalric and Cyneric were busier, and the little princesses constantly bickered over who got to play with you. Gisila, Odilia, and Asmin would steal you from each other, drag you around, and brag to anyone who'd listen that you'd be their future mate and the next king. You ended up begging our father to stop bringing you with him, and he promised he would after just one last day. Mother was still away as a field doctor, and he needed to find a nanny.

That day, Gisila dragged you onto a rooftop to hide from the other princesses. They eventually found you both, and the princesses got into a scuffle. When Gisila tried to bite you—thinking she could mark you like a stupid hatchling would assume—you jerked back and fell off the roof. You cracked your head open on the stone floor and fell unconscious. The princesses panicked and surrounded you, thinking you were dead because you were bleeding a lot. The stupid things didn't even notice your breathing or heartbeat.

Your memory didn't have any sight, but it had sound. I remember hearing them talk to another hatchling around the corner who told them to bury you. 'Hide the body,' he'd said. I'm pretty sure it was Cyneric now. He never seemed to like you much. I think he was jealous that you'd have a stronger dragon than him someday.

Cyneric? Fuck. That bastard had tried to get rid of me twice now. I needed to think more on this later.

Anyway... Toast sighed. *The princesses dragged our unconscious, bleeding body to the garden, where they started digging a hole. I'll never, ever forget what felt like hours of listening to little shovels digging your intended grave, Keyon. Never. I'll never forget how they spoke about you. Not as a person, but as an object. That it was a shame you'd died, not a tragedy.*

I'd been buried alive? Elpis's fingers dug into my thigh after I told her, and I reached down to stroke her hair while my heart pounded. Shit. This story was fucking insane.

Toast's tone became darker. *They apparently didn't do a very good job digging because the hole wasn't deep enough. They covered your head, though. I remember dirt pressing against your nostrils, and you ran out of air. The groundskeeper—we owe that male our life—found the princesses trying to pack the dirt over you, and he yanked you out of the ground. They tried to order him to secrecy, but he wasn't having it. He was old, curmudgeonly, and really didn't give a shit about anything other than saving a little hatchling who'd been buried alive.*

No wonder Toast had always encouraged me to say hi to him.

I remember hearing a commotion with the doctors—who were also all males, Toast said. *Your life was hanging by a thread from head trauma, blood loss, and asphyxiation. I'm certain that had you not been strong, destined to be the absolute dominant with me, you would have died. You were just strong enough to pull through with the help of the doctors.*

I heard them bring in a witch who was asked to isolate that year of your life and lock it. They didn't expect me to come along and bypass that magic. It wasn't strong enough to keep me away.

I heard the king visit you in the hospital with our father while you were still unconscious. He'd ordered his best doctors to treat you, but after that, he lied to Father about how we'd gotten hurt. He'd told him we'd climbed onto a human's horse without supervision and had gotten bucked off. Our father never believed it—said that not only would you never mount a horse without permission, you also knew better than to go near them. You knew horses were afraid of shifters.

Nothing traumatizing happened after that. The king had protected his daughters but took pity on you and spent a little time with you. He ended up liking you and decided you'd study with his best warriors and tutors if you still wanted to try and be the knight general when you grew up. The rest you should remember. That was all that the witch locked away, Toast said and went quiet so I could process the hard truth of his trauma.

After relaying the last to Elpis, I followed Toast into speechlessness. I rubbed my face with both my hands, hardly able to believe I'd almost died before I was old enough to hold a sword—not to mention at the hands of three little females. No wonder Toast had balked at flirting females. He kept flashing back to the princesses hurting me by trying to own me. That had been the first thing Toast had seen after waking. Father, the king, the groundskeeper, and doctors had all been males in the memory and cared for us. The only females in that memory had hurt us. Males were good. Females were bad.

"Toast had to carry that memory all by himself for years," Elpis said, sniffling. "Why'd he hide it?"

Because it was fucking terrible, and I didn't want him to relive it, Toast answered, and I relayed it back to Elpis. *If that meant suffering alone, so be it. Keyon was still a hormonal teenager, and I had no idea if he'd confront anyone about it. I thought I was protecting him.*

"Toast, can you come out so I can hug you again?" Elpis pled with a trembling lip. I scrubbed a hand over my face to hide a smile. That was fucking adorable. Toast laughed, sharing my sentiment.

Hug Keyon. I'll feel it, he said dryly. *I'm too tired to come out again. I need to rest.*

When I repeated his answer, Elpis stumbled to her feet and tackled me with a sniffly, whimper. She hugged me in her typical fashion—fiercely, unrelenting, and full of heart. I smiled and leaned into her, closing my eyes and savoring her affection. She was sweet, and my feelings for her rooted deeper by the day.

Elpis drew back and grabbed my face with both her hands. She looked deep into my eyes and said, "Toast, you are so brave to share this with us. I am so p-proud of you!"

She helped, Toast said tiredly. *All while suffering her own traumas.*

I relayed the message, and her eyes flickered, searching my own eyes. "Why do I feel like there's more to you both?" she murmured to herself.

Does she suspect? Toast asked. *Perhaps her beast is coming soon.*

I don't know, I replied, intensely distracted by Elpis's suspicious stare. *It's possible.*

"What could be more," I replied jokingly to diffuse her suspicion, "is some clothing. Pardon me, Elpis." I stood to get dressed, unable to stop thinking about everything Toast had shared. I might even get nightmares tonight.

I noticed with some interest that Elpis had changed into a nightgown. Though she looked tantalizing in it, I knew the gown wasn't as warm as her borrowed pajamas. We both could stand to find some water to clean up in and wash some clothes.

I ate more of the meat and cooked some for tomorrow. The stress had made me ravenous. I looked over at Elpis, who was checking her arm. "That healed fast too," she mumbled and glanced up at me. "I got a deep gash earlier. I suppose my beast is to thank for this…"

Gods, and I'd almost lost her today too. What a fucking day. My head was a jumble of thoughts and emotions, but I was starting to go a little numb. I needed to sleep, and I needed the comfort of my fated mate.

I marched over to kidnap Elpis like a barbarian, lifting her then reclining us both on the blanket. She didn't seem to mind in the least, especially when I trapped her under a wing per usual to keep her warm.

Sleep well, Toast… I need some time to sit on what you've shared. It's a lot. I'm sorry you were alone with it. Love you, big guy, I said sadly.

Good night, Keyon. Love you too.

Elpis then turned to face and stare sleepily at me. "I wish I had been there to kick their butts," she said, angling her face away to yawn. She rubbed sleepy tears from her eyes and grabbed my hand in hers, placing it between us. "I would have protected you."

I grinned lazily, barely able to keep my eyes open. "I'm sure you would have. I'd have let you march me around and call me your fated mate too," I mumbled, realizing a little too late that I probably shouldn't have said that.

I cracked an eye open and blew out a sigh. She'd passed out, and I sent a drowsy prayer to all the fuckin' gods, thanking them that she hadn't heard that.

I woke with the sunrise only to notice that Elpis had left her sleeping spot by my side. I scented her nearby, so I wasn't alarmed, just mildly concerned. When I walked around a corner, I found her curled up on the ground, wrapped in her blanket, and under a number of clothes to keep warm. She tilted her drained and exhausted gaze to mine, sporting rings under her eyes and blue lips.

"Elpis…" I chastised with crossed arms, "why did you sleep over here?"

"I didn't want to wake you," she mumbled and looked away in shame.

"Your heat? I thought we were past the embarrassment, Elpis," I said, feeling a little hurt that she'd pulled away from me last night.

"Toast just opened up to us. He was vulnerable. I didn't think it was right to ask," she said with a frown. I could tell she was getting cranky by her tone and disgruntled expression.

"So you just stayed out here and suffered in the cold?" I returned her frown. "I'm not happy with that."

"You're not the only one," she grumbled.

I sighed and scrubbed my face with my hands. "And the heat spike is over? You don't need relief anymore?" I asked, and she shook her head. "Ok, well, let's get some food in you. I'd like to let you rest more, but considering the attack last night, I'd like to get out of this area."

"That's a good idea…"

I moved to provide breakfast but froze and grinned when I realized something. "Elpis," I said in a playful voice, turning to look at her. Her head swung up to stare curiously at me. "Guess who finally gets to start carrying their own weight around here…?" I said in a sing-song voice with a broader grin. Her eyes lit up, and I think she knew exactly what I was going to say.

You're going to say it's me, aren't you? Toast said grumpily, but I knew it was an act.

"Toast!" I shouted, rushing to lift and spin her to make her laugh. I put her down and she wobbled.

"So he'll carry me?" Elpis asked excitedly. Her smile faltered when she added, "He won't... drop me like that other dragon did... right?"

"Not in a million-fucking-years," I said, gently poking right below her collarbone. "That means we'll reach our destination in a matter of hours today! Oh my fucking gods, it's miraculous."

Yes, yes. Truly a miracle, Toast said, continuing his dry charade.

Elpis, once again, didn't have much of an appetite, but she got ready in a blink. For the first time, I went to say bye to her before shifting into Toast. There was only so much of my affection I could hold back, and it took all of my effort to keep from kissing her. I approached her completely naked, wrapped her blushing form in a hug, and leaned into her hair to breathe in her scent. I dug my fingers into her back for just a moment before releasing and enjoying her bashful smile.

"See you in a while." I grinned and jogged away to shift into Toast. My colossal dragon ambled toward our female and eased into the gentlest nuzzle. He was so strong that his new fear was simply hurting her on accident. It gave him little solace that she was a fast healer.

Elpis clutched onto his snout and squeezed, laughing in delight at seeing Toast again. I felt my dragon's heart launch, and his joy washed over me like a warm bath. Yes, this was how it should be. Now we just needed her beast to awaken so Elpis could identify us as hers. We were so close. I could feel it.

Toast tried to pull away from Elpis, but she clung on, giggling mischievously as she became airborne by a foot. He shook her gently, snorting in amusement until she released him, landed, and picked up my bag. Toast carefully gathered her in his hands, crouched, and launched into the air past the treetops, flapping his wings to reach his preferred altitude.

Toast had caged her in his hands but left gaps so she could still look at the scenery. She'd screamed at first, then complained about her ears popping, but then her noises turned into laughter and gasps of amazement that we could barely hear over the wind. "Oh my goddess! We're so high!" she screeched in astonishment and laughed again, clutching Toast's fingers while she gaped at the scenery.

Toast was pleased as fuck because Elpis never stopped praising him and exclaiming about the view. He was going to be a smug bastard over this, and I couldn't be happier about that.

Imagine going from living in a cell to this, I said to Toast. *Her mind must be exploding.*

We'll take her flying whenever she wants. Those days are over, Toast asserted firmly.

Let's veer west a bit toward the river. I think she'd appreciate a chance to clean up, I suggested.

I have a better idea.

Toast found a possible stop higher up on the snowy section of the mountain range, and Elpis was beside herself when she saw where we were headed. "What's that?" she gasped. "Is that a pool? Why is it steaming?"

Toast descended and held Elpis in one hand after landing on a snowy ledge. He walked cautiously to the hot spring to test the temperature and acidity, but Elpis jumped recklessly out of his hold and ran toward the pool. "Toast, this is amazing!" she sang.

He panicked and shifted into me, not wanting to hurt her with his teeth and claws in an attempt to grab her. I raced after her, shouting, "Elpis, wait! Don't g—"

She jumped with a squeal, fully clothed, and landed in the steaming water with a giant splash. I jumped in after her and scrambled to find her in what I'd discovered was scalding water.

"Elpis! Where'd y—" I screamed, and my hand finally found a waist. I ripped her out of the water and held her up over it. "Fucking shit, Elpis!" I shouted, expecting to see burns all over her pale skin, but her flesh was flawless. "What?" I exclaimed, thinking I was imagining things. "Why are— Elpis, this water is almost boiling! You sh— I…" I was a babbling idiot, and she was just wrestling with me to get out of my grip.

"Nay... What are you talking about? I'm fine!" She showed me her palms and pointed to her clear face. "It's not that hot!"

"What?" I asked breathlessly, narrowing my eyes in confusion.

"I'm fine! See? I don't know what you're talking about," she complained and reached down to splash water at me. My jaw swung open, and my body froze while my eyes jumped from one section of her exposed skin to another. I slowly moved back and set her on the stone ledge of the hot spring.

"Elpis..." I said, still gaping. "This water is almost boiling. Your skin should be... you should have third-degree burns. That was... incredibly... stupid!" I was getting angry now that the fear was replaced by confusion. "I shouldn't have brought you here," I snarled. "Or I should have done a better job warning you, but you should know better than to just..." I snapped and turned away from her to stride farther into the pool. My wings exploded from my back, and I dug my claws into my palms, trying to quell my fury. I was so confused! I was pissed off!

Only dragons are heat resistant, Keyon... Toast murmured.

I know! I just... I don't... I was so flustered. *She... She just doesn't seem like a dragon, though! I thought for a minute I'd be dragging her dead—or near dead—body out of there! That scared the fucking shit out of me! My heart almost stopped!*

Me too...

"So can I come in?" Elpis's small voice asked. I turned to see her toying with the laces on her dress, frowning. "It'd be nice to get clean. Haven't bathed in a while..."

Test her, Keyon. There's snow nearby if it goes wrong, Toast suggested nervously.

I frowned and waded toward where she was sitting, not liking the idea too much. I frowned deeper in disapproval when I saw her dip her feet in the water. "Keyon?" she asked with a puzzled expression when I moved between her splashing feet and reached behind her ear to pull forward a long lock of her lustrous white gold hair. This would be the safest part of her to test.

"One minute, moonflower," I said gruffly, brought her lock to my mouth, and parted my lips to breathe out my coolest flame. The ends of her hair didn't blacken and sizzle into a tight curl like normal hair would. I increased the heat little by little until I was blowing a little blue flame over it. Nothing. Her hair was as shiny and healthy as ever, and Elpis was just watching with wide-eyed curiosity.

"Not possible..." I murmured. Even my blue flame burned other dragons. I looked up to meet her stunned gaze. "Clothes off, Elpis," I ordered and stood back to give her space. She furrowed her brows but pulled her dress over her shoulders and tossed her underclothes to the side. She shrugged and elevated her arms a little, not sure what I wanted her to do.

I cradled her arm and blew a small, cool flame across it. I looked up with raised eyebrows and asked, "Did you feel that?"

"It was warm," she said, peeping down to look at her clear skin. I blew a hotter flame over it and sent her the same question with my eyes. "Just warmer," she murmured, eyes glued to her arm. "I've never really tried to touch fire before, and Adelmar doesn't brand his slaves."

I nodded with a hum. Yeah, most people didn't go around sticking their hands into fire. I shifted nervously and blew an extended flame over her arm. That should have given her blisters... but it hadn't. "Felt nice," she said thoughtfully. I scrubbed a hand over my mouth and stared at her arm. Dare I? All signs pointed to her being able to handle it, but I was scared.

I licked my lips, swallowed heavily, sent a prayer to the Sun God, and then blew a burst of blue fire across her beautiful, soft skin. "Ooh!" she said, laughing. "That was a bit hot there!" I looked up in disbelief at her amused expression, my lips still parted from breathing fire.

"That's not supposed to feel 'a bit hot,' Elpis," I said carefully. "That should have..." I clenched my teeth, unable to believe what I was seeing. This wasn't possible. Not possible for a dragon, and there was no way she could be an absolute dominant either.

My mind shifted to our compatibility issue. If she could take my blue fire, could she carry my hatchlings? It was an exciting prospect, and it got my blood rushing, but I needed to see more to believe it.

I methodically worked from her hand to her shoulder, testing her resistance to my blue fire. I cautiously huffed some jets over her chest and belly, fighting arousal that surged in my groin when sweat dripped down her breasts.

I leaned against the ledge between her legs to breathe small flames slowly up her neck to her jawline. Nothing... she was just sweating. I blew gently over her ears, then her cheeks. I stopped there and just stared at her patient face. Her eyes were closed serenely, but her heart was drumming in excitement.

"Elpis..." I whispered, and her large, brown-sugar eyes fluttered open. I was speechless for a moment while I tried to make sense of her. "You can take my fire," I breathed in wonder. "You can take me at my hottest," I murmured and slid both my hands up her slender neck to palm her blushing cheeks. Her soft, pale lips parted, and her pulse bound into a racing gallop. "No one can do that, Elpis," I said, stroking her cheek lovingly with a thumb. She looked shocked, but—unless I was imagining it—she looked hopeful too.

She was so beautiful, but she glowed when she was full of hope. Her pale skin seemed to have fully recovered from her time in the cages. It was healthy. It was now smooth, shiny, and pearlescent, just as nourished as her white gold hair. The Sun God had been good to her. She looked to be in full bloom now, my moonflower.

"O-oh..." she said softly, barely above a sigh. Her face drew into a tender expression, and she asked, "Does that mean I could be pregnant?"

I sighed and leaned into her to press our foreheads together. I took a calming but ragged breath and clung to the comfort of the secret mate bond. If she was with hatchling, I hoped she could forgive me.

I pulled back to look her in the eyes again, still cradling her face. Her glittering eyes flickered between mine expectantly. "Yes... I'm sorry, moonflower. It's very possible," I answered apologetically and hoped she could feel my genuine regret.

What I wasn't expecting was the slow smile that spread across her face from my words. It was my undoing. My hands slid to cup the back of her head, and I crashed her lips into mine.

Chapter 22

Sir Keyon

I wasn't thinking. I was just feeling, and Elpis's reaction had yanked me up into the clouds. I pressed my lips hungrily into hers, unable to get close enough to my oblivious mate. She didn't know how happy she'd just made me that I'd found my fated mate and that perhaps we could have a family after all. I didn't know what she was, but I didn't care so long as she was happy, and she seemed very happy.

She returned my ardor just as fervently and opened her mouth at the same time I did to deepen our kiss. Her beast hadn't fully awoken, but we seemed to be in sync. Her hands landed on my ribs and slid around to grab my back just below my wings. I moved one of my hands to her lower back to press our chests together. Desire shot through me and escalated at the sensation of her soft, full breasts. The two hard bumps sandwiched between us said she was just as eager as me.

She pulled her lips from me and panted, her cheeks flushed from our heat. "K-Keyon... tell me, are there any other signs for fated mates?" she implored breathlessly. I tilted my head back to the sky and shut my eyes tight, feeling completely torn. There was one the coven mothers neglected to mention. Would there be any harm in sharing it with her?

Tell her, Toast encouraged. *I don't want any more lies between us and our mate.*

I sighed and said a silent prayer to the Sun God. He was right.

"There's one more," I said, glancing up at the cerulean sky for one last moment of peace, hoping everything would be ok. I licked my lips, swallowed heavily, and looked her in the eyes. "Fated mates have an enhanced sense of smell for each other. Everyone smells different, but fated mates can pick up more details of their mate's scent. Usually, it's a natural scent like… a wood or a plant… or sometimes it's something edible. It's heady and addicting; you can't get enough of it." I realized I'd made another mistake on that last sentence. I'd made it sound like I knew what it was like, and her eyes seemed to sharpen when I'd said it.

She tilted her head thoughtfully, and her stare became penetrating. Her fingers fidgeted on my back, and her palms slid across my chest before coming to a rest on my shoulders. I tried to look relaxed and clueless, but I was wound tighter than a coiled viper. She couldn't know. Her beast hadn't fully awoken.

Her beast seems to be exhibiting power, though. Could it be slowly leaking recognition? Toast asked worriedly. *I was expecting all this to happen at once…*

Me too… I replied, swallowing heavily again as Elpis studied me.

"Keyon," she said, glancing furtively away while she gathered her thoughts. "Why do you smell strongly of incense and ginger? It's not your soap, is it?"

I felt the blood drain from my face at her obvious line of thought. I became flustered and searched for a response, but I knew that—above all—I had to be truthful. "I… I didn't know that I smelled like that," I replied hesitantly. "My soap is just… regular soap…" My hands were getting sweaty, so I removed them from her skin.

Elpis shut her eyes tight and tapped one nail nervously on my shoulder. She took a deep breath, opened one eye in a squint, and asked, "You're my fated mate, aren't you?"

My breath came out in a rush. There it was. She'd figured it out and was coming to me to verify. She hadn't waited for her beast and had been too clever to miss the signs. Toast and I couldn't help doting on and spoiling her. She'd seen me reject female after female. She'd seen my eagerness to mate with her but my dedicated respectfulness in letting her choose. Perhaps she'd noticed how I scented her whenever she was close. Before we'd discovered our unique compatibility just now, the biggest tell might have been how I'd put her first over my duty as the knight general. Every choice I'd made had put her at the center of my priorities, and it had shown.

Elpis waited with bated breath, and her other brown eye opened, though her brows were still drawn in her vulnerability. When her eyes began to swim with unshed tears, I rushed out my answer. I couldn't keep her waiting any longer. She'd gone out on a branch, and she'd felt the wind blowing.

"Ah…" I nodded slowly, feeling guilty. "I am. I wasn't suppose—" I began to say, but she cut me off by kissing me more fervently than she had moments ago. I groaned into her lips, awash with more emotions than I could sort. She wrapped her arms around my neck and pulled me down over her. Legs still in the water, I propped myself up on my elbows to keep my weight off her but cradled her head with a palm. She deepened the kiss, and I slipped my tongue into her mouth to caress hers. She tasted wonderful, and I couldn't stop. I'd been wanting to kiss her for so long. So fucking long.

Her scent and pheromones had been building up since she'd removed her soaked dress, and I had a feeling that verifying our bond had triggered her heat. Her movements were becoming more urgent, and I felt my primal instincts stirring. I wanted to fight it this time, though. I wanted to savor the moment.

Her fingers slid up into my hair to muss it up, and her legs wrapped around my waist. She pulled her lips away and gasped,

"Keyon… what is this marking I'm hearing about?" She moved her lips to my neck, and I groaned, leaning my head into her and shuddering in pleasure. Little did she know she was very close to the marking spot.

"It's… Ahh…" I moaned between her kisses, barely able to talk. "How mates finalize the bond. It's like consummation an— Ah! V-very permanent. You grow closer… can feel each other's emotions and… Ahhnggg… mind-link," I groaned, feeling like I was about to explode. Every inch of me was thrumming with pleasure.

"Mind-link? What's that?" she murmured while nibbling my neck.

"Ahh fuck!" I hissed when she hit a particularly sensitive spot. "It's talking without words… like you do with your beast."

"I want that… let's do that," she asserted, kissing me again. My eyes widened.

"Are you sure?" I gasped when she released my lips again. I was surprised that she was already prepared to dive right into forever without her beast being fully awake. She gave an aggressive nuzzle and hummed a 'yes.'

Toast, what… what are we doing here, big guy? I asked feverishly, barely able to think straight.

She wants it, so give it to her, he replied simply.

But how does she mark us? She has no fangs… No canines… Nothing, I asked.

We'll have her do it later when she gets them, I guess? At least this way we'll always be able to find her.

Right… I could see the logic in that. It'd be a good safety measure too. I felt Toast crawl into the back of my mind to give us privacy.

I pulled from her lips and growled, "Alright, Elpis, I'll mark you, but you'll have to wait to mark me, and don't you dare rush your beast." She nodded and stared up at me through half-lidded eyes. "Fuck, Elpis, you're so beautiful!" I exalted in a moment of disbelief.

I crashed my lips into hers once again and dragged her hips to the edge of the pool. I was already aching to be inside her and couldn't wait a minute more. I braced myself on a rock and flexed my hips to push against her core, realizing very quickly that she didn't need any extra stimulation. I released her lips and leaned forward to slide the head of my cock past her folds to nestle against her threshold. I pushed slowly and pumped inch by inch until I was fully sheathed inside.

I groaned into her hair and kissed the top of her head. She replied with a soft moan and wrapped her legs around my hips once more. "You feel amazing," I whispered into her ear and kissed it. "So warm and ready. So soft yet so snug." She shivered below me, and I smiled at her response. Everything about this moment was surreal. Be it a dream or not, all I could do was go along with it. Happily.

I kissed her again, reverently this time. I swallowed her whimpers when I pulled my hips back to slide inside again. Slowly, I retreated and invaded, enjoying gliding through the shape of her channel and the tightness of her walls. Even her core was pure poetry, and had I been a touch more emotional, perhaps I would have wept. When they said a fated mate was made for you, there truly was no denying it. She was my utopia, unequivocally.

She squirmed beneath me as I rolled my hips, and I released her mouth to ask, "What is it?" I brushed our lips together while I waited for her response.

"M-more! Male... please! I want you!" she whined and arched in her frustration.

"But you have me, my female..." I rumbled into her ear. "The goddess gave me to you. She gifted you a blue-breather... and only you can satisfy his appetite." I nibbled her ear, and she began to tremble from head to toe. Her mind and body were whisked away into the wild, and nothing gave me more pleasure than feeding her feral mind. Teasing her senses was as addicting as breathing her scent. "Best brace yourself, female. My appetite is growing." I thrust my cock into her to make my meaning clear.

I straightened up, gripped her hips firmly, and began ramming into her sex. She arched her back, like her body was missing mine and was searching for me. I snarled at her erotic display, trying not to lose myself to my instincts with her writhing, sensual form and rocking breasts. I wanted to remember this joining as clearly as possible.

I barely noticed the cold mountain wind or the scalding water I was sloshing everywhere. All I could think of was my Elpis and how she'd soon be forever mine. My heart swelled at the thought, and I had to snarl out a breath of blue fire to vent both my physical and emotional heat. I shuddered with arousal. I felt more ready by the second to mark her; my fangs itched like mad, already extended and ready to claim.

I hooked my arms under her knees and pulled her up to face me. "Elpis," I said, kissing her lips and her cheeks to bring her to the present with me. "Elpis, are you ready?" I groaned and tried to meet her gaze. She shook her head and blinked a couple times to clear her mind, gripping my shoulders to steady herself.

"Mmm, what?" she asked, coming out of her haze.

"Are you ready?" I asked urgently and started rolling my hips into her clit. She gasped, and her channel clenched deliciously around me, making me grunt and turn my head to hiss out some fire. Fuck, she was like a vise.

"Y-yes!" she shouted, panting and red-faced. She whimpered under my grinding pelvis and melted with every rub. I spurred into her, gasping and growling to give her the gift of pleasure. Her hands dug into muscle, her back arched slowly, and her stomach clenched. I continued at the same pace in speed, knowing she was almost there, and I just needed to stay diligent.

Her mouth opened soundlessly for a moment, then let out a furious wail. She rolled against me as she climaxed, shuddering violently. I was not far behind her. I slammed her to my chest and roared out a burst of blue fire, bottoming out and filling her with my seed.

I wrapped us with my wings, clamped onto the soft tissue between her neck and shoulder, and sank my fangs in to permanently mark her. She screamed this time and alternated between grabbing at and punching my shoulders in her thrashing. I felt her second orgasm hit her, and I nearly collapsed as she continued to pulse around me. I let my venom sink in a moment longer before I relaxed my jaw and pulled my teeth from her.

There it was. I stared at the mark on her shoulder, struggling to divide my attention between my ejaculations and her wound. I gasped when I spent my last drop and eased her down so I could rest a moment over her. The puncture marks never left my sight. I was terrified that if I turned away, she'd heal again, and our bond would be incomplete.

Her emotions swelled into me, and I was unprepared for how hard it hit. She was in euphoria, unable to do anything but exist in the moment and feel pure happiness. I bit my lip through it, tortured by the distraction. I wanted to enjoy this moment, but I was anxiously waiting. Elpis healed fast... would this heal?

"Keyon?" Elpis asked breathlessly. "What's wrong?"

"I'm waiting... I'm worried your mark will heal and disappear," I answered, swallowing hard. I was repeatedly holding my breath and exhaling sharply. The wait was killing me. If the bond didn't take, I didn't know how else we could do it.

Please don't reject my venom, I begged. As if it heard me, the angry red swelling around the puncture marks began to fade, and the bite marks scabbed around the border. It seemed to stop healing at that point, and the dead skin flaked off, like her body was sweeping it clean.

The scars were there, and I stared at them. I didn't feel anything change. I could still feel Elpis's emotions, which were getting more anxious by the second. After another minute, I just collapsed on her chest and allowed my vision to blur from moisture and relief. I couldn't believe it.

"We did it, Elpis..." I said, dripping tears like a silly hatchling. They beaded and streamed down her soft, sweaty skin. "The bond took."

Elpis

I held a lightly crying Keyon to my chest and felt an unimaginable surge of completion. No longer would I ever feel like I couldn't get close enough to him. I had a part of him within me; I could feel it. It settled like a brave sentry, posted in my soul to watch over me.

For the first time, not only did my body welcome poison, but it also celebrated it. The venom was exactly where it should be, and my body knew to nurture it, allow it to change parts of me for my protection. It knew my fated mate had claimed me and accepted all he had to give.

"Don't cry…" I said to Keyon, massaging his rippling back affectionately. "Don't cry, sunflower."

"Can you"—he sniffed, and I felt another tear drop down my chest—"please pick a different endearment?"

I laughed from a deep, joyful place in my heart and squeezed him in a tight hug. A small chuckle escaped from his throat, and I beamed. It felt good to make my mate laugh.

My mate… I was so happy. Keyon was the best male.

"Ok, I promise I'll try to think of a better one. Sunflower is just so good, though." I laughed again and tried to reach for my bag while he was still on top of me. He sighed reluctantly, kissed between my breasts, and pulled out, letting me grab what I needed to bathe. Every movement he made had me sighing in pleasure.

I tended to him first, feeling an immense sense of gratitude for everything he'd given me. "It's a world of a difference," I said thoughtfully while massaging his scalp with shampoo, "to go from belonging to someone to belonging with someone."

"I can't even imagine," Keyon replied gently.

"How long have you known?" I asked him, and his muscles became particularly rigid. "I won't get mad… I can't imagine Toast made it easy."

I made it as difficult as I possibly could've, a new voice said in my head, and the shampoo bottle I was holding went flying. It was deep, warm, and gravelly. Each word sounded like it had been born from a furnace and grated across scales. *Sorry, mate. Didn't mean to startle you.*

"Fiddlesticks, that scared me! By the Sun God's fire, is that you, Toast?" I gasped and Keyon looked over his shoulder to smirk at me.

It's a one-way link until you figure out how to mark us, so talk out loud when you wish to speak to me, he informed politely.

"Oh, that's great... actually. I really don't want you hearing the nonsense that comes out of my beast at random," I replied with wide-eyed relief. "I'm so happy to hear you, Toast!"

Keyon dunked under the water to rinse and came out to hover over me. He palmed the back of my head and pressed his lips to mine, massaging my lips sensually with his warm ones. My stomach did a somersault and fluttered with tiny dragons.

"I had no idea kisses could be so good," I murmured against his lips. I'd been forced to kiss so many... I'd hated every single one. Even though I knew it was Keyon, I occasionally had to open my eyes to make sure. So many bad memories—like with my breasts.

He narrowed his entrancing copper eyes. Could he feel my unease? "You will only be kissing me from now on," he asserted, stroking my parted lips with a rough thumb.

I leaned into him, wishing my body didn't feel my memories. Now that I knew the pleasure of a good male, the bad memories felt so much more violating.

"I'll make you forget about them, Elpis. I'll work every day to wipe those bastards from your mind so you can be free of them," he said, crushing me against him. I felt him pull back, and he leaned to whisper into my ear, "I'll kiss you, worship you, and mount you until all you can think about is me."

I shuddered, and he nuzzled my cheek affectionately, then gently began to wash me.

Wash them from my mind like you do my body, I pleaded silently.

"Since the dance," Keyon said minutes later while lathering my hair.

"What?" I asked.

"That's how long Toast knew. He knew when you brushed against my hand at the mansion. He didn't tell me until after I removed your chastity belt," he clarified and brushed the tangles out of my hair with his fingers.

"You mean after I found you moaning my name with your fist around yourself?" I asked innocently.

"I said 'Elpis?'" he mumbled the question to himself. "I'm not ashamed..."

"I wish I had known," I said softly as we finished up washing. "I was so confused about what we were," I confessed. "It was painful."

Tell her, Keyon, Toast said, and I gave him a curious look.

Keyon opened his mouth, looked away in thought, and then said, "The witches... also wanted you to come to the conclusion yourself when your beast woke. They're worried you'll push her to come out, which could hurt her or destroy your bond. You must be careful with her, Elpis. Promise me you will!" He became more impassioned as he spoke.

I balked at the warning. I had no idea that my connection to my beast was that tenuous. Keyon's gaze intensified, and he reassured me by saying, "I'm not going anywhere. You have all the time in the world to mark me, ok?" His brows drew in as he stroked my face, overflowing with worry.

Also, I still can't look at another female without gagging... so... Toast rationalized.

I burst into a sharp laugh at Toast's comment but sobered and said, "I promise." Keyon relaxed and brushed his wet hair aside. I added, "I yearn to feel complete, but I'll be patient."

"We're complete no matter what, moonflower," he whispered and lifted me up to meet his starved lips. My poor male had gone so many years without a female's touch; I was excited to make up for that lost time.

I wrapped my legs around his narrow hips, and he walked us out of the pool that should have cooked me. He grinned wickedly when he set me down and dried my body with his fire. I squealed when he lingered a little too long on my breasts, but he just chuckled and moved around to finish drying my hair. I snorted with delight and good humor when I looked at the dry but frizzy strands.

"Ready to go, moonflower?" he said once I was dressed. I nodded excitedly, and he claimed my lips for one last heated kiss before backing up and shifting into Toast. I waved at my favorite dragon, the other half of my fated mate, and he snorted affectionately. Bracing myself, I stepped carefully onto his fingers, and he scooped me up before launching into the air.

Flying was terrifying while simultaneously being the most wonderful experience in the world. I wasn't supposed to be so far from the ground, but I knew my mate would take care of me. I winced as my ears popped and shouted my question to Toast. "Is my head going to explode? This happened last time!"

He released a chuff-like noise and said, *No, but I should have been more careful on my ascent. I will go slower next time, mate. I'm sorry. Dragons are not as sensitive to altitude change. I forgot. Yawning helps to clear the pressure. Try that.*

I breathed a sigh of relief and yawned while staring at the scenery. It took a little while, but sure enough, it worked. Less distracted now, I noticed that the ground was starting to look a little marshy, and fog was crawling over massive hills that were just small enough to not be considered mountains. Farther into this new area, any trees that remained appeared quite dead.

"It seems that the Sun God does not favor this spot," I shouted to Toast, and I barely heard his rumbling growl.

Perhaps this place does not wish for the Sun God to see its secrets, he said forebodingly.

We know a witch lives here that Gunel seems to dislike, Keyon's voice said. *Who knows what else might be lurking.* Despite the dark warning, my heart warmed; I'd forgotten he could speak from Toast! Keyon hummed a chuckle, and I realized he may have felt my excitement. This new bond was very intriguing.

Her house is going to be tucked around the next hill, Toast, Keyon said with an edge to his voice. Toast and Keyon were silent for several minutes, and I began to get nervous when Toast's claws flexed slightly, cutting off my view of the scenery.

Mate, Toast said anxiously, *we are scenting dragons in the area. They may not be hostile, but they have a smell we're unfamiliar with. We'll take a detour to avoid them, especially since you're still in heat.*

I patted and rubbed his palm in acknowledgement since I didn't know if he'd be able to hear my response. I tried to stay calm, not wanting to overwhelm my mate with my fear.

I'm starting to think flying straight here was a bad idea, Keyon murmured over the mind-link. *Elpis, the ride might get a little rough. Hold on to one of Toast's fingers.* I squeezed my hands between Toast's fingers to wrap my arms around one, then sent a desperate prayer to the Sun God, hoping that He could pierce the fog to watch over us.

There was a massive lurch, and gravity shifted dramatically. I was disoriented for a moment, and it seemed like my dragon had turned left, then shot straight up with several pumps of his wings. I whimpered but tried to stay calm for the benefit of my mate. Being kept in a miserable state of suspense chipped away at my body and mind, not knowing when Toast would switch directions, and I found myself nauseated.

It's ok if you have to throw up, mate, Toast said. *I will endure it. I care for you.*

As it was Toast, the sentiment was... shockingly generous, and I definitely had a feeling that my stomach wouldn't tolerate the blind ride much longer. What was worse, though, was not knowing what was happening. Keyon and Toast were quiet for long stretches of time, and my anxiety spiked beyond my control when I heard roaring through the wind.

"Don't leave me in two darks," I begged at the top of my lungs. Could they hear me? "Tell me what's happening. I can't bear not knowing!"

They have King's Poison, Elpis. We are trying to avoid them, but we've never seen it ejected like breath. Something isn't right with these shif— Keyon's update was cut off when Toast made a sudden turn and roared. I realized that my mate wouldn't be able to use his front claws because of me, and I became deathly afraid for him. I fought the fear viciously, focused on Toast, and sent all the positive energy I could muster.

I'll stir up essence... move blinders, my beast announced tiredly. Her voice startled me. *Can extend to hot bread.*

You did this before, I said. *Help me help our mate!*

Easier now... with marking, she said falteringly. *Tiring. Not quite awake... I try...*

How does it work? I asked, trying not to panic at the wasted time talking.

Shine to shame. Poisoned heart just as blind... is how.

But how do we give it? Did we already do it? I sensed that she was gone and yelped at a series of lurches and snarls. Clutching at Toast's finger, I shut my eyes tight and tried to give him all my hope and what I thought could be brightness. I thought about the Sun God and imagined myself as Him, just for a moment.

Shine, shine, shine! I begged, having no clue if any of this was making a difference. There was a huge impact that stunned me, and I heard a number of pained roars. Then Toast descended, and I screamed.

Chapter 23

Elpis

"Toast? Keyon?" I shrieked. There was no response, just small lurches as Toast struggled with something. I couldn't help it; what was left of my composure shattered. I screamed at the top of my lungs as we fell, having no idea how far we were from the ground. I couldn't take this again! Not again!

Toast seemed to right himself and flap haphazardly until we came to a brutal, rolling crash. I fell inside his grip and was knocked back into his hard palm, dazed and disoriented. Crawling back to my feet, I wobbled and tried to balance myself, but everything whirled. I felt around the back of my aching head and drew my fingers forward to find blood. Oh gods.

I couldn't hear Toast breathing, and I wasn't sure if I was feeling a pulse beneath me through his thick skin and scales. Was Toast ok? How badly was he injured? I tried to push against his claws to get out, but my progress was slow, torturous. When I finally pried his fingers apart, I whimpered at the sight of my unconscious—but still breathing—mate. My eyes swam with tears; it pained me so deeply to see him hurt.

I squeezed out to find a number of dragons landing around us. Most of them seemed off-balance and ended up running into their comrades, who snapped irritably at them. Despite the anxiety that overtaxed my heart, I was deeply and bitterly pleased to find most of them nursing blackened burns that exposed muscle and bone. Many had torn or broken wings, and a handful were missing limbs outright. My mate would have slaughtered this Inferno under normal conditions.

In that moment, with how they all stared at me, I knew I was going to be taken. As one male approached, I did the only thing that came to mind, which was to hastily leave whatever I could of myself for my mate. I bit my arm until I drew blood, then wiped it on Toast's hand. I yanked out some hair and draped it as well. I even spat. It was a stupid idea, and I doubted any of this would heal him, but I had to try something, and my brain wasn't working particularly well after that impact.

"Go away!" I shrieked mindlessly at the male and the surrounding dragons. I couldn't leave Toast and Keyon's side! What if they killed him while he was unconscious? I ran pathetically around Toast to avoid the approaching shifter, keeping what I hoped was a healing hand on my dragon—loathing how weak I was. Once I was grabbed, I kicked, shrieked, and headbutted, but he didn't loosen his grip. He didn't seem stable, though, and even tripped a number of times.

He threw me roughly toward a dragon who caged me in a blackout grip like Toast had. "You touch him again, and you're dead!" I screamed as loudly as I could, going out of my mind with fear and fury. "Do you hear me? I will kill you all!" They were all unnervingly silent and gave no reply.

I bared my teeth and kicked at my living cage, my blood boiling in my heart and ears. I could only hope they were too blind and injured to focus on Keyon and would just head home. I tried to feel which way the dragon lurched and took my best guess.

"They took me north!" I screamed to my unconscious mate. He couldn't hear me... not through his forced sleep and my living cage.

"North! North! North!" I repeated the shriek until I felt him completely disappear. I didn't even know I could feel his presence until it was gone. I clutched at my heart, already aching from emptiness.

I screamed in rage once more and felt around for anything that could hurt this dragon. I bit flesh and yanked at scales, reckless in my fury. My cage lurched as the dragon shook me around in its grip to punish me. I grabbed my head and groaned as my body surrendered. Stumbling over the uneven floor of fingers, I threw up and fell unconscious.

A violent jerk woke me, and I found myself being slung over a shoulder, the impact stealing a lungful of air. Winded, I tried to smack the head of my kidnapper but could only manage a weak flop. Gods, my head was killing me. I looked down to note that the male holding me had four feet. No, that couldn't be right. I tried to focus my vision, then gave up, closing my eyes outright. I was too dizzy. My stomach also hated this position.

His stomping on dirt turned into stomping on stone. A door grated open, and his steps multiplied into echoes. I peeked through my bravest eye to find us walking down a dark hall with stone walls. Even with my cloak, it was uncomfortably cold and damp. Little clusters of moss grew greedily around patches of light that broke through the damaged ceiling, and I could hear the occasional drip of water plip and echo. This place looked like it'd been in its prime far too long ago.

The hall opened into a colossal circular chamber. Murmurs and scraping told me that there was a crowd wandering over to my kidnapper. "You're back, Meino," a male said in a sharp, forceful tone. "Was the lead accurate?"

I scrabbled at his shoulders when he hoisted me over them, but he still tossed me painfully onto the stone floor. I yelped and was tempted to rub my bruised bottom but not in the company of these loathsome strangers.

"Who are you bastards?" I yelled furiously at a giant dragon but quickly realized that it was an enormous stone statue. Too mad to be embarrassed, I wobbled to my feet to try to deliver my glare to the right person.

"They removed her collar," Meino said. "She may be ruined. The beast is still asleep, though."

"Don't ignore me!" I protested and turned to punch Meino for calling me ruined, but he just brushed my fist away like I was an annoying hatchling. I tried to kick his shin, but he just held me at arm's length, which was possibly longer than my legs. The more I felt like a harmless toy, the angrier I became.

"I can see that," the sharp voice remarked, ignoring me, and I squinted to watch a different dragon-shifter approach. I bared my unimpressive teeth, and the shifter studied me for a moment. I glared right back, willing my vision to try to focus on his features. Short grey hair and four small black eyes—no, two. Two beady black eyes beneath two straight brows. Those were eyes that didn't look like they ever missed anything, and they unnerved me.

The nostrils on his large, aquiline nose flared, and he shuddered. "She's in heat. Get her into a cell before one of our own tries to rut her, please. When is Mantegazz arriving?" he snapped, turning to face another shifter. My blood turned cold at the word 'rut,' and I shrank into myself, no longer wanting to draw attention.

"Someone's fetching her now. Should be an hour," they replied tersely. Two males grabbed a wrist each and dragged me from the room.

"I'll get the kit," a different shifter said from the large room while I was being forced down a new hall.

I had many things on the edge of my tongue that I wanted to yell, but my life as a slave came rushing back to me when I saw the cell. I became paralyzed by fear, knowing that the 'safety' I'd experienced at Adelmar's mansion wouldn't repeat here. I wasn't even remotely protected now. Death and rape were two very real possibilities. This place was going to make me fight for my life.

Did I want to tell them I wasn't a precious virgin anymore? No, they'd just kill me like the collar had intended. If it made me useless, I'd still pay with my life. I snapped out of my paralysis and struggled against the two males' grips. When I started kicking, one of them lost his patience and slapped me into a daze. Then they pushed me into the cell, and I fell into a pile of hay.

I fought tears and bared my teeth in frustration. I turned to watch the males depart but shrunk away when three more rounded the corner. The one in the middle had a case, and I paled when I saw that the other two were carrying large jugs and some clear tubing.

They're going to kill me, I thought and crawled into a corner of the cell to vomit. *Drained dry.*

Soon, my beast mumbled.

Soon is too late, I thought sadly to myself. I didn't know if it was worth talking to her again. My hope was drying up, and that alone made me feel like dying.

I still couldn't give up and did everything I could when they opened my cell. I kicked, spat, wrestled, and headbutted. I bit and screamed, but none of it mattered. I was weak, and I hated myself for it. Perhaps they'd allowed me to thrash as much as I did because it sucked the fight out of me. I lay panting on the hay, watching tearfully as they slit down my wrist and shoved the tube in to catch the red blood that poured out in a heavy stream.

After about fifteen seconds, my body pushed out the tube, and the skin healed shut. I laughed bitterly at their frustrated faces, and they cut into my skin again. I gritted my teeth harder and wailed from the agonizing incision. "Tell Franco this will take a while," the one placing the tube said. I froze at the name.

"Franco?" I asked after I caught my breath. "Was the one who spoke out there Franco?" Franco, the notorious slave trader, and the purchaser Adelmar risked pissing off to save me as a child? I guess it verified that these were the same people. How patient they'd been for me. How important was I to them? What was I to them?

The male didn't answer. Like the rest, he ignored me like I was an inanimate object. "If you're going to kill me, grant me a dying wish, and at least tell me why you're killing me," I begged sluggishly. "Please... what harm would it do?" Fighting aggressively wasn't working, so I'd try a different approach—that is, if I could function through the shock. If I couldn't tug at their heartstrings, then I'd resort to another tugging activity I'd rather not bring back into practice.

The male was quiet for a moment, then muttered to himself, "I don't need to disclose anything to an ingredient." I frowned at being called something so degrading, though I'd prefer insult to injury any day.

He cut my wrist again to insert the tubing, cursing irritably at having to redo it every fifteen seconds. I winced at the pain every time, and even though I knew I could push out infection, the tubing hadn't been cleaned in front of me, and I grimaced at the thought of something dirty getting shoved under my skin.

I changed my tactic, giving in to my last resort. "Nay, you don't, but you could disclose something to an ingredient with breasts and a practiced hand..." I breathed, looking up at him through my eyelashes. I knew not to lay it on too thick. I tried to sound innocent and hesitant. Males had always seemed to respond well to it.

"Heard she was a pleasure slave..." one of the other men said in a low voice.

"Franco said not to touch her," the third said, but he didn't sound adamant. The male collecting my blood dropped the tubing and cursed again. Making my move, I reached to brush my free hand against his thigh.

"Can someone please hold her down? She's in heat, and I can't fucking focus." He growled while cutting my wrist again. I looked over at the jug, ignoring the two idiots bumping into each other to help hold me still. There was only an inch of blood in there. At least my body was fighting an internal battle to preserve my life, and I decided to save my energy to let it do just that. It bought me time. There had to be something else.

Very soon, my beast said in my head, and I wondered if that was soon enough, after all.

The male continued to struggle with collecting my blood and eventually sat back, glaring at his supplies. He looked at my other wrist and said, "If I keep opening that other vein, can you two collect it in that second jug?" The one holding my other wrist nodded and was handed some tubing. Both of my wrists were slit, and they started draining both.

I shuddered at the discomfort and coldness, and my eyes watered from pain and panic, but I tried to hold back my tears. My body needed all the water that was left. I doubted that even I could heal from nothing. Soon, I broke into a cold sweat, becoming overwhelmed with pain and shock.

Several hours passed, and they'd collected a decent amount, but it didn't seem like nearly enough to kill me. "What is your progress?" a sharp voice asked, and I gazed bleakly over to see Franco standing by the cage. He was quiet. I didn't like that.

"Slow," the male spat bitterly. "She heals too fast. Her body just spits the tubing out."

"And you're resisting her heat?" he intoned harshly.

"Yes, Franco," he said with an aggrieved sigh. "She hasn't spiked yet, but it's getting worse. I'd like to see you focus with an erection."

"I see you have at least enough for Mantegazz to make a first attempt. You're all dismissed for the night. Wait until her heat passes. I'm not risking it," Franco ordered dispassionately.

"Attempt at what?" I asked tiredly, doubting I'd get an answer. As expected, Franco turned and strode off while the three males gathered their gear, hurrying to leave. No answers. I sighed and shivered from the chill of blood loss. Then I crawled into the hay pile but backed out when I smelled mold. I hated the musty stench and ended up settling on top of the drier fodder.

"Attempt at losing their humanity," a familiar voice croaked from the neighboring cell. I let out a bizarre combination of a yell and a squeal, nearly startled out of my skin. Still though, I was struck by disbelief, and I shuffled toward the voice, unable to trust my ears alone.

"L-Lord Adelmar?" I whispered, grabbing the iron bars with both fists. In the next cell, he was just a lump of clothes in another pile of hay. His familiar chuckle hit my ears, and he sat up awkwardly. Something was wrong with the way he moved.

"I'm deeply disappointed to see you here, little sunrise. I thought I'd left you in good hands," he said with a shake of his head. It was him, my old owner. He was in poor shape, looking wan and bruised.

"I came to destroy them," I muttered, rattled by his appearance. "I wasn't expecting an entire crowd of murderers, though. Why are you here?"

"Oh sunrise, that is so stupidly cute." Adelmar snorted with derision. "I doubt you're alone, but I won't pry. No, I'm here because Franco hates me, and he needed someone he hated."

"Why's that?" I asked, too curious to be insulted. Adelmar held up a shoulder, but the entire sleeve of his coat was empty. I gasped and fought roiling nausea. "The bastard took your arm?"

"Indeed, he did," Adelmar uttered darkly, staring at his missing appendage. "We're both ingredients, it seems." He sighed. "Witches are so troublesome."

"Yes, I've met your Gunel," I replied. "She's the one who told me to find the witch here." Adelmar's eyes lit up at the mention of the woman.

"Ah, my dear Gunel. How is she these days?"

"Cranky," I said shortly, and he laughed quietly before falling into coughs. "She told me what you did," I added and wiped my hands nervously on the bars. He sobered and tilted his head.

"I imagine she did," he murmured but didn't add anything.

"I won't ever forget the torture you put me through, but I will thank you once for saving my life," I said, hating the words as they left my mouth, but they needed to be said. I could move on now… if I survived this place.

"Apparently only saved it for a little longer than they'd originally planned," he replied darkly.

"Why'd you sell me, then, if I was so safe at your mansion?" I asked bitterly.

"Oh, you weren't. Franco's men had been sniffing around, and I knew it was only a matter of weeks before they found you," he answered. His willingness to share emboldened me to ask more questions.

"But to a male? Gero would have killed me with that curse! You knew about it!" I accused.

"Oh please." Adelmar scoffed. "I did my research. I knew that the famously good-hearted and very chaste knight general would take you in, especially when I dangled you in front of Gero. At first, I thought it was good fortune that Prince Cyneric offered to connect us with a deal. Unfortunately, Sir Keyon and I'd been played."

I giggled and rested my head against the bars. Perhaps I was going mad, but I couldn't stop laughing. My nerves were shot.

"What's got you so amused, sunrise?" Adelmar inquired, curious.

"He's"—I gasped and whispered between bursts of laughter—"my fated mate." I snorted and smacked my hand against the bar, convulsing with amusement. Adelmar started laughing with me, and we both succumbed to madness.

I pulled my long hair back and showed him the mark Keyon had left, snorting again. Adelmar sobered and waved at me. "Put that away!" he hissed. "Don't let them see that!" His gaze cut to the corner of the room as he listened for footsteps. When none came, he relaxed and pressed his lips together.

I crawled back to the hay and lay down on it again, but I was starting to feel warm. I knew what that meant, and I covered my face with my hands.

"You need to try to keep your wits about you," Adelmar warned quietly. "If they discover that scar, they'll use you and kill you."

I didn't reply, but I'd do the best I could. I couldn't afford to go wild here. I buried my bottom half in the damp hay, grimacing at the state of it but accepting the solution.

Need food, my beast demanded.

There's no food, I replied miserably, resting my head in my arms.

Dry grass has food for blood. Make more.

Can I even digest that?

Don't know... better than not. Need something. Anything.

I picked up a twig of hay and wrinkled my nose. The fresher blade smelled sweet, but I doubted it'd taste very good. I popped it in my mouth and chewed slowly. It was bland and difficult to soften, but I worked at it. I grabbed another piece and ate that too, hoping I'd be able to digest it. It was less edible than a salad but more edible than a stick, so why not try.

I ate as much as I could stomach and moved my focus to my heat. I pressed my thighs together and pushed my hands against my sex, as if I could keep it from sharing my state. I yearned for Keyon to relieve me, but that only made me think of how I'd been torn from him. Was my mate ok? My heart ached fiercely, deeply, wishing we were safe at the cabin together and that none of this had happened.

I squeezed my eyes shut and writhed in the hay. I wanted to take my clothes off, but I resisted. When my mind called for a male, I just focused on Keyon. He was my male. He was my only male.

"Wow!" another familiar voice exclaimed, accompanied by slow footsteps. "They were not exaggerating." My dread sank deeper into horror, and I grimaced, gagged. I could practically hear his greasy double chin wobbling.

"What are you doing here, Gero?" Adelmar asked in mild surprise. "I thought you hated Franco. He was your biggest rival."

"Oh, I do. I hate the bastard, but you know what they say about keeping your enemies close." Gero chuckled. I suppressed a moan and turned toward the wall, unable to look at the disgusting creature outside of my cell. I could barely focus on the conversation he was having with Adelmar. I was getting a headache on top of my heat spike.

"I heard what he was cooking up and simply had to pay a visit."

"Surprised he let your ugly mug in," Adelmar muttered.

"Well, I mean, I did tip him off about Elpis's location," Gero said smugly. I scowled into my fist. How'd he know? When had we gotten near him? "Who better to put down the knight general and catch her for me?" I stiffened at his words. What?

"Catch her for you? You can't possibly be thinking he'd give her to you," Adelmar snapped.

"Oh, I don't want to take her away. I just want to take her," he leered. "I volunteered to check her purity since I was the only one familiar with her. The guards should be at my guest chambers in about thirty minutes to escort me here." He snorted with laughter and said in a sing-song voice, "I got here early."

"Franco won't only kill Elpis, Gero, but he'll kill you too," Adelmar warned.

"No, I'll be long gone. I get to taste what I've been craving and ruin Franco's plans! This might be the greatest moment of my life!"

Adelmar laughed darkly. "Not a high bar, especially for a dragon."

Keys jangled in the lock, and I jerked into a sitting position. I was panting and burning up, but Gero revolted me down to my very soul. I wouldn't let him have me.

"Scream, Elpis!" Adelmar shouted, and I opened my mouth to do that, but Gero lunged at me. I stumbled out of his way and bashed into the cage wall I shared with Adelmar. I shrieked as Gero rushed again, but I felt Adelmar's hand snake through the bars and push me to the side. His clawed hand snagged Gero's coat, who snarled and shrugged off the garment, not wanting to waste time wresting it from the other prisoner's grip.

When I screamed again, it was due to a sudden, cracking pain in my skull. Gero cornered me as I staggered and moved his hand to cover my mouth. I struggled to orient myself through the agony so I could defend myself. A piercing shriek in my head had me lashing out in reflex, and I stomped blindly on Gero's foot. Then I kicked him in the shin and rammed into him. A haze took over my senses, and it wasn't long before I was drenched in blood. I stared down at Gero's lifeless, mutilated face and stumbled back, hyperventilating.

I screeched at the top of my lungs when several bones dislocated for no reason. Once I collapsed, that was the end of what I thought pain was. A new kind of pain was everywhere. It penetrated so deeply that I lost sight of everything else. I didn't know my name, I didn't know what species I was, and I didn't know if I was alive or dead. All I could feel was pain and my body parts moving around as though carried by thousands of ants.

I felt some semblance of form take shape, but it didn't feel like what I'd known my entire life. The pain receded, and all I witnessed was myself returning it. Males flooded the cell and tried to restrain me, but I saw nothing but blood and none of it was mine.

Chapter 24

Sir Keyon

Toast and I woke with a start, and he scrabbled deliriously to get to his feet. He stumbled and fell sideways into a rock wall, off-balance from his quick rise. He lurched and threw up yellow bile; we could still scent trace amounts of venom in it.

Elpis! I screamed.

Mate! Toast cried and roared in despair when we couldn't find her scent, not a fresh one.

"Hey! Hey, hey, hey! Toast! Calm down, you handsome devil," a smooth voice that we immediately recognized shouted from the ground. Toast's head jerked down to find a waving Leofwine.

Damnation, I've never been happier to see that bastard, I said to Toast.

Shifting... Toast warned, and we returned to my form. I fell to my knees, and Leofwine came running. I clutched at my chest, feeling Elpis's absence like cold water in my veins. It doused my inner fire; my furnace faltered.

"Where the fuck did you go, Leof?" I gritted through my teeth. "I waited!" Angry tears dripped down my cheeks as I glared at the ground.

"Found your note... Found the coven... The king is dead," he announced breathlessly. "So is Prince Odalric."

I couldn't have heard him correctly. "What?" I croaked out, moving to rub a tear away only to notice Elpis's blood on my hand. I gazed down to find several strands of her hair scattered about. My heart clenched to find that this was all that remained of her. A bleak smile tugged at the corner of my mouth. Had she tried to heal me?

"No one knows the details, and there are a lot of rumors going around, but Prince Cyneric has ascended to the throne. My spies can't infiltrate, but we've noticed that his Royal Gene is very much... activated. That means the king and Odalric are dead.

"I need your help, Keyon. Everything has gone to shit! Even the new knight general is a sticky yes-man," Leofwine rushed out anxiously. "There's even talk that he'll legalize slavery again, but I don't know how the fuck he's going to spin that one."

What? I held up a hand to let him know I'd heard him. "I need... a moment... to process," I said, falling into shock. I'd never been this vulnerable before meeting Elpis. Her abduction, in addition to this news, had dropped my mind into a tailspin.

"Where's Elpis?" a small voice asked timidly. I glanced up to find Adelais pop out from behind a rock wall. She jogged up to Leofwine, who held a comforting hand out for her. She pressed herself shyly into his side and stared worriedly at me.

The question forced me to say aloud what I could barely accept in my mind. I felt my mental supports weaken, and my emotions surged. I spun away from both of them, grabbed my face, and released a shrieking roar. I couldn't tell if my shoulders shook from my anger or my sobbing. "They took her!" I shouted through my teeth, watching my tears plop and seep into the dead earth. "They took my Elpis! They took my mate!"

"Who?" Leofwine asked in a dark voice.

"Coven Mother Gunel said that Elpis was sold as a child to someone who planned on draining her of her blood when she came of age!" I growled and Adelais's breath caught. "It never happened because her last owner stole her. Her original buyers are still hunting for her, so we wanted to take them out. We'd just gotten information on where to find the witch who was involved when we got ambushed. They were King's Poison spitters, Leof! Spitters! I've never seen the like! Something unnatural is going on! I was completely overwhelmed!"

"You were overwhelmed?" Leofwine asked, shocked and disturbed.

"Toast and I did what we could, but we got knocked out. I can't believe they didn't finish the job while I was unconscious." I snarled and dug my claws into my palms.

"Shit," my friend cursed quietly, and Adelais whimpered.

"We have to help," she said to her mate. "They saved me... I care about Elpis!"

"I know, I know. We will," he replied hastily, and I heard him kiss the top of her head. "Keyon, we're going to get her back first. She's still alive. You would have felt her death. You know that, right?"

I glanced up at him and nodded, unable to steady my shaking. "She's still alive. I just wish I knew for how much longer! I can't wait anymore, Leof! I have to go! I'm going out of my mind!" I stood too quickly and wobbled. Leofwine shot forward to steady me, and I cursed. "Fuck! I can't lose her! I can't lose my mate!"

"So, you finally marked and mated? How did Toast even manage a hug?" Leofwine asked curiously, trying to diffuse my spiraling with a question.

"I marked her, yeah. Toast had a couple of wake-up calls that pushed him to tolerate more as time passed," I said, grimacing at a mild headache that hit my temple. I rubbed at it with a jittery hand.

"Well, now his mental balls will match the size of his actual balls. That's a good dragon, Toast, you virile devil," my friend complimented, but Toast was in too black of a mood to appreciate it. His wrath leaned into me, pushing me to get moving.

Leofwine took an offered canteen from Adelais and handed it to me. I drank heavily from it, parched from my body's fight with the venom.

"It's going to be dark in a couple hours. Since you marked her, we can trace her, but I'll be flying you both," my friend directed. "Can Toast deal with you sitting next to Adelais?"

I can if it means we get Elpis back. Adelais doesn't seem to be the worst female ever, Toast answered.

I repeated exactly half of that back to Leofwine—the first half. I also knew not to argue his plan. Leofwine ran our spy network, and this was his expertise. His dragon, Simmer, was also smaller and looked like a slice of the night sky itself. Toast was built more for making... colorful entrances.

Leofwine grabbed my bags and walked me over to their hidden camp. "I want to scout again when we get there," Adelais murmured to her mate. He blew out an aggrieved sigh and rubbed his forehead with a palm. This seemed like a topic they'd previously argued about.

"Please?" she pressed.

"Have you been teaching her espionage, Leof?" I asked seriously. I would have been joking about it had I been in any other situation than my current one.

"We took a detour before coming here," he confessed and grabbed his mate's hand to massage it. "Taught her some take-downs assassins used. They work surprisingly well in her cat form."

Adelais looked up at me and stared straight into my eyes. "We practiced on the fake soldiers who... did what they shouldn't have done to me."

Leofwine stroked the back of her hair. "She's actually very good at sneaking about. They're all dead now."

"Well done, Adelais," I praised solemnly. "You have a long road to go in your healing, but you took your justice."

"They were false," she muttered. "Leof said that Cyneric's been hiring mercenaries to fill in the ranks. Some of the old soldiers didn't like how things were changing... These new fighters don't care about the people. They're a danger to them. I wasn't going to let them target..." She shuddered, and Leofwine wrapped his arm around her. He rummaged in his bag with his other hand and tossed me a ration.

After getting Toast's permission, I told Leofwine about both of my deadly encounters with Cyneric. "He really doesn't want you around, and that makes sense," my friend said. "You'd have never supported a return to slavery. He needed to replace you with a minion."

"Leof," I began hesitantly, "what happened to my Inferno? I went to where they'd been ambushed, and all I gathered was that they'd been betrayed and poisoned."

"They're all locked up... They're alive but locked up," he replied with a scowl. "We think Cyneric's going to accuse you and your men of aiding the traffickers if he gets his claws on you."

"That's absurd," I spat, mirroring his scowl.

"He is absurd."

"So, what's the plan? Take Cyneric down and let one of the princesses rule?" I gave a dour laugh. "I suppose, as a people, we could survive stupid over psychotic. Hopefully they won't be burying anyone alive anytime soon."

"Certainly not promising," Leofwine mumbled, chewing on a ration bar. He pointed a zealous finger at me. "You and I have sworn to always serve the people, Keyon. Letting Cyneric stay king is going to bring a rot upon this country so destructive we may never recover from it. I can tell you right now that we will lose our thin, fragile relationship with the lycans and the wolves. Slavery is punishable by death over there. They can't abide by their friends doing so. We will be vulnerable. We certainly don't have any friends in the cats to the west." He paused and looked at his mate. "Except for you, shadow kitty." She smiled weakly and leaned against his shoulder to close her eyes.

"The kingdom is definitely at a crossroads. So is my life with Elpis missing," I said numbly and ate the rest of the bar. I rubbed my forehead, irritated that I couldn't get rid of my headache on top of everything else.

"Why didn't she mark you?" Adelais asked but then winced. "Sorry, that was probably too personal of a question."

"It's fine, Adelais," I replied and sighed. "We still don't know what she is. She hasn't shifted yet and doesn't seem to have a way to mark someone. No fangs… no canines… no venom. I assume cats mark like the dragons, lycans, and wolves do?"

She nodded and pointed to Leofwine's neck, who pulled his shirt down and smirked with deep pride. Adelais's bite mark on him looked slightly torn, like it'd been violently delivered. That must have been quite the night. "You got him good," I commended. "Bastard had a good bite coming to him." Leofwine snorted and let his shirt collar spring back.

"I can't think of a species that can't mark," he said. "Nothing that isn't already extinct."

"She's also immune to my blue fire," I added, and my friend's face turned to stone.

"You're fucking with me," he accused, and I shook my head.

"She must not be a predator," Adelais mused, placing a finger on her elegant chin. "We're all predators. Fangs and prominent canines. I can't think of any prey shifters, though."

"If they still want her blood after several decades, she clearly is a rarity they see worth hunting," Leofwine added. "Perhaps the only of her kind, at least in our known territories. I certainly hope this is the last batch of people looking for her."

"She doesn't deserve a hunted life," I snarled, feeling my wings twitch in anger.

"She deserves you," Adelais said quietly. "You must have been fated because you're the best one to protect her. She's something precious worth protecting."

"I fucking failed at that," I replied, riddled with self-loathing and massive anxiety.

"Not yet, Keyon," Leofwine said confidently. "Not yet."

Night touched down after it escorted the Sun God to His rest. I wished I could see the stars through the dense fog so the Sky Gods could hear me better, but I sent a fervent prayer regardless.

"Do you recall the number of spitters with the poison, Keyon?" Leofwine asked after securing his bag and handing it to Adelais.

"I'm not positive because they were ambushing through the fog, but I'd say eight at the most. They might not have all been spitters," I replied, grabbing both my and Elpis's bags.

"Shit," Leofwine replied. "Ok, so you're going to have to communicate with me through Adelais. You'll tell her which direction you're sensing Elpis in, and we're going to find the best angle to approach. Spitters can't echolocate, so we have a very good chance at completely avoiding detection coming in at night."

"Right," I agreed while Leofwine shed his clothes and handed them to Adelais, who took the opportunity to appreciate his nudity.

"We'll find a decent spot to land. Wherever Elpis is contained, there's bound to be a door less guarded. We'll send Adelais through that, and she'll get a very quick sense of the layout. She won't dally, and she'll come back immediately," he said, giving his mate a stern expression. She nodded vigorously and tried to suppress an excited smile with a hand.

"So," I said, rubbing my temple with a forefinger, "if we do encounter dragons, we'll need to engage with them under low ceilings to prevent them from shifting on us. Even with you at my side, Leof, I'm not keen on grappling with that many spitters. Unnatural shits."

"And me?" Adelais asked, and Leofwine's lips pressed together. I understood exactly what he was feeling. Leofwine and I had several decades of fighting under our belts, but Adelais had only started training less than a week ago. There was also a big difference between taking one enemy by surprise and engaging with multiple who could all target you simultaneously.

She was also his fated mate. To allow the other half of your soul, your female, to put herself in danger went against our very nature, especially as males. We both also led our own teams of strong warriors and knew what it took to be successful in a mission. Times were changing, though, and more females were willing to fight tooth and claw to join the males on the battlefield. It seemed like Adelais's heart was more than ready to fight alongside her mate. They'd have to find some kind of compromise while she learned, though. The overeager and unexperienced often ended up dead.

"You, kitty cat, will follow behind us until we find Elpis. If we need to secure a route out first, you'll watch over her. We may need to strap her to Foray if she's not well enough to walk," Leofwine said, and Adelais nodded, seeming pleased to have a role to play. Leofwine looked at me and jerked his head upward while asking, "You ready?"

I nodded, and Leofwine shifted into his sleek, shadowy dragon. His hands were a little smaller than Toast's, so it'd be a little cramped with Adelais, but Toast was mentally prepared for it. It was for his mate; he could manage the discomfort.

Simmer caged us, and I hooked an arm through one of Adelais's to keep us more stable in his grip. The stealthy dragon crouched and launched into the sky. I noticed that Simmer's ascent wasn't as steep as it usually was, and I smiled; Adelais must have complained about the pressure change too. It made me think of Elpis once more, and my heart clenched. We'd save her. We wouldn't be too late. Elpis would fight until we got there. I had to believe she was strong enough.

After I told Adelais the direction we needed to start in so she could relay it to Simmer, she turned to face me. "Why do you say these spitters are so unnatural?" Adelais asked, casually stroking Simmer's palm.

"Because King's Poison is neutralized in the air. Dragons with it have to inject the venom directly into the flesh for it to be effective. There's no way that a dragon could spit King's Poison and still have it be effective. There must be witchcraft at work here," I answered, and she grimaced at my explanation.

"I agree... a change like that would otherwise be decades of evolution..." she murmured, looking through Simmer's claws.

I directed Adelais throughout the flight, and we were only in the air for a half an hour before it felt like we were right on top of Elpis's location.

"She's down there!" I hissed to Adelais, who relayed the message to her mate. She leaned down to peer between the gaps of his claws and focused with deeply dilated eyes.

"Some kind of run-down temple," she said, and her gaze flickered about for more information. "There's only one dragon out, and he's on the west side. There are tracks on the east side that suggest a second entrance, just like Leof was hoping for."

I peered down next to her. I spied the lone dragon-shifter, but I couldn't make out the tracks she mentioned. It was black out there, and even though Toast and Simmer had excellent night vision, Adelais's cat surpassed us both. She really would be the best one to scout.

"You both make a beautiful team," I complimented. "I'll let you both decide on where to land."

"I think so too," she replied softly, sounding deeply content. "And yes, Leof and I are discussing..."

Simmer landed silently behind a hill that propped up the remains of a very large, dead oak tree. Toast and I'd always marveled at Simmer's quiet movements. I'd love to have my presence announced with a broken twig at my very loudest and clumsiest.

Leofwine shifted back and dug through his backpack for a spray bottle. I politely looked away when he embraced Adelais and kissed her. When she shifted, he began to spritz her with the chemical that shifters used to hide their scent. Leofwine worshipped the stuff, and I was pretty sure he always had a small bottle on him. It was pretty critical for his line of work.

He ran his fingers over Foray's coat to rub in the chemical and slapped her playfully on the bottom. "Don't spend a second more in there than necessary, mate," he growled, and Foray's tail lashed. The black jaguar stalked soundlessly over the hill and headed toward the entrance to the temple.

I don't know if you can hear me, but hang in there, moonflower, I thought, trying to reach her through the mark I gave her. *We're here! We're coming to get you!*

We're coming, mate! Toast hollered.

 Delais

What's it like in there? Leofwine asked through our link.

Dark... cold and damp. It's not much better than it is outside, but there are torches. I'm in a long hallway, but it's opening up into a large circular room, like an audience chamber. There's no seat, but there is a dragon statue... a rather large one at that. No one seems awake or patrolling... I hear snoring, I reported as Foray padded forward, slinking silently along the walls.

Perpendicular to the last hall was another corridor. I noticed that one wooden door had a silhouette of light around it, but I was drawn closer by the conversation coming through. Foray hunkered down, and we listened to what was being said.

"—enough for Cyneric and the others?" a sharp voice asked.

A dark, disturbed cackle nearly spooked us into retreating, but we held fast. "Oh sure, but can't say certain what this will even do now," the creature sneered. "You strong males can't keep a female a virgin," it cackled again. "How embarrassing for you. Now you have to wait several hundred more years for another. So sad!"

"Well, isn't there something you can do to adjust for it? I couldn't get to her. Cyneric wanted in, and he promised he'd deliver her whole," the sharp voice seethed.

"Doubt it. You should have done it yourself. Relied on royalty. Stupid dragon."

"Well, since he failed to keep her pure, he can enjoy a botched
potion... I admit, I am curious to see if it'll do anything at all
before we destroy her," the male with the sharp voice mused.
"Prepare one dose, Mantegazz. I think I'm due to pledge myself
to the new king. I have just the coronation gift."

Elpis was still alive! It was good to hear it from the enemy's
mouth. We just needed to find her now... I was having a hard time
dragging myself away from this conversation, though. This was
incredibly juicy information. Leofwine and Keyon should know
about this gift for Cyneric... whatever this potion was.

"Good luck knowing if work or not." Mantegazz snorted
wetly. "You won't know if removed his human side or if just
forced him to shift."

"Maybe he won't know either. If we can't reach our fucking
goal now, I'll settle for legalizing slavery again so I can get back
to work," he snapped, sounding impatient for Mantegazz to put
the dose together. The clinking of glass sounded lazy, and I could
hear his teeth grinding.

"Why you shifters here reject your humanity? Why not just
stay shifted? You truly wish to lose your body so your dragon
can be free?" Mantegazz muttered, chuckling occasionally.

"Humans are weak. Witches are weak. You are weak,
Mantegazz. I'm a drain on my dragon. They're made to rule
alone like they once did. You're all meant to be slaves. You're
fodder. You go against the natural order."

"Don't recall a time when dragons weren't shifters. Where
you get your facts from..." Mantegazz muttered. "But yes, this
weak witch took the sacred blood from the unpure pure, and the
flesh from your hated one. This weak witch made the sacred
healing blood recognize human as a poison. Sacred blood is
vengeful blood, but yes, only the weak know that. So weak. If
potion work... your weak humanity looks like poison and potion
kill it. Leave only dragon. I am so weak to be able to do such

things. Know such things. This sad, weak witch. Please take pity. Oh mercy. Have mercy. Mercy, mercy, mercy! Bahahahahahaha!"

The witch sounded anything but sad and weak. In fact, the longer it spoke, the more terrifying it sounded. Its voice became gravelly and layered, as though others spoke with it. It didn't seem to have much humanity left in it at all.

"You sound more unhinged by the day, Mantegazz. Like I said... weak," he noted darkly. "Perhaps you should drain what you can and slaughter her after I leave. She's marked, and that means whoever marked her will be coming. Perhaps the old knight general. Kill him if your busy schedule allows for it," he snarled.

"Oh, so wise, Franco. You truly think things I do not!" Mantegazz wheezed. "Do you need this Gero body? Can I eat? Has lots of fat," the witch asked while making slurping sounds.

"Ugh!" the male named Franco sputtered and walked toward the door. Foray slinked into a dark corner, and we watched him depart. He turned left from the large circular room; he was leaving by the front entrance. I linked my mate and repeated everything to him.

Franco! Slippery bastard. If he's going to the castle, we might finally be able to end his operations for good, Leofwine said enthusiastically. I glowed with pride to have given my mate such good intel.

I crept a little farther down the hall and noticed some bands hanging from the wall. They looked large enough for dragons to wear and seemed to be made from something stretchy. There were eight of them, and each one had an identical series of symbols on it—definitely looked like witchwork. Foray collected them all in her jaw and peered down the hall to see if there was anything else to investigate before we left.

Our heart leapt when we saw the edge of a cell, but we backed up when we scented blood from many different bodies. The floor by the cells was covered in pools of red, and I lost my desire to explore. There'd been a slaughter back there... I retreated down the hall and crept out of the temple, completely undetected and completely disturbed.

Chapter 25

Sir Keyon

Leofwine breathed out a huge sigh of relief when Foray returned to our hideout under the deceased oak tree.

"Foray, you did well, sex kitten," Leofwine whispered in her ear. "Remind me to give you a little positive reinforcement when things quiet down, Adelais. My sources reported you have a job for me. I'm happy to send someone in..."

I would have laughed at my friend's version of dirty talk, but I was about to go out of my fucking mind. Leofwine repeated everything that Adelais had seen as Foray, and it was enough to make me lose my shit at the slightest delay.

"He mentioned killing her, Leof! We're going now!" I snarled, and he nodded, wrapping some rope around Foray's abdomen and stashing the odd bands she'd brought back into his bag.

I ran toward the unguarded entrance and walked carefully down the stone hall. The temple was eerily quiet, with only the sound of popping torches filling the air. I jerked in surprise and scowled with impatience when Leofwine spritzed me with his scent remover. I gave him an irritated look, but he just shrugged and pointed ahead of us.

The hall opened into a huge, circular room like Adelais had reported. We were startled by a door slamming, followed by heavy footsteps, and I ducked into the shadows with Leofwine, but Foray raced forward to hide behind the dragon statue. I felt Leofwine tense, and he swore under his breath. I'd never seen Leofwine so shaken, and I put a firm hand on his tense shoulder.

A shifter walked in and nodded to another male who passed him. This must be a changing of the guard for the front entrance. I could see Foray's haunches shift left and right in anticipation; she was going to attack, damn it. Which one, though? Would she wait until one was out of hearing range? That wasn't likely to happen because they were both equally near doors. I hoped Leofwine was telling her to let it go because we'd soon have the entire bui—

Leofwine hissed a list of profanities as Foray silently pursued the new guard down the hall. We heard a scuffle, but the other shifter retiring for bed simultaneously released a loud belch, covering up the noise of Foray's takedown, and exited through a door. Leofwine's hands slapped over his face, and he staggered from frayed nerves. I placed a hand over my mouth to hold back an incredulous, anxious laugh. Fucking shit!

Foray appeared in the hall and pawed at her face to clean off the blood of her target.

That was lucky. Toast gaped. *Let's go. She's left... left hall.*

Yeah, I feel her there, I agreed and motioned for Leofwine to follow me. We rushed across the large chamber and entered the perpendicular hallway. A bloody door grabbed my attention, not only because it smelled like Gero, but because I also scented Elpis's blood behind it. It also reeked of rot.

"This was the witch's room," Leofwine whispered while scratching Foray under the chin. I didn't scent anyone around and realized the blood was actually a poorly written message. Some letters were backwards, and some words were missing or spelled wrong. It didn't look like a human had written it either. It was too… wild looking. It read:

"Digesteen food. This weke witch cant finish job becaz jus oh so weke. Too human, so weke! So sad! Took my weke poshuns an went. Maybe you fine dragon witch? Strong! Not me. So weke. Hahahaha. If Night Jenral show, you kill yourself. I take credit? Too weke. Hahahaha!"

I swallowed some bile that threatened to come up but took comfort in the fact that the witch hadn't killed Elpis before leaving. I opened the door and saw an empty workroom. There was a drop or two of Elpis's blood on the central, dusty table, but that was the only part of her in there. The scent was mostly overwhelmed by a large puddle of gore on a side table. I wrinkled my nose and shut the door. Gero was definitely what the witch was digesting. I held back a dry heave and gestured for the others to follow me down the hall. Elpis's scent was getting closer but so was the smell of dead bodies. This place was disgusting. I wanted her out of here now.

We passed hooks on the wall where Foray had found the bands. I was hoping those were what allowed these dragons to spit King's Poison. If we'd grabbed them all, we wouldn't have a problem taking down the rest of the shifters here. I could have even done it by myself, but I was extremely grateful for the help. I was too anxious about Elpis's safety, and having another keep an eye on her was a huge relief. Having Leofwine at my side was basically overkill at this point. After my last defeat, I welcomed overkill. I needed this to end. I needed her safe.

The hall curved slightly, and there was blood all over the floor as Adelais had also reported. This had been where she'd retreated, and I couldn't blame her. Seeing one dead body was unnerving, but gazing upon multiple while their gore mixed was a nauseating sight. No one's mind came back from their first battlefield unscathed.

There was a sweeping noise, and several bodies were pushed into the hall where a dragon we couldn't see proceeded to cremate them. He released bursts of weak fire in a rhythm, like he was bored.

"I'll jump in on his next burst and drop him," I whispered to Leofwine, and he nodded. I crept forward and hovered at the corner of the hall. I sensed that Elpis was also around the corner, so I had to be extremely careful. I skipped an opening because I scented another familiar dragon. What the fuck was Adelmar doing here? I snarled silently, furious at the unknown, and jumped into the dragon's next jet of fire to rip him apart. The shifter died without a scream. Good.

I stepped over dead bodies as Leofwine and Foray hurried to catch up to me. Quickly now, I followed Elpis's scent of misted grass and agave to a cell where I stopped breathing. I placed both my hands on the cage bars and stared with a loose jaw, unable to understand what I was seeing. My mate was limp. She'd finally shifted, and she was covered in other people's blood. She must have fought hard before passing out... if the bodies littered around her cage said anything about the encounter.

"She's... unconscious. Is... What is she?" Adelais asked. "That's... Elpis's beast... but..." I heard a sob escape her lips. "She's exquisite."

"I've never seen anything like her before..." Leofwine murmured, awestruck.

I squatted by the cage and reached in to pet her white gold hair. Tears formed in my eyes because, like her human form, she was the most beautiful thing I'd ever seen or heard of in my lifetime. Her body reminded me of a horse, though it looked stronger and a bit shapelier. Her four robust, sinewy legs ended in wispy white gold fetlocks that pointed down to wickedly sharp cloven hooves. Her tail was long and short-haired, like her body, with a luscious spray of long, white gold hair at the very end. A wild mane, also of white gold, draped messily across her thick, powerful neck and splayed across the filthy floor. It was matted with sticky blood, and I longed to clean it. She was far too lovely to be left in such an awful state. Two pointed ears, a little longer than a horse's, rested stock-still in her sleep. Like her neck, her face was very much like a horse's but seemed sturdier, and I figured it had to do with needing shock absorption... Shock absorption for the long, slightly curved horn that jutted from the center of the beast's forehead. Underneath the dried blood, the horn looked as sharp as a dragon's claw, and I guessed it was the main weapon used in her defense.

"These corpses are covered in stabs, lacerations, broken bones, and other high-impact injuries..." Leofwine analyzed, moving a body out of the way. "Those hooves look almost as sharp as that horn, Keyon. Careful waking her," he warned.

"Yes, it'd be a shame to have her wake up only to find she'd killed her fated mate," Adelmar's voice said tiredly from the next cage. I didn't look at him, and I fumbled around the shifter's pocket for the cell keys. I unlocked Elpis's cage and tossed the keys to Leofwine.

"Leof, can you please go deal with that?" I said, gesturing idly to Adelmar's cell. I had tunnel vision for my mate. Nothing else mattered.

"My pleasure," my friend said and went over to speak to the caged slaver.

I frowned when I opened the door, realizing that Elpis's beast would absolutely not be able to fit through the opening. If I had to guess, I'd say that she'd killed every shifter who tried to go into the cell to restrain her. They had to drag out the bodies so more could attempt to get in and subdue her. Perhaps they weren't done draining her but eventually had to give up once too many of them had died.

"You bought us time... well done, moonflower," I whispered to her. "I'm so fucking proud of you."

I pondered my options as I looked around the cell. I had to either get her to wake up and shift back or melt a section of the iron cage. The latter would take longer, so I squatted by her side and tried to wake her.

"Elpis," I said, rubbing her beast's shoulder while keeping a hand safely on her cheek. "Can you hear me? We're here for you, but you need to wake up, moonflower. Moonflower?" I rubbed her shoulder a little harder, but the beast didn't move. I could hear the steady thumping of her heart, but her breathing was a little shallow. Had her beast been forced into an early shift? Did she hurt herself or put pressure on her bond with Elpis? I couldn't tell! "Elpis!" I said urgently and gave her one last push before I surrendered and studied the iron bars.

"This is going to be an awkward exit, Foray," I said to the black jaguar who turned to look at me from her post at the corner. "I can't get her to shift back, and it's too narrow here for me to shift into Toast and carry her out. Leof and I might have to carry her beast form out in our human bodies, so we'll be relying on you to scout ahead."

The cat-shifter nodded and went back to watching dutifully around the corner. I began to torch the iron bars with my hottest fire when Leofwine and Adelmar came over to help. I narrowed my eyes when I saw Adelmar, and Leofwine stopped momentarily to explain. "He's agreed to let us escort him out, and he'll surrender to arrest. He's lost an arm. He's too weak to fly off."

I scowled, not trusting any deal Adelmar had to offer, but continued to heat up the bars until I could fold and shape them out of the way. Leofwine and Adelmar couldn't get the metal to bend on their own, but they sped up the process for the cold iron so I could do it within minutes.

Once I bent the cell wall back far enough, I crouched and got a grip under Elpis's beast's hips while Leofwine supported her head and torso. I snarled viciously at Adelmar when he offered to help with his remaining arm, and he backed away with his palm out. I trusted my mated best friend to help, but I did not trust her old owner. She'd never suffer his touch again! Filthy bastard.

Foray took the lead, and Adelmar fell in pace behind her like I'd ordered. I wanted him where I could see him. There wasn't anyone in sight when we entered the round chamber, but a door opened, and a male shouted a warning when he saw three shifters absconding with their prisoners. He jumped forward and shifted into a dragon in the larger space, then lunged toward us, but Adelmar burst from his clothes to intercept him. They collided with a quaking fury that rattled the wood and stone supports. Dust sprinkled warningly from the rafters.

"Go, go, go!" Leofwine hissed, and we rushed toward the next hall where the exit was. If Adelmar wanted to hold the enemy back, so be it. I had plenty on my plate, and if he died, he'd be one less thing on my mind.

We burst through the door and ran out into the cold night air. We deposited Elpis's beast under the oak tree and witnessed a large number of dragons stream out of the temple.

"Foray, cover Elpis up and watch her!" I ordered and shrugged my clothes off to shift. Toast and Simmer were going to clean up real quick before leaving.

I unleashed Toast to get his revenge on the dragons who'd previously resorted to witchcraft to attack us. These were likely the same ones, and we waited eagerly to see if they were now without their King's Poison. Toast banked and gave a dragon a wide berth, studying to see if it'd spit at him. The dragon merely roared and raked at the air in frustration.

Simmer must have enjoyed the distraction we'd created because he claimed that one as his first kill. The black dragon darted out of nowhere and removed the dragon's head from its long neck. The body fell the long distance to the ground, and the remaining enemies swarmed in panic.

Definitely no longer spitters. Such false confidence given to them by that witch, Toast sneered. He looked down, bobbed his head as he considered the timing, and dropped like a stone to land on another dragon. He ripped its wings off and threw it high above the fog, letting it eventually fall to its death. It was possible it'd survive the fall but equally possible it'd bleed to death.

A dragon barreled toward us, but Toast grappled with the attacker and slammed him into another advancing dragon. He unleashed his blue fire over both stunned shifters, and they fell to the ground as a smoldering tribute to an absolute dominant's vengeance.

Should not have come between us and our mate, Toast remarked coldly, decisively.

We sensed a change in the air currents and rolled to receive an attacking shifter, but Simmer sniped his left wing, and the dragon careened into the temple's spire, sending stones crashing down to the main building. Toast rolled away to find a new target and spat several jets of blue fire to take down another two who tried to stay out of our reach. Toast was darkly amused; no one was out of his reach.

His thoughts briefly flashed back to playing with Elpis under the pine trees, and he was even more resolved to finish up here. He slashed, scalded, and crushed several more before the air became silent. Simmer passed us, and we followed him back down to the dead oak tree. He seemed to be in a rush, and I grew concerned when he immediately shifted back into Leofwine and ran toward where our mates were hidden.

"Woah!" Leofwine yelled, and I burst through the oak branches to see him struggling alongside Foray to hold down Elpis's beast.

"Back off!" I ordered, not wanting them to get hurt. Leofwine snatched Foray away like she was a tiny kitten and backed off with her, putting a large, gnarled oak branch between them and my mate. The horse-like beast rocked desperately as it tried to go from its side to its feet, eyes rolling in fright and nostrils puffing warm clouds into the cold night air.

I squatted, grabbed her beast's shoulder, and leaned into her to help her stand. She scrambled to her feet and squealed, so I backed up out of kicking range. She snorted and skipped away several paces, her heart and lungs racing at a speed that frightened me. She was too scared. I had to calm her somehow.

"Elpis," I said, putting my hands up. "Moonflower, it's me! It's Keyon! Your fated mate. Do you remember me?" I edged towards her, and she pranced back in a spooked response.

She's prey animal, Keyon, Toast reminded. *I don't know how to approach prey.*

Slowly... I replied. *Like a scared hatchling.*

Hatchling steps...

I took another step forward and held out a hand for her to sniff. I glanced into her beast's eyes, and my heart ached painfully. She had Elpis's deep, sweet, brown-sugar eyes. "You're so beautiful, mate. You're complete perfection. I wish you knew to trust me," I said softly to her. "Elpis, moonflower..."

Some of the rubble in the temple shifted unexpectedly, and Elpis's startled beast bolted into the night.

"Fuck!" I cursed and turned to face a stricken Leofwine and Adelais. "You two get going! Bring those bands to the Solar Coven. Find out what they are, then we need to draft a plan for Cyneric. I have to catch Elpis and get the mothers to check on her. We'll be there soon!"

"Good luck, Keyon," Leofwine said with a worried frown, looking off to where Elpis's beast had disappeared.

Adelais wiped a tear away and forced a smile at me. "W-we'll see you both real soon!"

I shifted into Toast, who grabbed our bags, and launched into the sky again. I could tell he was tired, but nothing would stop us from reclaiming our mate. Between her galloping sounds and her gleaming white hair, it didn't take long to find her. We stalked her south, which was interesting; it was as if she knew there was nothing but dead plants and bog water in the northern region. Was Elpis awake in there, or was it just her beast? Were her memories intact?

We flew over her as she raced, trying to find the safest place to intercept her.

That horn is sharp, but it only points one way. We have to grab her from behind, Toast said.

Try to glide down and cage her, but keep that horn away from our belly until she recognizes us. Bite her neck, I said. Toast growled an affirmative and descended. The beast screamed and thrashed, but we landed smoothly with her in our grip. Toast's teeth were gently clamped around her neck as she fought against us.

Should we let her tire herself out? Toast asked.

Let's try to reach her first. Try talking through her mark again, I suggested.

Mate! Toast said to Elpis and her beast over our one-way mind link. *Mate, don't fight us. It's Toast and Keyon! We freed you! Come back to us!*

Elpis! I shouted. *Moonflower! You're safe now! Shift back so we can talk! Shift back so I can take care of you!*

The beast's thrashing slowed, but I couldn't tell if it was from fatigue or something else. Once she slowed to a wobble and an occasional pawing, I shifted back into my human form and kept a firm hand on her back. Her muscles bunched, and I jumped onto her before she could escape me again. Shit, I sorely wished I knew how to ride a horse!

She tried to trick us! Toast sputtered. *Smart prey.*

I dug my heels into her side and tightened my grip on her neck as she tried to buck me off. "Mate," I growled softly as she kicked about. "Calm down. You're safe with me." I rubbed her neck affectionately, but she broke into a gallop, squealing.

Shit, I groaned to Toast. *Doing this without pants was a huge mistake!*

Perhaps death by blue balls was preferable to this.

I adjusted my grip and shouted, "Elpis, I swear if you don't stop your beast, we'll not be able to have hatchlings at this rate!" Being soothing wasn't working. I had a threat to hang over my mate's head… her dangerously pointy head.

The threat didn't seem to sink in, and I growled.

Is she in heat? Toast asked. I had no idea. Beasts like this didn't blush or send furtive glances. I leaned into her galloping shoulders and took a breath. I scented her estrus pheromones, but I couldn't tell if they were contributing to her wildness. I wiped some white, foamy sweat off her, getting more and more concerned for her health.

Elpis, my fated mate, I thought to her. *This wasn't how I wanted to mount and ride you. Do you need relief, my precious moonflower?* I ran a hand down her neck suggestively, hoping she'd shift back in desperation. If there was anything Elpis had a hard time resisting, it was my dirty talk.

The beast stumbled and crashed into the ground, squealing again. I jumped clear and ran toward her as she shifted back into her human form. My fated mate crawled to her feet and appeared lost. Elpis seemed confused and wild-eyed, but her scent staggered me. I was slammed by her pheromones and felt desire shudder down my body.

That was a good call, Toast. I wonder how long she'd been stuck in heat without relief? The spike didn't fade?

Go claim her, Toast said and crawled into the back of my mind.

Elpis turned once again and looked hesitantly at me. Did she recognize me? She retreated and stumbled while I approached warily. Something looked different about her face, and that was when I noticed she still had a horn on her forehead. I paused in surprise, gaping. Was that the cause of the migraines? Had her horn been pushing to come out but had been obstructed? I couldn't even imagine what that must have felt like. Was this her natural human form now?

"Oh, Elpis... sweetheart..." My heart clenched at how much unnecessary torture she'd been forced to endure. She hadn't been allowed to be who she was supposed to be and had suffered deeply for it. I cornered her trembling, naked body against a rock wall. Her large eyes stared up at me in the darkness, looking scared, lost, and lonely. I reached out to caress her short white horn. It was only around two to three inches long now.

A pleasant spark lit up between my hand and her horn, but she flinched and ducked out of my arms to run from me again. I gave chase, not willing to let discouragement faze me. Like the first time I'd joined with her, I scented her getting progressively more aroused the longer she sprinted. I snorted smoke out through my nostrils and moved to cut her off, but she was faster than the first time I'd chased her; Elpis's beast must be helping. She evaded me, and I growled a warning at her to stop running.

Perhaps the pursuit wouldn't be as easy this time. Her stubbornness and the drops of her arousal she'd left behind on the ground spurred me into action. I couldn't toy with her anymore; this was a real chase now. I had to get to her before she wandered too close to another dragon.

The anger and fear triggered my feral instincts, and soon all I saw was a fleeing, fertile female that I needed to take for myself. I could have sworn I had already claimed this one, though. Why was she fleeing me? Why was she disobeying and putting my potential hatchlings at risk?

I roared to let her know I was serious and breathed a jet of blue fire to herd my female back toward the rock wall, where I could corner her again. She somehow managed to recall that she couldn't be hurt by my fire and jumped right through it. I snarled and continued hunting her, barely gaining ground on her fleet-footed escape.

I heard her whimper and stumble. My blood heated at the chance to catch up, and I burst through a dead tree line. I realized very quickly that we were at the edge of a cliff, and my wild female had begun a descent. I grinned down at her climbing form with my elongated fangs and growled, "Female, that was a bad decision if you wanted to escape me."

She froze and looked up at me through her thick eyelashes. The canyon's wind ripped at her hair, tossing it about in a mesmerizing dance. I released my wings and crouched to grin at her. I let a blue flame trickle up my lips so I could see her better, and she was glorious. Her chest heaved as she tried to catch her breath, and I growled at the sight of her breasts and nipples rubbing against the rock wall. Her soft lips were parted from her panting, and I could barely recall through my feral mind how they'd felt wrapped around my cock. The curves of her perky bottom followed her hips as she adjusted her footing.

"Didn't recall the first time I mounted you, female?" I asked in a low voice and reached down to trace under her jaw with a claw, urging her to continue looking at me. "Didn't recall I prefer cliffsides?"

I glanced around for a decent ledge to take her on and grinned when I spotted one that would do. It was a little narrow, but I'd make it work. There would be no shifting into her beast on that platform. There'd be no getting away from me.

Chapter 26

Sir Kenon

I took one more look down at my female during her ador-
ably impossible escape before I wrapped both my hands around
her hips and pulled her up to meet my gaze. She squealed and
kicked her legs a little, as though she wanted to keep running,
but she didn't make contact with me. I stared challengingly into
her face, waiting to see if she'd try to headbutt and kill me with
her small horn. I had to test my female's loyalty now that she'd
run from me.

My female didn't even look like that thought crossed her
mind. Her nostrils flared, and her cheeks pinkened as her kicking
subsided. She snorted softly, and her breathing slowed a little,
which pleased me.

I leaned in to draw a lungful of her scent and pheromones,
feeding my already awakened cock. "Stay, female, and I will care
for you. Run, and I can't promise I won't be a savage," I rumbled
into her neck. I groaned at a surge of lust when my words pulled
some of her arousal from her. Was I finally getting through to this
wild female? Would she remember she was mine?

I kissed down my female's neck as I continued to hold her off the ground, wanting to show her my gentleness as proof that I could be this way. She would want to choose this over a savage male. I left saliva behind from each kiss, only to breathe out fire and evaporate it, letting her enjoy the hot and cold sensations on her sensitive flesh. I reached her marking spot and bit down but didn't penetrate her flesh; I planned on penetrating her elsewhere. My female's body rocked and convulsed with need as she cried out in pleasure. Her legs kicked, and I scented a fresh stream of arousal from between her thighs.

There, perhaps she'd know not to leave now. She knew I could give her what she needed, so running was utterly pointless. I slid my lips back up to her ear and murmured, "Remember, I'm an absolute dominant, female. You wanted me to pick you."

I set her down on her feet, and she collapsed, whimpering and writhing. She got onto all fours and pressed her chest into the ground, putting her sex on display for me. I crouched next to her and stroked her back. "That's a good female. You remember now…" I purred softly and nibbled her earlobe, appreciating the curve of her spine and the roundness of her rump.

Instead of flying her to my ledge or positioning myself behind her, I decided to care for my female before rutting her. Although I was roused by the blood of her enemies splattered across her body as evidence of her strength, I wanted to purify her. Water was a good cleanser, but nothing purified like fire.

"I'm going to clean you first, my female…" I purred again and let a pleased growl rumble through my chest. I pressed a hand down between her shoulder blades, pulled her hair out from under her, and breathed blue fire across her head, hair, shoulders, and back. Everything that wasn't my female turned into ash that I either brushed or shook off her.

"What a good mother you'd be for my offspring," I growled approvingly and shifted down to burn any blood off her hips, rump, and legs. "You'd slaughter anyone who got near them." I rubbed her bottom appreciatively before turning her on her back.

I blew a sweeping flame down her face, making sure to remove every impurity there was marring my female. I blew another flame over her horn just to watch it catch the light. "Yes, a strong, protective mother," I growled and felt her shiver beneath me.

I continued grooming her neck and shoulders but spent a particularly long time purifying her breasts. I wiped the ashes away and grabbed both of them. "A good providing mother too. Imagine these full of milk for my offspring. They would never go hungry," I rumbled breathlessly and leaned down to take as much as I could of her right breast into my mouth. The female started and bucked, crying out in surprise. I sucked and pulled back until her nipple left my mouth with a slurp and sprung back into place. I blew fire across her breast to dry it and glanced up at my female while she mewled in pleasure. No, she definitely wouldn't be running now.

I treated her left breast differently, lapping over every inch of skin to moisten it. I laved with my tongue, enjoying the softness and heaviness of her providing flesh. In my attempt to put her first, my arousal was straining my own overly engorged, hardened flesh. Pre-cum dripped down my thigh, and I knew I should speed up lest I waste my seed. It should be in my female, not on the dirt.

I suckled on her nipple and released it with a small spray of fire, letting the heat wash away the cold. I grinned when my female gasped in ecstasy. She was squirming feverishly, and I had to hold her down while I finished breathing blue fire across her. I quickly pulled her up to brush away the ashes of the fallen and lifted her. She promptly wrapped her arms and legs around me, and I growled in approval.

"Good female," I murmured into her now-purified hair. I would bring her to a spring later to get the ash out of it, but this would have to do for now. I still had a task, which was to ease my fertile female during her heat. Perhaps then her mind would come back to me.

I jumped off the cliff and landed on a narrow ledge, my heavy and uncomfortably long erection bobbing on impact. I held my female close as I settled with my legs dangling from the edge, then I turned her around to see the view. She whimpered when I sat her on my lap, the end of the ledge mere inches from her knees.

"Worry not, female. Enjoy the view," I soothed and slid an arm around her waist to make her feel secure while I checked her readiness with my right hand. I palmed her abdomen, then slid my fingers down and into her sex. I tilted my head back and released the wave of lust I felt through a long, guttural groan.

"Drenched. You are too good to me," I snarled and gritted my teeth through the pulsing desire that hardened my cock to the extent that only she could. Unable to wait a moment longer, I lifted her, lined her entrance up, and began to slowly impale her. Slick folds parted for my head, and I allowed gravity to squeeze my girth past her threshold.

Once she was able to stretch and accommodate me, she whimpered and squirmed. The muscles of my abdomen contracted with anticipation and pleasure as I lowered her, but she got impatient and slammed down her hips, sending me deep inside to bottom out. I tilted my head back again and roared in ecstasy, not expecting an aggressive move like that. As she grinded against my lap, I dug my fingers into her hips, barely able to see straight after that move. She was exquisite. She always was. She gripped me like a hot, slick fist. Nothing could match how we fit each other.

"Such an impatient female," I growled into her ear and raised her along my throbbing cock. "You could have been doing this instead of running from me, you know," I snarled and bit down again on her mating mark to punish her with painful pleasure. She arched her back and shrieked, letting the canyon carry the sound of her euphoria far and wide. Her channel clenched around my cock as more arousal spilled from her. I lifted her up until I was almost out, then pushed her back down until her bottom was pressed into my lap, seating myself completely inside her again.

She moaned and leaned forward as I took control of her hips, sliding her up and down my length in a fluid motion. I took my time to enjoy the view, watching her sex glisten around my invading member that was preparing to spill into her hungry body. I loved the silhouette of my fertile female. I loved how her wide, offspring-bearing hips narrowed gracefully into her waist. Softer in places, leaner in others, and made to receive me. Her head turned slightly to the left, and I stared at her horn in wonder while I continued to slide her channel along my ravenous cock.

This female was mine. Precious to me before I knew what she was and precious now. I needed to protect her, keep her. I slammed her hips down on my lap possessively and grunted in response to her cry. I lifted her up and slammed her down again, groaning at how her tight, smooth channel gripped me. It clenched to keep me from pulling up again, but I fought against it and slammed her hips down a third time. She gripped my legs and allowed me to rapidly fuck her, lifting and yanking to impale her again and again.

She wailed, arched, and clawed at my legs in her rapture. As a pool of her arousal collected under her, I snarled and lost all sense of reason. I just needed this female. All I needed was her.

At some point, the female escaped my grip and began to ride me with unbridled adoration. She panted, and I nearly roared from how fucking erotic it was to see her sweaty, soft body bouncing away on my lap. My sound came out in a groan instead, and I released blue fire into the sky, unable to contain my arousal in any form. It was bursting through my skin like sparks of light, and I knew I wouldn't be able to take this much longer. I needed to tend to her first.

I tried to regain control, but she turned her just head enough to show me her bared teeth. She didn't like that at all. "Female," I croaked while trying to snake a hand around her hip to rub into her swollen, sensitive flesh. "Let me please you before I c—"

She pulled recklessly off me, and I jerked my hands forward to steady her, making sure she wouldn't fall. She turned to face me and fed my soaked, heavy cock back into her tight, hot channel. I hissed through my teeth, surprised once again by her aggressive movements.

She rode me again, harder and faster this time, and she leaned forward to lick down my neck. I gripped her ribs and tried to gently push her away because she was arousing me too much, and I wouldn't be able to get to her first. She didn't like that either. Adamantly, she dug her fingers into my shoulders, and I felt them slightly harden and sharpen. They weren't dragon claws by any means, but she was showing me she was serious.

"Female, please..." I snarled and felt my muscles contract when she repeatedly lapped over the marking spot. Each lave of her tongue fed a drip of carnal pleasure so deep inside me that I didn't even know where it went. My entire being was preparing for something that I couldn't fathom, and all I could do was follow the igniting sensations within my body.

The female rode me with abandon, panting into my ear and lapping it affectionately on occasion. She moaned and rubbed her swollen breasts into me, spreading her pheromones and mingling our sweat. She did everything she could to get me to explode within her, and my resistance was faltering. She was too fucking seductive, and I'd never been harder.

"Fill me. Male, please," she whined and whimpered. It was so sad, so desperate that my emotional wall collapsed. I surrendered and stopped fighting, tilting my head back to let her take what she wanted from me. I grunted with each impact and felt the coil in my abdomen tighten. My cock felt like it was stretched so tight that it was about to burst. My heavy sack tightened, and I gave in to my female.

I roared out through my teeth and came into my desperate female, unloading my seed by the rope. I heard her soft, pleased moan and something stabbed into my marking spot. I screamed at first in pain, but it was quickly replaced by a pleasure I'd never experienced in my life. Something swept through my body and caressed all my nerve endings, sending me spiraling into another orgasm.

I gritted my teeth as my hips jerked up into hers, filling her while she filled me with a part of her soul. She settled in me like a calming hush and spread to offer my body her eternal protection. I felt a bond snap in place, leaving a part of my female with me always. Her horn pulled from my shoulder, and she collapsed on my chest, succumbing to an orgasm I hadn't realized she'd obtained. She mewled and clawed at me, mindless in our releases.

I clutched her closely, fiercely, and protectively as I spilled my last rope within her. She nuzzled into my heaving chest, and I groaned, barely able to process what had just happened. We sat on that ledge while we recovered, and my mind slowly returned to me.

Releasing a long exhale, I looked down to see Elpis's calm face staring into the dark distance. Had she marked me in her own fashion? Was our fated connection complete?

Elpis...? I tested our link hesitantly, frightened that it hadn't worked. Part of me was still scared that we weren't compatible, especially now that I knew she wasn't a dragon.

Keyon? her voice replied in my mind, and she sat up to look at me.

"Mate..." she whispered. "Mine."

Elpis

My mind finally returned to me when I uttered those two words. Those two words were tiredly whispered to me from my beast before she fell asleep, exhausted from defending us, suffering the claustrophobic cell, and running. I felt emotions flowing parallel to mine, swelling slowly until they settled within me like another beast. Disbelief... happiness... relief... I knew they weren't mine. Were they Keyon's?

Two warm, rough hands cupped my face, and gentle lips met mine.

Thank you, moonflower, Keyon's voice rang in my mind, clear and beautiful as a bell. *Thank you for accepting me as your mate. I'm so happy... I can't even begin to describe it.*

You don't have to, I replied, and I felt a tear trickle down his cheek as he kissed me. *I can feel it. I can feel your relief... I am relieved too.*

He deepened the kiss before he released me, licking his lips. He had such an affectionate expression on his face, and it almost brought me to tears. His soft lips were parted as he took in slow, calm breaths. Dark brows drew sweetly up and inward while his large palms moved to rest on my hips, caressing me slowly with his thumbs. His brilliant copper eyes flickered between my own and my forehead, and I drew my hand up to feel where he was staring.

Something was jutting from my forehead, and I was confused for a moment, thinking it was an injury before instinct told me what it was. "Where have you been all this time?" I whispered as I felt my horn. It wasn't very long, not even close to my beast's horn, but it was sharp at the end.

"I don't know, but I'm glad it wasn't there when you head-butted that dragon-shifter." He chuckled and tilted his head. "That night would have ended differently."

"I'll have to be careful..." I said quietly. "That female really pushed my buttons. I don't like hurting people... but I don't like feeling inferior either. Not after the life I've had."

"You'll never have a reason to feel that way, moonflower," he murmured and massaged my hips. "It's actually really funny because her attack was quite backwards. You're the one that can handle me. She'd get burnt to a crisp, even with fireproof lingerie."

I burst into laughter and nodded. My eyes then drifted to his neck and shoulder, where there was a scar from a new puncture wound. "Is that how...?" I asked no one in particular as I brushed it with a thumb. I was starting to recall it, the moment my brow itched to pierce his marking spot. Keyon groaned when I touched it, and I smiled at his response.

"Yeah. You skewered me pretty good, moonflower. It was amazing, though," he said with his eyes closing. The knot in his throat bobbed as he swallowed, and I slid my hand down to caress his shoulder.

"We should rest," I said and stood carefully to allow his cock to fall from me. Unblocked, I felt a gush, and a large amount of his seed drained down my thigh. If I wasn't pregnant before, I definitely was now. Keyon looked apologetically at me as he stood, keeping me secure on the narrow ledge.

"Marking is messy business, I guess." He sighed and picked me up to return to the top of the cliff. I could tell he was extremely tired, but he was trying not to show it. I looked around for our bags while he made a campfire.

"Where'd our things go?" I asked, trying to recall the last hour of my life.

"Several miles away," he said with an unhappy exhale. "We had to drop them. You and your beast gave us quite the chase."

I scrunched my face up. "I'm so sorry."

"Nope, not your fault. The cult—or whatever they are—caused all of this." He gestured loosely with a hand. "I'm going to quickly grab our bags and come back. Don't leave. Mind-link me if anything happens, but I don't sense anyone nearby," he said and kissed the top of my head before jogging off into the darkness. I inched toward the fire, shivering and unable to wait until I could wear something. Shifting was very inconvenient if you had to keep dressing and undressing all the time.

I was a little thrown to see Toast return instead of Keyon. He dropped the bags near me and settled close, only several feet away from where I sat.

Hello mate, Toast said tiredly. *Keyon and I don't trust this area, so I'll be sleeping next to you. No person or creature will fuck with me… as Keyon worded it.* He laid his head down, and I stood to give his snout a hug and a kiss before wiping Keyon's seed off my legs and crawling into some clothes.

That was nice. Thank you, Toast replied sleepily.

We're just too tired to travel right now, Keyon admitted. *We'll fly to the coven tomorrow if your heat is over. If not, we'll stop by the spring and clean up. You still have ash in your hair.*

I combed my hair with my fingers and noticed the fine grey particles. Huh... maybe I'd remember more about this tomorrow. I grabbed my blanket and curled up where Toast's neck met his shoulders. He drew his wing over me to trap in his body heat, and I sighed in relief, feeling much cozier than I should on the dirt in a dead forest.

Mate? Toast asked uncertainly while yawning.

"Mm-hmm?" I mumbled.

Does your beast hate me? he inquired, sounding insecure.

It's not possible to hate you, Toast, I consoled. *She was scared and confused. I'll bring her out soon for a proper hello.* I patted him on the scales, and he soon fell asleep. I felt his worry and would do my best to fix that when we were all a little more awake.

Warm arms squeezed me into a hard surface, and I yawned sleepily, opening my eyes to a dead campfire in a dead forest. It was later in the morning than when we usually woke, but yesterday had been near crippling. I could sleep for a week. Keyon peppered my neck and cheek with kisses, and I squealed in delight, kicking my feet and laughing.

"Breakfast," he said, kissing my ear and standing to hand me some freshly cooked meat. I ate a little but felt like something was missing. I looked around, noticing that all the plant life was dead, and felt myself salivate. I couldn't stop thinking about fresh... something. Something green.

"Do you have any more rations?" I asked, having eaten about half of what he gave me. I liked the meat... but I needed something else. The rations had nuts in them. Keyon looked in his bag and tossed a bar towards me. I caught it with a grin and ripped it open, sinking my teeth into the nutrient bar. This would do for now.

Keyon was studying me and said, "You know, animals like horses, deer, and goats are herbivores. Your beast looks similar to them. Perhaps she is craving some grass." I chewed and considered his words. Herbivore. Herb. Plants?

Veterinarian? my beast asked.

Vegetarian! Th— Wait, are you all better? I asked my beast, hoping she'd respond.

I am feeling better. Yesterday was a whole lot of wow, she replied, and I had an urge to clap with glee like a hatchling. She replied! She replied to me!

Clap with glee like a foal, you mean? We are not flagons.

Yeesh… You mean dragons? I asked. Oh, great Moon Goddess, was she ok?

Ah… yes… she replied, sounding quite abashed. Maybe she needed time to… catch up to my memories and learn… words.

What is your name? I asked and held my breath, hoping she'd continue to talk to me.

Rein, she replied.

"Rein!" I shouted loudly at Keyon, startling him. I must have been louder than I thought. "Her name is Rein!"

"Rain, rein, or reign?" he asked with a wry smile. "Rain like water from the sky? Reins that you put on a horse's head, or reign as in ruling over a kingdom?"

Did you hear our mate's question? I asked her.

Yes, and… I don't know what he's talking about. They all sound the same.

"I heard her." He chuckled and finished up the meat I didn't eat. "We'll keep teaching you spelling. You got hit with another homophone there." He smiled happily at me, and my heart fluttered. His own happiness glowed within my chest, and it drew a smile out of me as well. "Hello, Rein."

Hi mate. Uh, other mate. The beast mate. I mean, Rein, Toast chimed in nervously. I frowned at how worried he was. I hoped he didn't think Rein would try to murder him or bury him alive.

Is that the hot bread? Rein asked, and I placed my hands on my face. Keyon just erupted into laughter and patted my shoulder.

"How are you feeling, Elpis?" he asked, and I peeked through my fingers to see him squatting in front of me. "Think your heat is gone?"

"I'm not sure. How do I smell?" I asked, leaning forward and turning my neck to him. He growled and leaned in to scent me. I shuddered when his nose and lips grazed my skin, delivering the sparks I was growing to know and love as the mate touch. He pulled back, looking like he was trying to restrain himself.

"I smell a little, but it seems weaker. Let's stop by the spring and see how you feel. I just want to get the fuck out of this place. I had to go pretty far to find game to hunt," he said and closed up his bag. His cheeks were flushed, and I caught sight of his eager member before he shifted into Toast. I rubbed my neck in awe; he certainly didn't react like it was weaker! I grabbed the bags and let Toast fly me to the springs again.

So high, so high, so high, so high! Rein worried restlessly. I could almost hear her tail swishing in the back of my mind. *We are not meant to be this far up!*

We are now, I said with a happy smile and patted one of Toast's fingers. *We're mated to a dragon!*

Yes, you are, Keyon said smugly.

I w-won't drop you, Rein, Toast said, and his hold on us tightened. I couldn't see as much after that, but I felt Rein's anxiety lessen.

Toast landed but didn't place me on the ground until he dipped his tail in the water. *Not acidic, Keyon,* Toast said before finally releasing me. I dropped my bags by the hot spring and threw off my clothes.

"Let's bring Rein out," Keyon said, hugging me from behind. "See how she handles the water. I have a feeling she'll be the same." He kissed me and stood back, grinning and crossing his arms.

I frowned and said, "How... do I shift?"

I guess I'll try to come out... Rein said, and I yelped when my body began to change. I had a vague memory of this happening before, and it definitely wasn't as bad. It was quicker too, but by the goddess, it still hurt a little!

"It'll get better over time, moonflower," Keyon said as he approached Rein. She turned her head to face him and snorted, then nickered softly. I felt her tail flick, and she took a step toward our mate, who held his hand out for her. "You've been through a lot, Rein," he said gently as she pressed her muzzle against his palm. "Shall we get you a bath?"

Rein looked toward the steaming water, and I could feel her uncertainty. *Go ahead, I encouraged. It feels wonderful.* She walked slowly to the edge and dipped her horn in it. I felt an odd sensation through her, like her horn was testing for and clearing out... impurities. After she seemed satisfied with the water, she jumped awkwardly in, creating a large splash that drenched a chuckling Keyon.

As Keyon lathered her coat and washed her mane, Rein became more relaxed around him. He spoke gently to her like he would a hatchling, and my heart filled with warmth. He cared just as much about Rein as me. I was beginning to understand how difficult it must have been for Keyon and Toast to manage that phobia all those years. To be at odds with a part of yourself and be unable to escape it... that was an unavoidable test of strength and stamina. It must have been exhausting.

I continued to watch Keyon care for Rein and saw with different eyes how much he cared for me. I was comfortable with my feelings now and validated by our bond. There was obviously no going back on what we'd done, but my mind, my heart, and now my sense of self had caught up to my body. The feeling that had been burning for a long while in my heart could no longer be suppressed out of fear. It could no longer be ignored. It was hotter than Keyon's flames and would soon melt me if I didn't share it with him. I loved him. I loved him so much. Yes, I think I was long overdue to tell Keyon that I'd fallen in love with him.

Chapter 27

Elpis

How do I shift? I asked Rein when Keyon was done rinsing her clean. I got mildly distracted when Keyon began to tend to his own body. Gods, he was well sculpted.

I guess just... push forward, she answered. *It's almost like clam memory.*

Clam memory?

Maybe that is the wrong shellfish, she mused. *I can't imagine any of them having good memory, though.*

I gave up trying to get help from her and attempted to push my sense of self forward, imagining her legs becoming my limbs. It took a minute, and it kind of felt like patting my hands about in the darkness to find my body, but I was finally able to return to my human form. However, I sunk fairly quickly when my feet couldn't find the bottom and realized that Rein had wandered into the deepest end.

Help... Keyon, it's too deep! I said, not panicking too much because he was nearby. *Take me to the shallows!* I suppose I could have shifted back into Rein, but I was so proud that I'd shifted back; I wanted Keyon to see me!

I was amused to feel his panic, but it quickly turned to amusement when he felt my emotion. How odd it was to communicate so quickly without words. It would take some adjustments, and I wondered how many misunderstandings it could cause.

He picked me up out of the water and looked me in the eyes while I caught my breath. "Why were you laughing at my distress, mate?" he growled into my ear and nipped it.

"Because I knew I was safe. You were around," I answered honestly, grinning as he walked me to the shallows. He paused for a moment.

"That's... very sweet, actually," he said, looking down at me with a thoughtful tilt of his head. He pressed his lips to mine and murmured, "Remind me to give you swimming lessons when things settle down." He deepened the kiss, slipped his tongue into my mouth, and groaned when he massaged a breast but then reluctantly released me. I felt his cock harden as I slid past it, and I looked up at him with a silent question. "No... No... If I start anything, we'll never get to the coven," he said woefully and waded out of the water with me.

"I'm not feeling a lot of heat symptoms, so maybe they'll let me in," I said while he dried me, feeling a little regretful that my heat was coming to an end. It was inconvenient, but by the Sun God, that time spent with Keyon had been hotter than the sun's fire!

I pouted and dressed, keeping my disappointment to myself the best I could; I didn't think it'd be possible to hide anything from Keyon now. I was surprised when his hands grabbed my hips roughly, pressing my butt to his hot erection and my back to his chest.

"Oh, moonflower... Don't think the fire's gone with the heat," he whispered into my ear. "I'll take you every chance I get, and when this is all over, I may not let you leave my cock at all. You'll be overflowing with my seed and have a belly stuffed full with my hatchlings." He released me roughly, and I gasped. Electrical pleasure shot straight to my core like lightning. Tiny dragons fluttered around in my belly, making me nervous and excited. I got a little dizzy from the spike in arousal and turned with a wobble, fanning my heated face. The tease had already shifted into Toast, who was waiting patiently for me to climb into the safety of his claws. Great goddess, I was a flustered mess! He was too skilled at dirty talking!

Ready, mate? Toast inquired, and I nodded with a smile, crawling on and clinging to him as he launched into the sky. I looked up to see what I could of his face. Toast was wonderful, and I loved him too. He was sweet and surprisingly polite for a creature of his aptitude. I felt some remorse that our beasts weren't sexually compatible. He deserved to feel the joys of intimacy after everything he'd been through. I hoped it was enough to live vicariously through Keyon and me.

Rein, I asked my beast through what I hoped was a private mind-link. *What do you think of our mates?*

Keyon is kind. I am growing fond of him. Warm bread seems nervous, though, Rein replied hesitantly.

His name is Toast, and he's the best dragon in the world, I said, smiling broadly and enjoying the view. As odd as she was, I felt less lonely. She filled up a space that I never knew existed, and it was comforting. *Have you caught up on all my memories yet?*

Not yet... I am having a hard time watching them, Elpis. I don't like the memories of your torture. They make me panic.

My heart sank. I hadn't anticipated that. I was overwhelmed by deep sadness and wrapped my arms around my knees. *Do me a favor and talk to Toast privately about that. I think he'll be able to help you more than I can.*

If you say so... she replied, sounding ambivalent.

I insist, I replied. *Trust our mate. He will help.* After that, I mind-linked Keyon privately—I hoped—to let him know I was ok before he checked on me. I curled up in Toast's grip and tried to fall asleep, more upset than I was willing to admit. It was yet another thing that made it hard to move on from the mansion. I couldn't wait until I could put it all behind me for good.

Toast woke me when we arrived, and Keyon shifted back to get dressed. I stared at the Solar Coven, getting a better look at it during the daytime. It was much more impressive than I remembered. The main coven building was flanked by two massive cliffs that were sprinkled with lanterns. I took a closer look and noticed windows in the cliffsides. The witches must have hollowed out the inside to populate their coven. Proud banners depicting their worship of the Sun God hung from the street lanterns that followed the many different stone paths throughout the central area. Any ground not taken by road or building was covered in different types of bulbous, fleshy plants. Some looked like they'd be rather painful to touch; I'd never seen any plant with needles before now. There was definitely an aura of power surrounding their massive domain—strong and a bit severe.

Keyon took my hand and led me down the stone path toward the central building. I smiled with delight to see Arevik waiting for us at the door and waved enthusiastically. After all I'd been through, it was wonderful to see another friendly face. Arevik smiled and gestured us in to rest.

"Ah, there's our unicorn," Tesni's voice sang out from the hall, and she joined us by a fireplace. She embraced me, and I sent her a quizzical look when she sat down next to Arevik.

"What's that?" I asked, sitting down on a couch next to Keyon, who grabbed my hand again.

"That's your beast. She's a unicorn. Monoceros, sun-mare or sun-stallion, wardeer, warhorse… so many names, but they're all archaic… antiquated," she said with a wave of her long, elegant fingers.

"Elpis?" a familiar voice rang out, and I saw Adelais rush around the corner with an earnest expression on her face. I jumped up, and she swept me into a tight hug. "I'm so, so, so glad you're ok!" she exclaimed, clutching me like a devoted friend would. I sighed and relaxed, enjoying the comfort she brought.

"I'm ok now." I stood back to see Leofwine standing by us with a forced smile; he seemed relieved too. I went to hug him, and he patted my back.

"Good to see you in one piece, Elpis," he mumbled. "We were worried. Your beast was wild."

I stood back and gestured for them to join us, glad to see more familiar faces. "You were all there?" I asked. "I can't believe you risked yourselves for me. Thank you..." It was humbling, and I felt embarrassed, guilty even, that I'd ended up in such a bad situation.

I sat back down, and Keyon took my hand once more. I had to hide a smile of delight at his need to touch. Then I looked around and asked, "Where's Gunel?"

Tesni adjusted her robe like she was trying to find the right words and said, "She left the coven to take care of unfinished business. Now that she's no longer a coven mother, I'm allowed to do some divining in regards to her activities. I did some scrying, and let's just say she's currently... witch hunting." She frowned and patted Arevik's slumped shoulder. "I didn't look past that. Who knows if she'll return or survive. That's up to Fate."

I looked to Keyon, who mumbled, "Hopefully Mantegazz is still in a food coma." He noticed me staring at him, waiting for the explanation, but he shook his head adamantly. "You really... don't want to know." Both Adelais and Leofwine seemed a bit queasy, and I decided that Keyon was probably right. I didn't need any more darkness. I changed the topic to the questions that were burning a hole in my mind.

"So, what does it mean to be a unicorn? Are there others of my kind? Why doesn't fire hurt me? Why did those people want my blood?" I asked, unable to pick only one question, so they just flew out of my mouth.

Arevik held up a placating hand and said apologetically, "I know you must be very overwhelmed right now, and I'm sure those aren't the only questions you have, but most of those will be better answered by the guest who's arriving tomorrow."

I deflated and felt my body droop in extreme disappointment. I wanted answers so badly.

"Who's arriving tomorrow?" Keyon asked while scrubbing his palm over his stubble. He squeezed my hand and sent soothing emotions to me over the bond. I was taken off guard, not knowing we could do that. That was a pleasant surprise, and I greedily drank up the comfort.

"The Sun God," Tesni said casually, as though it wasn't something extraordinary that would make any person question their hearing.

"Wha—" I said, unable to form proper words and just gaped like the goldfish Adelmar used to keep in the mansion. Adelais mirrored my shock, batting her wide eyes and placing a hand on her pursed lips. Leofwine merely scratched his jaw and nodded thoughtfully.

He said, "My team has brought word of the gods using vessels. The Sun God has chosen the red wolf; I imagine that's who we're expecting. Surprised it's not one of His children, but now that I think about it, it's probably best that we don't have another powerful dragon to contend with. Perhaps it was a wise decision after all."

"We can be downright bastards," Keyon agreed. "Our current situation is a perfect example of that."

"Speaking of which," Leofwine said, changing the topic. "No pun intended," he murmured as his eyes rolled to the snickering witches. "What are we going to do about Cyneric?"

Keyon adjusted his shirt and replied, "I think we need to take away as much power as we can before we engage him. He's a fucking king now, so he's going to be a tough opponent even with an Inferno at our side. First, I want to free my Inferno. We'll need every knight we can get. I also want to find a way to draw him from his castle, if possible, but I'm not sure there's a way. The less resources he has, the better our odds will be of killing him."

"If we piss him off enough. Cyneric's not exactly the most prudent," Leofwine said darkly. "You wouldn't be, killing your brother and father."

"What does he value?" Adelais asked, looking at her mate.

"Power," Keyon snarled, angry. "What's new? Tried to kill me twice because I was a threat. We also know he wanted to shed his humanity because he thought it would strengthen his dragon. Seems like that's all he thought about since he was a child."

I could feel Keyon's ire and leaned over to hug him. "What if we took slaves away?" I asked thoughtfully. "If he's involved with Franco, surely losing free labor would madden him."

"Labor costs money. There'd be a lot of pressure on him to support those who relied on it to remain wealthy," Adelais added. "The treasury may take a loss if he's forced to pay people off. I don't know if he sees it that way, but... as a merchant's daughter, I know money is power."

"That's a long shot." Keyon sighed, rubbing his temple.

"We do love our treasure, though." Leofwine smirked. "They'd be safely hidden, of course, but we could also spread the rumor that the slaves are volunteering to form an army against Cyneric's reign."

Someone say my name? my unicorn said, and I ignored her with a resigned sigh.

"But how do we find the slaves to free? It takes forever to find leads. You know that, Leof," Keyon argued.

"I think I can," I said, raising my hand timidly.

"What makes you think that?" Keyon asked, turning his head to look at me with drawn brows. I didn't feel any disbelief from him; he just seemed quite intrigued. Leofwine and Adelais were staring at me in anticipation, but when I glanced over at the witches, I almost barked out a laugh. Tesni was painting Arevik's nails, and they both had pressed lips and raised brows, like they were trying to stay inconspicuous during the conversation. Perhaps they were glad the others were there so I'd stop asking them questions.

"I... uh..." I started saying, mildly distracted by their odd behavior, "I don't know what's considered normal to you all, but... Keyon, you recall that wealthy community south of here? The one that's locked up behind a gate now?"

"They gated Astertrove?" Leofwine interrupted, swiping a hand over his jaw. He jutted out his lower lip in thought, almost pouting.

"Mm-hmm," Keyon hummed to both of us and twisted in his seat to give me his full attention, crossing an ankle over his knee.

"Well... I know there are slaves there. I don't know how, but I felt a colossal sense of hopelessness about the place." I rapped my chest with my knuckles and said, "It's pure instinct. I don't really need to think about it. Now that Rein is awake, I might be able to get more information or feel them from a longer distance. It's something that... I think is worth exploring." I put my most assertive face on and waited for someone to say something.

"It's pretty close," Leofwine commented, resting his head on his hand now. "Extremely convenient to test her beast's abilities. Also doesn't make sense for so many wealthy people to feel hopeless."

"So... I just want to check... none of you can feel someone's hope?" I asked hesitantly, twisting my lips in apprehension. "That's not... normal?" They all shook their heads.

"It's normal for you, Elpis," Keyon said, gently poking right over my heart. "I can feel your unease. No one thinks you're weird."

I puffed out my cheeks, then blew out a gust of air. "At the mansion, we'd gotten a new slave. Just a hatchling at thirteen. Dagmaer was her name. She still had a little hope in her heart, and I tried to feed it. It made me feel better. I didn't realize I was the only one who felt that," I said, feeling myself drift away into darker memories. I glanced at Keyon. "With such a strong name, we cheered her up. Said she'd become one of the king's knights someday. I hope she's safe..."

"Well, I guess we'll have to find the hatchling and train her after this." Leofwine shrugged.

"She can be our first female knight." Keyon nodded approvingly.

"Uh... What if I want to teach her to be a spy?" Leofwine argued in a serious—but subtly playful—tone. "Maybe the hatchling would be better off under my wing because... Toast."

"Hey, Toast is much improved," Keyon retorted, sounding more dubious than he likely intended. "And what makes you so qualified to teach hatchlings?"

"Hey! I've never taught a hatchling, but I think I'd be pretty good! I'm a patient dragon! I can be fatherly. Could even open a small academy... We could even open it up to pups and cubs." He attempted to put an innocent but heavier emphasis on the word 'cubs.'

I noticed Adelais fanning her rouged face with a hand, and she quickly got up to excuse herself. Leofwine scented the air, found her excitement, and grinned. Keyon tried to hide a smile with a hand that he scrubbed over his mouth, but I could sense his amusement. Leofwine leaned forward and whispered conspiratorially, "How fucking awesome would cubs with dragon wings be?" He stood up, straightened his coat, and strode out while saying, "Now if you'll excuse me, I have to investigate why my mate has suddenly gone into such a state. What a mysterious development. Perhaps I can be of some assistance... Hmm..."

"Well!" I slapped my hands down on my knees and gave a wide-eyed smile of defeat to the remaining people. "There goes the planning party."

"That's not unusual for Leof," Keyon said, laughing as quietly as he could while brushing strands of hair from his eyes. "When he goes off to chase tail, it just means he's going to think about things and get back to me." He snorted and looked up with a wry expression. "Though, having his mate here could make him more distracted than usual."

"Speak for yourself," Tesni muttered in a low voice, and the coven mothers tittered in their seats. Keyon raised his brows and shrugged, not minding the accusation.

"Let us show you to your room," Arevik said, standing with her nails spread. We followed her to a guest room that was similar to the one I'd woken up in before, but it was a bit larger. The bed was clearly wide enough for two now.

"Also, congratulations on your marking and mating," Tesni said, gesturing to our necks. I placed a hand over my mark and felt my cheeks heat with embarrassment, but Keyon just stood tall and proud, crossing his arms. The mother then gestured for me to follow her. "I want to give you that follow-up health exam, Elpis." I set my bag down and waved to Keyon while he curiously watched our departure.

I followed Tesni into a very bright room that was lit by windows and steady lanterns. Everything was spick-and-span, from the floors to the raised bed. The walls were covered in bottles and containers, labeled neatly in clean handwriting. I looked with some trepidation at a tank housing some kind of aquatic slug. Wasn't a fan of that…

I hopped onto the bed and let Tesni examine me. She checked my ears, my eyes, and even listened to my chest. I squirmed a bit when she asked to examine between my legs, and I winced at her poking and prodding. Lastly, she inspected my horn, measuring it and taking notes.

"Finally came in! Must be nice to be free of those headaches," she said, jotting down observations.

"Yes…" I said and wondered what the point of this exam was. I waited and she looked up at me with a smile.

"You seem all healthy! Your beast is keeping you in tip-top shape!"

I hesitated and bit my lip with indecision. Finally, I asked, "Am I pregnant?"

Tesni shook her head. "Nothing in there," she said and guided me out the door. She left me to find my way back so she could take care of an urgent matter. I sighed in disappointment, wondering if Keyon and I were truly compatible. I was sure Tesni would have mentioned it if we weren't. I'd been in heat, though! Wasn't that when I was the most fertile?

The door to Keyon's and my guest chamber opened before I could touch the doorknob. I started in surprise but smiled faintly at a concerned Keyon, who closed the door behind me.

"What's wrong?" he asked. "You're disappointed, moonflower."

I sat on the edge of the bed and looked around, not really sure what I wanted to do with my free time before tomorrow. I also wasn't sure I wanted to share my disappointing news. I was so certain that I'd be pregnant after four matings.

We don't have any mini bagels, Rein said to our mate, and I groaned. I had to wonder if she was starting to do this on purpose. That one was particularly atrocious.

Mate wants pastries… maybe the witches have a bakery, Toast suggested, completely oblivious to Rein's flub.

"Uh…" Keyon tilted his head to ask for clarification. He wasn't sold.

"We're not pregnant. Not that I was ready to share that," I mumbled. "She meant little Toasts. Baby dragons."

Mate forgot my name? Toast asked, sounding hurt.

"Oh gods, now she hurt his feelings," I whispered to myself and rubbed my temples. I spoke louder and looked up at Keyon, who wore an inscrutable expression on his face. "Toast, please forgive her. She's having a hard time catching up on my memories. She's got a lot to learn, and it's overwhelming."

Ok, he said sullenly. Fiddlesticks, I could feel his sadness. That really ate me up, and I longed to make him feel better.

Keyon came closer and put his hands on either side of me on the edge of the bed. His nose was almost touching mine as he said, "Moonflower, it's not a big deal. It happens when it happens. Just you being in my life makes it complete. Many couples can take a year to get pregnant."

"A year?" I gasped. "I had no idea…" I pursed my lips as a burning question ignited in my mind. "How do you know so much about the female body? You seem to be able to answer all my questions, but you haven't been with anyone in a… long time."

"Oh, ho, ho, ho!" He laughed and waggled a finger. "No. I had one way to get around Toast's phobia, and that was through medical journals in our library." He jumped onto the bed and lay down with his hands under his head. "At some point I'd gotten so frustrated with him that I'd go to the library, pick up a book on female anatomy, and learn as much as I could. He didn't even like me looking at real women, so I was going a bit mad. They'd become forbidden fruit, and so I absorbed as much as I could in ways Toast could accept." Keyon raised his brows and said jokingly, "Plus, some of those illustrations had very nice breasts."

"I have noticed that you like breasts," I replied with a chuckle and marveled at how easily he could cheer me up and make me laugh.

"Only yours," he growled, glancing down at my chest. The knot in his throat bobbed, and he licked his lips. I was surprised to see his fangs slightly elongated; I wasn't in heat anymore, at least I didn't think I was. "Yours are utter perfection."

I do have those, Rein said proudly.

"What?" I asked, confused.

Keyon burst into laughter and eventually covered his red, oxygen-deprived face with his large hands. He sat up and dragged me down to lie with him, barely able to speak while he tried to catch his breath. "We really... need to finish teaching... you and your beast spelling. These mix-ups will be the death of me!"

I still didn't get it, but his laughter was contagious, and it got me giggling a little bit. When he calmed down, I looked over at him and asked, "Can we fly to Astertrove, Keyon? I'm anxious to see what I feel. We don't have to get close..."

"I don't see why not..." he said, studying me with his keen eyes. "It'd be a quick trip. You good with that, Toast?"

Yeah... fine... he grumbled, surprising me with his surliness.

"We can put it off for tomorrow..." I said hastily. Toast did not seem to be in a good mood. "Maybe it'd be a good time to let Rein and Toast meander outside? They haven't properly met..."

Maybe you should apologize, I said privately to Rein.

I guess I should... he's taking it rather hard for being such a tough dragon, she replied uncomfortably.

I think he's just hungry for affection now that he knows we are safe.

I haven't gotten that far in your memories... she admitted, sounding guilt-ridden.

I sat up and looked at Keyon. "Does he want to go?" Keyon's lips pressed in a thin line, and he sighed in defeat, turning to snuggle into my shoulder. "Best do the introduction another time. He's hibernating right now."

Violin twigs, Rein cursed sadly to me.

Exactly, I groaned.

Chapter 28

Elpis

I held Keyon to my shoulder, and he nuzzled closer, tilting his nose to scent the base of my neck. I felt terrible that Toast seemed to be facing issues with my beast. I didn't really know the extent of his struggle, so I trusted Keyon to work with him. I'd do whatever I could to help, but Keyon would know best.

I had to wonder if he saw Rein as a separate female from me. Certainly, we'd gotten to the point where he'd allowed me to show him affection, which I could tell he really appreciated. Rein, though... I was beginning to worry that I was blocking her mental development because of my history. She couldn't learn about my world if she didn't absorb all of my memories.

I couldn't imagine anyone having an easy time watching memory after memory of me being forced to please males. They'd used me in disgusting ways, given me illnesses that'd made me sick time and time again, and my handler had tortured me more times than I wanted to remember. Was Rein being traumatized with each approach of a memory?

I knew she felt my discomfort when I did, but did she feel as violated? The physical flashbacks still happened, but I was always quick to latch on to Keyon's calming skin before I started to feel too nauseated. The Moon Goddess had truly blessed me with him. If anyone could make me feel safe, it was Keyon.

I held him tighter to me and closed my eyes, feeling like I was overflowing with gratitude and love. As we lay there, I wondered if our bond spoiled the surprise of telling him I loved him. Surely, he could feel it, but I hoped it was different from hearing it.

<hr>

A knock on the door made me realize that Keyon and I had fallen asleep on the bed. I opened it to find a slightly hyperactive witch with cloudy, sable hair. She smiled and gave a little wave. "Good evening, Elpis Eudokia and Keyon Kenelm! Sunlight preserve you! The coven mothers have ordered dinner for you, and it's waiting in the western dining room. They are too busy to join you, but I can escort you there if you don't know where it is!"

She caught her breath, bounced on her toes with a grin, and waited expectantly. I looked sleepily at Keyon, and he gestured for me to go first. "Would appreciate that. And you are...?" Keyon asked politely as we walked through the coven halls, glancing around to take in the fascinating rock walls like I was.

"Sunniva!" she answered cheerfully. "Isn't our architecture beautiful? I still marvel at it!"

"Witches are a remarkable people," I complimented. "I wish I had seen more of this growing up! You are most fortunate..." My eyes widened when we walked down a windowless hall that seemed to be made entirely of black rock; perhaps it was obsidian? Little blue crystals nestled in crevices glowed, and I was so enthralled that I jumped when I felt a finger poke my shoulder.

"Eee!" I squealed, and Adelais's laughter came from behind me. I turned and snorted, shaking my head in playful disapproval. Leofwine smiled at me before striking up conversation with Keyon, and I fell back with Adelais. That was when I noticed her very subtle limping.

Dare I ask? I thought.

"Have a good 'talk' with your mate about that cub academy?" I asked her discreetly, giving her a meaningful look.

She smiled so broadly that it seemed like it'd turn permanent. "Yes, quite."

"Rough lover?" I snorted and gestured slightly to her limp.

She laughed, showing off her sharp canines. "No, I'm afraid I'm slightly more aggressive than him. This is my own doing. I really should have dialed it back…" Her face sobered, and she looked down at her hands. "To be honest, Elpis—and I feel safe sharing this with you because… I know you used to be forced to do unspeakable things—being rough and losing myself in Leof helps me forget what I survived. Being in control is… comforting. Thank the Sun God that he's incredibly secure in his masculinity to let me," she whispered that last part so quietly that I almost couldn't hear it. A smile tugged at one corner of her lip. "He finds it thrilling, actually. He says it's a very welcome change of pace."

I smiled, chuckling silently so my belly and shoulders just bobbed in good humor. "Take the victories and hold them tight. Leofwine was chosen just for you," I said and stopped her, feeling an intense urge well up inside me. My forehead itched the longer I was around her, as if it was responding to her injury. Its intensity forced a frown onto my brow, and I rubbed my temples.

"Adelais, let me please try something. Your injury is very distracting—not that I blame you!" I said and turned her to face me. I grabbed the sides of her head and touched my horn to her forehead. I tried very hard to be careful, but I still slightly pierced her skin. Fiddlesticks! My horn was sharp, but at least I didn't seem to hurt her more than a pinprick, thank the goddess.

"Sorry!" I cringed and let my instincts guide my actions.

Only a second passed before she breathed a sigh of relief, and her posture relaxed. "Elpis, what have you done? I feel all better!" Fortunately, the prick on her forehead from my horn also left without a trace.

"She healed you," Keyon said softly but proudly, standing tall with his arms crossed over a puffed-out chest as he smiled lovingly at me. I could feel his pride directly, and I basked in it. It spread through all my limbs, warming me from my heart to my skin. "She healed me too when I was sick with King's Poison... though that was through a different form of physical interaction. Perhaps it is faster with her horn."

"Ah... yes... I think... maybe that is technically correct...?" I slapped my hands to my cheeks as my face reddened. Goodness, that was a bit more than I'd wanted to share, but I simultaneously loved that he wanted to brag about me! I laughed nervously and gestured for us all to keep going. I noticed that Sunniva had disappeared, but Leofwine and Adelais seemed to know where to go.

I linked arms with Adelais until we arrived at the dining table. "Don't think you're using me, Adelais," I said to her when I let her arm go. "I feel a desperate need to be useful... so please come back whenever you feel unwell. Please." She wiped away a tear and hugged me, whispering 'thank you' before we sat to eat.

When I saw a large salad placed before me with several strips of chicken on the side, I nearly fell out of my chair in excitement. I gaped at sliced carrots, apples, cucumbers, and other little greens I didn't recognize. For the first time, I felt like I was feeding both the unicorn and the human in me.

Keyon must have felt my extreme delight because he leaned over to deliver a soft and sweet kiss to my cheek. "Enjoy, moonflower," he said with a smile that curled my toes in their slippers. I certainly would!

Perhaps I was making too many moans while I enjoyed my meal because Keyon nudged me. *Knock those noises off before I haul you over my shoulder and fuck you 'til next week,* he warned me. I stared at him, aghast, because now I was truly aroused.

Do you realize what you've just done? I accused, pressing my thighs together and adjusting my napkin on my lap to try to hide my scent. My sex was threatening to announce my arousal to the entire table.

He didn't answer; he just took a bite of his roast, and a smirk tugged at the corner of his lip while he chewed. I glanced over to Leofwine and Adelais, who were exchanging bites of food affectionately. I narrowed my eyes at Keyon and tried to find a way to get revenge. We were almost done eating by the time I formulated my strategy.

I scooted my chair and plate closer to him and offered him a bite of my chicken, which I oversalted on purpose. My unicorn enjoyed the extra salt, but I doubted my mate would like it. I batted my eyes at him innocently while he accepted the bite, though not without giving me a suspicious look. He could sense my mischievousness but not my plan! When he went to take a drink of water to wash down the salty meat, I slipped my hand into his pants and groped his warm cock. He spat the water out in surprise and fumbled for his napkin.

I moved my hand to pat his back, sending my fork flying away from the table. I massaged his cock several times to get it nice and excited before I slipped my hand out and said, "Oh fiddlesticks! Could you grab my fork? You startled me! Are you ok, by the way?"

Ha! Now everyone will see his erection! I thought victoriously. *Justice for females everywhere! Making us aroused in public places...*

Instead of fetching my fork, he grabbed me by the waist and said, "Good night, Leof. Sleep well, Adelais. I'm off to punish my mischievous female." He threw me over his shoulder and marched confidently out of the room, not caring about anyone seeing the massive erection that was putting up a good fight against the front of his pants. Laughter erupted behind us when we left the dining room.

You're in trouble, moonflower, Keyon said, and I could almost hear his grin in my head.

You started it! I accused. *I thought it was a rather clever plan…*
For a civilian, yes. I'll give you that, he replied and opened
the door to our room. He tossed me gently onto the bed and was
naked in seconds. I scrambled up the sheets, feeling the prey in
me get nervous and the mate in me get excited. His gaze was
quite predatory, and I laughed apprehensively as he crawled onto
the bed toward me.

His metallic eyes narrowed as he approached, staring intensely
into mine. Yes, I felt very much like cornered prey! "Toast may
not be so, but I am a very confident male, Elpis," he growled.

Something occurred to me as he said that, and I paused. I
placed a hand on him to stop his actions, and he froze instantly.
He sat back and tilted his head, sensing my change in mood. I felt
bad for distressing Toast with my beast, and I felt the urge to do
something special for Keyon. I hadn't shown him all my skills
yet, and I had a feeling he'd really like something in particular.

"Close your eyes, Keyon. I'll be back," I said gently and
scooted off the bed. I took my bag to the bathroom and rummaged
inside for several items. I'd noticed that the lady in the clothing
store had snuck free lingerie into my purchase and pulled that out
along with the lubricant. I readied myself as quickly as possible
and stepped out of the bathroom.

I watched my mate as he sat with his eyes closed. He raised
a brow, sensing I was near, and he waited patiently for his next
order. I smiled sadly, realizing that I didn't want to tell him I
loved him until our beasts were more comfortable with each
other. It was really important to me—and possibly to Keyon as
well—that Toast and Rein felt like they were part of the moment.
They were us and we were them.

Until then, I'd show him in a different way. A fun way.

Until I felt like it was the right moment to say it, I could show
Keyon my love through one different way, and that was through
my attentiveness. I paid attention to his likes and dislikes…
though he didn't seem to have any dislikes when it came to me.
At least I hadn't heard any complaints thus far.

Looking back at when the shopkeepers spoiled me with extra gifts and donations, I realized how special those little gestures were. It made me feel cared about, and I wanted to share that feeling with my mate. I wanted to make it even more special by customizing my gift to his tastes.

I knew it would bring up bad, uncomfortable memories, but if Toast could practice around his trauma, so could I! Part of me had to wonder if what I'd planned was considered too vulgar for a free female to do, especially when done to show gratitude. I suppose I'd get feedback later... It's just... when I'd been a slave, no one ever thought about me without wanting something in return. Receiving gifts was a new thrill, and I genuinely wanted to give one.

"Keyon, lean against the edge of the bed," I ordered gently and watched my mate scoot to the foot of the bed. He sat against it with his legs relaxed and slightly extended. His cock wasn't as excited as it was before, and I could feel his worry for me. He was as sweet as he was handsome, and it made me want to please him more than ever.

I grabbed a thick pillow, spread his legs with the back of my hands, and placed the pillow down so I could kneel at the right height. I gently grabbed his cock, and he started, slightly surprised.

"You can open your eyes now," I said softly and looked up at him through my eyelashes while I lazily stroked his length with my pre-lubricated hands, starting slow. His eyes shot open, and they dilated when they fixed on mine. His gaze lowered, and his lip curled in a silent snarl, releasing a lick of blue fire. I sincerely hoped he could control that, or this bedroom would be ashes by the time we were done.

"I didn't realize I was playing with fire," I said in a seductive voice, reaching up to trace the bottom of his lip with the back of a finger. Most of the mansion's clients hadn't requested dirty talking from me, desiring me to either shut up or make pleasing sounds. This was an opportunity to see if I could match Keyon's skill.

"You definitely are," he growled in a deep, low voice that rumbled attractively in his sculpted chest. "Fuck, f— Elpis. You look like a sex goddess." I nearly burst from the compliment, and his eyes raked once more over my silver lace babydoll. I'd kept one strap purposefully longer, and I made it slide down one shoulder with a shrug. The fabric was scantily hanging onto the swell of my breast, barely covering the nipple. His claws extended and dug into the bedsheets. I could see the veins in his hands pulse, but they didn't pulse as hard as his cock.

"I wore this just for you," I said while arching my back, pretending to stretch. "I know you prefer me naked, but perhaps it's my turn to tease you for having such a filthy mouth." A gravelly, rumbling groan escaped his throat, and he clenched his teeth to keep his fire in check. I observed his inability to reply and said, "Oh, how interesting... Your filthy mouth appears to have surrendered..."

Now I had to feed his erection. I slid my fist down his cock, released once I got to his base, and imitated the action with my other hand. I slid one after another down his length to make it seem like an endless stroke, and he hissed, baring his teeth to expose his elongated fangs.

"Do you like that, my male? My absolute dominant?" I asked provocatively. "Do you like your female at your feet, worshipping your thick, heavy cock?" I stopped my motions and waited for his reply. I smirked internally as he nodded, swallowed hard, and released his breath to free another long groan.

I placed my hands on his to keep them from wandering and stood so I could speak into his ear like he did so often to me. "Perhaps my dominant deserves something even better for taking such good care of his female..." I whispered and dragged my tongue up his earlobe.

He growled, and his hands shot out to grab my wrists. He turned his wild copper eyes to mine and asked, "Better? Does that mean I get to moun—fuck you now? You're going to turn me feral, Elpis! Careful!" His eyes gleamed, and his entire chiseled body tautened with excitement. I didn't know when it happened, but his wings were out in all their glory.

Oh goddess, he was reacting very differently than me! I thought he'd melt. This was not melting! Perhaps I should rush to give him my gift now. Any additional teasing, and he might not let me stay down there.

"Release me, my male," I said, baring my very unimpressive teeth to show my displeasure, "and I will show you." Something in his jaw ticked, and his grasp loosened.

I pulled back, pulled on the string that held my babydoll closed, and exposed my breasts to him. Before he could grab me—and I could see the muscles in his abdomen, chest, and arms contract to do exactly that—I pressed my breasts together and dropped to my knees, smoothly sliding his long erection through my cleavage.

"Ahhh...!" He gasped and leaned forward a little in his shock, bucking slightly in reflex. Keyon's expressions went from disbelief to elation, then to fiery lust. His hands flexed restlessly, and the thick cords in his neck strained. I slid my pre-lubricated breasts up and down his cock and gazed innocently up at him. "I learned this a long time ago, but... I have to wonder if it's too vulgar. Shall I stop?" I asked with wide eyes, knowing his answer already. I bobbed slowly along his length while I waited, encouraging out some pre-cum.

"No. No. No. Fuck no times forever!" he snarled adamantly, his gaze fixated on the creamed valley where his cock appeared and disappeared between my cleavage. His cheeks ruddied, and his expression was nearly one of disbelief. "Shit, Elpis! Fuck! Fuck! Fuck!" he growled loudly, shivering and staring with bared teeth. Small blue flames trickled out, and his chest heaved. Though he wasn't exerting himself, a sheen of sweat broke out on his chest, causing droplets to trickle down the valleys between his clustered muscles.

"It's no wonder you're so confident, my male," I said, squeezing his shaft as tightly as possible with my soft flesh. "You've the largest member I've ever seen. It's a wonder it even fits inside me," I praised, lowering myself enough to brush the tip of his cock against my lower lip. Perhaps I was pushing my luck with my teasing, but I couldn't resist; I was enjoying it too much. "It's fortunate I've enough breast to handle it..."

"You. Certainly. Do," he replied in a raspy, deep voice, sounding more feral by the second. Even though I wasn't being sexually pleasured by the act, I enjoyed the texture and heat of his skin on mine. I was deeply pleased by the response I was getting out of him, and I knew I'd picked the right act. I was also getting extremely aroused, and based on his flaring nostrils, I suspected the time I had was limited. I might as well pull out all my skills.

I stared demurely up at him while biting my lower lip, occasionally licking it suggestively between small moans. I also made encouraging little noises and switched up the pressure and speed, never taking my eyes from his face. I wanted him to see me looking in admiration at him whenever he was able to rip his gaze from my breasts and his overly engorged bobbing and sinking head.

He didn't last long after that. "I warned you, female!" he announced savagely. He snarled, yanked me onto the bed, and laid me on my back. His hands grabbed mine and slapped them to the sides of my breasts, telling me without words what he needed me to do. I obliged by squashing them together and watched him climb over me, straddling to kneel right over my ribs. He placed his hands down by my head and jerked his hips forward to squeeze his cock between my breasts again. Now that he was in control, he began driving wildly through the middle, growling nonstop as he did so.

"You've gotten in my head, female," he hissed. "If you tease me with my fantasy, I will lose control every time." He sat back and placed his calloused hands on the peaks of my breasts, gripping them along with my hands as he pumped his hips. He leaned his head back and released a deep, rumbling groan that made my abdomen clench. More blue fire decorate the corners of his parted lips, but he managed to keep it under control. His wings would even flap haphazardly on occasion, as though he was trying to burn off extra energy.

"Uh!" he exclaimed, much louder and more vocal in his pleasure than he'd ever been, as he repeatedly forced his erection through the tight slit I'd made. "So fucking soft! So fucking tight! Oh my gods!" He massaged the front of my breasts with his fingers, rubbing around my nipples and occasionally pressing into them while he jerked his hips back and forth. "Uh! Sun's fucking fire, you're exquisite!"

I bucked and writhed with pleasure, squeezing my thighs tight to try to quell the ache that was growing within me. Between his rhythmic, masculine grunting, the heat between my breasts, and his massaging fingers, I was starting to wish his cock was elsewhere.

An agonized and strangled bellow pushed its way past his clenched teeth, and he crouched back down over me to pound into my cleavage feverishly. One of his hands fisted my hair, clutching possessively at my head as he rode me. My entire body lurched into the bed with every thrust. I tried to hold back a thrilled cry, but a rush of arousal finally tore it from me. I could sense his ecstasy grow and roll through him over our bond; he was lost to his feral mind and buried deeply in carnal pleasure. The stronger his emotions became, the harder it was to tell where he ended and I began.

He leaned down to muffle a loud roar into the blanket. Then he slammed his fists violently into the mattress before climbing down my body, shaking with need. He spread my legs and lurched his hips forward in one slick move to bury his hot length in me. I gasped at how fast I was forced to take in his enormous size and scrabbled at his back to stabilize and balance myself. His head nudged urgently at my cervix before he started moving again.

"I need you, female," he growled and propped himself on his elbows so he could grip my head and kiss me wildly. His mouth claimed mine aggressively as his hips rolled. "The only place I will spend my seed," he said into my lips, grunting while he pumped his cock into me, "is between my female's legs to feed her womb."

He reached down between us and massaged around my opening. The sparks and warmth of his mate touch were incredible. If I thought he was good with his hands before my beast woke, he was practically a god now.

"Come while I fuck you, female," he ordered into my ear, and I felt tiny flecks of flames caress my ear. I opened my mouth in a soundless cry. Somehow the tables had turned! I was speechless, and he was talking!

"Come so I can fill you with my offspring," he snarled, pumping his length in ardently. I groaned and shut my eyes, savoring how his heated cock traveled along the stretch of my channel. I was nearly undone by how his girth forced my tight walls to repeatedly make way for his grand appearance. I was also growing to love how his tight sack slapped against me, as though it had the final say in all matters.

He leaned down to put pressure on my mark with his fangs, which made my sex clench and forced a wail out of my throat. He groaned in response and dug his teeth in harder, making me writhe beneath him. I maintained enough sanity in my thrashing to turn my head so I wouldn't hurt him with my horn.

He growled and slowly punctured my skin with his fangs, making me scream in pleasure. My legs flailed, my body arched wildly, and my core went into a full blooming climax. My sex throbbed and gripped my mate's straining, sliding cock like a vise. His motions slowed as my muscles held onto him, and he roared into my shoulder, muffled by my flesh.

His body spasmed furiously as he came inside me, hissing and groaning past his teeth in rapture. Through my own blind waves of ecstasy, I gripped his hips with my hands and jerked him as close to me as possible while he spilled his seed. His head pressed up against my cervix, and I imagined his seed squeezing right on through to my womb. I urged them on in my mind, hoping someday to have proof that I could carry hatchlings for my mate.

Chapter 29

Elpis

I clutched Keyon fiercely and possessively until he finished filling my core with his own burning gift to me. I stroked his back gently and prayed to the Sun God and the Moon Goddess for a hatchling. I noticed that he was gasping for air while trembling and struggling to keep his weight off of me, so I leaned up and gently nuzzled his cheek with the side of my horn. He seemed to stabilize a little after a couple strokes from it. After, he mindlessly and apologetically licked my bite wound and rolled off, wiping sweat from his brow and chest as he fought to clear his head. Goddess, he'd nearly lost his mind.

I smiled inwardly and turned on my side to face him so I could idly caress his shoulder. When he shook his head and blinked his eyes rapidly, I knew he'd returned to me. He rotated his head and stared at me for a while, just breathing slowly and blinking occasionally. I let him recover and stretched my legs a little to ease the pressure on my hips. I was already mostly healed from any roughness that'd occurred from our joining, and a part of me preened, knowing that any other female would have been burned and battered. Not me! I was made for Keyon, and I loved it!

Keyon turned fully on his side and laid his hand on mine. I could feel his happiness and sexual satisfaction, but I was dismayed to find embarrassment coming from him. "Why are you embarrassed?" I asked with a concerned frown. "Did I embarrass you? Perhaps I should not have done that. It's hard to tell what is normal pleasuring between mates and what is not no—"

He stopped my babbling with a kiss, scooting up closer to wrap his arms around me. He released my lips and said, "No, Elpis. You just discovered my very private sexual fantasy. Not ever female would offer to do what you just did, so I never would have had the courage to ask."

"Seems a lot more harmless than oral sex," I murmured, letting my lips brush pleasantly against his. He laughed slightly through his nose.

"Yet somehow it's weirder," he said, emphasizing the last word. "I was probably… inappropriately loud for being in a guest chamber," he whispered with a wince, but that just made me swell with pride at how well I'd done. "I think I was also pretty rough. I'm sorry," he apologized and pressed his lips delicately to mine in a gentle and sweet kiss.

"I enjoyed it…" I hummed, sighing in happiness.

I crawled off the bed to turn off the lanterns and get a damp towel, then returned to my mate to wipe us down a bit before bed. I was sad to have to wipe away some of Keyon's seed that'd escaped me. I wondered how many tries it would take to…

"Come here, moonflower," Keyon said and pulled me under the covers with him. He lay on his back—wings long since gone—and cradled me against him. "Perhaps some of the embarrassment was from how vulnerable you made me." His voice was quiet in the darkness of the guest chamber. "I couldn't believe how wild you got me. You found my weakness alright." His voice warmed as he smiled.

Before he could say anything else, I said, "My fantasy has already been realized, Keyon." I closed my eyes and let the sound of his breathing relax me as I became drowsy. "I'm a free female with a fated mate. With a past like mine, it doesn't get better than that. You're my weakness and my fantasy," I added, my murmur turning into a tired mumble.

"You're so unbelievably precious," he said, stroking my belly with a finger. "I know you've at least one more fantasy right now." His full palm spread flat on my stomach, just below my belly button. "Who knows? Perhaps this time, the fire caught."

I was a wide-eyed mess of nerves when I woke the next morning. I stared out the window as Keyon slept, waiting impatiently for the sun to rise. I wondered if the Sun God would show up at the coven's doorstep as soon as the brilliant golden orb popped into the sky. Certainly, the sunrise would mean He was awake. Did He have anything else on His godly agenda before visiting us today?

Not wanting to risk being unwashed before His arrival, I rushed to the bathroom to bathe and put on clean clothes. The witches had laundered all of our clothing, but I wasn't sure when or how it'd occurred. It truly made me like them all the more. I wished I could learn that spell!

Keyon eventually woke and bathed after making sure I was ok. I didn't realize that I was tapping my foot on the floor until he pointed it out, and I hoped that wasn't what woke him. We ate breakfast in the western dining room, but I couldn't pay attention to anything or anyone. I didn't even process who was at breakfast. I just kept looking from the windows to the doors nervously, waiting for a witch to waltz in and announce the Sun God. Even Keyon's touch would make me jump on occasion, and that was pretty much when he decided to herd me outside to get some fresh air.

"Come on, sweet moonflower. Let's get your jitters out," he urged, opening the front door for me. He guided me up the path, and we found a place to stretch and embrace the sunshine.

Laughter erupted from the coven's entrance, and I turned to see Leofwine and Adelais coming to join us. "Elpis! I need you to settle an argument. Do you think that y—" she began, laughing and shoving Leofwine aside before she wobbled with a startled expression.

The hairs on the back of my neck rose, and I spun around to see a red wolf approaching from a trail. I could feel Keyon's indecision in that moment; he was tense, but instead of stepping between me and the wolf, he kept me at his side. Then my mate simply wrapped an arm around my shoulders and studied the approaching figure.

A large bang had me squealing and jumping a foot into the air. I whirled to see both coven mothers leaving out the front door and moving to join us like Leofwine and Adelais had. If my nerves hadn't been shot before, they were now. In fact, they were absolutely shredded. Keyon rubbed my arm, reminding me that I wasn't alone.

The red wolf stopped within five feet of us. It seemed small for a wolf, or at least I'd imagined something much bigger. What wasn't small, however, was the creature's dominance. Both Keyon and Leofwine abruptly and simultaneously fell to a knee, like they were receiving a king. Adelais was crouching with a lowered head, shaking almost violently. I desperately wanted to go and comfort her, but something told me not to interfere with anything. I looked back to see both coven mothers kneeling in a prayer position, smiling.

I returned my gaze to the red wolf and didn't know what I should do. Its aura was crushing in its dominance, but my being merely accepted its position of power. I'd move if it told me to, but otherwise, I was fine where I was. I gave an awkward wave and curtseyed, hoping that was enough. In hindsight, that probably made me look like a silly foal.

Fate's timing is impeccable as usual, the red wolf said.

"All is as it should be, so says the Moon Goddess," Tesni replied with a smile and returned to her feet, helping Arevik stand as well.

Up, favored dragons. Stand and show your father your faces, the wolf said to Keyon and Leofwine. They returned to their feet, strong and sturdy, like nothing had happened. Leofwine, however, looked dismayed at his huddled mate, who was left alone on the ground.

Cat... rise to your mate's side. The Sun God welcomes you to His family.

Adelais cautiously stood and inched toward her mate, who held out a hand for her to grab. I was in awe at the power the Sun God's mere presence had on all of us. What drew more wonder was how all that power could be contained in such a small creature. What a miracle it was to be a vessel. I truly couldn't comprehend it.

The Sun God turned the wolf's head to regard me and said, *Greetings, favored daughter. I'm here because once again there is work to be done, and I need to set you up to succeed.*

My lips parted, and I couldn't bring myself to yell out all my burning questions like I'd done yesterday. All I could say was, "Greetings, Father." My mouth snapped shut, and I waited for his next words.

There is a sickness in my favored lands, a sickness that continues to rear its despicable head since the goddess helped me birth my dragons, the god said, beginning to pace as He spoke.

"What sickness?" I asked in a tiny voice.

A mental poison... Greed. The god snarled. *The one thing I could not beat or threaten out of my children's nature. Oh, I love my dragons. They are powerful, glorious creatures of the sun! They are brilliant creatures of brightness, heat, and destruction, but they lust for wealth. They lust for luxury. They lust for laziness!*

"That they do," Leofwine agreed quietly.

And you, Leofwine, and my other hatchling, Keyon, know the result of this. Of how one acquires wealth while doing nothing!

"Oppression... enslavement," Keyon said, keeping his voice low as well.

And my daughter... Elpis, you know what my favored lands feel like. Tell me, Elpis, what did that nearby, gluttonous town feel like? The god jerked its wolf head in the direction of Astertrove.

"Hopelessness," I said, shuffling my left foot in the dirt.

It seems, the god said with a growl, *that no matter how many times I ask Fate to create a unicorn to purify my lands, the poison always comes back. But now,* the god snapped, *as much as I loathe to predict upon uncertainties, I see that there is a chance that most of this sickness can get wiped out for go—*

"Am I the only one?" I cried out loudly, stricken, unable to hear anything else. "Is there no other?"

The wolf froze in its pacing and stared at me. *You are the only one.*

I staggered. My head spun, and I sat down to avoid stumbling. Had I heard him correctly? Keyon crouched next to me while I heard Arevik clear her throat. "She did just find out she was a unicorn," she said tactfully.

I am aware, the Sun God stated.

I placed my hands on the sides of my head, trying not to hyperventilate, but my lungs weren't listening to me. I choked on my tears and panicked, all sounds muted under my galloping heart. All I could do was squeeze my eyes shut to hide in the darkness.

"I'm alone," I moaned frantically. "I'm alone, I'm alone, I'm alone!"

I'm here! Rein cried, and I felt her reach out to me. *I'm here, I'm here, I'm here!*

Moonflower! You're not alone, I'm h—

Mate! It's going to be o—

Closing my eyes just seemed to amplify the pain and discomfort my body was feeling. My gut clenched from the emotional agony of what I'd just realized. "What was the point?" I screamed and fought at hands that tried to hold me. "You birthed me only to allow me to fall into slavery? To put me through the very thing you're trying to get rid of?" I cried and struggled against hands and voices. "I don't understand! Why would you let that happen to me? They tortured me! They violated me! I choked on a thousand fucking cocks just to stay alive!"

I was swiftly losing my mind, and I didn't care. Rein tried to take control of my body, but I fought her. I fought everyone. I kicked until all my limbs were held down, and all I could do was shriek and sob uncontrollably.

"You abandoned me! You abandoned me like you abandoned Pelagia! You forgot about Dagmaer, Dagrun, and Zosime! Would you have ever remembered us?" I rattled off all the names of every slave I'd ever known and spewed more vile insults at the god than any sane mortal would.

After a particularly piercing wail, noise just stopped coming from my rent throat, and all that escaped my mouth was raspy air. Unable to protest any further, I went limp and accepted my defeat. I couldn't open my eyes. I'd lain waste to my surroundings and couldn't bear to see the insanity I'd created.

There was murmuring as I was lifted off the ground, and my body was eventually slid onto a bed, then covered with a cool, soft sheet. A door closed and the room quieted. The only individual in the room was the cat-shifter who crawled onto the bed and curled up next to me. She was close enough to offer comfort but far enough to give me space while my mind tried to stitch itself back together.

I rubbed my swollen eyes as I slowly woke from my emotional collapse. It had been dreamless, and I wondered if the witches had anything to do with that. I felt like it should have been riddled with nightmares.

It seems my approach to our first encounter was more upsetting than I'd anticipated, Daughter, the voice of the Sun God said. He was close. Perhaps if it had been anyone else, I would have tried to pretend to still be asleep. It simply wasn't the case. I propped myself up with a pillow and gazed wearily at the red wolf resting near my feet on the bed.

"I apologize for the filth that I allowed out of my mouth," I said numbly.

Let us continue this differently, the god said and rested His head on His paws. *Ask your questions. I will exercise patience, which I do not often offer.*

I swallowed hard and nodded. I could do that. Perhaps with more context, my life would make more sense. "Why is there only one of me?" I asked, addressing the topic that had carved a lonely pit in my heart.

There used to be herds thousands of years ago, the god said, and though I parted my lips in mild surprise, I was still quite numb. *When I saw the Moon Goddess create Her children, I became inspired and asked Her to help me with mine. I wanted children that represented everything I cherished. They had to be powerful and pay their respects through flight and fire. I wanted them near me.*

My children disappointed me when I discovered their tendency to take what was not theirs. They not only stole items, but they also stole individuals, overpowering them and forcing them to do things they wished not to do. To further my humiliation, their habits had inspired other species to practice slavery. Their sins spread like poison through water.

I consulted with the other gods and decided to balance my dragons with a new child. I created a creature that was designed to burn out the plague my dragons had wrought. They were expected to pull out the poison and cauterize the wound... but it turned out they were too weak.

The worst of my hatchlings started targeting and killing them, partially to prevent change and partially to covet their horns as trophies.

I placed a hand to my own horn and shuddered. The thought of someone taking it put me into a cold sweat, and I tugged the sheets up to my shoulders.

The god sighed and looked down at the blanket. *I tried everything. I blessed them with advanced healing, but the dragons could still bite them in two. I blessed them with speed, but the dragons outflew them. I blessed them with a sword, but their charge was not enough to protect them. I blessed them with fire immunity and the power to blind, but it couldn't prevent the inevitable. Soon, all my unicorns had perished.*

I was crying softly at this point and had wrapped my legs around my knees for comfort. "But if they're all gone... how am I here?"

I went to the Moon Goddess for help in negotiating with Fate. To avoid disrupting Fate's plans, Their singular offer was to turn your species into a conditional species, and I accepted that price in my desperation. They said that every three hundred to five hundred years, a unicorn will be born to a witch and warlock, who will have conceived under my sunlight. That way, my purifying foals would never die out. That is where you came from, Elpis.

"But one unicorn... what's to stop me from dying if entire herds were wiped out so easily?" I asked, rubbing a bleary eye.

That was why I created the absolute dominants, the Sun God said, eyeing me knowingly as the topic perked me up a bit. What did we have to do with each other? *The Moon Goddess recommended pairing up my foals with strong mates to protect them. I took Her advice seriously, as She is the expert in such things. I blessed those with the most virtue to become a new type of dominant, and She promised to pair them with my unicorns.*

Keyon has fulfilled his role admirably, considering the mess my other hatchlings have created. No dragon can challenge my absolutes other than a king or queen. It was the best I could do to protect my foals. I advised my godling, the Dragon God, Corona, to make special considerations for my absolutes when the king's seat becomes empty. That way, a new line can begin with a virtuous king and an excess of offspring. In my attempt to keep them from going extinct, I've made my unicorns very fertile.

"So, it is possible..." I murmured, feeling the relief of a weight falling off my shoulders.

It is so. You conceived last night, the god said simply, and I gasped. *And before you ask, worry not about the offspring. Unicorns do not miscarry. Your offspring will arrive safely as long as you live. I have been very thorough, Daughter. Ask another question. We still have much to discuss.*

I was still shocked and wanted to run out to find Keyon, but I slapped my cheeks gently to get myself to focus. Focus! Ahhh!

"Ah... Um..." I said, trying to clear my mind. "Oh! Why did that cult need my blood to be... virgin?"

Yes, I am aware of that encounter. The god sneered in extreme distaste. *I am not Fate, but if I were, I would find witches to be a particularly painful thorn in my side.*

Witches may be skilled in creating their spells and potions, but they have a penchant for drama. Many of the wilder ones read too much into signs and the nature of creatures. The purity of my unicorns is in their cleansing nature, not in the state of a tiny piece of flesh. How wretched their insult is to me.

Tell me, Daughter, do you see a pregnant dragon, a mother-to-be, as some unwholesome whore? the Sun God inquired heatedly.

"N-nay!" I said. "I find the sight of one quite sweet, actually."

As you should. It is in mortal nature to breed. To cast shame upon the act is unwholesome.

"Wait..." I said as a thought came to me. "So, the witch's potion will work? Our king will lose his humanity?"

If the potion fails, it won't be because of you, I assure you, He answered.

"Oh gods!" I swore, then winced at the curse. "Pardon me. Keyon must know this!"

We've spoken.

"Oh," I said simply. How much had they discussed?

You may call your mate in if you feel he must be here, the god said with an impatient sigh. *Do hurry, though.*

K-Keyon? I asked in a mind-link, hoping he was available. *C-can you join us?* I was ashamed over my meltdown and was certain he'd look at me differently now. How ugly it must have been...

The door opened immediately and Keyon stepped in, closing the door quietly behind him. I gestured for him to sit next to me, unable to meet his gaze. He reclined and didn't say anything, just slowly reached to slip his fingers through mine. Some tension drained, and I took in a deep, steadying breath.

"S-so..." I said in summary, "it was completely unnecessary that they made such a big fuss over my virginity... In hindsight... I have to be grateful for the stupidity of the witches. It kept me from being... er... deflowered while I was a slave." I frowned and found myself back to where I'd had an emotional collapse.

"But... I still want to know why you let me fall into slavery..." I asked quietly and wiped a tear away before it could fall. Keyon squeezed my fingers gently and sent me soothing sensations across our bond.

That is nothing I had control over, Daughter, and I grieve in my own way for your time spent suffering. You were taken from your family, sold, and became a slave because Fate decided it so. The Moon Goddess, should you ever get the opportunity to speak with Her, can explain just how challenging it can be to get Fate to bend even the slightest of things. The way your life has turned out, none of that would have been negotiable. Events have shaped you into who you are today. It is not all darkness. Remember that.

I sighed miserably, feeling deflated and wishing I had someone to accuse. It wouldn't do me any good, though. Fate didn't seem to care about my thrown fits.

"So, what now? What do I do now to fulfill my role?" I still didn't know how I felt about being born to do a specific job. I didn't know if it made me feel special, honored, or objectified. There was so much to absorb.

At first, I was satisfied to let you proceed normally, but I've grown uncomfortable with the witch's involvement. They've offended me with their manipulations of my hatchlings. The spitters who took down my absolute, Keyon, were the final insult.

I felt a sensation of biting shame come from Keyon, and I looked tearfully up at him. I hadn't known he'd taken that defeat so hard. A wolf growl startled both of us, and we jerked our gazes to the mercurial god.

Do not let defeat muddy your mind. Snap out of it, hatchling. Pay attention, He barked with raised hackles. *As I was saying, the spitters were the final insult. I want Toast's claws to be free, so I am offering you a blessing, Elpis. Do you wish to receive it?*

"Wh-what is it?" I asked nervously, feeling little dragons in my tummy again, but they were not there from excitement. The prospect of a god changing anything about me was frightening, and I was just starting to get used to my body!

The blessing of flight. A way for you to keep up with your mate. This is technically blessing Rein's half of you.

R-Rein? I asked my beast. *D-do you want this?* I asked uncertainly.

If it helps Toast... she said nervously. *Then... yes?*

"Ah..." I cleared my throat. "We accept," I said, trying to sound as confident as possible.

Then receive your blessing, the Sun God said, sitting up and facing me. I climbed out of the sheets and knelt before Him. *Secure your mate, Keyon. This will be painful.*

Oh no.

Oh no, Rein echoed.

Keyon held my back to his chest, and halfway through a steadying breath, I was hit by a wave of heat. My bones felt like they'd been engulfed in flames, and I screamed. I barely registered a handful of people running into the room as my body came to a broil. My veins thickened as molten lava coursed through instead of blood. My organs incinerated, one by one, and I clutched my belly protectively, crying in fear. I screamed once more as I felt layers of myself unfold and turn to ash.

Then it was over. The silence was deafening when I collapsed against my mate's chest. I barely registered Rein crawling into the corner of my mind to hibernate and rest. For the first time, Keyon's hands felt cool to the touch, but it was only for a minute. They rubbed my forearms gently, and he was murmuring about how strong I was. I grunted weakly as I tried to open an eye. I was terrified that I'd find my skin black and peeling, but it was as healthy as ever.

Take care of your mate, favored one, I heard the god say through my haze. *Do not fail me. You are close to purging this poison for good. Remember all I've said.*

"Yes, I will. It will be done," my mate said sternly, sounding like a general now.

The dominating presence left, and the mood of the room relaxed significantly. I blinked my eyes clear, and Adelais rushed forward with a cup of water.

"Thank you," I said hoarsely and drained the entire cup. I was parched, but my throat didn't hurt. The pain from the blessing was lessening by the second, and every new breath brought relief.

"Can we get you anything to eat?" Keyon asked over my shoulder, pulling some of my hair aside to straighten it.

"N-nay… not yet…" I said unsteadily. That blessing had been an ordeal, and I wasn't convinced I could hold food down quite yet.

"Well, no shit…" Leofwine smirked, sounding amused.

"He wasn't joking, was he?" Adelais added, barking a short laugh in surprise. Keyon's chest rocked as he chuckled silently.

"Elpis," Leofwine demanded, "say 'no.'"

I sent him an apprehensive look and said, "Nay…"

"No, moonflower. Not 'nay'…"

"I am! Nay!" I asserted, having no idea what they were talking about. Adelais broke into a fit of giggles, becoming red-faced while she leaned into a laughing Leofwine for support. "I don't understand..." I said while looking around, confused.

"I thought..." Adelais choked out, gasping for air. "I didn't even notice before he pointed it out!"

"Alright, let's give her some quiet. Stop making fun of her, you frolicsome feline." Leofwine chuckled, herding his cackling cat out the door. "How did he put it? 'Let it not be said that the Sun God doesn't have a sense of humor.'"

"Wha—" I protested as they shut the door behind them, leaving me alone with a joyful Keyon.

"Don't mind them, moonflower," he said, turning me around to plant a soft kiss on my lips. "Let me just take care of you while you recover from all that."

I gave up and melted into his care, feeling like I needed a year to process everything that had just occurred. Someone was also going to have to explain that joke to me...

Chapter 30

Sir Keyon

Elpis was a swirl of emotions for several hours following the Sun God's departure. She told me about the history of her people and how absolute dominants came to be. The despair I felt from her made stomaching the story a challenge. I tried not to feel guilty about my ancestors killing hers, but it weighed heavily upon my conscience. She tried to comfort me when she noticed, and soon we were simply wrapped up in each other's hugs, trying to come to terms with all we've learned.

When we went to the dining room later, Leofwine and Adelais were there like before, but we were also joined by Tesni and Arevik. I squeezed Elpis's hand when I felt her anxiety spike and tried to calm her. She was radiating embarrassment, nervousness, and anticipation, and I was pretty sure I knew why.

Elpis cleared her throat when she sat down, trying to seem put together by sitting straighter than normal. "Everyone…" she called softly to get the table's attention. The mellow chatter stopped, and the table turned to listen to what she had to say. "I wanted to apologize for my outburst earlier… outside. I'm…

r-rather embarrassed, and"—she took a deep breath, trying to blink away fresh tears—"I said things that were a little extreme. I'm r-really sorry." She sniffed and looked down at her hands when she could no longer stand holding anyone's gaze.

Adelais raced around the table and wrapped her arms around a lightly crying Elpis. Arevik placed her fork down and said, "No apology is needed, sweet one. You let out a lot of poison in your own heart by doing that, I believe. I was glad to see it."

"That's an intriguing perspective, Arevik," Leofwine mused. "Don't worry over it, Elpis. I would have been a blubbering mess if that'd been me. Probably would have pissed myself too."

Elpis choked on a laugh, and I felt her unease decrease a little.

"It's true," I disclosed, gesturing to him with my cup. "Leof has a very weak bladder. Pees himself constantly."

"It's a problem when I'm on the job." Leofwine nodded solemnly as we passed each other our bullshit story. "I'll be doing surveillance, and if a spider comes out of nowhere—bam! I'm wetting my pants, and my hideout is completely compromised. It's a wonder I'm still the spymaster."

"Those cellar spiders, I tell ya," I muttered the inside joke to Leofwine, who grinned devilishly.

Elpis had come down with a case of the nervous giggles, and Adelais was pulled along into it. Tesni sniffed and said, "If we're done talking about urination at the table…"

Leofwine and I snickered like two impetuous fledglings. Tesni didn't look very upset, though; I could tell the coven mother was holding back a smile. Gunel would have had a fit.

"So, for those who don't know, Leofwine and I discussed the next stage of our plan," I said and took a small bite of food so I could keep talking. "You're going to take a team to free my Inferno?" I asked again, just to hear him expound his plan at the table.

"I have a handful of my best in mind. A small team is preferable for this particular extrication, but I will inform the rest of my official spies—obviously after Keyon's Inferno's release—that they are welcome to join us. If they don't, I'll harbor no ill will.

Choosing between your king and your country is not an easy decision, especially for those with family in the capital. We'll be escorting the Inferno to Keyon's cabin, where we can patch them up and prepare for our first raid."

"Astertrove?" Elpis asked eagerly, and Leofwine nodded, taking the moment to shovel some food into his mouth.

"When do you think you'll be back?" I asked.

"Probably by tomorrow evening if all goes well. It's a short enough flight, and I don't want to stay a second longer at the castle than necessary."

"And you're certain you don't need me to come along?" I pressed, and my friend snorted.

"You? I don't want a one-male parade coming along on my extrication." He laughed, and I balled up my napkin to throw at him, but then I remembered where I was, so I settled for gesturing a vague death threat.

"So, what do we do in the meantime?" Elpis inquired, looking up at me with her soft, parted lips and her large, brown-sugar eyes.

Sex! my brain said impulsively, but that was not leaving my mouth. Gods, she was distracting. I tucked a rogue strand of her shimmery hair behind her ear.

"I think we need to figure out your blessing and get Rein and Toast more comfortable around each other. The road ahead will likely get pretty rocky, and we need them to be able to work together," I replied, feeling really proud of myself for not saying sex. What was wrong with me today? Focus!

Is it me or does Elpis smell better today? I asked Toast.

Mate always smells perfect, but today she is more, he replied, seemingly unconcerned.

Huh. Must be the tail end of her heat or something. Toast huffed at my unintentional joke.

"Also, when you're there, Leof," I said, pointing to him with my fork, "keep in mind that potion might actually work, but we don't know if Cyneric has already taken it. I expect Franco will also be sculking about."

"Right-o," Leofwine acknowledged, nodding. "Adelais and I will leave after we finish up eating here."

"Be careful..." Elpis said with a worried frown, but the mated pair just flashed a couple of feral grins. They'd be just fine.

I woke holding Elpis from behind. When we'd gone to sleep early last night, she'd turned to face away for a very specific reason this time; she was extremely paranoid about injuring me with her horn in the middle of the night. I admit that having a dagger in the bed was useful but not necessarily when it was attached to my mate's face.

I wrapped my arms tighter around her waist and buried my nose into her neck to take a deep breath of her scent. Still sweet and earthy, but something was different. Maybe I just didn't remember what she used to smell like before her heat. Her heat scent was intoxicating and arousing, but this one was calming and satisfying. She still smelled absolutely amazing, though.

I felt her wake before she stretched her arms and legs, and I kissed her neck in greeting. "Good morning, moonflower." Happiness radiated from her at my words. Unfortunately, she arched into another stretch, and her pleasing, round rump discovered my 'happiness' on accident.

"We should get up," I mumbled into her ear, but she yawned, shook her head, and reached between her legs to pull the front of my pants down, letting my cock spring free. Oh... if the lady insisted...

Always give mate what she wants, Toast said tiredly. Interesting.

You sticking around for this, Toast? I asked, moaning slightly when Elpis hiked up her nightgown and tucked my cock between her thighs. No underwear? What a naughty unicorn.

Just... thinking about things. I wonder if things would be easier with Rein if we were the same species. Sex seems to be... a good icebreaker, Toast answered. He seemed lost in his thoughts, like he was totally unaware that I was thrusting my cock between Elpis's now-wet thighs.

Love is love, Toast. You can very well have that without sex, I replied distractedly, sliding Elpis's nightgown up to use her generous breasts as handholds. I gritted my teeth and held back an orgasm when she tightened her thighs. *Sex can bring two together, but love is what keeps two together,* I said, feeling like my activity wasn't really adding to my point; I was currently busy sliding my erection against my mate's sex, rubbing across her primed folds.

I guess… I don't know what to say when I see her today. How does a beast court without sex? She's Elpis, but she's not. What do I say?

Whatever comes naturally… females like compliments. Compliment her, I answered. In a very strategic, smooth move, Elpis lifted her thigh and tilted her hips back so the head of my cock caught on the front of her sex's opening and redirected my length to her heat. I gasped and shuddered in surprise. Electricity burst from my chest and trickled down into my abdomen to feed my thrusting. *Tell her,* I said, barely able to think while I pumped to squeeze inside her, *that her mane is pretty, or*—I grunted and started bucking my hips into my moaning mate—*you know what, Toast? I can't think right now. Can we talk about this in a little bit?* I almost laughed out loud; the conversation was poorly timed.

Sure… he said a bit sullenly.

I slid one hand back up to her breast while the other slid down between her legs. "This is a pretty convenient position, moonflower," I groaned into her ear. "Look at how easy it is to finger you while I fuck you."

She was surprisingly easy to finish this morning. Already pretty wound up, Elpis bloomed into a climax and spasmed against me. I moved my hands to her hips to find my own release and slammed wildly against her soft bottom. With the erotic sounds coming from her throat and her smooth channel kneading my

length, it only took several more slides into her brutally clenching sex to explode.

We were a tangle of bedsheets, limbs, moans, and thrusting
until I was spent. My mate hummed in satisfaction, and the head
of my cock rested happily against her cervix, pleased it'd done
its duty in the service of the knight general.

"If that's how you say 'good morning,' moonflower," I mumbled into the back of her head, "I could definitely get used to
that." She laughed, and I dragged her out of bed to start our day.

<hr/>

"He wasn't very specific when he said Rein could fly..." Elpis
lamented as we stood at the edge of coven territory by a cliffside.

I guess let me out and we'll see... Rein said through our
bond's open mind-link.

I'd already shifted and let Toast out, who was pacing anxiously in front of the western-facing cliff. It looked like he was
there to keep them from trying to fly rather than the opposite.
He was very nervous.

Elpis shifted and let Rein out to properly meet Toast for the
first time. The mare—I assumed you'd call a female unicorn a
mare—stared up at Toast with the same brown-sugar eye color
as Elpis.

Remember Toast, I said privately to him, *this is Elpis, just a
different side of her. They even have the same color eyes.*

Toast didn't reply and merely stared down at the mare, who
also said nothing.

Say hi, T— I began.

Hi mate, Toast said, and I breathed a sigh of relief. *How are
you today?*

I am fine... Toast. How are you? she replied, also nervous.

You remembered my name... Toast said, surprised, and I could
feel warmth in his heart.

I am sorry for that. I'm not done catching up with Elpis's memories, and some words confuse me.

Why is that? It didn't take me nearly as long, Toast asked, and I cringed.

Rein's ears pinned back, and her shimmery tail swished in the sunlight. We could feel her annoyance, and though Toast's question was innocent, I couldn't blame her for being offended.

Excuse me for not having it easy like you! Rein snapped.

I-I didn't s-say I d— Toast stammered, thrown by the smaller angry mammal.

I'm trying to get through years of memories of Elpis choking on people's c— Rein shouted.

Woah! Rein. That is enough! Elpis interrupted. *That was uncalled for! Toast, you have to tell her your story yourself. She hasn't gotten that far in my memories.*

Before that, I said, fixated on what everyone seemed to have forgotten. *Where are your wings, Rein? Didn't the Sun God mention flight?*

Rein turned her head to the side and let out a dismayed squeal. *I don't seem to have any,* she replied, sounding a bit lost.

Maybe she doesn't need them. Maybe it is more magical than that? Maybe she can run in the air? Toast suggested, but Rein took one peek over the edge of the cliff and stepped back, looking more than dubious. *There is only one way to find out.*

The mare's head snapped up to gawk at him, and she groaned loudly. *Wh-what? You mean jump?*

I will catch you, Toast said firmly, sounding more like himself now. *You won't get hurt.*

It was Rein's turn to pace anxiously now. Her stress was coming in pretty strong across the bond, and her rippling, equine muscles were beginning to shake. Before I could suggest anything, Toast leaned forward and clamped his jaws delicately around Rein's neck to stop her from moving.

Calm down, mate, he said soothingly. *We won't try until you're ready.*

Instead of fighting him, she relaxed and bemoaned. *And today had started so well too…*

Toast released his gentle grip on Rein and moved to the edge of the cliff. Rein backed up a bit more and bobbed her head as she took in the distance to what probably seemed like certain death. She side-stepped nervously and swished her tail in agitation.

I don't know if I can do this. My cloven hooves are meant for the ground, Toast! Rein whimpered.

Have I told you that you look pretty today, mate? Toast asked, and I perked up in surprise.

Rein quivered with a bout of flustered, nervous giggles as she side-stepped. Her movements had a bit more of a prance now, though it was subtle. He used my compliment idea but did it to destabilize her anxiety. Smart strategy.

Thank y-you, Rein said. *O-ok… I'm ready to try! You're going to catch me, right? You swear?*

If you don't sky-run, I will catch you. Just think of it as jumping into my hug, Toast rumbled and backed up a bit more, angling his wings to prepare to follow her. Shit… It turned out my Toast did have a tiny bit of game in him. Maybe I needed to stop giving him advice and let him do his thing. This was going to be fun to watch.

Rein reared onto her hind legs several times—as though fighting her own survival instincts—and raced toward the cliff. She got within four feet of it when she squealed, dug all her hooves in, and came to a panting stop.

Try again, mate. You can do this. You're a warrior, Toast encouraged. With her shimmery, lion-like tail tucked in shame, Rein retreated some distance to try again. She walked anxiously in a circle before facing the cliff again.

Come on! Attack the sky! Charge! Toast ordered and spat a blue flame over the threshold.

I felt Rein's anger, though not aimed at Toast, spur her into action, and she charged as my dragon ordered. She even pointed her horn toward her goal, and all her muscles rippled with power as she leaped off the cliff.

Then she fell.

Fuck!

Toast slid off the cliff, falling like a rock with his wings folded. He propelled himself with ease until he maneuvered under her, turned on his back, and caught her. He rotated and glided away before returning to the top of the cliff, gently petting Rein's mane with a couple claws. She was a squirming, wriggling mess of nerves.

That was a wonderful first try. Very brave! he praised, putting her down gently. She walked away on trembling legs, looking mildly traumatized with her wild eyes and heaving sides.

What a time the Sun God must be having, watching this ground-born creature try to fly, Rein said while trying to catch her breath.

You are as much a child of the sun as I am, fated mate. You belong up there with me now, Toast reminded her, and I felt a flush of pleasure bloom from Rein's emotions. They both knew they could never join like Elpis and me, but that didn't stop affection from growing. I was glad to see some kind of start to that.

I will try again... she said and charged off the cliff.

She fell... again.

Toast caught her, brought her back up, and she tried a third time. She failed once more, but she seemed to get more of a thrill from falling than last time, knowing she'd be gently caught by him.

Alright mate, we are taking a break. Let's go flying, Toast said, opening his arms for Rein to come closer. She trotted toward him, her emotions swaying between disappointment and curiosity. *I will fly low so it will be less scary.*

He launched off the cliff and headed to the northeast side of the mountains, where there was more grassland than trees. He kept Rein secure in his grip as he glided down the cliff face. When he leveled out over a grassy field, Rein felt safe enough to pop her head out between his claws. Her white gold mane fluttered in the breeze and danced around her horn as she looked down at the weeds and meadow flowers. She was feeling joy, which made both Toast and me swell with warmth. Elpis was quietly observing everything, but she was happy too.

Toast adjusted his grip, making Rein squeal with fright, but he held her so that she was hovering upright over the plains with her hooves dangling mere feet from the ground. She relaxed once she realized he wasn't going to drop her; he was simply holding her like a parent would a hatchling over water for a first swim. Her legs broke into a run instinctively, and I imagined that it must seem pretty wild for her to be moving that fast over the ground without actually running.

Yes, mate, Toast said, sounding like he was smiling, *feel what it's like to fly.*

Rein released a giggle through the mind-link, and her emotions flooded with hyperactive glee. She was thrilled!

There is a lake. We will rest there. You like grass to eat? There is plenty, Toast said and secured Rein in his claws again before he landed on the soft ground. He released Rein, who trotted around, adrenalized and curious about what could be edible around the lush lake bed.

Toast moved to drink some water, but Rein said, *Toast, wait. I will fix it.* She lowered her horn into the water, and the lake became crystal clear after a minute. The change was surreal, and though I'd seen it before, it was still hard to process. Never had we seen water this pristine outside a mountain spring. *Ok, good to drink now.*

Toast took a long drink, and his gaze shot to her in surprise. *You are remarkable. This is the best water this dragon has tasted...* he said. We felt Rein preen as she pranced off to graze.

You are welcome... mate.

Progress. I loved to see it.

Toast lounged lazily on the grass while he waited for Rein to finish eating. She came over, and Toast said, *I must tell you my and Keyon's story now, mate. I need you to hear it.*

Rein nervously lay across from him in the soft grass to listen, her slightly longer ears facing forward like an attentive rabbit.

Toast started from the very beginning. He told of how he woke within me and watched the hidden memory. He explained how it traumatized him and how he wished he'd watched my memories in the correct order, that perhaps he wouldn't have been so shaken if he'd done that.

He detailed how his developed phobia had negatively impacted my life and nearly cost us our fated mate. He fervently expressed how he'd worked extremely hard to get past his fears, and it was all for me and Elpis. He still struggled to be near any other female, but he didn't really care because all he needed was his unicorn and her Elpis.

I had to hand it to Toast; he'd spun that pretty romantically, and I definitely decided to stop any advice-giving. My hands were officially off the reins at this point. He could handle his own Rein now.

Rein was a blubbering mess after his story was over, and she leaned against him in despair. *Rein...* he said, trying to get her to stop mourning, *I am better now. I am happy. You need to face your challenge now.*

I was expecting her to bite back on that one, but she didn't. *I don't know how! Watching her suffer is unbearable! The things they've done to her...*

I learned a trick from growing up around the scholars, Toast said, and that caught my attention. I didn't know about any tricks. *The scholars at the castle told of a practice called speed-reading. I learned to apply the skill when I had to watch any of Keyon's uncomfortable memories. If I hibernated to avoid an interaction Keyon had with Elpis, for example, I could get a sense of what happened without having to relive every second of it. I can't avoid things entirely, but I could speed up the process, which made it more palatable.*

Flaming shit, I had no idea. What else had my dragon not told me?

That's really clever... Rein said. *You think I could use this to get through Elpis's memories? It's taking me forever. I often need to take breaks, and I just end up becoming a crumbling mess...*

I know you can. We can do it right here, right now. Lie down, mate.

Rein settled in the grass, and Toast circled to curl protectively around her. *Look at the next memory, but instead of zeroing in and picking up at the start, try to get a bird's-eye view of the entire memory. Like reading... oh right, Elpis and you don't completely know how to read yet. Um... Just stay pulled back and drift through conversations instead of listening to them word for word. For activities, it's like peeking through a door to see what happened in there instead of going through every movement that every person makes. The point is to get an idea of what happened without subjecting yourself to the most painful details.*

I'll give it a try... Rein said uneasily, and Toast lowered his head next to her, showing he'd be there while she went inside Elpis's mind. He even spread his colossal wing to umbrella them both and keep away distractions.

Elpis, I said privately to my fated mate.

Yes? she replied, sounding as emotional as she felt.

Let Rein do this. We can figure out flying another time if it gets late. We won't need her to fly tomorrow anyway since Astertrove is practically around the corner.

Ok... I think that's a good idea. They seem to be doing better, don't they? she asked fondly.

I'm just discovering that my Toast has pretty decent game! I'm thrilled. Elpis laughed, and we waited patiently to see how Rein did processing her human's memories.

Hours passed, and Toast never moved a muscle. You would have thought he was a statue in his sentineling. This was a good spot for them both right now, and it was nice to just rest outside. The sun was on Toast's back, and the air swirled lazily under the smallest breeze. I could forget, even if it was just for a moment, every trouble we were facing. This could be any moment in the future. Perhaps the next time we did something like this, the kingdom would be sorted, and we'd have a home of our own. Perhaps Elpis would be pregnant with hatchlings by then. That'd be nice.

Rein finally stirred just as the sun was kissing the western mountain ridge. *I'm done...* she said. I could feel her colossal relief flow through the bond, followed by an intense burst of love and gratitude. She leaned a cheek against Toast's snout and nuzzled affectionately. *It was a struggle, but you helped me. I couldn't have done it without you. You are the best dragon.*

Yes, you could have, but yes... I am the best dragon anyway, Toast replied, preening.

I owe you, Rein said sadly. *But I don't know how to repay you.*

Just keep calling me the best dragon. I like that, Toast said simply. *Best dragon mate. Best provider. Best snuggler. I accept all as currency.* Was Toast flirting? I held back a laugh, pleased beyond words.

I'm sorry your baguette won't fit in my oven. I regret we are different species, Rein said. Toast burst into raucous laughter, which really surprised me. I thought he'd be flustered at best. Seemed like Rein still enjoyed word play, even after being fully educated with Elpis's vocabulary. Perhaps that would be their inside joke now.

We don't need mating. Keyon said that love is what keeps two together. That is what's important, Toast replied with a shrug. That was my big guy.

Then it's good I am growing to love you, then, Rein said decisively. Toast was finally thrown a little off his game, standing and nervously flapping his wings back into place.

Well... m-maybe I am t-too. Let's go back n-now. It is getting dark, mate.

Ok!

Chapter 31

Elpis

We returned to the coven and decided to eat a quick dinner before traveling to the cabin. Rein was overwhelmingly happy. I knew she was still unsettled from having to watch my life of slavery, but the misery she had endured was drowning dramatically under her growing adoration of Toast.

It seemed like everything for those two had snapped into place once they'd addressed their injuries. Did beasts fall in love faster than their humans? They seemed to go from strangers to attentive mates in the span of a day. Or perhaps those with similar injuries could connect sooner on a deeper level. It was hard to say, but I knew that today had been incredibly meaningful for both of them. For all of us, ultimately.

We said our goodbyes to the coven mothers and left the grounds. I gave Toast an enormous, wet smooch on his snout and crawled into his grip to be carried southward.

Thank you, mate, Toast said happily and launched into the sky.

Since it's getting dark, should we pass by Astertrove? I asked Keyon and Toast. I want to see if I can sense anything.

We can pass on the eastern side of the town. The majority of buildings there face the west because of the view. It's all cliff face on the eastern side. Should be safer, Keyon suggested, and Toast growled an acknowledgment.

I tried to keep my watery eyes open through the night wind's cold sting as I looked for the town's lanterns in the distance. Once we spied the twinkly lights of the taller buildings, Toast shifted east to approach from a more covert angle.

"Oh!" I cried and slapped a hand to my mouth.

Elpis? You ok? Keyon asked, alarmed.

Ah... yeah. I'm just... I took in a breath to try to brace myself against the hopelessness that was pouring from the town. *Oh, great Sun God! There are hundreds under there!*

So, you do have a stronger sense now, Keyon said thoughtfully. *That will make our search easier. Once we do our raid, do you think you'll be able to 'sniff' them out? Would you be able to point out where they could be?*

I think so! I replied optimistically. *It's just very overwhelming. I don't know what it'll be like when I'm down there. Oh goodness, this is rough. I'm not going to be sick, but... I can feel my stomach turning a bit. L-let's go.*

We're going, mate, Toast said comfortingly and flew us the remaining distance to the cabin.

They're here! Keyon exclaimed, beside himself with excitement. *Toast! Look!*

Toast sank through the trees to land in front of the cabin. The entire outdoor area was full of people, tents, supplies, and campfires. There was a massive reaction to Toast's arrival, and individuals came clamoring to greet him. When Toast shifted into Keyon, he was inundated by his knights before he got a chance to finish dressing. Keyon fended them off with a hand while he turned to me, trying to put a shirt on with one hand.

"Give me a minute, moonflower." He laughed, struggling to get the collar of the tunic over his head. "Let me deal with my Inferno first. They're a bunch of lost hatchlings without me."

"Not so, you absolute coxcomb!" one knight shouted in good humor, and Keyon whirled to playfully yank the outspoken dragon-shifter into a rough headlock.

I nodded and crept to hide behind our bags to watch the celebratory reunion. There were dozens of males around Keyon now, but I saw Leofwine break through the crowd to make his report. From the grins on their faces and the back-patting, it seemed like everything went smoothly, which was a relief.

Two large blond males followed Leofwine through the throng of shifters, and I recognized one as the blacksmith we'd met at the farmer's market. I supposed the male next to him was his twin. Did they both defect to join our cause? Their family must be around here too. How many people had Leofwine brought back?

Seeing the quiet little haven turn into a village made my anxiety spike, and I hugged myself. So many people... I desperately needed a distraction.

The only people who hadn't run to greet Keyon were either civilian-looking folk or warriors who seemed to be injured. A male with a broken leg shouted a hello to my mate from his campfire, who gave him a friendly wave in return. I itched to go to him, but I felt so shy.

Eventually, the impulse to heal him bothered me so much that I snuck past the crowd and scampered to greet the injured male. The brawny, freckled redhead looked up at me as I approached and gave a thin-lipped smile. With his pallor and the tension in his body, he looked like he was in a fair amount of pain. His eyes flickered up to my forehead, and he did a double take.

"Ah, hello miss..." the male said, trying to look me in the eyes, but his gaze kept sliding up to my horn.

"Elpis Eudokia," I introduced myself shyly. "I'm Keyon's fated mate."

"No shit!" boomed the deep voice of a colossal male from behind me. I jumped in fright, squealing embarrassingly.

"You scared the lady, Sir Gerfrid," the male before me chastised.

"'Pologies," the large, bald, and bearded male said, settling next to me with some gauze and ointment. It looked like he was tending to some wrists that had been abused under shackles much too tight for someone his size. His poor hands were quite swollen.

"Never woulda thought he'd mate and mark someone," the male with the broken leg remarked in wonder. "Must have known to wait for the right one! We expected he'd die a virgin! The men will love this!" He laughed boisterously along with Sir Gerfrid.

"And you are?" I asked, wanting to get his name so I could offer to heal him. I could barely pay attention to what he was saying, and my right foot tapped away with gusto.

"Sir Stroud," he said with a polite nod.

"Please, can I fix that broken leg? It's driving me crazy," I asked, and both men gave me an odd look.

"That's a strange way to ask, My Lady, but… you can look at it if you think you can do better," Sir Stroud said, shrugging his mouth. I sighed in relief and shuffled up to grab both sides of his head. "Woah, woah, M'Lady, that's not my leg!"

"Shhh!" I ordered. "Don't move or I'll hurt you on accident."

The male grimaced and held still as I pressed my horn against his head. Like Adelais had, the male relaxed considerably after several minutes and groaned in relief. Then I sat back and gestured to his leg.

"How do you feel?" I asked. He felt healed, but I wanted to hear it from him. Would these strangers think I was weird? Would they think I was too bizarre to be their leader's mate?

"Fucking shit!" Sir Stroud shouted and jumped up onto his feet. "You healed it!"

"What?" Sir Gerfrid sputtered. "Lady Elpis, what about my wrists, eh?"

I turned with an excited grin and placed my horn against his shaved head. His wrists were healed in seconds, and I sat back, feeling warmth spread inside from how he gaped at his fresh skin. He tugged at his cloudy, black beard and cursed a string of words.

"And there, my dear friends," Keyon's voice said loudly from behind us, and I started again, nearly scared out of my wits, "is my fucking amazing fated mate, Elpis Eudokia." I blanched to see Keyon grinning with all of his people hooting and hollering behind him.

The boisterous crowd was demanding a celebratory lap for their general's new mate, so Sir Stroud and Sir Gerfrid picked me up and paraded me from campfire to campfire on their shoulders. It was pretty obvious that Keyon kept a wine cellar because everyone here looked like they'd had a cup of something. I might need to look for hard cider myself if this continued much longer! Most of the shouts were jesting jabs at Keyon for no longer being a virgin, slights that he seemed to take with levity. I only witnessed him doling out several death threats.

"Elpis? Elpis!" I heard a female yell out my name, then scream it. I looked around frantically and spotted a smaller hand waving to me from behind all the massive, rowdy males. I knew that voice!

"Let me down! Let me down!" I patted the males frantically, who set me down quickly, sensing my urgency. I ran through the crowd toward the voice with tears beading in my eyes.

"Elpis!" the female screamed, and I crashed into her embrace, sobbing like mad.

"Zos-s-sime!" I bawled, crushing her against me, unable to believe it. She was here! After a minute of near-violent crying and us checking each other to make sure we both had all of our limbs attached, Zosime dragged me to a campfire where a number of other people were sitting and eating. A female hatchling looked up and jumped to her feet, eyes wide with excitement.

"Dagmaer!" I sobbed and ran to lift her into my embrace. She was heavier! I kissed her cheek repeatedly until she started complaining, and I released her, only to have her cling to my skirts.

"H-how are you here?" I gawked, and Zosime gestured for me to sit by the fire. I looked at the brawny male next to her and gasped. "You! You were at the smithy! The farmer's market!"

The smith's son's jaw dropped, and he looked at Zosime while gesturing to me. "Is this Elpis? We met her and the knight general at the farmer's market! They're the ones who encouraged us to visit Uncle Sigivald."

"Granpa Sigivald!" Dagmaer corrected firmly. I looked down at her in surprise and back to Zosime.

"Mind filling me in here?" I asked, confounded.

"I know!" Zosime said to me with wide eyes. "So much has happened in such a short span of time!" She propped her chin up with her palms and rested her elbows on her knees. "After we were liberated from the mansion, they rehabilitated us at the castle. They gave me odd jobs to work so I could start earning a bit of coin." She frowned and looked over at Dagmaer. "They separated us, and I asked if I could adopt her, but I needed to prove that I could earn income and give her a good home first. There was also an adoption fee I wasn't able to afford yet, so it seemed impossible.

"I took every job I could find and worked myself to the bone," she said with a nostalgic laugh. "Almost a week had passed when I scented my fated mate, but it was like we were playing hide-and-go-seek. We couldn't quite find each other!" My eyes moved to the smith's son, and I was certain I knew where this story was going. "Days passed until he finally tracked me down in the garden! I was weeding, and Sigeweard practically kidnapped me back to his family's home."

"Uh, sweetling, let me remind you that you did not require any convincing whatsoever," Sigeweard said low so Dagmaer couldn't hear. "It almost became publicly indecent." Zosime's face turned red, and she cleared her throat to keep talking. I didn't bother to hide my smile. I could already tell they were happy.

"S-so, Sigeweard didn't want me toiling away for work anymore, but I told him I had to in order to adopt Dagmaer. I didn't want her going to a family who didn't understand what she'd been through... My male put down everything he was doing that very moment and went out to initiate the adoption. So... Dagmaer's our daughter now." Zosime beamed and moved her hair aside so I could see the mark Sigeweard had given her.

Pulling Zosime into a tight side hug, I looked tearfully at Sigeweard. "You have no idea how much good you've done. Th-thank you... on behalf of every Reborn looking for a fresh start." I cried a little more and rocked Zosime, melting at the thought that all three of us had found exactly what we needed.

"Things are getting better," he replied and rubbed his mate's back. "She still has nightmares, but she can be around more people now. She's working hard. Both my females are." He grinned affectionately at his adopted daughter, who was sporting a fine milk mustache.

Zosime pulled back from my hug eventually and decided to finally address the glaring change in my appearance. "Elpis," she said tactfully, "you didn't use to have... a horn." She put her fingers to her lips as she glanced up at it. "What happened to you after we were rescued?"

I told her almost everything that had happened since Keyon arrived at the mansion. Zosime and Sigeweard smiled broadly when Dagmaer jumped excitedly about the 'spy' part. I said that Keyon ended up being the 'spy' that I predicted would come as a sign of being rescued. Keyon might just have a little fan now.

"That's remarkable, Elpis. I can't imagine how difficult it's been, but oh! You have a fated mate now too. I'm so happy!" she said, embracing me again. "We three... we're so fortunate. I couldn't ask for more!"

I felt a part of me soften, a part that'd been high-strung since day one. I glowed from my hope and theirs, the ones who meant so very much to me.

"Pardon me, Lady Elpis?" a male's deep voice said from behind me, and I turned with a small smile. I could sense his injury before he even spoke. His wrist was sprained, and it looked like he was coming to see if I could help him like I had the other knights. This male was dressed all in loose black clothes, and I wondered if maybe he was one of Leofwine's spies. "I tweaked my wrist earlier, and I was hoping..."

"Of course!" I replied excitedly. I loved finally having something to offer other than sexual acts, and I loved that it was my choice to give. It made me feel like... maybe I could have another profession. It made me feel... respected! That was it! What a strange feeling, the way it elevated me.

The male went off grinning, and another one replaced him, hesitantly asking for help with the nasty rashes he'd gotten while shackled. I healed him and felt more hope grow with me. I was in my element and thriving! This felt good! My instincts loved using my skills on these warriors. These were good people and deserved my assistance. They'd help free people like me. Soon!

My smile faltered when I noticed a line had formed. I froze as the next male knelt so I didn't have to stand to heal him.

A line. I had a line.

My body chilled and locked, minus the mild shaking from my arms and legs. My breathing became fast and shallow, and panic sprouted in my chest. A hazy wall wrapped around me.

"Sigeweard, she shouldn't b—" I vaguely heard Zosime say in a distressed tone. "Her breathing is too fast..."

"Already on it," he said and appeared by the male near me to disperse the line. I heard the words 'Reborn' and 'trauma' and distantly wondered if I'd ruined my first impression with Keyon's men. My mind was in two places now, and my body was back to feeling dirty and used. Tears streamed down my frozen face as I recalled the parties at the mansion. The filthy hands on me...

"Elpis? What happened here?" My mate growled softly, sounding more concerned than angry. I couldn't look at him; all I could do was stare straight ahead, held down by several vicious tethers. One tether made me feel so disgusting that if I moved, I'd feel even more violated. Another tether was one of fear. I was horrified that everyone had seen me crumble into this state. I was too afraid to look at faces, to see what they must think of me now. I didn't want to realize how embarrassed I should be. Numbness was my only shield. If I didn't move, nothing would change.

"Help me bring her inside, and I'll tell you, Knight General..."
Zosime said quietly. Keyon carried me to the master bedroom,
where it was dead quiet. Adelais had discovered us on our way
up and was asking anxious questions.

Zosime told Adelais to run some cold water, the colder the
better, and instructed me to dunk my face. I could either hold my
breath or scream, whatever helped. I did as she asked, and after
a few plunges into the shockingly cold water, my mind began to
clear, and my body started to relax.

Zosime then made me run in place for several minutes, which
I didn't feel like doing at all, but she insisted it'd help. A medic
and scholar at the castle who'd been treating her trauma suggested
four ways to break out of these... heightened states of distress.

Finally, they put me in bed where Zosime taught me how
to take long, counted breaths and perform an exercise where I
had to flex my muscles individually. It was strange, but she was
right. By the time we were done, I was feeling a great deal of
relief and exhausted enough to sleep.

Zosime pulled Keyon and Adelais to a corner and spoke in a
low voice. I could barely hear them, but I knew she was telling
them about the mansion's parties and the lines that would form
for my 'services.' I pulled the blanket over my ear to make dou-
bly sure I wouldn't hear any details, but at least I felt grounded
now. Thank the Moon Goddess that Zosime was here... I'd been
doing ok with the crowd at first, which was an improvement, but
the line had shattered my composure.

I felt Keyon's muted rage through our bond, and I knew he
was struggling to stay calm for my benefit. I couldn't blame him
for being upset though. Had he been through the same, I would
have been livid. After they finished talking, both Zosime and
Adelais left while Keyon came to lie down and hold me.

"We have a strategy now, moonflower. Tools to work with.
We'll use those techniques if this happens again. Until you're
all better, ok?" he said, kissing the base of my horn. "You're so
generous, Elpis. Just don't overdo it. Promise me?"

I nodded, then asked, "Did I embarrass myself? Do your knights hate me now?"

He snorted. "No. I'm sure I'll be surrounded by a bunch of sniffly, concerned dopes when I go back outside."

"Ok…" I said, laughing slightly at the funny mental picture his words instilled and forced myself to stop thinking about it. He cupped my cheek and turned my head so he could kiss me properly.

"Your horn is a hazard." He laughed, moving around it to lay his lips on mine. The kiss relaxed me even more, and I sighed with the renewed alleviation. He stroked my horn lazily while he kissed me and played with its shape. He released my lips and asked, "Does this feel good? I've been wondering."

I was going to shake my head but thought better of it. "Nay. I can barely feel you touching it. I think it's for the best if it's being used to stab through bone," I informed him, a touch dryly. He laughed quietly, rocking me gently with his quaking chest.

"That's a very good point… pun intended." He smirked and tapped the tip of my horn to test its sharpness.

"Don't! It cuts easily," I hissed and swatted at his hand. He frowned and pressed harder with his thumb.

"Elpis, it's not cutting me. It feels sharp, but it won't cut," he murmured and showed me his hand. "Odd sensation."

I grabbed his hand to give it a closer inspection. "Maybe because you're my mate?" I asked. Sure enough, his hand wasn't bleeding. It certainly should be. It should have been skewered with the pressure he'd put on it.

"Oh, thank the gods!" he exclaimed and kissed my horn. "Now we know you can't maim me in the middle of the night," he said, tickling me slightly to get me to giggle. He kissed my lips once more and nuzzled his nose into mine. "I have to go back out now, moonflower. We're sending out a couple scouts tonight so we can strategize for the raid tomorrow. I'll come to bed in a couple hours, though, ok?"

I nodded and smiled, feeling much better now. I closed my eyes, thought about all the wonderful people in my life who were now safe, and fell into a deep sleep.

I woke to a bunch of females trying to feed me breakfast and laughed when a little girl attempted to blow raspberries on my cheek to get me out of bed. I ate with Zosime, Adelais, and Dagmaer, then left to see where Keyon was. I needed to know if I should join the raid as Elpis or Rein.

Oooh, me, me, me! So that I can see Toast again! Rein gushed.

I smiled at her enthusiasm and found Keyon strapping a large, wheeled cage to one of his shifted knights. He was wearing a loose, armor-plated jacket that looked like it'd be easy to toss off if he needed to shift. His pants also had sections of metal plating and... made his butt look rather nice.

He turned and grinned at me, knowing exactly what I was feeling. I skipped up to him, feeling incredibly refreshed, and asked, "So what now? When do we leave? Should I shift?"

He kissed me and said, "Morning, moonflower." Right!

"Morning!" I added, sheepishly. "I'm just so excited!"

"Oh, I can tell." He grinned, setting the last strap in place, and led me from the cage. "And no, I don't think you should shift right away, mostly because Rein might not fit in every doorway."

That is... very true, Rein mused.

It just means you have a lovely butt, Toast added, and I nearly choked on my own spit. Keyon pressed his lips together in suppressed shock and mirth. Toast! You rascal!

"And uh... yes, we'll be leaving in about an hour. Leof and I want to hit them early today. The sooner we get to these dens, the better. News will spread fast about Leof's team defecting and my Inferno escaping. We'll be met with more resistance as we make progress. Hopefully that resistance will be sloppy considering the males Cyneric's filling the ranks with."

Oh gods, I had to wait an hour. I wandered off while Keyon finished preparations and looked for something to keep my mind occupied. I was soon interrupted by a number of males apologizing about last night and offering small gifts to earn my favor. I told them it wasn't necessary at all, but they insisted, so I accepted the offerings with mixed feelings. Gratitude was still at the top of my heart, though. For a bunch of scary-looking men, they could be rather sweet.

I wandered around more discreetly after that and kept my senses alert for any injuries that would truly hamper the rescue effort. I privately healed several more sprains and another pair of beat-up wrists that were rubbed raw from shackles. When Keyon finally called out to me, my heart fell into a full gallop; it was finally time to leave!

Interestingly enough, we weren't flying to Astertrove. Keyon and Leofwine wanted to keep a low profile to make sure no one saw where our departure originated. They wanted to keep the cabin's location a secret for as long as possible. That meant keeping to the ground.

We finally arrived at the gilded gate, and by that point, I was well past miserably uncomfortable. My stomach roiled from Astertrove's acute hopelessness. Keyon stroked my back and said, "Stay close to me, moonflower. You tell me where to go, ok? We'll find them. My men will take care of the rest. Leof already took out their messengers."

I nodded and drew a deep breath. I could do this!

Chapter 32

Elpis

The knights didn't give any of the guards at the gate a moment to process what was happening. Two males—who were already shifted—ripped the gates open, and Keyon's small army surged into Astertrove. Leofwine's team worked on the perimeter, apprehending anyone who was trying to escape the raid. Apparently, the cage we'd brought was not for the slaves but for those who were suspected of being slave owners or sympathizers.

I strode down the main road and felt my attention being pulled in several different directions. I followed the largest pull first, thinking that maybe it would be the closest location that hid slaves. When I pointed to the gate of an estate, several knights who were escorting Keyon and me ripped them off their hinges. The strength they possessed was frightening, and I was certainly glad they were on our side!

A team of guards raced to engage us, but they were quickly overpowered, apprehended, and shackled with a metal that apparently couldn't be melted by normal dragons. They were also masked with the same metal to keep them from breathing fire.

Once Keyon burst through the entryway, we were met with very little resistance. Maids and servants scrambled to escape, and I followed the intense despondency to the kitchen.

I frowned and looked around for a hidden door. "We're right over them, Keyon, but I don't know where the entrance is..." I said, shuffling around the large kitchen and peeking into cabinets. Keyon told his two knights to spread out, and he joined my search. I walked into an adjoining room and found the larder, then Keyon squeezed past me and kicked a hole through the wall, which turned out to be a door. He reached around to try to figure out where the handle was and finally exposed a hidden passage.

I teared up and frowned deeply at the door's chosen location. The larder was filled to the brim with food that was locked behind a metal grate. How cruel to force slaves to walk past that every day. Anger boiled inside me, and I followed Keyon down the stairs into a room that housed slave pens. There was only one guard down here that immediately moved to attack Keyon.

"Anyone past hidden doors, Elpis," he said almost casually as he sent a thread of blue fire through the male's heart, "is fair game. These people know what they're doing." He dug through the guard's clothes, found a heavy set of iron keys, and began unlocking the doors that imprisoned the slaves. Both of Keyon's knights had found us and waited patiently while Keyon explained what was happening to the poor, abused, and disoriented souls.

"You are all being freed per the knight general, Sir Keyon. Please follow my knight, Sir Adalbern, out of the mansion to a safe location where you'll be treated and fed before eventual rehabilitation," he announced and checked each cell to make sure no one needed help standing. "The raid is occurring throughout Astertrove, so your departure will be protected." He turned to Sir Adalbern and said, "Let me know if there are any issues, but we have several more locations to get to. I trust you to handle this."

Sir Adalbern nodded and began gathering the slaves. Some looked shocked, while others cried from relief or laughed from frayed nerves. I looked forward to returning to the cabin after this raid and taking care of the injured. It itched within me as much as freeing them. I was beginning to see what the Sun God meant about His unicorns. It felt like I was burning out a sickness and drawing out poison. It was deeply satisfying, and I was compelled to keep going.

Once we left the estate, Keyon called a second knight to escort us to replace Sir Adalbern. The next location ended up being two neighboring shops and an enormous inn that shared one large holding area underground. There were easily another hundred slaves in there, perhaps more. The conditions were much worse than the estate, and many of the slaves were sick from one illness or another. The air was thick with disease.

"I don't think some of these people will make it if I don't treat them now, Keyon," I whispered worriedly as he unlocked the cells. I wrinkled my nose, trying to get out the sting of impending tears.

"How many do you think you need to treat, Elpis? We just need to get them back, so you have to pace yourself. There are still many more to free," he replied just as quietly. "You need to be honest with yourself here."

I frowned and paced by the cells as one of the knights organized the survivors. I tried to pick out who the sickest were, the ones who couldn't walk and the ones with heart problems or breathing difficulties. I rubbed my temple, feeling anxious about making a judgment call.

"Sixteen," I said firmly, worrying at my hands. *Please don't say no...*

He sighed and unlocked the last cell door. "Fine... pick them out, and we'll bring them to a private corner where you can heal them." I slumped in relief and pointed out the sickest to a second knight, who helped me while Keyon gave his speech to the slaves. The knight made sure the slaves didn't get a good look at me so I wouldn't be pressured to heal more than I could handle if they started begging on their friends' behalf. It killed me that I couldn't heal them all right now.

I worked through the sixteen slaves and ended up on the floor, leaning against a cell. Breathing hard and sweating, I felt like I'd just done pushups with Keyon. I wiped my brow and looked up at a concerned mate, who crouched and grabbed my hands. He pushed some of his energy across our bond to help me recuperate, and my grateful heart accepted it, drinking deep.

After a minute, he helped me stand, and we returned aboveground to go to what felt like the last location. Another knight joined us, and I led Keyon to a larger mansion with a private landing on the cliffside. There were a surprising number of guards at this location, and it took the knights a little more time to subdue and chain them.

"Be faster if I just killed them," Keyon muttered darkly. His mood was getting progressively worse the more he saw of Astertrove, a town built on broken spines.

When we entered the mansion, we quickly realized why it'd been so heavily guarded. There were a number of portraits of Gero littering the entryway and halls. All of which made him look more attractive than he really was... or apparently used to be. I had to remind myself that he was very much dead now—his portraits brought horrific memories. *He's dead. He's dead.*

"Guess no one got the notice that he was dead," Keyon muttered, his thoughts following me as closely as his stride. No, and I doubted he had any legitimate heirs to take over this place either. Distracted by dark thoughts, I struggled to pinpoint the location of the slaves and ended up zig-zagging through the mansion in confusion.

"I think there's more than one holding area," I said, backtracking into the previous room. I snorted in frustration and tapped my toe, trying to focus on just one. A knight returned to us, saying that they found a trapdoor in the wine cellar, and we followed him. Keyon forced it open and sighed in relief. This definitely seemed to lead to one group, and we descended to find several floors of penned slaves. There were no guards here; I had to assume they'd joined the other guards to defend the property, so they were likely already in custody.

It took longer to free these slaves, but we finally got through them all. Like the others, they were either in shock or extremely emotional, but the level of despair I felt had dropped considerably. There was just one more location I had to find. It was smaller and upstairs, but I had a bad feeling about it.

I jogged up the stairs and followed my senses to the western wing. The area reeked of Gero, and I faltered in my steps to gag. I covered my nose and mouth with my arm and walked into the master suite, additionally revolted because I knew what I would find. When I pointed to the walk-in closet, Keyon kicked a hole through the hidden door, not wanting to waste time searching for the hidden handle. He reached in, opened the door, and walked in first, then backed out immediately.

"Elpis... I don't want you coming in here. I'll send the girls out to you," he said in a voice void of emotion. The warning made me sick. It must be bad. I stayed with the other knight and received the young women one by one. They weren't communicative at all, choosing to just stare into the distance as we gathered them.

"I'm getting Leof to escort Adelais here. I want her to bring them back with our knights. They'll feel safer," he said. His entire body was on edge from what he'd seen. His neck was corded with tension, his quivering knuckles were blanched, and his jaw was clenched so hard I could hear his molars grinding. If Gero wasn't already dead, I felt like Keyon would take his time killing him.

Adelais arrived and herded the women out as fast as possible, wanting to get them into fresh air and far from the nightmare they've been trapped in for who-knows-how-long. Keyon took my hand in his, desperate for comfort, and I yearned to give it. We reached the mansion's exit when Keyon pulled me toward the privacy of the cliff landing and yanked me against him. His tears dampened my cheek as he clutched me, like he couldn't get close enough to receive what he needed so badly.

I rubbed his back and made calming noises while he released his grief away from his knights. "There's always something worse, Elpis," he croaked. "Every time I think I've seen the worst..." He was so vulnerable right now, and all I could do was hold him and send him as much soothing energy as I could.

He pulled back and held me at arm's length. "I don't know what I'd do if you'd been in there. I... If I hadn't met with Adelmar. If I hadn't taken you from Gero's bid." His arms shook in his distress, and his eyes searched mine, still brimming with tears. "This is probably the absolute worst time to say this, but... moonflower, I lo—"

His words were cut off with a choke, stopped by the arrow sticking out of his throat. I shrieked, and when I turned, I saw my old handler with a bow. I was disoriented for a second. I thought I'd never see her again! Tofa swiftly nocked a second arrow and released it, hitting me in the stomach. I stumbled backwards with a pained cry and clutched at my abdomen.

Get it out, get it out! shrieked Rein. *Our hatchling!*

I tried to yank it out, but the resistance had me screaming in agony. It was lodged in deep, and I was too terrified to pull on it. I glanced over at Keyon, who snapped off the head of the arrow penetrating his throat, yanked the shaft out, and blew blue flames at the next arrow that came flying. I didn't know what the arrows were made of, but it didn't get hit hard enough to divert. It landed firmly in the side of his chest, where there was a small gap in his armor, and the impact was punctuated by his scream. Keyon's flames extended farther and enveloped a shrieking Tofa, giving her a brutal cremation. My mate stumbled back, coughing up and choking on blood as I hobbled toward him as fast as I could.

"Keyon!" I screamed, trying to reach him before he got too close to the cliff. His face paled, he fell to his knees, and he collapsed toward the right, which was far enough to take him over the edge.

I shrieked and jumped off the cliff after him.

REIN, YOU HAVE TO FLY! I cried, knowing that if Keyon died, I might as well too. Rein forced her body out and screamed in terror as we descended. There was no time! No time! The treetops were rising, and I wondered if this was finally it. No one else was close enough to catch us. We didn't know what we were doing, and we were all going to die.

Pain laced through Rein, and she was taken over by a violent shift. It ripped through our body at a fast and brutal pace, almost causing us to black out from the pain. This was new. This was unfamiliar—terrifying.

We were in between bodies and following our fated mate to our deaths. Everything became smaller, and Keyon became a lot closer. Rein reached out and snagged him with jaws that were way too large to belong to us. Somehow, we met with wind resistance, and Rein flailed with her limbs, trying to slow our fall with that resistance as a compass.

The ground came fast, so Rein curled herself around Keyon and leaned into the sloping cliff wall to break our fall as much as possible. We hit the forest floor with a stunning impact and rolled to a stop, our ears filled with the sounds of our shattered bones crunching. Rein released Keyon's body and stumbled to her feet the best she could, wobbling and struggling to balance. So much pain... we were in so much pain...

Horn! Where's our horn? Heal him! HEAL HIM! I screamed madly, my nerves completely shattered. Rein bent over him and shakily nudged his head with a horn. He was limp and bleeding heavily, and she pressed against him as gently as possible. She was making odd, breathy noises as she cried, and I noticed her front limbs were no longer hooves, but large, white, clawed hands.

After what felt like an eternity of absolute torture, Keyon's wounds closed, and his chest finally pushed out the second arrow. It rolled to the forest floor, soaked in blood. Rein's chuff-like crying became uncontrollable as he stabilized and took in steady breaths. His heartbeat strengthened, and we weakened, but it was a trade I'd make any day. The healing we'd done had exhausted us, and the new shift had depleted us. Rein finally succumbed, falling on her back to avoid pushing the arrow in farther, and we both fell unconscious.

Sir Reyon

I groaned and rolled onto my side, feeling like I'd been thrown into a tree at best. I slowly blinked my eyes open and stared at a solid wall of scales. Where was I? Why did I scent Elpis but didn't see her? Then it all came back to me. The fucking handler from Adelmar's mansion had been at Gero's place.

She shot us… Toast's voice said groggily, but then it sharpened. *SHE SHOT ELPIS! REIN! WHERE ARE THEY? WHERE'S OUR MATE?*

The realization struck me like another arrow.

I stumbled backwards from the wall of scales. "Not possible…" I murmured in shock, realizing that the large creature next to me was no stranger. I should have known. There'd be no dragon in the world this beautiful that wasn't our mate.

R-Rein? Toast choked out as I walked around the unconscious beast, stunned.

She wasn't as big as Toast; no one was. I found her gentle face and cradled her snout in my arms, crying softly. Then I ran a palm across her lovely white gold scales and took in her state. She was still alive, but her body was wrecked. Lightning struck my heart at the sight, and nothing else mattered.

I sent a desperate call to my Inferno. *I need a knight to come to me immediately! There's been an accident off the cliff! Let Leofwine know as well!*

Sending someone, a knight reported immediately, and I waited for help to arrive. I wiped tears from my eyes and ran a palm up her long horn, the one part of Rein that was still a unicorn. I felt around my neck, then fingered the hole in my coat where the arrow had pierced.

She finally flew, Toast said, grief-stricken. *She caught us and healed us. I can't believe she did that in the amount of time it takes to fall from that height.*

She looks completely drained, I said, wiping away another wave of tears with a quivering hand. *She can't even heal herself right now. I feel so fucking guilty! That was such a stupid fucking place to stop.*

It's done. We can't help our mate by kicking ourselves, Toast said, though it sounded like he also needed to convince himself.

A knight landed by the edge of the cliffs and hurried over to survey the situation. *Reporting as requested, Knight General,* he said, gaze darting from me to the unusual-looking dragon.

"I need you to head north and veer slightly west toward the Solar Coven. They're located on the west cliffs. Go and ask if they can send a healer out for the unicorn. Tell them it's an emergency," I said and pointed northward with a hand that wouldn't stop shaking. "Sir Eadwine, this is my mate, Lady Elpis. I need you to be swift about this!"

Leaving immediately, Knight General! the knight replied, backed into a clear space, and launched into the sky. I crouched to give Rein my full attention, trusting that Leofwine and our teams had everything under control in Astertrove.

So, the Sun God just gave Rein a second body? That's unheard of. A shifter only has one beast body.

As far as we know, I said with a sigh, gently laying Rein's head down on the ground so I could look at the rest of her injuries.

Seems like it would have been easier to have just given her wings or something, Toast pondered.

I don't think you can just slap wings on any animal and expect it to do well in flight. The Sun God would probably have to completely redesign Rein for air movement. Seems easier to just slap her into a dragon's body, I reasoned and looked sick at the state of her wings. I couldn't even bring myself to touch them for fear of doing more damage. The membranes were intact, but the bones were... just destroyed. They were broken in so many places.

Maybe so, or He didn't want to change the body of His unicorn. She'd be something new. This is making my head spin, Toast admitted.

I think we need to take it at face value, Toast, I said, realizing something. *This could even be a reward, giving us both compatible beasts.*

Let's not… discuss that over her unconscious body… Toast said uncomfortably, and I hummed an agreement. I walked around and discovered that the arrow was still lodged in our mate's belly. It'd have to be cut out if her body couldn't reject it. The arrowhead used was deeply barbed and would shred her insides if I was to yank on it. I had no idea if her being shot and going through two shifts made the internal damage worse. All I could do was try to give her energy and wait for help to arrive.

I need out, Toast said firmly, and I nodded, moving to get undressed. I tucked my clothes by a tree and shifted. Toast stalked over to lie by his mate, extended a wing over her battered body in a protective manner, and nurtured her through the mate bond while we waited. He growled viciously at anything that came near, including a squirrel.

I need a knight to bring us, the knight general, a fresh kill, Toast ordered our Inferno.

Food will let us give her more energy, I agreed tiredly. *Good idea.* Toast ate the entire buck brought to us and settled protectively by Rein again. Another hour passed, and Sir Eadwine landed on the forest floor with a witch in his palms. Toast shifted back, returning my body to me so I could talk to the witch about what'd occurred. I dressed and waved her over to Rein's body.

She approached with a hand held up in greeting. "Eloise at your service. I see the unicorn is in a different body," the brunette said, tucking her short, straight hair behind her ears.

"The Sun God blessed her with flight. We were ambushed with arrows and fell off the cliffside. She shifted into this form for the first time and saved us but seems to have sustained a plethora of injuries from the impact," I answered, trying to not let my voice waver from emotion. "She still has the arrow in her belly."

"I see, I see, I see," the witch said and climbed onto Rein's stomach to assess the injury.

"It'll have to be cut out..." I said, not feeling very helpful, and went back to holding my mate's snout in my arms, cradling it. I watched the witch remove her backpack and unroll a sleeve that contained surgical instruments. She sterilized one and made an incision into Rein's belly.

This is hard to watch, Toast said in a strained voice. *But I will, in honor of her pain and sacrifice.*

I didn't have anything to say to that and just followed the witch's progress. Eloise dug into Rein's abdomen and excised the arrow, then threw it bitterly to the ground. After that, she started on the other internal injuries, and I cringed as she swapped between magic and surgical tools. The witch looked like she was playing a game of chess with how focused she was. It seemed like the coven mothers had sent a practiced healer, and I was grateful for it.

We should find a way to thank the Solar Coven for all their help. I'm not sure how we would have coped otherwise, Toast commented quietly.

When this is over, we will, I agreed.

The witch sealed up her injury and worked her way around Rein's prone form, applying a sedative before setting bones. "Until she heals, do not let her fly or shift," the witch ordered while setting the tenth break in Rein's wings. "Once she wakes, make sure she eats plenty of food. This dragon is... uniquely herbivorous, so make sure she gets greens. Her nature hasn't really changed, Sir Keyon. She just has a dragon's body. Likely has the same abilities too, if she healed you as you said."

"Understood," I said, absorbing every detail.

She continued to work for another several hours and finished after setting a dislocated joint in her back left leg. The witch left me with a pouch that contained herbs and bark that acted as painkillers and would help her sleep. We thanked her profusely, and Sir Eadwine left to return her to her coven. I shifted into my dragon form so Toast could act as sentry again. All we had to do now was wait for her to wake. She was too fragile to carry.

It wasn't until sunset that we felt her heart rate and breathing change. *Mate's waking!* Toast yelled and rose to eagerly watch her face. Rein's eyes slowly opened, displaying the same sweet brown sugar-colored eyes that she shared with Elpis. Toast's heart melted at the sight, and he nuzzled her snout. *Mate, you gave us a scare,* Toast said gently. *We are so glad you survived that fall.*

And thank you for saving our lives... I... I sighed in frustration, but I was too emotional, too relieved to berate her for putting her life at risk for ours.

And do not shift! Toast said hastily as Rein tried to right herself. *The witch who helped you said not to until you're all healed.*

Oh... o-ok, Rein said in a trembling voice. *What happened to my body? I feel... strange.*

The Sun God gave you a second body, I think, I said to Rein. *You are currently... very much a dragon.*

I had a feeling, I heard Elpis murmur. *I saw our claws and...*

Rein turned her head slowly to look at her body and balked. *I never would have guessed this was what He gave us!*

He seemed desperate enough to do something this extreme, I replied, relieved to finally hear Elpis's voice. *As desperate as the Sun God can sound, I suppose. Are you able to stand? We can't risk carrying you, and I want to get some food into you as soon as possible. I'm not comfortable staying in this location for long.*

I will try, Rein said and managed to hobble to her feet with Toast's gentle assistance. Fortunately, her wings were bound, so she didn't have to worry about catching them on branches or shrubbery. The walk back to the cabin was a long and painful one for Rein, and we had to make frequent stops to let her rest.

I ordered a knight to request a favor from Leofwine; I needed him to send someone to discreetly pick up a bale or two of hay for Elpis. It was the easiest and fastest thing I could think of to get in bulk for her. She needed as much energy as she could get as soon as possible.

They ended up having plenty of time to find the bales because we didn't arrive at the cabin until well into the night. I saw that we'd set up a camp for the ex-slaves a little farther south from the cabin in a well-covered, heavily forested, and remote part of the mountain. A small team worked to weave branches over the camp to diffuse the smoke from the campfires and provide better camouflage from aerial searches. Protecting the new Reborn was our highest priority.

Rein finally dragged herself to the side of the cabin where the bales had been delivered and ate ravenously. I was relieved to see that she had an appetite because that meant her body was ready to put that energy into healing. She ate an entire bale, spreading grass everywhere, before flopping over and closing her eyes.

Leofwine was finally able to get away from our teams to check on us and was quite shocked when he laid eyes upon our mate. He patted Toast's arm and said, "Great Sun God, can't believe what I'm seeing. She's alive, Toast. That's what matters. We'll get her back in shape soon. She's a tough survivor, right? Prettiest dragon you've ever seen, I bet." He nudged Toast playfully, trying to cheer him up and lighten the mood as best he could.

Toast just nodded morosely and stared at his exhausted mate, unable to take his eyes off her. Leofwine gave Rein an affectionate pat on the head and walked off to get some rest himself.

Keyon? Elpis's voice asked tiredly.

Yes, moonflower?

You know female anatomy... right?

Er... Yes, why are you asking? I replied. Where was she going with this?

Do you know if that arrow hit our womb...?

No, Elpis... you got hit right in the belly. Your uterus is much lower. Why are you asking? Are you worried about permanent damage? You'll be just fine.

Rein's body seemed to relax further with my answer, and her tremulous voice filled our heads. *Ready, Elpis?*

I don't want to wait until the next time we fall off a cliff, Elpis replied nervously. Now they were making me nervous. Toast was getting tense. What was about to happen?

Rein tilted her head to look into our eyes, and I could see Elpis's array of emotions in her gaze. I could feel their hope, worry, relief, and affection. All four of us were held tight in that moment and were unable to sense anything outside of us.

Toast... Keyon, we're carrying your croutons.

Chapter 33

Sir Reyon

Toast let out a surprised snort and crept forward with wide eyes. He bobbed his head slightly, trying to scent her better while I tried to find words to express my shock and elation.

Hatchlings? I asked in astonishment, needing to hear it again, perhaps with words not chosen by Elpis's playful unicorn. *Elpis, is this true? Are you pregnant with our offspring?*

If this is a joke, Rein, and you are simply holding several pieces of baked bread in your claws, I will be very cross with you, Toast said, but he didn't sound serious about that threat. He just seemed full of wonder as he continued to sniff at Rein's neck, belly, and slightly under her tail. Rein surprisingly didn't kick him in the face for that last one. I supposed beasts were less shy about that kind of physical checking than humans.

The Sun God verified... Elpis said nervously. *I was trying to find the right moment to tell you.*

When did we... I asked again, slowly starting to make connections in my brain. This must have been why she was smelling differently!

Ah... she murmured shyly. *The night I discovered your fantasy.*

Oh right... that makes sense. That was the only time in between... I replied, distracted by the exquisite memories of that night. I desperately wished that Elpis could shift back so I could kiss her, please her, and care for her until she fell asleep. *My gods... Elpis, I can't express... I...* I was absolutely tongue-tied. *Flamin' shit, we're going to be a father, Toast!*

We're going to be a father! Toast echoed, but he seemed way more in the present than I was. What shocked me even more was when he started grooming Rein. Not only had I never seen dragons groom each other in public, but this was also my squeamish dragon doing so.

Rein was covered in dirt and a little blood from her fall, and Toast seemed displeased enough to take care of it. My partially gynophobic, absolute dominant dragon alternated between licking her scales and blowing little bursts of fire. He didn't give a shit about who was watching.

When he was done, he settled himself next to Rein and gently swung a protective wing over her. Toast nuzzled a very pleased and relaxed Rein as he emitted a low rumble in his chest, beside himself with happiness.

Are... you happy... Keyon? Elpis asked me privately, sounding anxious. Toast was making a huge display of his joy with Rein, but I was struggling to communicate without my body.

I decided I would describe what I wanted to do. *Elpis, I. Am. In. Euphoria! So beyond absolute joy. I want to pick you up and parade you around the camp, screaming that my mate is carrying my offspring. I want to lay my entire hoard at your feet, you exquisite being. I want to give you everything you want. I want to kiss you, hold you, care for you, and fall asleep with my head on your belly! I want to make love to you if that's what you want to do. I want to provide for you. It's driving me insane that I can't do any of that! I can't express my joy the way I want to!*

I will accept all those things when I shift back, she said, a warm glow in her voice. I felt her worry dissipate, and it was replaced with the pleasures of deep satisfaction, happiness, and well-being. Despite all the excitement, Rein and Elpis were soon fast asleep.

I ended up resting, but apparently Toast chose to stay up all night to keep watch over our pregnant and injured mate. When dawn came and the night shift went to rest, Toast reluctantly let me get back to work.

I shifted back and went to check in with my knights. As I made my rounds, I discovered that some of the Reborn had chosen to leave the safety of our encampment. We knew it was possible, but that didn't make it any less of a disappointment. They were free to do as they wanted. I'd just hoped that they'd all stay to accept help until they got back on their feet.

Then I met with Leofwine to discuss the potential routes we'd take Elpis along in our search for slaver dens. We targeted wealthy areas and locations that were close to multiple trade junctions.

"And now that I don't have to dig up enough dirt on Franco to get permission to raid his properties, we'll swing by those too," Leofwine said with a demonic grin. "Never thought I'd be so happy to defect! Gods, I can't wait to take him down." He rubbed his hands together gleefully.

"And the locations we've considered for housing the Reborn? We can't fly them all back here," I said, looking over the map for the spots we'd marked.

"They've been scouted, but I'm waiting to hear back from one more," he said. "You mentioned leaving several knights behind at each location to keep an eye on them. I think that should be enough if we're quick about our raids. How is Rein doing?"

"She's healing a bit faster after her meal last night. I'm hoping she'll be better by this evening. Her healing powers are pretty fucking potent," I said, glancing over my shoulder toward the cabin, but both her and the building weren't quite in sight.

"Good, good." Leofwine nodded. "See if she's up to a morning or afternoon departure when she's healed. If not, I can just use another day to do more scouting and get more intel."

"Sounds good," I said, slapping my hands down on my knees to get up and check on my knights again.

The day was pretty much centered on getting the Reborn to be self-sufficient in our absence. There were plenty among them who were strong enough to hunt and provide food, and I made sure they all knew where to find water. I prayed to the Sun God that they'd behave and that no one would get hurt while we were gone. A couple knights were enough to provide guidance but not regulation for the number of humans and shifters we had.

Everything seemed fairly well oiled by the early evening, so I returned to the cabin to be with my mate. Rein had finished the second bale and was currently stripping bark off a nearby pine tree. She ripped at it with gusto, and we felt her satisfaction through the mate bond. Though I knew some pines were toxic, I gave up worrying about that with Elpis and Rein. Their furnace just so happened to be in their stomach.

"Hello, Rein," I asked, walking up to rub her scaly arm. "How are you feeling?"

All better! Can we take the bandages off now? They're so uncomfortable! And itchy! Rein replied excitedly.

"Well," I said, scratching at my jaw, "if you're sure you're better, I can cut them off."

Yes, yes, yes, yes, yes! Rein said gleefully and lay down so I could reach her wings.

She's been going stir-crazy for hours, Elpis said while I sliced at the ties made by the witch. *Something tells me that Rein is not fond of bed rest.*

"I don't think most people are," I mused while I worked on her other wing. "Oh, Leof wants to know if you're ok with a morning or afternoon departure tomorrow. If you're not up to it, we can wait another day."

No! Elpis said, rejecting the idea vehemently. *I'm ready. I want to start the search quite badly!*

But uh... how hard is it to learn to fly? Rein asked with a cringe.

Not hard, mate, Toast said. *Instinct will guide you. Let's take a little fly now, and I'll show you.* At that cue, I stripped and shifted into Toast so he could take her through the process. He did, however, spend several minutes rubbing against Rein and nuzzling her before he remembered what he was supposed to be doing.

He led her up the mountain and found a short cliff for Rein's first attempt. She wasn't nearly as nervous as she'd been as a unicorn, and I was grateful that the Sun God had given her dragon instincts too. Toast showed her which muscles to engage when she launched and how to angle her body to increase her altitude. She wouldn't get any assistance from thermals at this time of night, so he'd teach her about them another time.

After only one failed attempt, Rein soared into the sky, wobbling a little while she tried to maintain her balance. Instead of screaming in fright, she was just laughing at her own mistakes, completely high on adrenaline and the daring new experience.

Toast released his own dragon laugh and snorted at her wild enthusiasm. The longer Rein flew, the more stable her form became, and Toast was radiating pride. *Let's fly to the lake again, mate, so you may have sweet grass and water. I'm sure it's better than bark.*

Rein released a soft, growling hum and said, *It is not so bad, but fresh grass sounds very good to me.*

Toast guided her toward the lake, where they landed to take a breather. Rein cut off Toast before he could drink because she obsessively wanted to purify the lake again. *Just in case...* she said and made room for him to quench his thirst.

You will be a good mother, Toast complimented after drinking from the crystal-clear lake.

Even though I had nothing to do with making our hatchlings? she asked a little too innocently.

Th-that is not true, Toast sputtered. *They are in you. You nurture them as we speak.*

It's too bad I didn't get to experience the fun part, though, she said, sighing dramatically. She rubbed up against Toast's shoulder suggestively.

Th-the fun part? Toast asked hesitantly, eyeing her as she slid her tail under his chin. His heart started to pound, and his breathing quickened. I smiled to myself because Toast was getting worked up for the first time in his life, and I wondered how long he could hold out against her. Could he resist Rein's encouragement? This was fucking historic.

Toast growled quietly when she rubbed her scent into his chest again. *C-careful Rein...* he said a little more firmly this time. He backed up hesitantly.

What? she asked with a pout. *I'm just trying to butter up my toast...*

He growled louder and snapped lightly at her, but it didn't faze her at all. He snorted out a blue flame, but she shrugged it off, knowing she was immune to it. She dragged her tail along his chin again, teasing my poor virginal dragon. *Rein... You don't know what you're asking for,* he snarled, starting to sound a little feral.

Are you encouraging her, Elpis? I asked her privately, grinning at the show.

This is all her, Elpis said, already laughing. *I can't say she's not getting ideas from my memories, though.*

Of course I know what I'm asking for... Rein moaned sensually. *I just want to get your dough to rise.* Yes, she was definitely pulling inspiration from Elpis. *But I guess it needs more heat,* she sighed.

Toast finally lost his mind when Rein raised her tail in front of him. The hulking absolute dominant roared and crawled on top of her, caging the female of his species under him. He clamped onto her neck with his teeth, in the typical position that dragons take when they couple.

Oh my goddess! Elpis cried out to me. *Keyon, how do I hibernate? HOW DO I HIBERNATE?*

Just tuck your mind back, like you're scooting back into the dark to sleep, I answered, trying not to laugh at her distress. Why was she so scandalized? Our beasts were us. We'd give them privacy, but there was no need to panic...

You wanted a baguette, but you're getting a full-sized loaf, Toast snarled to Rein. *This is what happens when you tease an absolute dominant, female.*

Yesss! Preheat my oven! Rein simpered like a wanton.

KEYON, Elpis shouted. *IT'S NOT WORKING. OH MY GODS!*

Try again. Good luck, moonflower, I said with a grin and went to hibernate while my dragon finally got laid.

Elpis

It was sweet at first, then it was funny, but when Toast got that look in his eyes and approached Rein, I began to panic. Part of me was overjoyed that Rein and Toast could finally experience physical intimacy, but I wasn't ready for this! I hadn't known Rein long enough to share this much with her!

When I saw what the gods had blessed Toast with, I prayed for Rein's lady bits. I prayed hard. I just hoped that he knew how to wield that thing, or my poor unicorn wouldn't be able to walk for a week. I also tried desperately to avoid using her eyes because her gaze was fixed!

Then Keyon disappeared from the mind-link, leaving me all alone to figure out hibernation, and Rein was not helping. She was horny, distracted, and her wordplay was rampant. Toast was going a bit feral like Keyon sometimes did, and he was no longer flustered by her begging.

From what I saw, it's already reached the right temperature, female, Toast growled and readjusted his grip on her neck. Oh my goddess, I was out of time!

I scrambled and finally managed to tuck myself away in hibernation but not before hearing a triumphant, earth-shaking roar.

※※◎※※

I had no idea how to manage being in hibernation. It was like that state of being between asleep and awake. I was resting, but I simultaneously had some awareness. I sort of knew how much time was passing, and I still felt my connection to Rein, but it was muted.

I would occasionally check to see if they were done, but I was accosted by sights and sounds that I was not prepared to experience. Were our dragons fighting or mating? I balked at the violence and immediately went back into hiding, feeling more worried than ever. I hadn't even thought to check on her emotions. Rein was fine, right? She was tough. She healed fast. Right?

I waited much longer this time, and she finally nudged me. It was faint, but I heard her say, *It's safe to come out now.* She chuckled like my terror was all one big joke.

I warily removed myself from hibernation to find her grazing in her dragon form. As I feared, she was moving with a heavy limp and let out soft, rumbling groans every several minutes.

Are you... ok? I asked with a grimace.

Oh, he destroyed me, Rein informed, but before I could reply, she added, *and I loved every second of it!*

That's... good, I replied cautiously, not knowing what else to say. I tried to reach Keyon instead, hoping he was awake. *Keyon?*

I'm here, moonflower, you shy thing, he answered, laughing.

I would have blushed if I were back in my body. He knew I wasn't shy! This was just... different. *How is Toast doing? Rein is as happy as her limp is heavy.*

Oh, he's a real smug bastard. He's a new dragon. Rein's created a monster, and his confidence is through the roof, Keyon answered, complaining playfully. He sounded deeply relieved, though.

I guess we should go back now, I said to Keyon and our dragons. *We're leaving tomorrow, so… I need Rein to rest… and, er… heal.*

I was met with amusement over the bond from everyone, and Rein turned to wobble after Toast. He waited patiently for her before launching into the sky. Rein was definitely tired, and her head drooped on the flight back to the cabin. Toast rushed ahead to their nesting spot and lay down first so she could lean against him in her sleep. Just like Keyon did with me, he draped a wing over her, and they fell into a deep slumber.

I think Keyon could tell how deeply touched I was by Toast's attentiveness. The more Toast healed, the more he reminded me of Keyon. I had so much to learn about beasts—ours, in particular.

Do you see it now, moonflower? They're us.

I think I do now.

Rein was ready to go by late morning, and I was incredibly excited. I couldn't wait to find and liberate more slaves. As much as it was a deep craving, I hoped someday to have nothing left to satisfy that craving. I wanted them all freed as soon as possible.

"Communication between our teams will probably be our main issue when we're shifted," Keyon said with a sigh to Leofwine, looking westward from the cliffs. "Two different Infernos will be a challenge, but we'll make do. We've sorted our signals out. I just hope we don't come across anything unexpected."

I watched Leofwine frown and rub his chin. "I spoke to my team earlier, Keyon. Why don't we just merge the Infernos? We've all defected. Doesn't matter that we have two specialties. It won't change the teams."

Keyon snorted. "That's like asking two alpha lycans to share one pack."

Leofwine crossed his arms. "You know that's not true. I may be on the same level as you at the castle, but you're the dominant here. You should absorb my Inferno. I'll be second-in-command. The incredibly handsome mstovari knight, Captain Leofwine. That has a nice ring to it, yeah?"

My mate ran his hands through his messy chestnut hair and sighed. "That would make things easier. We can separate them again later."

"Then it's settled!" Leofwine clapped and turned to face his spies. "We're merging like I said! Get in line and sell your soul to Keyon." He chuckled and gestured for his team to make haste.

"Like you said?" Keyon sent his friend a wry look. "You assumed I'd say yes? I'm not that predictable." Leofwine grinned and placed his hands on his hips, choosing not to answer.

Keyon pressed his lips together, then addressed the first spy. "Do you—"

"Norbert Hallbjorn," Leofwine supplied helpfully.

"Norbert Hallbjorn, swear to defend the knight general's Inferno with your bravery, commit yourself to honorable action, defend the defenseless, and fly as commanded by your leader?"

"I do so swear," Norbert said, taking to a knee and offering his hand like a sacrifice. Keyon cut his own palm with a claw, then cut the spy's palm before clamping their bloody hands together and lifting him to his feet. I watched in fascination as the spy's pupils flickered to slits for the briefest of moments. Were their dragons acknowledging each other?

"I dub thee, Mstovari Norbert Hallbjorn of Knight General Keyon Kenelm's Inferno," Keyon said resolutely and waited for the next spy to approach.

This is going to take forever, but he looks quite kingly, though, doesn't he? I asked, staring obsessively at my mate, who had adopted a very serious expression. His brown locks occasionally flickered in the breeze, his brow was set, and he gave every dragon his full attention. *I'm glad we're shifted so no one can tell how aroused I am.*

Yes, it's good that Toast isn't doing this. Last night is all I can think about, Rein mumbled happily and curled up to sleep while surrounded by Keyon's devoted knights.

⚜

Keyon woke us several hours later, and we finally took to the skies with his terrifying, expanded Inferno. Finally! I couldn't believe we were finally doing this! I'd been waiting for this moment for days and days!

There were way too many of us to not attract attention, so we swarmed along our route as I focused on finding the slaver dens. I stayed as low as Keyon would allow, and I was surrounded by knights who kept watchful eyes for other dragons and ranged attacks. The first place we checked was clear of slaves. I sensed nothing at all, not even one slave, so we continued to our next destination, Nord'rove.

Nord'rove was another upper-class community, and when I dipped down a tiny bit more, I sensed what I was expecting from a place like this. Underneath all the finery was ugliness.

More slaves down there, Keyon, I reported, feeling pleased with my second discovery. *Not as many as Astertrove but still a significant amount!*

Excellent work, moonflower, Keyon said with a smile in his voice. *I shall have to reward you later.*

Tee hee hee! Rein giggled. *I helped. Toast, I want a nickname too!*

I already gave you one, he replied slyly, and Rein went quiet. What name did he give her?

It's not publicly appropriate... she eventually—and meekly—protested, but he just laughed. Now I was curious...

With our target in sight, Keyon ordered his troops to converge on Nord'rove. Rein landed, shifted, and I led Keyon and several knights to the closest location. We found about two hundred and fifteen slaves between several estates and another hundred and fifty in a mansion that was located in the center of town.

Since we weren't equipped to take prisoners this time, Keyon's dragons had to either scare off, subdue, or kill the slavers who tried to keep us from leaving with the new Reborn. If we wanted our mission to succeed, Keyon had no choice but to make some hard decisions. I saw that his Inferno tried very hard not to kill anyone, but a knight was occasionally pushed too hard and ended up executing the particularly relentless slavers. Also, the slavers and sympathizers who kept hostages during the raid had forfeited their lives, per Keyon's orders. He tolerated no threat to the Reborn, and Leofwine's spies slayed the captors without hesitation.

I tried not to focus on the violence and—with the help of several spies—carefully healed the Reborn who were at the highest risk of dying during relocation. Once we herded the ex-slaves out of town, Keyon left several knights to escort them to the designated hiding place. They were to follow the previous orders of settling them, getting them into some state of self-sustainability, and guard them until Cyneric was overthrown.

We had to keep moving to stay as far ahead of any reports as possible. Keyon said that once Cyneric caught wind of our activities, he would likely try to strike us hard and fast. Hopefully, the more slaves we ended up freeing, the more reckless he would grow. We were relying on their sloppiness to win this war. Each knight could take down a large number of mercenaries, and Cyneric himself might not be calm enough to focus on a winning strategy. He might underestimate the number and skills of those who've defected.

We passed over a large forested area in the northwest that was sectioned off for logging and liberated about fifty-seven slaves. There wasn't a lot of resistance, and the slave owners mostly looked on helplessly as we escorted the Reborn to safety. The group of ex-slaves was so small that Keyon and Leofwine decided to have them carried to another raid to combine with the next group.

We collected a heartbreaking two hundred and thirty-five from a quarry, and I had to hide myself behind a tent to cry after healing several dozen hatchlings with crippling injuries and a handful of adults with severe breathing difficulties. Keyon tracked me down, but instead of berating me for going off alone, he just picked me up and brought me back to his Inferno without saying a word. He ordered another escort for the near three hundred Reborn we had collected.

Rein and I were exhausted, emotionally and physically. Toast kept looking over at us, and I could feel our mate's worry grow until Keyon instructed his Inferno to land and nest for the night. I knew it was done for our sake. Perhaps the others could have done another raid, but Rein and I had nothing left.

Leofwine verified the safety of a location by clean, running water, and camp was swiftly made. Rein shifted as soon as we hit the ground, and I dragged my feet to the water, feeling worn down to the very marrow of my bones. I plopped down by the bank and pursed my lips, trying to figure out the best way to drink. Rein had become very particular about her water now, but running water didn't hang around after being purified.

I cupped water in my hands and leaned down to dip my horn into it. It was awkward, and I spilled a little on my dress, but it worked well enough. Then I heard footsteps from behind me, and I could tell that my mate was here.

Keyon simply sat, turned my head to his, and softly placed his lips on mine. After a minute of absorbing some of his energy and affection, I released a sigh into his lips and felt my body grow heavy. He continued to kiss me sweetly and brushed back a strand of my hair that the playful wind tried to lift.

He didn't say anything, and he didn't mind-link. He just kissed me. It was a blessed moment of silence, and it felt like his body was relieved to finally have a moment with mine since I told him I was carrying our young. His heart filled as mine did.

He cleared away the shadows that I'd collected today and left behind warmth and comfort.

Keyon massaged his lips into mine, and I enjoyed the rough sound and texture of his stubble scraping against my skin. Every motion of his jaw and pull of his teeth spoke of how completely focused he was on me. His warm tongue dipped to stroke mine, and his hands slowly slid to my waist, squeezing ever so delicately with his fingers.

He moved one large, rough palm over my lower abdomen and left it there, acknowledging the life that was slowly forming—the offspring he'd kindled within me. He'd been right that night; the fire had caught.

We stayed by the water, kissing and breathing each other in as the sun slipped away to rest. His palm never left, and his thumb stroked idly in affectionate caresses. He pulled his head back just enough to speak while brushing our lips together. The warm words floated on foggy puffs in the cool evening air.

"I love you, moonflower."

Chapter 34

Elpis

Keyon said he loved me…

He loved me!

I was going to say it first!

We were too slow, Rein said dreamily. *Toast already told me.*

What? I nearly shouted at her. He must have confessed while they were… baking together. So far, I'd put off watching those memories.

I couldn't tear my eyes from Keyon's to get a second to think. I was so elated that my brain stopped working for a moment. I knew… I knew he loved me in some form, but to hear it out loud was euphoric. My eyes watered, and I tried to blink away my overflowing emotions.

"Oh, Keyon, I love you too!" I gasped and wrapped my arms around his neck to kiss him soundly. His sigh into my mouth carried bone-deep satisfaction, and his hands slid up and around my back to pull me against him. Every movement he made with his arms and fingers was a silent dedication to cherish me, and it had me melting.

"I know it's pretty much a given to love your fated mate, but... Elpis, you're the most phenomenal female. I can't believe how lucky I am," he murmured into my lips. "You saved so many people today, you know that? Without you... all that could have taken weeks—if not months—of Leof obtaining intel to get raid permission and me having to tear an entire area apart to find hidden slaves.

"Elpis..." he said softly, pulling back farther to look at my face. "You're so beautiful, so clever, so kind." He smiled and playfully assessed me, dragging his palms down to cup my bottom and whisper, "So very fuckable, but most of all..." His smile faded, and he looked at me in earnest. "A force with which to be reckoned. I can't imagine anyone else I'd rather have by my side forever."

I bit my lip hard so as not to fly into a crying fit. "Ah..." I sniffed, feeling my chin wobble as I fought tears. "You give me too much credit!" I smashed my lips against his and pulled a groan from him, but he suddenly stiffened.

He pulled his lips away, wrinkling his nose, and became annoyed. "Leof is looking for me. Something urgent came up." He growled and stood up to go meet him. I grabbed onto his passing hand and used him to stand so I could follow. I was curious, but I also wanted to be near Keyon.

When I thought about it being urgent, I wasn't expecting Leofwine to have a massive grin on his face. His pearly white fangs glistened with his grin, and he gestured behind him to what had to be several hundred tired-looking warriors.

"The last spy I was waiting for verified the safety of the location, but it was already full of these guys," Leofwine said, pointing a thumb backwards. Keyon's brows shot up in surprise.

"I recognize many of these dragons. These are some of the king's soldiers. Have they defected?" he asked, studying the males in disbelief. Leofwine nodded, and his face softened as he looked back at the exhausted warriors who were settling down to rest.

"When they quit their duties, the king promised retaliation, so they evacuated with their families," Leofwine explained. "Their families were left safe and sound at the prior hideout, but this lot volunteered to join our ranks once my spy informed them of our goal."

"Fucking sun's fire," Keyon murmured, scratching his chin. "Cyneric's really messing things up. He still has more soldiers at his disposal than we do, but this is starting to even out the situation."

"Are you going to absorb them?" Leofwine asked. "I think you should. This is an all-or-nothing war, in my opinion." Keyon nodded, and I wandered through the new recruits. I knew I was fairly depleted, but I was compelled to check and see how they were doing. There were only a couple fractures and a sprain, which were fairly lightweight injuries, so I just took care of those. I gave my name and told them where to find running water, then returned to Keyon.

"You look wiped. You healed someone, didn't you?" he said, playfully accusing me.

"Not so bad... but food and sleep are on my menu," I mumbled tiredly. I shifted in private and let Rein graze. It was the easiest. Then I trudged to camp to sleep. It was a miracle I made it to my blanket.

※◎◇◎◇

With the sharing of rations, volunteering hunters, access to fresh water, and rest, all the warriors were looking revived by morning. My poor mate had stayed up late to bring every single one of the ex-king's soldiers into his Inferno. He'd gone to bed with a raspy throat, but Toast had healed it before I could.

We soon launched into the sky, and I felt some of Rein's scales flutter as a shiver raked through her. The size of the group following us was becoming quite the terrifying sight. Toast sensed our trepidation and moved to fly a little closer to us, letting his proximity offer some comfort. Rein and I resolved to not look back again, even if we knew we were safe.

Westrove was next, but it had a surprisingly small number of slaves compared to the other wealthy towns... until I discovered a camouflaged compound several miles east of it. Fortunately, I'd flown close enough to the holding area to feel the misery. It wasn't between our list of stops, and had I been farther west, I could have missed it entirely. It was a close enough call to make me shudder.

We reunited the two groups after taking down the slavers and the compound's guards. This engagement had been bloody because no guard at the compound wanted to surrender, and there were multiple attempts to take hostages. These poor Reborn seemed particularly traumatized, and it looked like the holding area was for pre-bidding. I was fairly certain these were all brand-new slaves who were about to be shipped off to sun-knows-where. I was hopeful, though, that many of the hatchlings could be reunited with their families if they were recently abducted.

The next location had Leofwine humming with excitement. Simmer was almost bouncing on the wind as we flew toward Franco's large property. As we approached, I felt Rein sneer at the amenities surrounding the mansion and neighboring estate. Her eyes traveled over a racetrack to the mansion, and the large...

Keyon! I cried.

I see him! he said and took a wide turn to approach a dragon that had to be Cyneric from the front. *Fall back with your guards, Elpis!* I felt Rein bite her tongue, not wanting to fall back, but did as our mate asked. Keyon's army then formed a colossal crescent behind Toast as soon as he landed.

Just for now, Rein. We can and will help once we have more information, I said firmly to her. We weren't the expert on warfare here.

There was no mistaking who Cyneric was. A dragon twice Toast's size sat up from behind the mansion and strode forward to stand before my mate. He was... surprisingly colorful. I was expecting an evil-looking black-and-red dragon, but Cyneric was a vibrant shade of teal. Another aspect that made him stand out as a king was the large, horned frill that sat just behind his skull like a half moon. The frill, his back, and wings were speckled with maroon; the end result was truly magnificent. I might even have called his dragon beautiful if he wasn't such an atrocious piece of garbage who'd tried to kill my mate twice. Rein growled low at the reminder. Today would likely be his third attempt, but we wouldn't let that happen.

His soul is so dark, so poisoned, it's like ink, Rein murmured to me. *I will blind that bastard so fiercel—*

I see you've squeezed me into your busy schedule, Keyon, Cyneric said, interrupting Rein's violent thoughts. How could I hear his mind-links? Was it because he was a king? Toast shifted into Keyon, and I whimpered, desperately worried for his safety. Keyon also didn't seem to care at all that he was gloriously nude in front of royalty.

"You know I'm here for the slaves," Keyon said, crossing his arms and standing tall. "You haven't turned into a sympathizer while I've been out freeing slaves... have you... Cyneric?" It looked like both of them have chosen to drop the titles.

Cyneric released a heavy series of snorts, obviously laughing. *By the Sun God, Keyon, you're such a sad waste of a dominant. By the way, I'm curious, the "neighboring country"—which was me, by the way—wants to know if you've brought the precious slave back. Where is the tasty little thing? Franco said his temple fell to ruin from some kind of rescue. Isn't that what you said?*

Cyneric looked down at a male who pushed away from the wall he was leaning against. Sure enough, Franco was here at his property with his king. "Doesn't matter," Franco said gruffly. "We harvested her blood like I said we would. You didn't ask for anything else. I'm just waiting for you to execute your end of the bargain."

Cyneric laughed again. *Have I not already? I've brought all your enemies here. Who cares if it's still illegal. Just take your slaves as you will once they're all dead.* He gestured with a large claw to Keyon's army. *Act like you're the top of the food chain, and you will be.*

Franco didn't look happy about that. He simply scowled and kept his mouth shut. Cyneric gestured to a soldier, and a large cage brimming with slaves was carted over to him. There must have been at least fifty individuals crammed in there, and my heart clenched painfully at the sight. Cyneric's dragon placed his clawed hand on the cage and pressed down, making the top collapse slowly. The slaves screamed in terror, believing they were about to be crushed.

Keyon tensed, and I noticed his right pinky twitch. Did he give some kind of signal? I warned Rein to not look around and draw attention. We just kept our gaze on our mate and the massive monster.

Why are you bothering with these creatures? Cyneric asked my mate, sounding genuinely confused. *If these were real dragons, they wouldn't have allowed themselves to be stolen and enslaved.* He kicked the cage, forcing it to roll onto its side. The slaves yelled, screamed, and cried out in pain as they toppled over each other. My anxiety spiked as I felt small injuries pile up among them. Rein shifted nervously, feeling both urges to heal and maim.

"They are your citizens, Cyneric! Civilians!" Keyon roared in anger, gesturing for two groups to flank him. They had their eyes on the cage where Cyneric once again rested his claws. "It's your sworn duty to protect them!"

That's a very human concept, and since we are not humans, I think not, Cyneric said darkly and lifted his claws to flatten the cage. Keyon's two groups charged, and Cyneric swung his tail to crush them, but Keyon's ground soldiers feinted and dispersed, leaving the king unbalanced. Cyneric growled victoriously when he caught the actual attack and lashed out at the knights who were coming from above his head and to his left. Rein nearly shrieked when that group feinted, and the cage by Cyneric's feet was instantly whisked away by three of Leofwine's spies, who'd jumped out from the shadows of the mansion. They flew off into the distance and disappeared. Rein uttered a relieved groan.

Cyneric, seething, tried to regain his earlier composure but only got halfway there. Black smoke curled from his nostrils and the corners of his dragon's mouth. The massive dragon froze for a moment and then huffed with quieter laughter.

You don't deserve the strength you have, Keyon—Cyneric scoffed—*so I'm going to execute you. You don't have a beast that's unbroken enough to be at the top of the chain, and you weaken all of us. You're a danger to us. Absolutes shouldn't exist at all. Nothing should be stronger than relative dominants.*

And now it's time to burn the sick and own the rest. There are no limits for an unrestrained dragon, and I would very much like to see no limits to my kingdom.

I saved this moment just for you, Keyon. I wanted my last words to be with you. I want you to watch my dragon purge its humanity. Perhaps the last thing I'll be blessed with seeing will be you pissing yourself, Cyneric said in a low, dark voice.

He leaned over and opened his mouth so Franco could pour the witch's potion into it. What Cyneric couldn't see was the smirk on Franco's face. Franco thought he was giving him a false potion, but... that probably wasn't the case.

Keyon's not going to be the one pissing himself, Rein said, but neither of us laughed. We just watched as Cyneric slowly went from being a monster to a horror.

If I thought that Cyneric was monstrous before, he was a behemoth now. I suppose it was inaccurate now to call him Cyneric. The male, the human part of the shifter, was supposedly gone, and we needed but wait to get that verification.

Keyon, however, had not wanted to waste that moment. He was sending orders out to his army, though I didn't know what he was saying. Sections of dragons flew off in different directions to meet with the charging army of the transforming king. The enemy had twice as many soldiers, but I believed in our warriors. We had knights, assassins, and the well-trained soldiers of the late king. We had skill, honor, and valor on our side. They had mercenaries and soldiers who were likely demoralized serving an unworthy king.

However, Rein and I were terrified. I had a picture of what would happen in my mind, but it was nothing like reality. Kills were not clean, and none of it seemed like a romantic dance or a beautiful display of skill. It was sickening. We were frozen solid as we watched guts spill onto a battlefield that was quickly becoming soaked with blood and bodily fluids. It was a nightmare. There were things I immediately wished I had not seen, and the fight had only started. I was already traumatized.

W-we need to focus! Rein all but screamed in my mind, as though trying to convince both of us. *Focus for Keyon. Focus for Toast. Focus for our army. Focus for the slaves! Focus! Focus! Focus!*

F-f-focus, I agreed as we stared at what used to be a king. The behemoth was now three times bigger than Toast and shook violently from its transformation. Its mouth grew wider and split well past its face. I had no doubt it could now fit the entire estate home into its maw. The space between its eyes shrunk, and its orbs no longer held the slits of a reptile but instead looked more like ones you'd see on a bird of prey.

Its eyes don't matter! I said fiercely to Rein. *Take them out!*

You read my mind, she seethed darkly and launched into the sky where we were followed by our personal guards.

Elpis! Rein! Stay back! Keyon said, panicking.

We're blinding it! I replied, trying to sound calm, but I was growing angry. I hated Cyneric, and I hated what his dragon had become. He'd partaken of my blood and had become something truly abhorrent from it. I wanted revenge for that. I felt more violated than ever. *We have guards. Let us do what we were meant to do, Keyon!*

We felt a bevy of emotions hit us through the bond. He was worried, anxious, panicky, but also proud. *Be safe,* he begged, and he was echoed by Toast. *We love you!*

We love you too, so very, very much! I said and urged Rein to get just close enough to be effective. I felt her dig deep; I didn't see anything, but I felt it. Oh, this time, I felt it. The power Rein collected pressed up against her skin and scales from the inside, as though it wanted to flee through her pores. Once the pressure built up to an almost unbearable sensation, she released it, and the behemoth raised its clawed hands to its face. I grimaced at its clutching, noticing that those claws were now serrated. Then it swayed slightly, as though it lost its sense of balance.

Focus! Rein reminded me. We turned to get to a safe distance, but the behemoth lashed out blindly, and its claws came careening toward us. Rein panicked, and I shifted. We shrunk into my human form, and I fell, becoming a much smaller target. The claws missed my head by a terrifying foot, nearly making me faint in complete terror.

One of my knights roared—likely pissed or terrified from my stunt—and snatched me out of the air. I patted his clawed hand vacantly as he retreated with me, but I had to immediately jump out when an enemy came flying at us. Rein shifted in midair again and glided away with our remaining knights. I turned, and Rein released a smaller burst, blinding the dragon who'd latched onto my knight. He fell off, confused, and the knight dispatched him quickly by gutting him, tearing his wings up and leaving him to fall to his death. If Rein had a slightly weaker stomach, she would have vomited.

I wanted to help more of our soldiers, but it was almost impossible to tell who was who. Perhaps if I had been in the Inferno, I would have been able to tell. That only left one dragon I was even remotely comfortable targeting, and that was the behemoth.

How can we help our army take it down? I asked Rein as we fell back to a safe distance.

Target weak spots, Rein said, watching Keyon rip through dragons to reach Cyneric's abomination.

Weak spots, weak spots, I murmured, studying the monstrosity. *Its wings hadn't grown with the rest of it. I don't think it can*

fly anymore, so targeting those is pointless. That leaves what?
Hindering movement and…?

In that moment, I remembered what the Sun God had told me about my people, how the dragons had removed their horns for trophies. Rein took that thought and sharpened it.

Hindering and removing its weapons, she decided coldly.

Our horn is very sharp, and that thing is practically blind. Perhaps we can latch on to a hand and declaw it? I asked, wincing.

Oooh, gruesome. A shudder moved through Rein that was born of both disgust and delight. *But it's a good idea. Those assassins seem to have a similar one,* she pointed out, and I saw them swarming around the behemoth's ankles, trying to sever some taut piece of flesh.

It's going to take so long to chop away at that thing, I replied, worried. Rein turned and flew us back toward the behemoth, girding her loins for what was sure to be a terrifying experience.

She nearly turned around when the creature let out a blood-curdling scream, one that parted the air like a slap. The shriek layered on top of a roar, and it sent vibrations through her chest. She whimpered, and nausea roiled like a poisonous fire in her belly.

We were still distracted by that vocal display when several of my knights shot toward the right and tore into a charging enemy. Rein started and nearly threw up out of shot nerves, severely rattled by how our knights ripped the dragon's limbs from its body.

Oh Sun God, oh Sun God, oh Sun God, oh Sun God! Rein chanted, and I quickly joined her. We were a whirlwind of shock and adrenaline. All our nerves screamed at us to survive.

My knights were severely displeased with me approaching the behemoth and tried to herd me away, but Rein stuck to her target, occasionally snapping irritably at an insistent knight.

What ended up making us stray from our goal was the sight of two females yelling up at the behemoth. Curious, Rein dropped to a lower altitude to see what they were saying, and there was an awful lot of pleading coming out of those two.

"Cyneric! Please! What are you doing?" a black-haired female around my age screamed, her curls bouncing furiously as she waved her arms.

"Come back to us, Brother! What is wrong with you?" another said. She looked very much like the other female; they had to be sisters. They both ran toward one of the behemoth's planted hands and tugged on it.

What are they doing? They're going to be killed! Rein yelped.

Are they the ones who buried Keyon alive? Oh gods, I can't think right now! Go grab them! If you can? I don't know! I yelled in alarm, confused about my feelings. Rein banked to take a large turn, but Cyneric's nightmare faced the two females who were tugging on it and lunged toward them with an open maw.

Oh gods! We won't make it! Rein squawked.

The females tripped over each other to escape, and in a horrifying display of sororicide, the curly-haired female pushed her sister into the gaping maw and ran to save herself. Rein turned sharply, left speechless by what we'd just witnessed. Was this what Keyon meant? When you thought you'd seen the worst, something came along to prove otherwise?

Our knights kept a tight formation around Rein as we flew off in shock. Deep shock.

F-focus, I said, shaken.

Focus... Rein agreed, and she turned to approach the behemoth once more. Rein wasted no time and latched onto a hand that had recently settled to take its shifting weight. She swung her head down a handful of times in quick succession and managed to sever two fingers before the behemoth ripped its hand up, sending us the short distance to the ground.

Unicorn! I cried and Rein shifted into her normal body, racing away from the other hand that came down to crush us. It missed in its blind fury, and we escaped under its belly to end up at the back where the assassins were working. The behemoth's tail was thrashing viciously and had already crushed several of Leofwine's spies. Rein sobbed at the sight and decided to sever what they'd been working on while she was back here. They'd completed one leg but were still trying to get to the next. Rein released a terrified scream that she couldn't hold back, dodged a shifting foot, and galloped past its back left leg, severing the taut flesh in one swipe.

The tail came crashing toward us, and I screamed, *Human!* Rein shifted into me, and I curled into a ball, rolling and barely avoiding the tail that brushed over me. *Dragon!* I shrieked, and she shifted, taking off as fast as she could while I quaked inside my mind, terrified beyond belief. I couldn't believe we'd survived that!

Once we'd put some distance between us and the behemoth, my knights caught up to me, and I knew that I was going to get a talking to if we ever got out of this alive.

There was a crashing behind us, and Rein turned to see what had caused the noise. Unable to bear its back weight, the behemoth had fallen into the mansion, crushing a portion of it into rubble. Upon its descent, nearly the entirety of Keyon's army converged on its neck, ripping savagely at flesh to find a precious artery. A battered and bloodied Keyon shredded at a particular spot, leaned in and ripped at a large tube, sending a scarlet fountain into the sky to pour down in a morbid rain.

The perversion of a dragon thrashed, and the army worked to hold down its limbs until it bled out. Rein turned, and we noticed that the late Cyneric's army had long since fled. I had no idea when that had happened. We looked down at the battlefield and balked at the number of dead. Our hearts clenched at the sight, hoping that none of them were ours… but that was a fantasy. Rein glided down to a safe spot, and I shifted into my body. I couldn't describe my feelings. I just knew I had more work to do.

I gestured at my knights. "I can't tell who's in our Inferno! Take me to anyone who's in critical condition, please!" I begged and stepped forward, waiting for a knight to offer a claw. One looked over at another, and they seemed to be discussing something. He eventually held out a claw, and I climbed into his palm, hoping there were some left holding onto life.

Fight! I prayed fervently. *Fight to live!*

The knight toured me around the battlefield, landing whenever we found someone who desperately needed my help. I lost track of how many soldiers, knights, and assassins I'd healed, but I fought to keep going. Nausea curled deeper into me after healing a soldier who'd concussed and nearly lost a leg, which I managed to save. I stumbled back to my knight's palm, but my vision tunneled, and I fell into darkness.

Chapter 35

Sir Keyon

The worst part of the battle had been, by far, leaving Elpis's side. I'd had such a hard time focusing because I was continuously being assaulted by her emotions. She'd felt the same way I did when I had fought for the first time. It was never how you pictured it. It was a nightmare that made you immediately wish you'd never fallen asleep.

I'd done my best to stay calm for her and focus on my task. Her blinding Cyneric's monstrosity had given us a significant advantage, and I was grateful she'd pushed to do it. I knew that'd saved lives. Her knights were constantly reporting her actions to me, which was how I received news that Cyneric's sisters were here. Apparently, Gisila still made a habit of pushing people to their deaths.

I'd almost lost my mind with fear when Elpis started her assault on Cyneric's dragon. I couldn't spare many glances, so I had to trust that my best knights would keep her safe. I didn't think she'd realized how many enemies they were intercepting on her behalf, and the knight's voices during their reports were getting increasingly more frustrated. I chose not to warn her, knowing she'd work better unaware. I couldn't stop her and Rein; they were dead set on helping take down the enormous dragon. I'd even felt her fury spike at one point, which surprised and almost pleased me. I was still more worried than anything, though—more worried than anything because she was my everything.

From what I'd heard, Rein's horn, being brutally sharp, was able to sever the giant dragon's fingers and tendon in a sweep or two. There was no doubt that my mate's efforts had significantly turned the tide, and I was so fucking proud... until I felt her collapse.

I left my army to manage Cyneric's dying nightmare and flew to find my collapsed mate, yelling at my knights to report.

I've got her, and we're retreating to the tree line, Sir Stroud said. *She asked us to fly her around to heal the critically ill because she couldn't tell who was in our Inferno.*

I knew she'd overdo it. I told you, Stroud, Sir Gerfrid said, annoyed. *We should have stopped at the fortieth soldier!*

Forty? Toast and I shouted at the same time.

Well, that's where we wanted her to stop, but she kept going like a vicious sow, Sir Gerfrid grumbled, then added hastily, *Sow like a mother bear, I mean! Not a pig.*

She fainted at sixty-two, Sir Stroud said, wincing. I arrived at their location, and Toast gave him a nasty look. *She really was very adamant.*

You're lucky you're indispensable, Toast snarled. I shifted back into my body and crouched down to slide my mate into my lap.

"Can someone get some water, please?" I asked, and Sir Havardr flew off to see what he could salvage from Franco's property. I stroked Elpis's cheek, not liking how pale she was, but her heart was still going at a firm, steady beat. "I think she's just exhausted," I said quietly, feeling slightly relieved. "She kept going until her body told her it was time to stop."

"Is this where the party is?" a tired voice called from behind me. I turned to see Leofwine and Foray trudging up to join us.

Leofwine's face was a mix of emotions. He looked pleased to be dragging a chained and unconscious Franco through the dirt, but I could see the pain of loss in his eyes. I wasn't ready to face the numbers myself.

Foray, distressed, trotted ahead to sniff Elpis's limp form. Leofwine's small, fake smile faded somewhat, and he asked, "What happened here?"

"She went about healing more people than her body wanted her to," I said with a frown. "Saved about sixty-two lives."

"So... did she just faint?" Leofwine asked, and I nodded while stroking her hair. "Well, I've got just the gift for her when she wakes up," he said, chuckling humorlessly. "It's wrapped up and everything." Leofwine twirled the chain attached to Franco's body. Foray draped her weight across Elpis's legs in a sweet gesture to keep her warm, and Leofwine petted the cat's neck affectionately.

Sir Havardr returned with a bucket of fresh water and a pile of clothes, and I sorted through it until I found several items that fit. There was one last obstacle to deal with now, and I had to dress for it.

"Leofwine," I said to get his attention, and he looked up at me. "I'm going to find our new queen and get our shit reinstated at the castle. I want my soldiers going home. Can you look after Elpis with my knights while I'm gone? I won't be long." He nodded, and I walked off to find the female who nearly killed me so I could place her greedy ass on the throne.

I heard her before I saw her. She was crying crazily by the doorway of the mansion, which somehow had not fallen when Cyneric's dragon collapsed. When my approach hit her ears, she looked up in shock and ran to embrace me.

"Keyon!" she cried dramatically.

Gah! Toast cried out, and I placed both my palms forward to stop her. *Don't let her touch us!*

"Princess Gisila, please listen, this is very important!" I said, utilizing my most authoritative tone, but unfortunately, she seemed to like that. Still, she stopped in her tracks, and her tears dried up rather quickly.

"What is it, Sir Keyon?" she asked. Good, she still recognized me as a knight. Perhaps this wouldn't be so difficult after all.

"You are next in line for the throne, and we are happy to escort you back seeing as how your brother's army up and abandoned you," I said, nodding in the direction of the castle. "In return, we need to be welcomed back to our lives and careers at the castle. I expect to be reinstated as the knight general and Leofwine as spymaster."

"I did find it hard to believe Cyneric's claims about you," Gisila said, sounding almost like an intelligent person. "I'll strike a deal with you, if you b—"

"That is the deal, Princess Gisila," I said, interrupting her with a warning growl. "I'm not negotiating any part of it. Take it or leave it. My knights, soldiers, and Leofwine's spies have risked their lives to save hundreds upon hundreds of slaves over the last couple of days! Then your brother"—I shoved a finger in her stuck-up face—"decides to target me and back the slavers. How will your future subjects see you if you don't bring back my Inferno? Don't you have to wonder that if you echo your brother's decision, they'll see you as a sympathizer too?"

Like the idiot she was, she grew afraid. She saw my speech as a warning, not a threat. I sighed internally, realizing she'd need a very strict panel of advisors to keep manipulators away from her. She was too easily swayed by words alone. Gods help this kingdom, but anyone was better than Cyneric.

"I-I see the wisdom of y-your words, Sir Keyon," she said with a lift of her chin. "Yes, please escort your future queen back to her castle, but don't think we're done talking." She held out her hand for me to kiss, and Toast gagged. I very quickly bowed over it and walked away before she could pull her trick.

After Cyneric's dragon finally bled out, I gathered my army and ordered the least exhausted of the knights to stay behind for cremation duties. We also had enough volunteers to fly the injured and the newly Reborn, but I suspected that Franco's property hid more slaves. We'd have to return later to do a thorough search of the place.

Hours later, my exhausted army arrived at the castle, and I purposely avoided Gisila, who had thrown a dickish fit when I refused to carry her here. I cradled my precious, sleeping Elpis after throwing on some clothes, then went straight to the hospital so a doctor could take a look at her. They verified what I suspected, which was extreme exhaustion. After a little attention from the doctors, Elpis finally woke. The doctors gave me some medicine and ordered bed rest for her.

I flagged a servant down on the way back to my chambers and asked to have two large, hearty meals with a variety of vegetables brought to my room. Elpis, sluggish but awake, gawked at the castle scenery. "This is your home?" she asked, staring at statues and other displays as we entered the south wing.

"No," I said and frowned at her. She looked confused and a little put-out, but then I said, "This is our home, moonflower." I grinned, and she weakly slapped my chest.

"You're the biggest tease. Did you know that?" she said with a tired chuckle.

"I did. I pride myself on it," I replied, pinching her bottom stealthily as I carried her. She jerked in surprise and smacked me again. I winced when she hit a tender spot, and her eyes widened.

"Oh nay! I'm so sorry!" she said and fumbled to move so she could heal what I was obviously not done healing. I pushed her back down against my chest and shook my head.

"No healing duties for you until you're better, moonflower," I warned, and she whimpered pathetically. She whispered another sincere, sweet apology right as we finally reached my chambers.

I smiled and nodded for her to grab the doorknob for me, which she did, and I eased us through the entrance. "Are we here? Is this it?" she asked, perking up and looking about the space. I chuckled, nodded, and kicked the door closed before turning into an adjacent room so I could tuck my mate in bed.

The scent hit me immediately, and I recoiled. What was she doing here? Gisila was spread out on my bed like she owned it, naked and obviously waiting. It brought my blood well past a boil.

Just like her fuckin' sister! What is it with these entitled pieces of shit? Get her the fuck out of here! That bed is for our mate! Toast roared, almost enraged to the point of coming out himself and burning her to ashes.

"Princess Gisila," I said warningly, barely keeping my fury in check, and pointed to the door. "You need to clothe yourself and leave. These are my private chambers."

Elpis simply gaped at first, but I could feel her shock turn into the wrath of a territorial female. She squirmed to get down, but I held onto her just a bit longer, not wanting this to get violent.

"Who is this little trollop?" Gisila said with an amused tilt of a brow. "Eh, it doesn't matter. She can watch. Now come here, Sir Keyon, so we can... talk," she added and lay back in a seductive manner.

"This," I said, sweeping my trembling hand over Elpis's body, "is my beautiful mate, who is perfect in every way." The princess's gall to be upset by my announcement was unbelievable. She shot up and gasped in outrage.

"You mated?" she shrieked, assaulting my ears with her pitch and volume.

"I did indeed," I said, tugging at my collar so she could see the mark.

"What is that?" She laughed and pointed at it. "Is she missing a tooth?"

"That's it." Elpis snorted furiously and jumped out of my arms. She started toward the princess, radiating murderous intent. The princess screwed up her face and pointed again.

"What in the blazes is that on your face? A rogue fang?" the princess asked with a disgusted face. I grabbed Elpis's arm and stared at the princess in bewilderment.

"Have you not been paying attention to current events? You don't know who she is? Cyneric never brought it up?" I inquired, and the princess shrugged.

"Haven't been paying attention," she dismissed. "Keyon, you are to be my king. We'll go to the witches to sort out removing that… whatever that is." She gestured to the mark on my neck.

I'd finally lost all the shits I had to give. Princess or not, her stay was fucking done. Elpis felt what I was feeling and said, "It's ok, Toast. I'll remove her."

No. I'm fucking over it. I'm done. That's enough. Fuck this shit! Toast snapped and took over my body. *Sorry, I need to borrow this real quick, Keyon.* I didn't fight it. I was too curious about what he'd do.

Toast made me walk forward and lean over Gisila, who looked pleased for a split second. Then he yanked her up by her waist and walked out of the bedroom, holding her away from my body like she was a bin full of trash. He set her down by the door, opened it, and shoved her so hard she stumbled out of my chamber and fell on her naked ass.

"Here, Toast!" Elpis called and shoved Gisila's discarded dress in my face. Toast snatched it and incinerated it. Now Gisila would be forced to walk naked back to her room. Toast nodded in approval, breathed fire over my hands to get her stench off of them, and returned my body's control to me.

Wow, Toast, I said. *That may have been your biggest victory yet, big guy, and we just won a war.*

I cut my irritated gaze to Gisila, who blew her disheveled hair away from her face. She finally stood, shaking with anger and humiliation. She glared at Elpis, and after a minute, a royal secretary ran up with a spare robe and asked, "You summoned me, Princess Gisila?"

Gisila ripped the robe from him and donned it. "Yes. I have two items to be carried out once I am crowned queen tomorrow."

"And they are?" the secretary asked, pulling out a notebook and a pen.

"This female," Gisila said, seething and pointing at Elpis, "is to be executed, and my upcoming mating to Sir Keyon will be announced the following day!"

Elpis

The royal secretary blinked slowly at the humiliated princess as though he knew he couldn't possibly have heard her right. His mouth pursed, and he dipped a little before saying, "Ahem, Princess Gisila, you do know we have laws dating back over several hundred years that someone must be accused of a crime and be found guilty before any sentencing can occur..."

The princess's cheeks burned in further embarrassment, and she snapped, "I said what I said! I expect to see her behind bars tomorrow!"

The secretary looked lost. "Do you not know who she is, though, princess? It is said she is the Sun God's favorite child, an—" Whatever composure Gisila might have had left was lost in that moment.

"BUT SHE IS NOT MY FAVORITE!" she shrieked and pointed for the poor secretary to leave, which he gladly did.

I was simply in shock this entire time. To think someone could just come along and kill someone's fated mate because they were jealous? It was absurd! I didn't know whether to be frightened, amused, or just... pity her. Perhaps I was simply too exhausted, but all I could do was watch with a gaping mouth.

Then a cold fury exploded in my chest until I realized it was coming from Keyon. His wings ripped right through his shirt, blocking my view of the princess and startling the ever-loving sunshine out of me! Oh my gods!

"Listen very closely, little hatchling," Keyon seethed quietly at the princess, and I tried to find a spot to peek through, but he was very thorough! "I'll help you understand what you just tried to do. You just threatened to kill an absolute dominant's mate. Don't do that. That'll end badly for you. If I hear one whisper about you thinking about this again, I will end your reign before it's begun. If you still don't understand the line you've just crossed, I recommend you ask around and get someone else to be horrified for you."

The princess gasped. "Y-you can't talk to me like that, Keyo—"

"Sir Keyon," he snapped.

"A-and you can't threaten me! I'm the last of the king's line!" she said with more confidence.

Keyon leaned farther out, and his voice lowered. "I can't? I can't threaten the female who pushed me off a roof and tried to bury me alive? I can't threaten the female who pushed her own sister into her brother's maw?" He laughed coldly. "Last of the king's line? I'll show you how little that means to me." His voice raised and he roared, "Now get the fuck off my doorstep!" I saw a flash of blue fire and heard a screech followed by the sound of bare feet slapping down the hall.

Keyon backed up to slam the door shut, making me lose my balance. I wobbled and sat down on a chair in the main room. He gave me a pained look and strode into the bedroom, where he replaced all the bedding and burned the ones Gisila had touched. He scooped me up and gently laid me down next to him on the fresh sheets.

"I'm sorry, moonflower." He sighed and cradled me against his chest. "This was supposed to be a safe place for us now. Maybe I should take you someplace safer during the coronation and perhaps the following week. She has no legal reason to attack you, and Leofwine would never order his assassins to kill you, but—"

"Stop…" I groaned and rubbed his shoulder. "I'm not afraid of her, Keyon."

"You don't have to be afraid of something for it to kill you," Keyon replied, upset. He wrapped his arms tighter around me.

"You don't understand," I said, nuzzling into his chest and sneakily healing his injury with my horn while he wasn't paying attention. "We just took down a colossal monster, Keyon. The princess is simply another monster. If she comes after me, I'll get Leofwine to gather evidence, and we'll remove her by whatever laws you must have. If that doesn't work, well, I don't want to kill anyone, but if it's me or her… I will defend myself."

Keyon was just breathing slowly, listening to me talk. "I will be at that coronation tomorrow. I'm not running anymore. I'm not hiding anymore. I'm a free female, and I'm demanding my right to be seen, heard, and respected! I won't be shoved from my place in society! Never again, Keyon!"

His chest rumbled under me in a soft growl. "I don't know if I've ever been so turned on," he said appreciatively and rubbed my back. He sighed and became serious. "We'll go. I'm expected to be there as the knight general, but you'll be at my side the entire time. No one will dare touch you anyway. We'll see what kind of absurd legal reason she has for attacking my Lady Elpis. Did you know you've a title now? Lady Elpis Eudokia."

"A couple of the knights called me that! Oh, it makes me sound fancy!" I said, carefully looking up at him so I didn't poke him with my horn. His eyes went round, and he let go of me, tucking me in before going to his closet and dragging out a heavy chest.

"Speaking of fancy," Keyon said excitedly.

Yes! Yes! YES! YES! YES! SHOW OUR MATE! AAAH, I AM SO EXCITED! Toast yelled, and I winced at his volume. What in the name of the s—

Keyon threw back the chest lid and grinned up at me with his sparkling copper eyes. "Elpis! This is our hoard! Look, it's all for you! Well, I have other chests, but this is one of them!" He jumped onto the bed with an armful of treasure and settled down, gleeful like an over-sugared hatchling.

"Oh, my Moon Goddess!" I gasped, laughing slightly at my mate acting like such a dragon.

Such a dragon, Rein agreed, tittering away with amusement.

I peeked throughout the impressive pile he'd brought onto the bed while he put jewelry all over me that he thought looked the best. There was an endless assortment of gems, chains, rings, bracelets, necklaces, lockets, cuff links, and other things I hadn't quite identified yet. If I hadn't known any better, I would have assumed Keyon was either a king or a pirate!

"Ah! I can't figure out what looks best on you," Keyon whined. "You make everything look good!" He replaced the emerald tiara on my head with a diamond one and nodded. "Maybe we'll just find the most expensive stuff in the whole lot and cover you with that?" He experimentally slid a ring down my horn and tilted his head in consideration.

"That will not bode well for horn or ring if I have to shift," I mused with a painfully wide smile. He sighed in disappointment and removed it.

"You're right…"

I was trying very hard to keep from laughing, but my composure was weakening.

I think we should have her wear a different set every day. We should show her the nice dresses and fancy gowns you've collected over the years too… despite my arguing, Toast admitted.

"The dresses!" Keyon gasped and launched off the bed. That shattered the crack in my defenses, and I burst into laughter. Did the terrifying knight general just run off to spoil his mate with fancy silks? I leaned back into the pillows, chuckling tiredly as my mate dragged more chests into the room. Warmth continued to bloom in my own chest, and he looked up at me with a shy smile.

"I love you," I said quietly. He came over and cleared off the bed, realizing I was still exhausted and looking a little embarrassed that he'd forgotten. He leaned down to nuzzle my nose and lay a soft kiss on my lips.

"I love you too, Elpis. No matter what happens, we'll always be together," he whispered sweetly. There was a knock on the door, and Keyon returned to feed me until I fell into a sweet, blissful sleep in the home I shared with my mate.

I was feeling back to normal the next day and walked hand in hand with Keyon toward the queen's coronation. We'd gotten up hours before sunrise so I could bathe and Keyon could dress me.

Even though the thought of Princess Gisila becoming the queen was putting a damper on the day, Keyon was still excited to put me in the best dress he had that would fit me and pick out my jewelry. He wanted to show me off to his people as his new mate but was also constantly reminding me that I didn't need all this to be beautiful. His fated mate side was at odds with his dragon side, and it only made him look adorable. He was trying so hard!

So, we strode out in our finest. Keyon wore his formal military attire, and I was dressed in a lavender gown that Toast insisted was 'the one.' That meant matching purple jewelry. Keyon said the set I had on were purple sapphires, and he said it with a very smug look on his face. I supposed that was good?

We walked up flights of stairs until we seemed to be near the top of the castle. Then we passed through a gate facing east and strode into a courtyard that led to a massively broad stone bridge. There were guards stationed everywhere, but Keyon ignored them as much as they ignored us.

I shivered once we began crossing the bridge and drew my shawl closer to me. There was very little protection from the wind's chill up here. Keyon frowned, let go of my hand, and pressed me against his side instead to keep me warm. He left his gentle, loving hand on my exposed skin to help keep me calm with his mate touch.

The bridge opened to a massive circular space in between two peaks of the mountain range. "This is Corona's Door, moon-flower," Keyon said to me as we walked toward an area that the royal court was utilizing. "We allow any citizens who wish to witness the coronation to sit in those arena seats," he added, gesturing to the thousands of people who were filling up the rows in the distance. There was a cliff separating the seats from the large arena; it seemed that, aside from flying, no one could cross between the two areas.

"See that huge depression in the mountain rock?" Keyon asked, pointing to the center of the arena. "See how it's reddish, like it's very hot? That's where Corona will emerge from. That's

Corona's actual door right there." I nodded with wide eyes and clung to his arm. Whatever was going to come out of there was much larger than Cyneric's behemoth... I was terrified.

"Don't be afraid, moonflower," Keyon said quietly. "Corona is a just godling." He stationed us by the dais that held chairs for royalty and the court. I kept my eyes away from the princess, who I assumed was sending heated glares in my direction. I just straightened my back and squared my shoulders. Even though I felt a little self-conscious about my horn, I shoved that fear aside too. Today, I would be confident!

"That's my moonflower," Keyon said lovingly and stroked my back in calming caresses. He wrapped his arm around me again as we waited for the sun to rise, which was when the coronation began.

I watched the Sky Gods prepare the day for the sun, fading colors into each other until a vibrant orange teased the horizon. When the blindingly bright sun finally peered over the edge and blessed us with a new day, the ground vibrated, and Corona's door splintered with fiery cracks. The entire circle heated up and melted. I started slightly, but Keyon held me tight.

That's just lava, moonflower. Melted rock. Corona is coming.

R-right, I replied.

Something that must have been at least twice as big as Cyneric's behemoth rose from the lava. The molten river never touched Corona, though. There was a black void between It and the melted rock, as though the godling was coming from some place very different from where humans and shifters reside.

Corona did not fully leave the door but merely rose as far as Its chin. I doubted Its body would have fit! My legs were shaking, and I wasn't certain I wouldn't pee myself from fright. The godling was enormous. Larger than I would have ever imagined!

Did we pee before coming? Rein asked worriedly. *I don't think we peed before coming here.* She sounded as faint as I felt!

The godling sniffed several times as It took in the surrounding audience. It was more than gold. If one could scoop the edge of the sun and mold something out of it, it would look like Corona. It looked very much like a dragon but more... evolved, more sophisticated, yet still so raw in Its purity. Its ears flickered like little rays of sunlight as It listened to the hush. The massive, golden maw opened, displaying hundreds, if not thousands, of teeth sharper than the sun's glare. Then, Its voice vibrated through the area, and yet I knew it must be but Its whisper.

"WELCOME, CHILDREN OF THE SUN GOD. RISE AND LOOK UPON US FOR WE CORONATE ANEW."

Chapter 36

Elpis

Corona's gaze wandered through the onlookers before it spoke again. "WE DRAGONS CARRY PRIDE IN BEING THE FIRST BEINGS TO TITLE A KING." The crowd cheered briefly, as though this was something Corona said at every coronation. "WE DRAGONS CLAIM RECOGNITION FOR BEING THE FIRST TO CREATE A KINGDOM." Once again, the crowd roared. "AND YOU DRAGONS SHOW YOUR FEALTY TO ME IN CONTINUING THIS TRADITION." More cheering came, and many blew flames into the sky to show their support. "IN A CEREMONY OF MY OWN NAMESAKE, WE ONCE AGAIN RENEW YOUR VOWS TO CORONA, THE DRAGON GOD, GODLING OF THE SUN GOD." The audience became a wall of fire as nearly every dragon blew their flames in piety.

"WILL THE NEXT IN LINE FOR THE THRONE APPROACH THE CORONATION PLATFORM," Corona commanded, and Princess Gisila stood to walk down a long golden carpet. She ascended several stairs leading to an unrailed balcony that hung over Corona's void, ending just before the godling's snout.

The princess bowed deeply, glanced back to give me a nasty smirk, and stood tall to face the epic deity. "Greetings Corona, Dragon God, Godling of the Sun God. We give thanks for your presence during this most cherished day."

She glared at my Elpis. Destroy her, Keyon. At your earliest opportunity, Toast seethed. *I fucking hate that little shit.*

I think she will eventually destroy herself, but I'll give it my best shot, Keyon said. Even though his tone was wry, I couldn't tell if he was joking or not.

The Dragon God leaned farther toward Princess Gisila. It was so close that I could see Its hot breath billow the princess's hair and gown. "PRINCESS GISILA ROMUALD, SECOND DAUGHTER OF THE LATE KING UHTRIC ROMUALD, DID YOU OR DID YOU NOT TRY TO MARK AN ABSOLUTE DOMINANT CHILD AGAINST HIS WILL?"

The gathered audience of citizens fell deathly quiet. Keyon stiffened beside me, and I went wide-eyed with shock. Gisila froze at the accusation, and I could only wonder what her face looked like.

Keyon? Are you ok? I asked, brushing my pinky against his tense fingers.

I... don't know. I feel rather exposed right now. Let's just keep watching, he said, disturbed. I felt fear from Toast as well, knowing that this would drudge up some ugly memories.

"ANSWER YOUR GOD, PRINCESS GISILA," Corona said in a tone that invited zero debate.

"W-we were but children, great Corona," Gisila answered in a quieter, tremulous voice.

"SPEAK UP FOR YOUR PEOPLE TO HEAR."

"We were but children!" Gisila defended again, and low murmurs rippled through the audience.

"IT IS A QUESTION TO BE ANSWERED WITH A YES OR NO."

"Then my answer is y-yes!" she answered, and she clenched her fists several times, as though she was trying to gather courage. Corona nodded slowly, appeased by her honest answer.

"THEN WE MOVE ON TO THE SECOND ITEM. PRINCESS GISILA ROMUALD, DID YOU OR DID YOU NOT CONSPIRE WITH YOUR SISTERS AND BROTHER TO BURY SAID ABSOLUTE DOMINANT CHILD ALIVE?"

"Great C-Corona, we thought he was d-dead!" Gisila pleaded, shaking. More murmurs broke out amongst the people, and I spied many appalled and disgusted faces.

"ARE YOU SO DIM-WITTED THAT YOU'VE FORGOTTEN WHAT I'VE SAID A MERE MINUTE AGO?" Corona seethed, and a rolling glow flared in the back of Its throat, like a furnace was being fed.

"I-I have not forgotten, Dragon God. I simply wished to exp-p-plain. I… my answer is… yes," she said loudly but much more meekly.

This is starting to seem very much like a trial, Rein said as another gasp rippled through the crowd. *I wonder if she'll still be crowned.*

She will be. She's a relative dominant. It is how it is, Keyon replied. *Perhaps Corona wants to rattle her into shaping up. I truly have no idea.* Rein was disgusted by the answer and turned grumpy while watching the ceremony unfold.

I was disappointed myself. She wasn't worthy. I didn't know her, but she truly didn't seem to care about anything, not even matters of law. That was dangerous and deeply disturbing. I could only hope that Corona did succeed in scaring her onto the right path.

"NOW WE HAVE THE THIRD ITEM. PRINCESS GISILA ROMUALD, DID YOU OR DID YOU NOT MURDER YOUR OWN SISTER BY PUSHING HER INTO THE JAWS OF YOUR BROTHER'S OUT-OF-CONTROL DRAGON?"

Gisila's posture severely cracked at Corona's question. She hunched a little, as though thinking it'd hide her from the onlookers, and gazed about fearfully.

Murdering a sibling for the crown isn't unheard of, remember that, Toast informed tiredly, knowing this wasn't an item that would stand out in history. I hated that.

"I was trying to escape, and sh-sh-she was i—" she began but faltered. "Y-y-yes, Corona. I did."

Even though it wasn't unheard of, I did see scowls deepen. Many spoke to their neighbors, and others simply looked on in continued shock.

"AND FINALLY, WE HAVE THE FOURTH ITEM," Corona said, staring levelly at the crumbling princess on the platform. "PRINCESS GISILA ROMUALD, DID YOU OR DID YOU NOT ORDER THE EXECUTION OF THE SUN GOD'S MOST PRECIOUS AND TREASURED CHILD—A CHILD HE WAITED HUNDREDS OF YEARS FOR—SO YOU COULD CLAIM HER MATE, THE AFOREMENTIONED ABSOLUTE DOMINANT?"

As soon as Corona mentioned my importance, Gisila fell to her feet and prostrated, sobbing uncontrollably. "I did! I did! F-f-f-forgive m-m-me, g-g-g-great C-Corona! P-p-p-please! H-h-have m-mercy!"

The crowd was muttering in complete contempt at this point. It was clear that Gisila had lost whatever respect she'd previously enjoyed. How she'd lead these people now was beyond me.

She may never gain their trust again, Keyon said. He was extremely upset having his assault exposed for all the kingdom to know. There was no doubt who the mentioned absolute dominant was, and his privacy on the matter had vanished.

It'll be ok, Keyon, I said, pouring all my love to him over the bond. *Remember what I said? I'll protect you, sunflower.*

I really wish you'd pick a different nickname, he replied dryly, but I felt his hidden mirth relax him, and the bond swelled with his deep love and gratitude. He reached for and held my hand, squeezing it in his adoration.

Corona drew Itself up a little to look down at the shattered princess. "I HEREBY FIND YOU, PRINCESS GISILA ROMUALD, SECOND DAUGHTER OF THE LATE KING UHTRIC ROMUALD, GUILTY OF ASSAULT, ATTEMPTED MURDER, MURDER, AND CONSPIRACY AGAINST THE SUN GOD'S FAVORITE CHILDREN."

What did that mean? I hazarded a quick glance at Keyon, who paled in shock. When I turned back to the scene, a long, thin tail emerged from Corona's door to hover before the princess.

"YOU ARE SENTENCED TO LIFE IMPRISONMENT IN MY DOMAIN AS MY FIRST AND ONLY SLAVE. NOW GO AND DEAL WITH THE SPIDERS IN MY WINE CELLAR," Corona decreed in a steely tone, grabbing the screaming princess with Its tail and ripping her down into the black void. The complete silence that settled around the scene was oppressive; I could hear the smallest shift of someone in their seat.

I don't believe it, Keyon whispered through our mind-link. I couldn't think of a response. I knew she wasn't worthy, but Keyon had been so dismissive. Had everyone truly thought that she'd be crowned?

How did Corona know about our inside joke with Leof? Toast whispered vacantly, as though he couldn't comprehend and address the more important part of what Corona had said. *Like sun, like son.*

What? Rein asked.

"WILL THE UNICORN, LADY ELPIS EUDOKIA, THE GREAT PURIFIER AND THE SUN GOD'S FAVORITE CHILD, APPROACH THE CORONATION PLATFORM?" Corona asked imperiously.

What?

I glanced up at Keyon, who licked his lips nervously and gestured for me to go as directed. *I love you,* he said, sounding strained. *Be brave, moonflower. All will be ok. I'm right here.*

Rein... Toast whimpered, not sounding as secure as Keyon.

I swallowed heavily, straightened my spine, and walked toward the largest being I'd ever seen in my life. Rein poured all her energy into my body, making sure my walk was steady despite our terror. We climbed the steps and stood before the godling, bowing deeply in respect as we'd seen Gisila do.

"LADY ELPIS EUDOKIA, DID YOU OR DID YOU NOT GIVE A SMALL FORTUNE TO A HUNGRY FATHER AND

HIS DAUGHTER?" the Dragon God asked. I... what? Had I committed a crime? Was that a crime? Oh gods! I didn't understand the free world at all!

"I did," I said simply and loudly, knowing the godling was not a fan of mumbling or explanations. Why would that be a crime, though? Certainly, I could do what I wished with my money, right? No, I did nothing wrong. I wouldn't accept that.

Please don't mention the bar fight, please don't mention the bar fight, please don't mention the bar fight, Rein prayed in a pious chant.

Corona seemed pleased with my straight-forward response and asked another question. "LADY ELPIS EUDOKIA, DID YOU OR DID YOU NOT FIND ONE THOUSAND AND THIRTY-SIX SLAVES FOR THE KNIGHT GENERAL, SIR KEYON KENELM, AND HIS ARMY TO FREE WITHIN A MATTER OF DAYS?"

We'd freed that many? I had no idea it'd been over a thousand...

"I did," I said with more confidence. I did, and I was proud of it! I wasn't even done yet. I still itched to go out and search until they were all free!

"ONE FINAL QUESTION," the godling said, and I made a desperate effort to not wipe my sweaty palms on my dress. I couldn't be seen as weak. I was a free person now! "LADY ELPIS EUDOKIA, DID YOU OR DID YOU NOT SAVE OVER SIXTY-TWO CRITICALLY INJURED WARRIORS ON THE BATTLEFIELD AT FRANCO'S ESTATE, PUTTING THEIR HEALTH ABOVE YOUR OWN?"

"I did," I asserted with finality. I definitely was proud of that one. I only wished I had been able to keep going. Those poor souls, dying for something that should have never occurred. May Franco rot in a cell forever!

"LADY ELPIS EUDOKIA, I HEREBY FIND YOU WORTHY OF THE TITLE QUEEN. PLEASE COME FORWARD TO RECEIVE YOUR BLESSED CROWN," Corona said, and I was certain I hadn't heard correctly.

What? Rein asked.

What did It say? I asked her.

Get your crown?

That can't be right.

I... don't know?

Corona closed Its maw, but I could see blue fire flaring behind Its rows of teeth. I smelled smoke, flesh, and metal all rolled into one scent. It was nauseating, but it soon cleared up, and black smoke curled out between the cracks, rising, dancing, and dissipating in the mountain breeze. Corona opened Its mouth, displaying a crown that was wedged onto one of Its massive front teeth.

I couldn't think, but the one thing I did know was that I didn't want to risk making this godling impatient. It gave me specific instructions, and I'd... follow them. The prey in me was terrified of going closer to those teeth, but Rein helped steel me, and I strode forward to lift the crown off Its tooth. I backed up and held it in front of me, not certain what the godling wanted me to do with it now.

It was an extremely pretty thing—gold with filigree depicting subtle, hidden images of unicorns. Small white horns jutted from the top of the crown, protruding all the way around in little spires. There was even a loop for my horn to go through, and I wondered if that'd make it a challenge to don.

"WILL THE KNIGHT GENERAL, SIR KEYON KENELM, THE GREAT DEFENDER, ONE OF THE SUN GOD'S FAVORITES, APPROACH THE CORONATION PLATFORM?" Corona asked, and I breathed a sigh of relief that I wouldn't be alone up here anymore. I was not risking walking away without dismissal.

Keyon stopped next to me, seeming less tense now. He didn't look my way, but he sent me comfort, which I returned to him. I was still in shock. Was Keyon about to go through the same interrogation? I would have prayed for it to go well, but there was no person more noble than my mate.

"SIR KEYON KENELM, DID YOU OR DID YOU NOT FREE THOUSANDS UPON THOUSANDS OF SLAVES

DURING YOUR TIME SPENT AS THE KNIGHT GENERAL?"
Corona asked, and I noticed that the audience had remained
silent for quite some time. Everyone seemed to be on the edge of
their seats, and many were staring at me. It had been a mistake
to look at the crowd. Now I was even more nervous. My hands
were practically dripping with sweat.

"I did," Keyon said in a professional voice, calm and confident.

"SIR KEYON KENELM, DID YOU OR DID YOU NOT
ASSIST IN TAKING DOWN A GROUP THAT CONSPIRED TO
REMOVE THE HUMANITY FROM DRAGON-SHIFTERS?"

"I did," Keyon replied evenly.

"SIR KEYON KENELM, DID YOU OR DID YOU NOT
SUCCESSFULLY LEAD AN ARMY TO TAKE DOWN A
CORRUPT KING WHO VIOLATED THE SUN GOD'S DESIGN
FOR HIS CHILDREN."

"I did," Keyon answered seriously for the third time. He
was a master at the straight face! I must look like a baby deer
compared to him!

"SIR KEYON KENELM, I HEREBY FIND YOU WORTHY
OF THE TITLE KING. PLEASE COME FORWARD TO
RECEIVE YOUR BLESSED CROWN AND ACTIVATION OF
YOUR ROYAL GENE," Corona said. "LADY ELPIS EUDOKIA
DOES NOT HAVE THE GENE, BUT SHE IS PERFECT AS
SHE IS, AND THE SUN GOD WISHES NO CHANGES
UPON HER."

Oh no, Rein squeaked privately to me as Keyon stepped
forward to receive the crown Corona was producing. *Am I going
to be able to handle Toast's royal co—*

Not a good time! I interrupted her hastily, having no idea if
Corona could read minds. I wasn't taking that chance.

Hey, it's not your lady parts on the line here! she grumbled.
That was sort of true?

Keyon stood by my side now, holding a golden crown dec-
orated with sapphires and blue inlay depicting flames. It wasn't
gaudy; it suited him quite well.

"SIR KEYON KENELM, PLEASE CROWN THE QUEEN," Corona said and watched as Keyon placed the crown carefully on my head, sliding my horn through the loop first before settling the rest.

"LADY ELPIS EUDOKIA, PLEASE CROWN THE KING," Corona said, and Keyon took to a knee, smiling subtly at me because I wasn't tall enough to reach. I held back a slightly crazed giggle, amused and nursing rattled nerves. I placed the crown firmly on his head, pleased to find that it fit just right.

"RISE, NEW ROYALTY, AND ALLOW YOUR SUBJECTS TO GREET YOU FOR THE FIRST TIME," Corona commanded, and the audience broke into a deafening roar, starting well before Corona was even done talking. Keyon grasped my hand firmly and squeezed. My eyes roved over the crowd, and the majority was smiling at me. I could hardly believe what was happening. Somehow, in the course of several weeks, I'd gone from being a slave to a queen... and the people already liked me. Loved us...

King Keyon

Queen Elpis and I were not allowed the luxury of time to nurse our shock. As soon as Corona sank back into the mountain, the members of the court surrounded us with questions and agenda items for the day. No one was prepared to seat a different queen— and they definitely weren't prepared to seat a king—so we were shuffled inside, where there were a number of documents to sign.

There was also the matter of picking a new knight general, and they told me I had some time to make that decision, but I already knew who I wanted. I requested for them to offer the honor to Sir Stroud and to offer Sir Gerfrid command of the King's Army. I desperately needed him to weed out the rotten dragons who'd been placed in there by Cyneric, and there was no better dragon to scare the piss out of them.

Leofwine was also reinstated in his previous role, and I made a note to call in Adelais to see what kind of career path she'd be interested in at the castle. Perhaps she'd want to join the spy ranks or work with Elpis. We'd have to see.

I thought that Elpis would be hiding in a corner during all this, but she grabbed onto what she could of her earlier adrenaline rush and dove into matters regarding the Reborn. When she asked about the rehabilitation programs, I called in Aiken to assist her. She was anxious to do something while waiting for me to finish my paperwork; she needed my help with reading and signing. I really needed to get her a tutor to learn properly...

I smiled as I overheard her chattering about the extra slaves we'd recently liberated and if we could handle the numbers. Aiken said it'd be a financial strain, but Elpis was insistent on learning more. My mate wasn't going to give up on the newly freed. After a little while, she came to me and shyly asked for my opinion on something.

"So," she said, tracing a nail along the carving of the desk I was using. "Apparently we have two treasuries."

"Oh?" I said curiously and pulled her closer so I could stroke her hands while listening to her.

"One is where the coin is. The other is just... overflowing with treasure, almost to the ceiling. It's like a massive hoard. Is there a reason we have that?" she asked timidly and looked around at the advisors. I regarded the advisors as well, waiting for an answer.

"It's, ah... the royal hoard," one answered, seeming confused, and looked to another advisor for validation.

"It's just the kingdom's treasures. Items of worth collected over the centuries," the other said.

"But it's just sitting there... in a vault," my queen said nervously. I could see where she was going with this.

"Is there a problem with selling any of it to fund Reborn rehabilitation?" I asked plainly and leaned my head on a fist.

"Ah, er... no... technically not..." an advisor answered, fidgeting like I was taking away his own hoard. I smiled internally at the difference between dragons and literally anyone else. We liked our pretty prizes. No doubt some would be unhappy about selling items from the treasury.

Too bad. Our queen had a good idea, Toast said proudly, and I agreed.

"There's your answer, beloved queen," I said, grinning up at her. "Do what you will." I trusted her, and Aiken would help. She'd get more confident with her own royal voice soon.

I finally finished my paperwork and called Elpis in to work on hers, which took quite a while. Then we were summoned for the Royal Flyover, a tradition that went back to the very beginning. Elpis and I had to shift into our dragons and fly over the castle and the surrounding city. I always thought it was a bit of a silly little parade, but Toast truly needed to come out, especially with his Royal Gene being activated.

Rein and Toast finally stood in front of a massive mirror, taking in his changes.

I almost don't recognize myself, Toast mumbled. He was recognizable, but he was definitely larger now, and Rein was looking a little terrified of his new bulk. Toast tried to look between his legs and murmured, *I don't think that got much bigger, if at all. We may have gotten lucky, Rein.*

Toast also had a kingly frill now with thick, sharp horns. The scales on the frill, down his back, and along sections of his limbs had turned a vibrant, cool green. It reminded me of oxidized copper.

You got corroded, Toast, I chuckled, though I was still in shock seeing him like this.

You're beautiful, mate, Rein said, and Elpis hummed in agreement.

Let's get this parade over with, Toast grumbled. *Are you ready, lingerie?*

I told you to pick a different pet name for my dragon form! she hissed, embarrassed.

After how you teased me last time? I don't think so, Toast chuckled and launched into the sky with Rein to fly over the city. Elpis and I had to hold back our laughter as they continued their very inappropriate, private conversation during the flyover.

What will you give me if I pick a different name, my queen? Toast asked in a kinglier voice.

I have a two-layer cake in need of filling and frosting... my king, Rein negotiated thoughtfully. I could feel Elpis's massive cringe. That may have been the most graphic one yet. Still though, my dirty talking was plenty graphic, and she'd always enjoyed it.

I can't believe how much has changed, Elpis said softly, gazing down at the cheering city folk. *Feels like just yesterday I was being tortured in a cage.*

Don't think about that, mate, Toast replied. *You're free, and you're with us now! We will treasure you and Rein more than any hoard in the kingdom.*

And our heir or heirs... I said, still in wonder about that. *We should have you see the royal physician tomorrow. Let them know you're carrying.* I felt warmth radiate from my mate. She was so happy, so proud to be carrying our offspring. We'd have a family in less than a year, and I was beside myself with joy.

Once the flyover was completed, we made our appearance at the evening feast and escaped as soon as possible to rest in our new chambers. Elpis, per usual, lost her mind as soon as we entered the royal suite.

"This is so much bigger than the suite we stayed at!" she screamed and ran off into different rooms to see what was there. I heard a squeal, followed by the sound of pots and pans clattering to the ground. I supposed she found the kitchen, and I started laughing again. I wiped tears from my eyes, but not all of them were from mirth. I was overwhelmed. Similar to what Elpis had been feeling, I remembered how miserable Toast and I had been weeks ago.

I sniffed and tried to wipe my eyes clear before Elpis noticed, but the bond gave away my emotions. She walked out of a hallway and went straight into my arms, squeezing me as tight as her arms could manage.

"Hard to believe, huh?" she asked quietly, and I nodded. "It will be incredibly difficult, but I can manage as long as you're here with me. I'll be here for you too, my love."

My heart swelled at her words, and I picked her up, cradling her to my chest as we wandered around in search of the bedroom. "Where the fuck is the bedroom?" I complained when we ended up in a room with a bathing pool. After several more minutes of exploring with Elpis giggling in my arms, we finally found the bedroom, and I lowered her onto the sheets.

I pulled her dress off while she removed my clothes. I needed her as much as she needed me. After a day that seemed more like a fever dream by the second, I craved to embrace the one thing I knew was real; it was my love for my fated mate, Elpis. My moonflower.

I kissed her as I leaned over her, stroking her delicate cheeks with my thumbs as I propped myself up on my elbows. I leaned into her hips with mine, grinding gently against her core to see if she was ready. She moaned softly into my mouth and reached down to glide her fingers down my cock. I groaned in response, shivering at her skillful touch.

She positioned my head at her entrance, and I pushed slowly down, wanting to savor the moment of the first joining. I slid inch by inch into the depths of her channel, gliding along the shape of her walls to feed her the entirety of my love. She wrapped her arms around my back and slid her hands along my working muscles.

Once I seated myself down to the hilt, I groaned in bone-deep satisfaction. Elpis whimpered and arched slowly and sensually into my chest. She wanted to feel me as much as I needed to feel her. I then leaned down to trail soft kisses down her neck, making her tremble uncontrollably.

I rolled my hips so I could begin making love to my Elpis, my everything. I wanted to show her another way that I'd treasure her, and it was in the way I'd worship her in bed. She could have whatever she wanted from me—wild or romantic. Nothing would change with our new roles. I'd still carry her to the bed and fulfill her every desire. No doubt she'd insist on doing the same.

"Gods, I love you so much, Elpis," I murmured, brushing my lips against hers. "Thank you for everything... I can't even begin to express how much you mean to me."

"I love you too, so very much, my Keyon," she replied and slid a hand to my chest. "You don't need words, my love. I can feel it right here." She kissed me, sighing in pleasure as I continued to slide inside her heat. "You saved me too. Too many times to count..."

It seemed like we both were overflowing with gratitude, and it made me want to burst from the emotional pleasure alone. I felt invincible with her at my side. I kissed down her neck and nibbled on where my mark was, making her gasp in pleasure. Then I slide a palm up her side to land on her soft breast, massaging gently as I grinded my hips into her.

A smile spread across my face as I laved her mark with my tongue, pleasuring her the way she deserved to be pleasured. She was a squirming, whimpering female under my ministrations, and I pushed further to get her to blossom for me. I increased the speed of my thrusting and bit gently into the mark on her neck.

She gasped, and her cries filled the royal suite as she came under me. I pushed for my own released and growled into her neck as I reached my peak. Her pulsing walls gripped onto my cock, taking everything I had to offer as my hot seed came forth.

We writhed together in bliss, finding comfort and peace in our coupling. My mate was in euphoria, not just from finding release, but from experiencing such a sweet, gentle way of joining. I pulled her to my chest, beaming with satisfaction. I could be a beggar in this moment, and I'd still be the happiest male alive.

I lay there in silence with my mate, idly stroking her hair. No words needed to be said. We were happy. We had each other, and now we had the means to make a huge difference in people's lives. Both of us were ready for the hard work; tasks were always easier when you were passionate about them and had someone at your side. Elpis would continue to be a force of nature, and I was so fucking proud of her.

"Are you ready to go liberate more Reborn tomorrow?" I asked sleepily, caressing her draped arm with a thumb.

"Always... so long as you're there with me..." she replied, just as tiredly, but I felt the supreme satisfaction and elation in her heart.

"Always will be," I mumbled, and we both drifted into sleep.

The End

Author's Notes

Why this Book was Written

Dear readers,

As I've done with *The Mistake and the Lycan King,* I am documenting here why this book was written.

If you've read the first book, you'll know already that I was sexually assaulted and later targeted by a second pedophile. You'll know that I entered DBT after I discovered I'd developed a personality disorder from all the trauma and abuse. You'll know it saved my life. You'll know that these books are part of my exposure therapy, an attempt to heal the memories my body carries, especially because I have no partner to help with this.

You'll also already know that I hadn't planned on writing so many erotic scenes. The more I did, though, the more I realized that the microscopic view of the sexual experience helped magnify the exposure and normalize the act. It doesn't matter how realistic or unrealistic it is, and sometimes it helps to get unrealistically graphic. It forces me into an uncomfortable experience that helps overwrite associations, ones that might trigger my trauma and summon an uncomfortable physical response. I can do this safely as long as I'm not cueing up too many negative emotions and constantly spiking my SUDs, subjective units of distress. Refiring is something I still struggle with, and I have a long way to go before I master the DBT skill of riding the wave.

I will now tell you what *The Dragon Knight and the Coveted* was specifically used for.

Everything that Elpis experiences, all her flashbacks that give her physical discomfort, are based off of how I feel in my body at any given time. Because of what I experienced as a child, I often do not feel comfortable in my own body. I feel like I'm being touched, but there is no hand I can rip away. There is nothing there. Sometimes it occurs when I'm dating and become intimate, and sometimes it occurs for no reason at all. It can happen in the grocery store where I feel a sudden sense of violation, something that makes me ill and deeply unsettled, but no one is there, and I'll have no idea what triggered it. Growing up, I never removed my bra because I felt too vulnerable without it. It was too easy to imagine being touched. I lived in it. I slept in it. I all but showered in it, and I bought the thickest ones I could find to feel more protected. Though I have improved a little since writing this book, and the 'ghost hands' have become less frequent, I imagine that I will be in therapy for many years to come. It's working, but it's slow going.

Keyon and Toast were the demonstrators of exposure therapy, and Elpis was my venting of the ghost hands. The journey they had to endure is the journey of recognizing, accepting, and addressing trauma. Then comes the practice of applying those skills progressively. Elpis was my outlet for many things but largely for her struggle to heal after being used for someone's(many, in her case) pleasure. I have no hope for some knight like Keyon to carry me off, and I'm not sure if I'll ever find love in this lifetime, but I do hope someday to be comfortable in my own body and able to live happily with that. I hope for that to someday be enough.

As far as the rest of the story goes, I wanted to write a shifter novel based off the medieval story theme of dragons, unicorns, and knights rescuing damsels. I merged the dragons with the knights and our lead damsel with the unicorn. Unicorns may be considered childish, but I brushed that off to write my story because the opponent to the dragon is often depicted as either the knight or the fabled unicorn. Maybe it's because I'm an assault survivor, but I do not believe in the trope of 'damsels in distress' or it being a negative concept. I believe that any person can find themself in a moment of powerlessness and distress, but it should not take away from their self-worth, potential power, or value as an individual. A 'damsel in distress' is a momentary negative label that I prefer to not be used at all because I do not believe there is anything devaluing about being in distress. If a person is having a bad week and needs help, there is nothing inherently wrong with asking for help. Everyone handles situations differently because everyone is differently equipped. Though needing rescue at first, Elpis eventually became equipped and could handle things at her own pace. She did the best she could, and Keyon encouraged her independence. People are complex, and that is how I attempt to write them.

Lastly, as you may have noticed, I use humor often to balance out the darker elements. Puns are my bread and butter—my buttered-up Toast, if you will. It's always been the most reliable way for me to calm down aside from utilizing the TIPS techniques, which I did mention Elpis learning from Zosime in the book. Including silly humor as I write helps to keep me calm and stay grounded.

I want to thank those who've read the book to this point. You were one more person who came along on the journey when I feared I was alone. If you've found something for yourself here, something you've gotten out of this experience, know that I will keep writing for a long time to come. I will keep enjoying humor, enjoying storytelling, enjoying world building, enjoying romance, trying to become more comfortable with sex, and hold on to hope. Healing Fate is now eight books in length. Soon, I will start the sequel series: Healing Chaos.

Sunlight preserve you,
Asha Nyr

Printed in Great Britain
by Amazon

37688951R00263